THAT GOOD MISCHIEF

THE NINE WORLDS RISING BOOK 3

LYRA WOLF

RAVENWELL PRESS

Cover design by Dominic Forbes

Ravenwell Press

eBook ISBN: 978-1-944912-33-8
Paperback ISBN: 978-1-944912-42-0
Hardback ISBN: 978-1-944912-43-7

First Edition

To Rafi, who is my rock in every storm, even though the storm might be me.
Sorry about that.

THE NINE WORLDS

SVARTALFHEIM

GROANING MOUNTAINS

MOUNT HEG

THEGH

HAMDUAR

GAROM

CARTHA OCEAN

N

ENCHANTED ISLES

BURNING MOUNTAI

IZGA

DARK ELVES

MOUNT ERBIS

NOAETH

LYNSVI ISLAND

LAKE AMSVARTHIR

ALFANOR

AFETHEMAR

NILHANOR

WHISPERING MOUNTAINS

EULALL

RIVER OF SORROWS

ONARA LAKE

ALFHEIM

MOUNT RUNNE

AFVADELL

FYLEN

BRETHA

LAKE CRETA

CYRROS

MELARTH

FALLROCK MOUNTAINS

BLAC

EPATHA

RED MOUNTAINS

DORN

FJDKLE RIVER

LEIRA

SEA OF AEGIR

IDAVOLL

ENSAE LAKE

SINENAE

VANAHEIM

SIRON DESERT

SOUTHERN ISLES

SOLEA

ELIVAGAR RIVER

MIST AND ICE

SHADOW LANDS

SHORE OF CORPSES

ELJUDNIR

HEL

GJOLL RIVER

BAY OF SERPENTS

BOILING TIDES

VEILED SEA

FROST GIANTS

...VE

...VA FIELDS

MUSPELHEIM

JOTUNHEIM

DECEPTION MOUNTAINS

AEGIT

MOUNT GLOKE

UTGARD

THRYMHEIM

GEIRSA

YMIR'S FELL

GULF
OF
THIEVES

IFING RIVER

GRAY MOUNTAINS

BLAUT PEAK

SPRITE LAKE

...RMT RIVER

RANDIR

ASGARD

HOWLING SUMMITS

MOUNT KASTEN

DYRDAL

KRET

...RMT RIVER

MYRFELL

IRONWOOD

ULM LAKE

MIDGARD

CITY OF ASGARD

WILD...

...I SEA

The road to Hell is paved with good intentions.

— Proverb

* * *

Do that good mischief which may make this island
Thine own for ever, and I, thy Caliban,
For aye thy foot-licker.

— William Shakespeare, *The Tempest*

1

BLADE AND BONE

Sigyn thrust her dagger between my ribs.

A punch of steel. A flash of white heat tearing muscle.

"I didn't want to do this," she said.

I know.

But that didn't make this any easier.

Blood spilled inside me, flowed warm over my stomach, filled my chambers and empty spaces.

I tasted copper on my tongue. Hot silk coated my lips and trickled down my chin.

Sigyn yanked out the blade, her skin taut over her rigid knuckles.

Pain followed, deep and searing and splitting.

The world shifted and blurred. I reached out to her.

I wavered. My knees buckled.

I fell.

My head struck hard earth, forcing dirt and rot and damp into my nose that burned with the blood coursing out my nostrils.

I choked on iron and stretched my fingers towards Odin standing over me, a tangle of roots and shadow behind him.

Help me.

But that wasn't how this worked.

His mouth moved quickly, chanting a guttural and ancient language brimming with dark magic.

His words drowned in the ringing that battered my eardrums.

Cold raced through me as fast as my blood raced out of me.

I crushed my hand against the jagged gash in my flesh, trying to stop my blood from emptying. Trying to stitch my torn sinew back together. Trying to survive.

I must survive.

Sweat coated my skin.

The wound wasn't healing itself.

Damn.

I'd already forgotten.

Of course it wasn't healing itself.

I wasn't a god anymore.

I was mortal.

I dragged in thin breaths that kept growing thinner.

So, this was dying.

2

NO REST FOR THE WICKED

Three Weeks Earlier

Midgard

Los Angeles, California

I tapped my black painted fingernails against a desk scattered with legal pads and student papers. Soviet posters of angry Russian women shushing me in bold reds and whites lined the grubby cinder block walls. Delightful.

Of course he'd be fifteen minutes late, and after I rushed with straightening my hair and doing my makeup—only an edgy look would work with this *divine* gray suit and its matching bra top. That pissed me off more than having to wait in his dingy office, rot filling my nose courtesy of the bookshelves crammed with Marx, Voltaire, and Foucault.

A key scuttled in a lock.

The jiggle of a doorknob followed.

Finally.

The office door creaked open and a middle-aged man walked in.

Clean shaven, a protrusion of fine hair dusted with salt at the temples, and a face that screamed *I interrupt conversations with "actually..." as often as I can.*

"Hello, Professor," I said, with that power bitch voice I loved when I was a woman.

His brown eyes latched onto my green ones. They widened, and a throaty wail burst out of his lungs as he dumped coffee down his off-the-rack tweed blazer and over his tasseled loafers.

This man really had no self-respect.

William's face scrunched as his fear melted into outrage. So, he was one of those. Good. It made this all incredibly more fun.

"Who the hell are you?" He sat his mug and stack of stuffed folders on the metal file cabinet beside him.

I flashed him a smile and chuckled as I leaned back in his worn desk chair that was held together more with duct tape than fabric. I ran my fingers along the silver chains hanging between my breasts— size C, because going Double D would distract him from the message I wanted to send.

"Does the university know about your penchant for harassing its students?" I asked.

His cheeks reddened further with a wash of that beautiful, growing anger I so desired.

William pushed his black plastic frame glasses up his wide nose. I tried to ignore the forehead grease clouding the corners of the lenses.

"How did you get in here? Did Mark let you in as some kind of twisted prank?"

"Why is it always changing the subject with people like you?" I said.

He straightened his spine and took a step closer.

"You can tell Mark I'm done with the Theology department and their continual hijinks," he said.

I took out my compact from my purse and flipped open the mirror.

"I'm not from the Theology department." I applied a fresh coat of dark red lipstick. "Although, I guess an argument could be made—"

He pointed his finger at my nose.

"Get out."

I snapped my mirror shut.

"Believe me, I'd love to leave this cozy—" I frowned, looking at a half-eaten egg salad sandwich sitting beside the worn keyboard, "—do you really consider this an office?"

I stood and walked around the desk, the click of my heels muffled by the berber carpet.

"As it is, I'm here on rather important business."

"What business?" He squared his shoulders.

He was trying to intimidate me.

The dear.

"Seems there's all kinds of nasty complaints against you from your students."

I stepped behind him and walked to the doorway.

"I'm only ever professional with my students."

I laughed as I closed the door. He was hilarious.

"You mean you didn't ask Lauren why she quit wearing skirts to class?" I said. "Or pull Kristen into *unwholesome* conversations under the guise of research? And then failed them both despite excellent coursework because they didn't find you as charming as you believe yourself to be? Is *that* the professionalism to which you're referring?"

I turned and faced him.

His jaw firmed. He stomped behind his desk and shoved papers off the yellowing campus telephone.

"I'm calling security."

He picked up the receiver and pressed the direct extension button. That's when he noticed.

The phone cord dangled, limp and frayed at the bottom where I had severed it twenty minutes earlier.

Oops.

He stared at the exposed wire and sweat broke out across his forehead.

"Afraid security can't help you." I locked the door. "And neither can anyone else."

I grabbed him before he grabbed his mobile from his pocket and shoved him against the wall of bookcases. He yelped as books toppled out of the shelves and struck his shoulders.

"You're probably thinking I'm a bad person." I coiled my fingers harder into his tweed blazer. "But you're wrong. I'm *far* worse."

I filled my eyes with fire. I let them burn bright and wicked with my chaos.

He screamed, but it died in his throat the second I pointed the tip of my dagger at the cleft in his chin. The sweat beading along his hairline ran down his temples as he lifted his hands over his head.

"Please...don't...don't hurt me."

I smiled, loving how he begged. Loving the reflection of my eyes blazing back at me in his glasses.

I leaned in to him until I smelled the spice of his cologne. Felt the heat of his panic rising off his neck.

"What you do leaves scars on a person." I pressed the blade into the thrashing pulse of his throat. "Just like nine inches of steel. If I hear one hint about you harassing students again, I will make you one appendage less, and I promise that will be very unpleasant for us both."

A disco beat of drums layered with claps and sharp plucks of a guitar pounded out of my vibrating mobile in my pocket.

Damn.

"Apologies," I said, relaxing into ease and charm.

I pulled out my phone and swiped right, shutting off the alarm before the melody soared into a chorus about some man named Rasputin. Time really did fly when one was enjoying oneself.

"Wish I could stay a bit longer," I said. "Unfortunately, I have a rather pressing appointment I cannot miss. Hope you don't mind?"

He shivered in response, his face frozen in terror and muscles rigid.

I patted his clammy cheek.

"Wonderful!"

I sheathed my dagger and stepped away letting him crumple to the floor. He huddled against the bookcases and drew in his knees, hugging them against his chest.

I swear humans never could keep their wits around flashes of the divine.

Turning, I put on my round sunglasses and walked out the door.

I had an important question to ask Sigyn tonight, and I couldn't be late.

3

WHY IS IT NEVER A GOOD SURPRISE?

I sped along Highway 101, twisting along the rugged California coast outlined by the breaking surf of the Pacific Ocean. Wind filled with salt tore through my hair as I hugged the sharp ridges and hairpin turns.

I downshifted a gear, and the engine of my black Audi R8 roared, accelerating and chasing the road that kept disappearing behind every bend carved into the sun-baked cliffs. Even though I had preferred the Lamborghini at first—Sigyn found it bumpy—the v10 was keeping up with me just fine.

Nothing beat this new age. Everything was fast and wanted to go faster.

Like me.

After saving everyone from a fiery end at Ragnarok by stopping Golda—*sorry,* Gullveig—Sigyn and I decided to call California home. Not because I had any fondness for Midgard, but because Odin and all the powdered arseholes of the Aesir high court highly suggested I stay and never leave—unless I wanted the other realms to find out the particular part I played in the whole ending the worlds thing.

Namely, causing it.

I know.

I had been in a rather bad place. Starting the apocalypse seemed like a great idea to get my revenge on all the gods for that five-hundred years of torture bound in a cave.

While that was all water under the bridge now, the other realms wouldn't see it that way.

The Dark Elves were already on the hunt for whoever caused firestorms to annihilate their entire crop of mushrooms.

I would not have my thumbs snipped off over a few sautéed morels.

And so, on Midgard I would remain.

Sigyn told me that if we were to live a Midgardian life, she would get a proper job, and attend medical school to become a proper surgeon. She had a true passion for medicine and healing, and knew more than any doctor already, having spent the last five centuries treating orphans in Alfheim while I...while I was otherwise *engaged*.

While she refused to accept my help with faking a few diplomas to skip the entire process and get right to work—it would be terribly easy—she acquiesced with a defeated sigh when she realized she did indeed need a believable background in order to even apply, since converting Elvish to Midgardian credits was rather impossible, given that Elvish credits did not exist.

UCLA accepted her without a blink.

As for myself, I chose to take a crack at something new. Something quite bold for me.

Retirement.

I spent my days laid out beside our pool, sunbathing in the nude with a glass of chilled white sangria in one hand, and a book in the other.

In the better part of a week, I had brushed up on all literature, philosophy, and science published since 1526.

It relieved me that humans finally got over their belief in humorism. Imagine thinking that bodies consisted of only four types of colorful bile? Horrifying.

I took up cooking next at the suggestion of my son, Fenrir, after he begged me to do something else. Anything.

It wasn't my fault that he always chose to video call me when I was au natural at sangria o'clock. The shrieks of the restaurant guests behind him had nearly burst my eardrums. Evidently, while humans had gotten over humorism, they hadn't gotten over their prudishness.

After filling the kitchen with copper pans and cast iron cookware, I had cooked my way through Mexico, Japan, and France. I perfected my Beef Wellingtons, Soufflés—the trick was whisking enough air into the egg whites—and claimed victory over the scourge that was the omelet.

That kept me occupied for a month.

Then I grew bored.

Quite bored.

That's when I dragged out my knives from beneath our bed, strapped my daggers at my hips, and returned to the only line of work that ever brought a smile to my face.

Was being a mercenary the most noble of professions?

Not really, as Sigyn kindly reminded me when I excitedly mentioned the Russian mafia paid double the Italian.

Apparently, decent people didn't help criminal organizations. And furthermore, we didn't need the money and I could take my principles and hang them on the nearest tree.

Fine.

She suggested I channel my energy instead into doing one random act of kindness every day. And the universe seemed to agree when I overheard Lauren and Kristen complaining about William Harlaxton while they prepared my usual cinnamon latte...*well*, fixing their little professor problem seemed the kind thing to do.

Surprisingly, I found doing these random acts of kindness had their own reward. They gave me quite the rush. It was new. Different.

I liked it and I wanted to keep chasing that feeling.

Shifting the gears of my Audi again, the exhaust lowered into a deep growl, and I pulled into our driveway. A sleek, five-bedroom, three bath Malibu Beach house—all straight lines, black windows, and 180-degree views of the Santa Monica Bay.

I walked into the foyer and dark hardwood floors spread through airy rooms, all white and modern and accented with Danish furniture. The crack of ocean waves against rock tumbled through the full-length windows and filled the open spaces with thunder as I bounded up the stairs and into our bedroom.

Kicking off my heels, I shimmied out of my blazer and trousers. I removed my makeup and undid the bra top and flung it on the bed draped in white sheets. I just didn't feel like a woman anymore. No matter. I flattened my breasts into a chest of lean muscle and narrowed my hips, returning to my male form.

I walked into my closet that complimented my fluid nature and riffled through layers of suits and gowns and red velvet trousers, all *Dolce and Gabbana, Gucci,* and *Versace*. Everything extravagant. Delicious.

Me.

But for tonight, I wanted something more subtle and chic.

Leaving the top two buttons of my white shirt open, I put on a black Prada suit, loving how the slim fit perfectly accentuated my tall frame. My lips pulled into a wider smile as I fastened a crown pin brooch to the silk lapel, the crystal accents giving that necessary bit of flash.

The entire ensemble set off my long copper hair that waved like flames around my angled cheekbones and sharp chin, and made my green eyes dance more than they already did.

Perfection.

I popped back downstairs and into the kitchen that gleamed with granite countertops and stainless steel appliances. Walking past the six burner range, I stopped in front of the double ovens and pulled out a venison pie. The savory scent of meat and carrot filled the house, bubbling beneath the golden crust flaking with butter.

Now for the wine.

I walked to the wine rack and trailed my gaze over twenty bottles capped in red and yellow foil. I slid out a Chateauneuf-du-Pape '47, a beautiful red that would blend seamlessly with the sauterne I'd serve with the crème brûlée. Of course, espresso and pear brandy would follow dessert and then a full night of vigorous love making.

But first...

I tugged open the wine cooler, grabbed a bottle of chilled Dom Peringon, and walked back through the kitchen, picking up the venison pie on the way as I went out onto the deck lined with glass.

The sun fell softly towards the hard line where a dark ocean met a sky smeared with pinks and purples. The Pacific pounded the coarse sand and rock, interrupted only by the crunch of ice as I twisted the champagne deep into the silver bucket sitting beside the table.

I placed the pie next to the canapés and beluga caviar, and covered it with a silver dome to keep warm.

Scooting out one chair, I plopped into the wicker and stared at the empty chair across from me where Sigyn would soon sit.

All I could do now was wait, and continue to let that single question I wanted to ask her burn me raw.

I shoved my hand into my inner pocket and took out a ring. It was a wide band of gold, decorated in Aesir patterns and carved with interlocking knots and runes and symbols. I had it specially made for her of my own design.

A smile tugged at the corners of my mouth as I brushed the smooth metal with my fingertip.

I loved Sigyn, and I wanted to bind myself to her. To be hers alone.

Now, everything rested on a single answer to a single question: did Sigyn want the same?

To bind herself to me.

To be my wife.

The door leading from the garage clicked open.

I pocketed the ring and turned and peered through the windows. Sigyn walked across the living room, framed by the teak wall unit behind her stuffed with books, ferns, and delicate glass trinkets she wedged between her collection of rocks and minerals.

She slipped the straps of her leather tote crammed with medical texts off her shoulders and dropped them onto the Wassily chair.

A flush of heat warmed me as she smoothed the puckers from her gray sweater over her curves, tugging the hem past her thighs squeezed into black leggings. Sigyn pulled a pen from her tied-back honeyed ginger hair that threatened to burst out of the elastic hairband and placed it on the glass coffee table.

I couldn't wait to dig my fingers into her curls and free them from being so rudely tamed.

I stepped through the sliding patio doors and walked into the living room.

"Well?" I leaned on the walnut sideboard. "How did you do?"

Her face of soft arcs and round cheeks brightened as her brown eyes met mine. Gentle and warm. Kind. Always kind.

"I passed the exam." Her face brightened further.

I smiled.

"As if there was any doubt."

She walked to me and brushed her thumb across the tops of my knuckles. Over the silver rings on my fingers.

"I wasn't so sure when they asked about the lymphatic system," she said. "Everything I ever knew fell out of my head. The various forms of immunoglobulin alone."

I squeezed her hands. Warm. Soft.

"But you got it right," I said, stopping her doubt. "And now, I think you need to take the next few days easy before classes resume."

Her brow twisted.

"You know taking it easy isn't something I'm good at."

True.

Sigyn was talented at many things, but relaxing was not one of them. Then again, she was happiest hunched over anatomy books at the table, highlighting paragraphs, dog-earing the corners of pages, and marveling at all the gooey bits of the human body.

Her ability to be giddy over something as pathetic as the spleen was one of the many reasons I loved her.

"Are you sure you want to do this the long way, Sigyn?" I said. "A few charms and I can make any degree you wish. I really don't understand why you—"

She pressed her finger against my lips, shutting me up. Playful teasing crept across her grin, making me smolder harder. She always could undo me without a word.

"We discussed this," she said. "If I'm to work here, then I do it honestly. Remember?"

I slid my hand behind her back and gently pulled her against me, cradling my body in hers, obliterating the remaining distance between us.

"I do, it's just I prefer remembering the discussion we had after..." I whispered, grazing her lips with my own.

Sigyn shuddered and lifted her chin, meeting me in a kiss that nearly punched the air from my lungs.

No matter how many times we lay together, every time was like the first time, and in those soft moments, I was whole.

She was so true. Good.

And I was...I was trying to be worthy of her.

She smiled against my lips. Laughter followed.

"What's gotten into you?"

"Can I not ravish you as soon as you come home?" I purred against her neck.

I slipped my hand beneath her sweater and raced up the curve of her spine.

My blood ignited, savoring her bare skin heating against my palm.

To hell with the canapés.

I led her to the sofa and sank into the buttery leather, pulling her onto my lap. My hips nestled between her thighs and she wound her fingers in my hair and lowered her mouth towards mine.

I braced for her kiss again, yearning to feel the silk of her lips on mine. To feel her...

"Is that blood on your neck?" she said.

I clapped my hand over a small splattering of crusted residue and rubbed it away.

Oh dear. I guess I got a little too carried away with Harlaxton.

"It's not mine, if that puts you at ease."

Her eyes narrowed, and she pushed herself back, sitting on my knees.

"Then whose blood is it?"

I gave her a sheepish grin.

"I must have accidentally nicked his skin in my excitement. I assure you he had plenty of other veins I left untouched." I looked at the red coating my fingers. "I didn't think he'd be that much of a bleeder. I swear, he's *fine*."

"Loki..."

"You told me I should help people." I wiped the evidence away on my trousers. "He was quite the louse and—"

She stood and crossed her arms, her cheeks hollowing as the most exquisite irritation settled in her features.

"I think you misunderstood my meaning of *help*."

I really didn't want the mood spoiled with this conversation again. Especially tonight.

I scooted to the edge of the sofa and reached out to her, lacing my fingers with hers.

"Before you start yelling at me, how about some champagne first?"

I stood and dragged her out to the patio before she could decline.

The edge of the sun peeked over the horizon. Stars blinked, filling the sky as pinks faded into twilight blues that faded into black ink.

The breeze from the ocean caressed us as I pulled the champagne from the ice. A *pop!* exploded as the cork flew out of the bottle. An arc of froth followed, cascading down the sides and over my fingers. I filled two champagne flutes.

"Is there a special occasion?" Sigyn picked up a canapé piled with caviar and stuffed it into her mouth.

I handed her a glass, delicate bubbles scurrying to the surface.

"Must there always be a reason for me to dote on you? Oh! What's this?"

I lifted the cover off the main course as she took a seat at the table. Her eyes widened.

"Is that—"

"Sylvia's venison pie?" I finished, sitting opposite her. "Yes. Took ages for me to replicate the recipe. But I recalled it being your favorite in the sixteenth century."

Sylvia had been Sigyn's maid back in Basel in 1526. She was a dear until she wasn't, and wouldn't think twice before trying to smack you upside the head with a pan if you crossed her.

"I still find myself missing Sylvia," Sigyn said. "She was my closest friend in those days."

"Whatever happened to her?"

"I actually had Falael search for her," she said. "I couldn't think of Sylvia struggling to find new work due to...well."

She didn't have to remind me. My throat tightened at the memory of Narfi and Nari, our twin boys we only knew hours before they were ripped from us. Before Frigg...

I scrubbed my arms, ridding them of the sear of venom, and set my eyes on the sun disappearing behind the Pacific, focusing on the beauty of the sea instead of the chill of rock and unending darkness of that cave.

I am safe.

I am not in danger.

"He found her and ensured all my assets, the house, the print shop, everything, be given to her," she said. "Apparently, she became a cut throat business woman. Never married, but had scores of lovers."

"Cheers to that."

Sigyn chuckled as I clinked her glass with mine.

I took a swallow of champagne, loving the bubbles snapping across my tongue.

"I also had him search for Simon."

I choked, a rush of fizz needling the back of my throat.

"Your brother?" I wheezed, trying to clear the prickle of champagne.

I didn't like the idea of Falael digging around this particularly thorny grave...especially since I was the one that put Simon in it.

My palms burned with the memory of his windpipe crushing

beneath my hold as I suffocated him. Cruel? Perhaps. But Simon was dangerous and made deals with even more dangerous thugs.

I ensured his death before he ensured Sigyn's.

"And did he find anything of Simon?"

Had the eels in the Rhine I tossed his corpse into not been as hungry as I thought?

"No." She glanced at her lap. "Falael checked every record book, and even as recently as last year sent my DNA to some database hoping to discover a match or relation. But, he found nothing. It's like Simon simply vanished."

The muscles in my shoulders I didn't realize had stiffened, relaxed.

This was definitely one skeleton I preferred to remain buried deep, deep underground.

If Sigyn ever discovered the truth of what I'd done...

"What a pity." I raked my fingers through my hair.

"I'll always be curious about what happened to him," she said. "I mean, it's obvious when one joins the military, but...it would be nice to know."

Even after all this time, her devotion to him remained.

"I don't see why you care." I uncorked the '47 and flooded our second set of wine glasses with the red blend. Hints of Syrah and Grenache diffused into the salty air.

"I *care* because he was my brother."

I snorted.

"He was a swine."

She tensed.

"I know you hated him. You don't have to always remind me."

She stood and walked to the edge of the deck and leaned on the stainless frame of the glass railing, and stared out at the ocean.

I cursed myself. I always had a talent for saying the wrong thing to her.

I picked up both glasses off the table.

She kept her eyes firm on the sea as I stood next to her.

"I'm sorry," I said.

She sighed and met my gaze, her annoyance melting until it disappeared entirely into forgiveness.

"It's alright," she said. "It's my fault. I shouldn't have brought Simon up. I know the bad taste he puts in your mouth."

I smiled and held the glass of wine out to her as a further peace offering.

"Yes. Unfortunately a taste that doesn't compliment the '47," I jested.

She chuckled, letting me know all was well again, and took the glass and gave the wine a firm swirl. Lifting it to her nose she breathed in the earthy tones.

"Let's not talk of the past anymore, and only of the future," she said.

"You read my mind."

I dug into my inner pocket and grasped the ring, the metal warm as I closed it in my grip that was unusually sweaty.

Was this nerves? This woman continued to bring out the oddest of sensations in me.

The wind skated off the ocean waves, cold and saturated with brine, and tousled through her hair. The lights from the house cast her in gold and shadow, deepening the hollows of her eyes and shading the curve of her jaw.

Sigyn was so beautiful and I never wanted to be parted from her.

She tilted her head and her smile widened, making my knees weaken further.

"You're being uncharacteristically quiet right now," she said.

"Is that a bad thing?"

"With you it usually means you're plotting something dangerous. Oh. You better not have Bananas Foster planned. I told you no more flaming desserts after the Cherries Jubilee incident."

I shook my head, reassuring her I kept my promise.

"Don't worry, there will be no flambéing of any sort this evening."

She breathed out in relief.

"I'm still finding exploded cherries all through the house, you know," she said. "Never. Again."

I laughed and neared her, planting my right elbow next to hers on the railing.

"Besides the cherries...Are you happy?" I asked. "With me?"

"Loki, you may sometimes make an art out of trying my patience, but..." She reached out and stroked my hand, love radiating from her. "Yes. I'm perfectly, and wholly happy. I love you."

My heart pounded harder against my ribs.

"Before I met you, I'd learned to live a half life," I said. "But you've made my life whole again, and—"

All I wanted to say. All I wanted to tell her—what she meant to me—it all turned to cotton in my mouth.

"Are you alright?" she said. "You look like someone who's accidentally eaten a bad prawn."

"I'm quite well. It's just..."

"Just what?"

"Sigyn, there is something I want to ask. Will you—or, would you ever consider—"

The roar of the ocean drowned in a deep and consuming hum that gouged my eardrums with invisible spears.

"What the bloody hell is that?" I said.

Sigyn didn't answer. She only stared through me, catatonic and her entire body rigid.

The hum ascended into a screech.

Her eyes turned black.

"Sigyn?"

A rush of energy stormed out of her, kicking me in the chest, forcing me to stumble back. Away.

The glass railing shattered, launching a million shards across the deck and over my head and shoulders.

I raced back towards Sigyn, resisting the urge to clap my hands over my ears that burned as the hum continued to burrow deeper into my skull.

The champagne flutes cracked and burst along with the bottles, a deluge of wine and champagne flowing over the table and flooding between the translucent slivers that crunched beneath my heels.

Sigyn's knees buckled.

She collapsed.

I caught her in my arms.

And I felt a force.

Power.

Raw.

Hungry.

I lowered us both to the ground littered with broken glass and food and wine and cradled her head in my lap.

I pressed my hand over her chest, trying to feel, to understand, what was happening to her.

The energy writhing within her center snapped and bit beneath my palm and...and a knowing darkened my center, recognizing the familiar growl. Recognizing it because I had felt this energy once before, writhing in Gullveig's heart.

Surtr.

Sigyn had pulled Surtr into herself to save us from Ragnarok. Her contrary element of hope and fidelity had smothered this lethal and consuming darkness. At least, that's what we all thought. But now... now that darkness raced through Sigyn's veins, pulsing and alive.

Awake.

Awake? That's not possible.

My heart pounded against my ribs like a pick against ice.

The hum died.

The rhythmic thunder of the ocean that the hum had drowned out returned.

Sigyn's eyes fluttered open, normal and brown.

Wincing, she sat up and leaned forward, rustling the surrounding glass.

"What happened?" She pressed the butt of her hand against her forehead.

I couldn't find my voice. I lost it in the tempest of terror and panic filling my mind, each fear worse than the next.

Her cheeks flushed taking in the surrounding destruction. Her eyes settled on mine. I wanted to break seeing the worry blazing in them.

"Loki..." alarm filled her voice. "What happened?"

"You passed out and..."

I gathered her to me and held her against my chest. I pressed my face into her hair and kissed the top of her head.

"I did this?" she whispered.

"Have you noticed feeling anything odd? Rumblings? Twinges?"

She bit her bottom lip.

"I thought they would go away."

My pulse quickened and my stomach burned.

"Away?"

"I thought if I ignored it..." she paused. "We've fought so hard to have our present. Our future. I didn't want anything to get in the way."

I held her tighter, caressing her upper arms with my thumbs.

I understood what she meant. Our futures always tended to blow up in our faces, and now this...

When could we just be happy?

"How long has this been going on?"

She huddled deeper in my arms.

"Two weeks...maybe a month. But never anything like this."

I stood, beads of glass racing down my shoulders, and faced the house, needing to collect my thoughts. Webs of fine cracks split the thick windows.

"A *month*?" I turned and helped her to her feet. "This explains the broken mirror in the bathroom from a week ago. Why didn't you tell me?"

"Because I know how you get when things like this happen." She shook the glass from her hair. "You tend to get carried away."

"I do not get carried away."

She shot me a look that said *are you serious?*

Perhaps she had a point. I could be a tad rash. I had tried to destroy the worlds, after all.

She brushed the collar of her sweater. She stiffened as her finger-tips grazed something resting beneath the fibers.

"What is it?" I said.

She tugged her sweater off her shoulder and...

I thought some invisible hand gripped my insides and clamped shut.

Horror filled her gaze as she stretched her neck and stared down at a crusted, black spot festering on the ridge of her collarbone. That wasn't there this morning...

"What's happening to me?" she said.

That question gnawed my insides further raw. Because I didn't have an answer.

You think you've stopped Ragnarok. That you've won. But Yggdrasil's roots remain shaken.

I hushed Gullveig's warning from my mind, but I couldn't hush Odin's voice that trailed after.

Time will tell, he had told me when I asked him if there would be a price for Sigyn defeating Surtr.

And time told, but I had no idea what it meant.

"I don't know." That thought made me sick. I hated not knowing. "But I know who might."

I hated that more.

"No," she said. "Not him. You can't trust him, or any of the gods."

"I know."

"With what they've done to us—"

"I know!" I pulled in a calming breath. "But this episode you've just experienced—we haven't the time to find anyone else who might be able to figure out what's occurring inside of you. What choice do we have?"

I wanted never to see him again, to *need* him again, and now, he was my only option.

Sigyn shook her head and took my hand in hers and squeezed, her nerves dampening her skin with sweat.

"But you're exiled," she said. "You can't return to Asgard. It's too dangerous. If you break the terms..."

I waved her worry away.

"It's just a measly little banishment," I said. "I'm sure the gods will make an exception."

She raised her right eyebrow.

"I'm sure if we go in the back way, we won't get caught and they'll never find out," I added.

I really could do without giving the gods the satisfaction of finally being able to spill their juicy gossip about me causing Ragnarok to all our neighbors, who in turn would spill my guts across their fields.

It was a mess best avoided.

No, it was better to be prudent and err on the side of caution, even though doing so really disappointed me. Besides, I had Sigyn to think about now.

I had a new life with her.

One I would not surrender.

Yggdrasil's roots remain shaken...

"I don't like this," she said.

I didn't like this either, but it was the only course to stop whatever was happening to her. Surtr boiled hotter inside of her and I swallowed a spark of fear.

"It's a quick jaunt via Bifrost to Asgard. We will return before supper gets cold," I said.

I lied, knowing what had to be done, and what we stood to lose.

4

SILENT AS THE GRAVE

Asgard

Rain poured out of a sky thick with clouds, soaking our hair and trickling off our brows and chins. My clothes stuck to my skin, and my socks squished in my shoes with each cold step.

I didn't want to be back here. And, it seemed Asgard didn't want me back either, throwing me an incredible metaphorical finger with this wet bullshit.

I grumbled, splashing through the third ankle-deep puddle.

Rivulets of water ran between cobblestones that gleamed blue in the dim light from shop windows and colorful limestone buildings. I tugged Sigyn tighter against me as we kept in the darkness, squeezing through city alleys and beneath archways.

We took a hard right on Gretha Street and slunk past doors that shut on either side of us.

Left we swung and slipped down Njoll. Shutters on windows snapped tight, snuffing out the remaining yellow light pooling in the shadows.

If there was one silver lining, it was that the storm drove everyone inside, making the usually packed streets sparse. If we were noticed before...

Before we make it to Odin.

Odin.

The thought of him alone turned my stomach.

Unfortunately, dark prophecies with a penchant for ultimate destruction were outside my territory, but they weren't outside of his.

As much as it pained me to admit, no one bested Odin when it came to understanding dark things—charms, spells, magic—and Surtr was as dark a thing as ever existed.

If anyone knew what this meant...knew how to stop whatever was happening to Sigyn...

Sigyn chilled against me, as if Surtr read my thoughts—my hopes —and laughed.

Lightning coated the city in flickering, garish white.

Thunder rumbled in the distant mountains.

The storm hardened, dousing the palace that lay ahead in curtains of rain. The building sprawled along the hill, halls of fine stone and leaded windows and tile shingles.

Though I would have preferred to use my secret passage, it was no longer an option after my last performance with the whole killing Balder thing. I knew the gods would have swept through and barred any crack or crevice that led inside to prevent any more of my fun surprises.

We crept across the gardens, mud splattering our legs as we squelched through a bed of tulips. I peeked over a hedge and scanned the grounds and walls for any guards roaming about.

The hinges of rusting metal squealed. I ducked with Sigyn behind the greenery.

Two guards marched out of an arched gateway, whining about the wish for a good fire and a pint of ale.

Once they passed through the tower door, I tugged her the opposite direction and fled beneath a covered walkway lined with pillars, letting us catch our breaths and wipe the rain from our eyes hidden in the gloom.

"Are you sure this is the best way?" Sigyn whispered. "Anyone could catch us. Or we catch them. I don't know how I'll react if I cross paths with that *monster*."

Frigg, she meant. I didn't know how I'd react either.

Lightning flared, glazing her face in white. Red flushed her cheeks. Fatigue deepened the fine lines around her eyes.

I needed to get her inside.

"It will be fine," I said. "Trust me."

Rolls of thunder drowned the crash of the Asgardian Sea as I grabbed her wrist and pulled her along the path. Our clothes hung off our shoulders, heavy and wet and dripping trails of water behind us.

I stopped at the back entrance and smiled as men heaved sacks of potatoes off a cart and flung them over their shoulders. They walked one after the next through the massive door and into the warm glow of the kitchens.

The staff and I had come to an understanding long ago. They stayed out of my way, and I didn't tell Frigg who nicked the mead. It was quite the lovely little symbiotic relationship. One I hoped remained.

But, just in case.

A bald man dug his fingers into the burlap sack and swung the potatoes over his shoulder. Keeping Sigyn concealed to my right, I snuck behind him and did the same, carrying the potatoes so they hid my face. A woman with a stubby nose buried in her ledger made a check mark without noticing us slip past her and into the roar of crackling fire, sharpening knives, and the curses of cooks.

The floor warmed my feet as we walked through the soot-stained kitchens, dodging the scrambling staff as they grabbed copper pans off shelves and tended the hearth, full of spits and boiling cauldrons.

The clatter of dishes and shouts at the scullions grew faint as we turned onto a black and white tiled hallway. Now where was...ah! There. I chucked the potatoes behind a statue of a boar, flung open the door across from its snout, and hurried Sigyn up a spiral staircase with steps so worn my heels nearly slipped off their sunken edges.

I clicked open the door at the top and peeked through the crack and into the feast hall.

Empty.

Perfect.

"This way." I led her between heavy oak tables battered from eons of feasts.

The hollow echoes of our footsteps on the flagstones rose into the hammer-beam roof, the carved wood richly painted in golds and midnight blues.

She faltered. I held her up, pressing us forward towards Odin's quarters.

I didn't even have to second guess if he'd be at his desk, quill in hand, scratching a million illegible notes into book margins. His excruciating routines infuriated me to no end.

Now, it's what I counted on.

I slid back a piece of paneling and shuffled us through a passageway. A mouse scurried past. Cobwebs clung to the fibers of my jacket. *Wonderful. The cherry on top of an already steaming pile of—*

We popped out into a marble hall filled with the drum of rain beating outside the open archways, and the scent of jasmine and oleander brought me back to times I wanted to forget.

Times with him.

Extinguishing such disgusting recollections, I knocked on the oak door of his rooms.

No answer. Probably busy feeding liver to his ravens. I would never understand why he enjoyed keeping such gloomy rats as pets.

I pounded on the door again. Louder.

Sigyn leaned against the wall and the pallor of her skin turned a nasty shade.

"I'm about to faint or vomit," she said. "I'm not sure which, but I know it will be one or the other. Gods. What if I get sick on the furniture?"

"Don't worry over such things. I've vomited on Odin's furniture loads of times after a night of heavy drinking and never thought twice—"

More color drained from her face and she wobbled.

That's it. If he would not answer...

I struck the door with my shoulder and broke the bloody thing down.

I expected a rush of curses. Rage.

Nothing.

Mildly disappointing.

"Odin?" I called.

Gathering Sigyn to me, I guided her around the splintered wood and walked into an absolute mess of books, and scrolls, and mahogany furniture that needed a good polish.

I darted my gaze to every corner, over tapestries and to his desk crammed with papers and pots of ink.

My throat tightened.

He wasn't here.

Damn.

I sat Sigyn in a leather chair by the fire. Kneeling on a sheepskin rug, I pulled off her wet shoes and socks and grabbed a wool blanket off a stool. I draped it around her shoulders.

"Don't go making a fuss," she said, her voice strained. "I'm alright now I can sit."

She was not alright.

Squeezing through the labyrinthine stacks of books—*this man, I swear. After all these eons, still a pack rat*—I walked to the small table wedged between bookcases of sagging shelves crowded with ancient trinkets and baubles. I recalled each.

"I just need to focus on my breathing," she said. "Whatever this is will pass."

For being practically a doctor, she was the worst patient.

Picking up a goblet, I filled it to the rim with claret, hating the familiarity of my every movement. Hating the familiarity of being back here.

I returned to Sigyn and handed her the goblet. She lifted the claret to her lips and took a large swallow. A small part of me relaxed as color started returning to her cheeks.

Where the bloody hell was Odin?

"Stay here," I said. "I'll be right back."

I left before she had time to argue and marched down the hall in search of him.

Of course, he would choose now to form new habits.

Clannggg!

I turned as a continuous metal ringing melted into an irritating spin.

Balder stood rigid at the far end of the hallway, his perfect mouth agape, a silver bowl whirling at his feet. Green apples rolled across the marble, one stopping at the tip of my Louboutin shoe.

My lips pulled into the biggest grin, I suspect with a hint of evil at the corners.

Balder the Beautiful. All blonde hair, chiseled jaw, and a smile so white it made everyone weak-kneed. Everyone except me. I often fantasized about pulling each tooth out with a pair of rusted pliers.

Maybe my luck had turned around after all.

"Hello, Balder." My voice dripped charm.

His eyes widened—so blue, so grating—and he took a step back, crushing an apple beneath his polished boot heel.

"Stay away from me," he said.

Every muscle of his lean frame tensed, pulling his shoulders up nearly to the bottoms of his ears.

I sighed.

Murder someone *one* time and they never forgive you.

"I just want to have a little chat," I said.

He rubbed the side of his neck, as if recalling our last meeting when I had rammed a spear of mistletoe into his jugular. One of the great highlights of my life. I smiled wider at the memory.

"Chat?" he echoed.

He took another step back.

I took one forward, putting up my hands. Trying to reassure him I came in peace.

"Yes," I said. "Won't take long. I need a bit of information."

He nodded slowly.

"What do you want to know?" he said.

I relaxed, lowering my hands to my sides.

Good. Maybe there was a functioning part of his brain after all.

"Where is—"

Balder spun on his heel and ran away down the hall.

That little shit.

I ran after him.

He stumbled on an apple, smashing it into pulp. He flung out his arms in a kind of pirouette to catch his balance and—I clawed into his tunic, tackling him to the ground.

His forehead smacked the stone, and I flipped him onto his back. Apples rolled past us as he scratched at my face, swiping at my eyes and my nose with all the strength of a pathetic kitten.

I straddled him, squeezing his waist between my knees and grabbing his wrists. At least, I tried to grab them. Layers of heavy creams made his hands so slick he kept slipping out of my grip.

"What do you smear yourself with?" I said, fighting to keep hold of him. "You're like trying to grab a slug."

"Don't kill me again!" he sobbed.

Of course. Always making it about him.

"Please, I've moved on," I said.

He winced as I finally wrenched his wrists above his head, pinning him still.

"Now," I said. "Where's your father? *Oh, stop it.* You know your blubbering has no effect on me."

"He's..."

He fought for breath beneath my weight.

"Yes?"

"He's in the stables. Must you grind your nails into my wrists?"

I smiled.

I suppose I didn't. But, I never could help myself.

"The stables?" I said. "Since when did he become one for manual labor?"

His muscles relaxed and that delicious spark of fear in his eyes dissolved into something malicious.

"He said it helps him forget."

"Forget what?"

A smile cracked his face, the kind of smile that always begged me to punch him in the jaw and shatter all those prized teeth.

"The gods won't like knowing you've broken your banishment," he said. "You shouldn't be here."

He thought he got me. How precious.

I lowered my face to his cheek, feeling the heat rise off his prickling skin.

"You shouldn't be here, either," I whispered into his ear. "You should be rotting away in Hel where I put you and...why do you still smell like the grave?" Mushroom and damp saturated his hair, rather ruining my threats. I got off him and wiped my hands on my trousers.

"It's nothing."

He pushed himself up and rubbed the red marks I left on his wrists away.

Dirt filled his fingernails.

Odd.

"I see it's been awhile since our last manicure," I said.

He hid his hands behind his back.

"I said *it's nothing.*"

I eyed him. It certainly didn't seem that way.

Whatever. I didn't have time for this.

I pointed my finger into his chest covered in layers of silk.

"One word about this meeting and I swear I'll—"

"I promise," he cut me off. "Not a word."

He held my gaze, telling me the conversation was over. Brave. Especially for him. Delight washed down my spine. I always loved it when he challenged me.

"Good. Then we're done."

I picked up his fruit bowl, the silver embossed with grapes and vines catching the torchlight.

"Really?" he said, a bit too brightly.

"No." I gave the bowl a flip.

He looked to the right just in time to admire the full force of the sturdy silver that I raced directly for his forehead.

Whack!

He dropped at my feet, a lovely indentation of a grape leaf stamped into his bruising skin.

"Terribly sorry," I said. "But for some reason, I don't trust when the gods make promises to me anymore."

I lifted his ankles and dragged him to a large chest with brass fittings pushed against the back wall.

Hoisting him up, I dumped him inside the pungent camphor wood.

He'd be fine. Although, if it did take a servant a day or two to find him...

I picked up an apple off the floor and tossed it onto his stomach and slammed the lid shut and gave the key a twist, locking him inside.

Straightening my lapels, I started off for the stables and threw the key out the window into a gardenia bush.

* * *

VEINS OF LIGHTNING shuddered in the roiling clouds. The stables fluttered in and out of blues and purples.

The ground rumbled with the growl of thunder.

I hated how my heart thundered louder.

I hated how I just stood rooted and stupid and staring at that damned timber building.

Knowing he was inside.

Thunder quaked again, this time closer, vibrating into the soles of my feet.

Enough of this. I swallowed whatever tightness lodged itself in my throat and marched across the cobblestones and into the stable.

Warm. Dry. Bursting with the sting of manure.

I rubbed the stench from my nose and walked across the packed earth towards Odin, though I wanted to remain planted.

He kept his back to me, scrubbing and scrubbing the side of a dappled gray horse.

Lanterns coated his broad shoulders in soft light and silhouettes. The straw in the stables glowed gold.

I opened my mouth to speak.

"I thought the idea of our agreement was to never see each other again," he said.

He picked up a bucket and sloshed water over the horse's back. Streams of suds slipped down the animal's shoulders and dripped off its chest. Odin circled his brush on its flank, lathering the soap into the stiff hairs.

"We've shattered so many promises to each other. What is one more?" I said. "It's tradition at this point."

He turned and faced me, a smirk hiding behind his short, dark beard.

Locks of his russet hair skated across his black silk eyepatch that covered his missing right eye. The patch complimented the striking and rugged lines of his face. The fierceness and danger of him that gave him an unslakable and hungry look.

He was a man as strong as a mountain, and as consuming as the storm raging outside.

I swallowed down that bitterness again.

Odin combed his fingers through his tousled hair, pushing it back off his forehead as lightning blazed, dousing him in seconds of white.

"So," he said. "Are we to be frank, or play the game where you pretend to be interested in how I'm doing and not what I can offer you?"

He dunked his brush into the bucket, swirled it three times, and pulled it out, an arc of soap and water raining out of the bristles and splattering his boots and the dirt floor.

I crossed my arms.

"Why does everyone think whenever I appear it's always because I want something?"

He scrubbed the horse's neck, his muscles flexing beneath his blue tunic with each stroke of the brush.

"Because I know you didn't come to watch me shovel horse shit."

I'd give him that one.

I took two steps towards him, careful to avoid piles of horse dung. Obviously, he wasn't very good at mucking out a stable.

Wind gusted through the oak beams, chased by a roll of thunder.

"Sigyn is in trouble."

His lips compressed into a thin smile, and he chuckled darkly.

"Yes. What else would it be to bring you here other than something that involves that woman you broke our blood oath over?"

My jaw firmed and I hated thinking how we still shared the same scar on our arms from when we mixed our blood. Now, that scar was nothing more than a reminder to me to remain rock.

"You broke far more to me far earlier than I ever did our oath," I said. "And *that woman* is soon to be my wife."

His smile disappeared.

He chucked the brush into the bucket, and a slosh of bubbles gushed over the rim.

"I know." He grabbed a linen cloth off a bench and wiped his hands.

Of course he knew. Those bloody ravens of his always kept track. I'd spotted Hugin and Munin several times circling our home, unfortunately always out of range of arrow or bullet.

I drew in a breath.

"Look," I said. "Something's gone wrong and I..."

Gods, this was the worst.

"And what?" He threw the cloth over his shoulder.

"And, I—*well*—I suppose..." I met his gaze and held it. "I suppose I need you."

He softened, his arms relaxing at his sides.

Another breath and he hardened again. Cold. Stone.

His hands curled into fists.

"Need me." His words dripped with scorn. "Just...just leave me alone."

He stepped beside the horse and ran his hand down the beast's front leg and rubbed the fetlock. The horse popped up its foot and laid it in his palm. He grasped a pick off a stool and started digging muck out of the grooves.

The bastard.

I marched to him and ripped the pick out of his hand and threw it across the stable. It banged against a wall full of bridals and saddles, jostling the metal buckles and leather straps.

"You must help her," I said, leaning into him, trying to ignore his hot breath on my face. The sage on his clothes.

"I must do nothing." He stood, not breaking eye contact. "You made it clear this is how you wanted things to be between us. I'm only honoring your wishes."

He pushed past me and leaned against a beam, staring out at the rain pummeling the cobblestones.

"But—"

"Now honor mine and return to Midgard," he said. "If you go now, I'll forget this disregard of the stipulations ever happened."

Hang the stipulations.

"You're always the same," I said.

He snorted and crossed his strong arms.

"And you aren't?" he said. "Again, you snub all I've done for you. It's because of me you got to be exiled to Midgard instead of some prison in Niflheim. It's because of me your involvement in Ragnarok is kept secret from those outside of us gods who would love nothing more than to have your head on a spike. Yet, here you stand. Without a care. Breaking, *again*, every condition I've set to protect you."

My jaw tightened. It took everything in me not to snatch the pick off the ground and lodge it firmly into his skull.

"Do you think I want to be here?" I said. "Do you think I want to see you? That I'm enjoying this? I'm only subjecting us both to this lovely reunion because only you can understand dark things—like Surtr."

Another stab of lightning washed us both in scorching whites, still not as hard as the silence settling between us.

"Surtr?" he said. "What does that have to do with anything? It's over. Defeated. Your dear Sigyn saw to that."

I flexed my hands at my sides, remembering the bite of power churning within her. Of that black spot growing on her collarbone.

You think you've stopped Ragnarok. That you've won. But Yggdrasil's roots remain shaken.

"What if it isn't over?" I said.

He turned and faced me again. His brow knit together.

"The prophecy said her contrasting element was to save us." he said. "It said—"

"It said nothing about the ramifications," I interrupted. "Prophecies always leave out those fun, little details. No one would want the job to be the *savior* or *chosen one* if they knew what it entailed."

Thunder crackled, and I tried not to think how very much like laughter it sounded.

He stepped closer to me, his shadow stretching the length of the stable.

"Loki, what's happened?"

"Remember when I asked you if there would be a price for Sigyn stopping Ragnarok?" I said.

"Yes."

"I think it's time to pay up."

5

A TWIST OF LEMON

I explained the entirety of the events to him. How I had felt Surtr roll in her veins. How the power exploded out and shattered the glass all around us. How Sigyn had collapsed and remembered none of it.

Each word I spoke made him grow more grim as we walked back to his quarters. Well, until his features melted into the purest irritation when we came to his door, ripped off its hinges and splintered beyond repair.

"Was it really necessary to break down the door?" he grumbled.

I shrugged.

"I was in a hurry. Had you been here—"

He put out his hand to me. "Shush."

I blinked.

Oh. He did *not* just shush me.

I opened my mouth to tell him exactly what he could shush.

"Listen," he whispered tersely.

Sigyn's voice tumbled out of the doorway.

She spoke with someone.

"He won't abandon me again," she said. "I'm not a fool. You're wrong."

Who was...

I stepped over the broken door and went inside, the fractured oak boards cracking beneath me.

Tapestries and wood paneling and shelves of books framed Sigyn who stood completely alone by the fire, the blanket still wrapped around her shoulders.

She stared at the corner of the room.

My body frosted.

Her eyes met mine for two seconds before latching on Odin following behind me. She stood straight, growing taller.

"Who are you talking to?" I walked across the patchwork of woven carpets towards her.

She tilted her head and looked at me as if I asked her the stupidest thing ever. She pointed at an exceptionally ugly ceramic floor vase in the corner that long deserved to be put out of its misery.

"To him."

Him?

Cold sweat coated the small of my back.

Odin's cheeks sunk.

"What?" she said. "Don't you see him?"

"Sigyn," I said. "No one is there."

Confusion tightened her face. I didn't like the sweat slicking her brow. She looked feverish.

"Shit," Odin said.

He walked to his desk and braced himself against the heavy oak.

"Yes, there is," she said. "We've been talking since you left."

"Damn." Odin shuffled through papers. Knocked over pots of ink.

Sigyn faced the empty corner again, her gaze receding, detaching. Her stare hardened further, and she scratched her collarbone beneath her sweater. The blanket slipped off her shoulders and fell to the floor.

"Sigyn..." I neared her, keeping my steps slow. Measured. "I think you are hallucinating."

"Impossible." She tore her nails faster across her flesh, leaving webs of pulsing red scratch marks.

Odin kept rifling through papers on his desk beside us.

"You must stop that." I reached out and gently grasped her wrist, stopping her from lacerating her skin raw.

Her eyes locked on mine, black and glaring and threatening to eat me whole.

More sweat beaded at my temples.

"What?" she barked. "I'm trying to listen. I'm having a hard enough time hearing a thing over Odin's ruckus."

I felt Surtr writhe and snarl within her as I had on the patio. But this time, I also felt anger. As if telling me I was not to touch her. To stay away.

I yanked back the neck of her sweater from her collarbone. The spot now spread and stretched over the delicate bone, roughly the size of my thumb, charring the tissue it ate.

My heart plummeted into my stomach.

She twisted out of my hold and shoved me back.

"If you keep touching Sigyn, it will be bad for you," she growled, her voice lower than I ever had heard. In fact, it was not her voice at all.

Something sulfuric entered my nose. It reminded me of Vigridr.

I reached out and grabbed her shoulder again, and her skin stung me deep into my joints.

"I said do not touch her!" she screamed.

A clap rang out and my cheek exploded in pain as she slapped me.

"Sigyn!" Shock filled my voice, and hurt bit my insides even though I knew this was not her.

One heartbeat more and she sucked in a rasped breath, as if waking from a nightmare.

Sigyn's eyes returned to their normal brown. To clarity. To her.

"I'm sorry. I'd never—"

She reached out and rubbed the burn away from my throbbing cheek.

"I know." I gathered her into my arms and embraced her. She pressed her face into my chest and clasped onto me tighter. Her heart pounded through my clothes, matching the pounding of mine. I hated this.

I hated not knowing what to do.

"What's happening to me?" Her voice trembled, as if she were on the verge of tears.

I combed my fingers through her hair, calming her, letting her know it would all be fine, although I wasn't so sure.

"Surtr is manifesting a figure from within her," Odin answered, hunched over a pile of scrolls. "Dammit all to Muspelheim."

He pushed off his desk and walked to the small table crushed between bookcases. He snatched a silver cup and grabbed the carafe of claret.

"Excuse me?" I said.

He filled his cup to the edge and gulped the wine down.

Sigyn pulled back and patted the wet from her eyes.

"Are you telling me I actually am having hallucinations?" she said. Her voice remained calm, steady, but I sensed the alarm beneath. "I saw him clear as day."

"No," Odin said. "This is far worse than simple hallucinations."

He kicked back another slug of wine. My mouth dried, wishing for a drink myself.

"Worse?" she said.

"Is this the kind of news one should be sitting for?" I asked.

He rapped his forefinger against his cup, his gold rings catching the warm firelight.

"I don't like your silence," I said.

He didn't meet my gaze, instead looking directly at Sigyn.

"Have you seen this being, this *him*, before tonight?" he said.

Her breaths jumped like staccato notes.

"No," she said. "I never would have believed he was..."

He stepped next to me, not breaking eye contact with her.

"What did Surtr say to you? Tell me exactly."

She sank into the leather chair, but kept holding Odin's gaze.

"It's like this darkness could peer into my depths. Into my fears," she said. "Surtr knew..."

She fiddled with the edge of her sweater. The fire popped and the logs collapsed further into cinders.

"What did Surtr say?" he repeated, voice low. Serious.

"That you are all against me," she said. "That I can't trust anyone."

Odin spat out a curse that even made me blush and walked to the leaded window and stared out. Rain clicked against the thick circles of glass.

"Can someone please explain what the blazes is going on?" I said.

"Surtr is possessing her and creating an avatar of itself because..." He scrubbed the dense whiskers of his beard. "Because the darkness is growing stronger and taking her over."

I took Sigyn's hand and folded it within mine.

"Taking her over? How?" I said. "Only my chaos can awaken Surtr. The element should still be dormant. Without my chaos it should remain harmless, and—"

"And I have a piece of your chaos in me," Sigyn said. "It's made Surtr whole."

Cold swept down my spine at that unfortunate truth.

I had made her a goddess. I put my chaos in her, igniting her element of fidelity. And in so doing, I made it so she had everything necessary for this sludge to thrive in her, awake and complete and lethal.

Odin turned and faced me. A grimness I'd rarely seen settled in the lines of his face, turning my bowels to water.

I wanted to squeeze her hand harder, but I didn't, not wanting to scare her more.

"Her fidelity might have been a contrasting element that could defeat Surtr—snuff the darkness out—but the chaos in her, *your* chaos in her..." He stopped. "Before Ragnarok, we only understood the basics about Surtr. Now, we understand what Surtr is. We saw the capabilities on Vigridr. Dark matter is rabid. Wild."

"Meaning?"

He sighed.

"Surtr's nature is to consume, and that includes consuming

Sigyn's element of fidelity. Her hope," he said. "She will soon belong to the darkness. She will become darkness. She will become Surtr."

My entire body sank with realization.

The very thing I sought to preserve, I now caused to die.

"Will Ragnarok start again?" she asked.

The fireplace spit.

"If you wish it to start again," he said. "After Ragnarok, I finally got my hands on that book of prophecy Falael kept locked away from me—"

Sigyn gave Odin a particularly frigid glare that I was happy to not be on the receiving end of.

"You mean you stole *The Foretelling of the Nine Worlds* from him?"

He shifted in his boots, the answer being an obvious *yes.* Surprise, surprise. He always did have sticky fingers.

"Anyway, the book taught me that burning the worlds is only one of Surtr's abilities. Yes, you can destroy the worlds, as Gullveig wanted, but you can also enslave the worlds to bend to your will."

I shrugged.

"That doesn't sound all that dire, then," I forced out of my tightening throat. "It sounds as if she is in control of it. She wouldn't be such a bad supreme ruler."

He laughed.

"You think she will keep her own mind? That this will turn out roses with Surtr's influence? That she will snap her fingers and make a utopia?"

"Well..."

"What are you saying?" Sigyn said.

"According to Falael's book, Surtr is limitless dark power devouring you, Sigyn. Infecting your mind. Warping your soul. Who you are now is slowly dying, as Surtr feeds on you like a parasite, and once the darkness possesses you completely, Surtr will corrupt you into becoming a being who only wants and craves and feeds—worlds, lives, freedom—all are at risk once you succumb."

"No," she said. "You're wrong. I won't succumb."

I caressed my thumb over her knuckles. Odin was right.

"I said the same about waking Surtr from Gullveig's heart," I said. "We all know how well that worked for me."

Her lips flattened.

"This isn't a matter of choice. It's a matter of time," Odin said. "That's the thing with being a god. We are our natures, our elements, and once Surtr consumes your fidelity—" He exhaled. "You will have lost your mind to the darkness, and you will be the darkness. You will be Surtr. And all our fates, all the worlds, will be yours to do with as you please."

You think you've stopped Ragnarok. That you've won. But Yggdrasil's roots remain shaken, Gullveig's voice ran through my mind again— cold and cruel and real.

A fresh roll of anger at myself burned my insides. I alone damned Sigyn to this situation, not only because she held my chaos, but because of my lust for vengeance. I started Ragnarok, endangering everyone, forcing her to suck Surtr into her and save us all from what I'd done, lost in my hatred.

Now, Sigyn was in danger again. And it was my fault.

I couldn't stand this thought.

I stood and walked over to the bookcases lining the back wall, needing space, needing to think of anything else. I roved over the knickknacks and trinkets, and picked up the ugly raven Balder had made for his father.

The only thing worse than Balder was Balder as a child when he discovered the joys of crafts. We'd all received some disfigured wood-land creature made from clay that Yule.

Mine had been a melted pig. He argued it was a fox.

I suppose it was sweet how Odin still treasured his glazed monster.

I had thrown mine away in the bin immediately.

"Now that we have the facts of this *wonderful* predicament, what do you suggest?" I pushed past the lump in my throat.

"Energy cannot be destroyed, it can only be transferred," he said.

I stiffened, running my fingertip down the raven's lumpy wings.

Over the tip of its squished beak. Anything to keep me grounded. To stay knit together. Steel.

"You mean remove it?" I said. "Last time that meant cutting out a heart..."

I squeezed the figurine, my knuckles turning white.

"But," Odin said. "This time Surtr isn't tethered to any heart, and I—"

A dull crack split in my palm as the head snapped off the neck.

Oops.

Odin looked at me.

I curled the decapitated raven tighter in my hand and hid it behind my back.

"And you what?" I said.

He eyed me.

"And I know a charm that can exorcise Surtr from her body, but it doesn't come without its own dangers."

I knew what he meant by *dangers.*

One of his dark spells.

I'd seen Odin perform enough of them. Quite entertaining, really. That is, as long as you weren't on the receiving end. Definitely best enjoyed as a spectator sport and from a good distance. If something went sour...well, I really preferred my organs remain inside my body.

I could still hear Herleif's screams.

But this...

This was something different entirely.

This was far darker.

"No," I said.

I shoved the fractured bits of raven behind a book.

He'd never know. At least, not until we were long gone.

"No?"

I walked towards him.

"You are talking about purging Surtr from her insides," I said. "About grasping a million roots of energy fused into her soul and sinew and ripping them out and it's...it's monstrous. Painful. Violent. I can't subject Sigyn to that."

"If you don't want her heart cut out, it's the only way," he said. "It might be barbaric, but it's all we have. Surtr is growing stronger. That's why the darkness is now manifesting itself a visible being and…and time is running out."

I shook my head.

"It's too uncertain," I said. I couldn't believe those words fell from my mouth. I lived for the uncertain. Uncertainty gave everything that zing, like a twist of lemon on an oyster.

"The only thing that is certain is if we do nothing, we will all be finished." Sigyn pushed out of her chair and stood.

"You promise if we do this, it will save everyone from this *dark matter* infecting me?" she said. "It will stop me from losing who I am and belonging to the darkness?"

"Yes," he said. "But, even if we succeed, it's not without risks to yourself. The effects—"

"What must we do?" she said.

"Sigyn, please reconsider," I said. "We can find another way."

"There is no other way," Odin snapped at me.

"Stop it," she shouted. "I'm doing it."

I wanted to rip out my hair.

"You don't understand what this all entails," I said. Begged.

The back muscles in her jaw twitched.

"This is my fate," she said. "I'm done having decisions made for me by both gods and mortals."

I gripped her shoulders, as if trying to keep her from slipping away. Needing to hold on to her. On to all we had fought for.

All our tomorrows.

It was all turning into sand and running between my fingers.

"I can't risk losing you," I said.

She stroked my cheek, a sad smile cracking her face brimming with determination.

"But you will lose me if we do nothing."

I fractured.

Everything in me shifted.

She was right, as much as I didn't want to admit it.

To keep our future, we had to do the very thing that might lose it all.

Odin cleared his throat beside us.

"Once I enact the spell and pull Surtr from your body, we will need a host," he said. "An object we can transfer the energy into and trap it."

"An amulet," I said.

I laced my fingers with Sigyn's.

Odin looked away and into the dwindling fire, the last embers glowing red in the ash.

"An amulet," he repeated. "One strong enough to hold an element."

Unfortunately, we didn't have any amulets of exceedingly robust magical properties laying about. No, acquiring such a rare piece would be tricky.

Tricky, if I didn't know exactly who could make what we needed.

The brothers Brokkr and Eitri of Svartalfheim. Exceptionally gifted. Exceptionally proud. Exceptionally gullible, but that last bit was neither here nor there. They were the best metal smiths in all of the Nine Worlds, and could make the strongest of magical treasures, no questions asked. Which was important when you needed something perhaps on the more devious side.

Not that I ever would. I cracked a grin.

I stepped away from Sigyn and pushed my sleeves to my elbows. Was Prada the best choice for a mountain climate? No. But at least I'd look good as I froze.

"Lovely," I said. "I guess I'll pop over to Svartalfheim. Then you can do this delightful spell of yours and get this sludge out of Sigyn."

I walked to the door.

Odin grasped my arm and stopped me, forcing me to face him.

"You can't go alone."

"Are you seriously suggesting we do this together?" I wrenched myself free and rubbed the sensation of his touch away.

"I don't like the idea any more than you do," he said.

"Out of the question. You'll only get in my way."

"Do you think I rejoice in this?" he spat. "Every minute counts. We can't afford any hiccups. If we stand a chance, we have to do this together."

"You underestimate me now?"

He rolled his eye.

"Oh, of course not," he mocked. "You always handle making a mess of things quite nicely on your own."

He really wanted me to kick him in the kidneys.

"Watch it," I pushed between my clenched teeth.

"Yes," he said. "Tell me how happy Brokkr and Eitri will be to see you again. How accommodating Brokkr will be after that last stunt you pulled with him."

I groaned.

"Is he seriously still sore about losing my head?"

"Head? What are you talking about?" Sigyn said.

Oh.

"Well—did I never mention this?—I—"

She put her hands on her hips, seeming to feel better. More steady.

"You what?"

I scratched behind my ear.

"I might have cut off Sif's hair," I said. "No more than an inch. Maybe twelve. Ok, it was all of it, but I did try to make it right by acquiring her new hair. Better hair. I even put my head on the line all in the name of thoughtfulness."

"Please," Odin said. "You tried to pull the wool over Brokkr's eyes with your *wager*."

I smiled. I really outdid myself with how I had wriggled out of that particularly sour pickle.

He looked at Sigyn and pointed his thumb at me. "He bet his own head, you know? And lost. But, because he is a cheater, he didn't have to pay up."

"It wasn't my fault he left the wording of our bargain vague," I said. "He said nothing about my neck."

"Do you actually ever think sensibly?" Sigyn asked me.

I shrugged.

"What's the fun in that?" I said.

She pulled her hands down her face.

"The fact remains, Brokkr will do you no favors," Odin said. "Unless you want to pay him what he still thinks you owe him."

I rubbed my throat.

Damn.

Brokkr was a nasty piece of work, even when he was in a good mood.

Maybe it would be wise to bring Odin along as a buffer. At the very least, he'd be useful to throw in front of Brokkr's blade if he came at me.

"Perhaps you're right," I said. "Best we journey together."

"Then let's go," Sigyn said.

"Afraid that's going to be a no," I said.

"And why is that?"

"You're too unstable to travel where we are headed," Odin said. "You will have good days and bad days, but the bad days will only grow more frequent as Surtr grows stronger, and this journey will not be helpful. We want to push off Surtr winning as long as we can, not speed it up."

She nodded stiffly.

"I see," she said. "So what then? I'm just supposed to stay in Asgard and rest? That seems like that would be worse given there are gods here who would see me as a danger. Again."

Odin sighed.

"You mean Frigg," he said.

Sigyn crossed her arms.

"I actually meant all of you Asgardian rats, but take my meaning as you will."

A rush of heat flushed between my legs. Gods she was incredible when she openly chastised the Aesir to their faces.

But her point stood.

"Frigg will learn that we've come. That I've broken the *terms* of my banishment," I said. "Balder has seen me, and he will tell mummy dearest. If she discovers what's actually going on with Surtr..." I paused. "I don't need to remind you what happened the last time she tried to stop a threat."

I shook away the horror creeping into my mind.

Odin's lips thinned behind his beard.

"We need to take Sigyn where no god in Asgard would dare step foot," he said.

I smiled.

"I don't like that look," Sigyn said.

I smiled wider.

Odin frowned. He knew where I was thinking.

"You can't be serious," he said.

"Do you have a better suggestion?" I said. "Sigyn will have a great time with her."

"When I thought you couldn't get anymore harebrained. Loki, I swear—"

"She just has to stay away from the demon bears. And the impaling fields."

"Who are you talking about?" Sigyn interrupted.

We both looked at her.

Perhaps this was a bad idea.

6

LEATHER AND STEEL

"Stop fretting," I said. "You and Angrboda will become fast friends!"

"She sounds like someone who kills after mating." Sigyn tightened the cords of her leather jerkin.

"Now that's hardly true, otherwise I wouldn't still be here." I tugged on a green tunic of dense wool over my head. Plain, boring, eternally itchy.

"You told me she once pounded a man's face into the floorboards because he wore a wolf pelt."

I covered my mouth so she wouldn't see me grimace at that unfortunate fact. It seemed a good story to tell Sigyn at the time. I never thought it would come back to bite me quite like this.

"I know Angrboda can seem hard as steel, but beneath all that..."...*is one giant spear*... "You will *love* her."

She sat on the edge of a chair by the fire and shoved her right foot into a sturdy boot. I removed the black nail polish from my fingers. I refused to deal with chipped edges the entire journey.

"I hope you're right," she said. "But, I feel like she and I are very different people."

She had a point.

Angrboda once left me tied to the bed, and not in the good way.

Gathering our tossed Midgardian clothing off the rugs, I bundled them together and walked across the room frosted in the pale light of morning to the wardrobe.

Odin thought it best we trade our Midgardian clothes for Asgardian and magnanimously provided us with the essentials while we remained holed up in his rooms.

I frowned at the lack of embroidery along the edges of my tunic, but this journey required rugged fabrics that could withstand trekking across the realms—each with their own delightful flavor of harshness.

Pulling open the wardrobe, I laid our clothes on the shelves, cramming in trousers and shoes. I hoped the Prada would forgive me. I peeked behind my shoulder at Sigyn. She kept fighting with her boot straps.

I breathed easier seeing a bit more color in her cheeks. A bit more strength in how she held her frame. It took an age to convince her to drink a second glass of red wine and close her eyes for an hour as I prepared our satchels. Quite the victory, as charming a wolverine was easier than getting that woman to rest.

I just wanted her better.

I refused to have this love end like all the others.

Angrboda and I had enjoyed the best of times together, and for a summer's day, I thought I finally had the family I always wanted.

But the wolves always feast at night.

And then Odin came.

He came and...promises were made. Promises I—

I slipped out Sigyn's ring from the inner pocket of my jacket, and the gold gleamed in my palm, warm and safe. I ran my fingertip along the engraving.

This time would be different. This time, love would not end in disaster.

This time, promises would not be broken.

The ring laughed at me.

Do you really think you can have a happily ever after? You don't deserve one.

I clasped my hand tight and shoved the ring into the pouch on my belt to shut it up.

It was wrong. I did deserve one.

And I would let nothing stand in my way of getting it this time.

The door swung open.

My muscles stiffened as Odin walked in, carrying a large satchel swung over his shoulder. He wore layers of wool in shades of gray and blue, a worn leather belt cinching it all around his flat stomach.

I finished stuffing our clothes into the wardrobe as he dropped his satchel on the chair at his desk, the wood cracking beneath its weight.

"Weapons from the armory." He flipped the flap over. "You're going to need more than just a dagger."

He pointed at my blade holstered at my hip. Sigyn who now fought the ties of her trousers.

"*Just a dagger*?" I repeated. "Alright, I can't even begin to tell you how wrong you are."

Laevateinn had been my mother's dagger that she had gifted to me as a child. She had told me it was named *Truth*, but Gullveig told me its real name was *Laevateinn*, or *Destruction*—I know, quite dramatic —and *Laevateinn* wasn't so much a dagger, as a way to channel magic, like a wand. A very sharp wand.

Odin sighed.

"Do you even know how to use *Laevateinn* besides slicing it through someone's throat?"

Leave it to him to ruin everything with logic.

"Please, these things are always straight forward." I dug through the sharp delights inside the bag. "Magic goes in, magic goes out. Honestly."

I waded through an assortment of sheathed blades and hilts wrapped in tough leather and shagreen, needing something with a certain...

Why, hello there.

I drew out a second dagger and inspected the blade. Dwarven steel. Nice bevel. Good balance. I secured the beauty to my belt opposite *Laevateinn*.

Odin rustled through the satchel, the clank of metal filling the room. His face softened, and he pulled out a leather case with worn corners.

My heart quickened.

Were they really...

"You still have these?" My heart raced.

He smiled, flicking the metal latch and opening the box, revealing a collection of throwing knives secured in rich velvet. Light and short. Clip point tips. Pristine. They were like seeing an old friend.

"Remember the last time you used them?" he said.

I lifted one out of the box and squeezed the concave grip, enjoying the chill of steel sinking through the black cord wraps. I smiled as battle roared in my ears and wood smoke filled my lungs. I felt the hot splatter of blood on my cheeks.

"When we stormed Utgard?" I said. "I never knew Jotnar could shriek so loud, but when you jump out of a pie in the middle of a theater production..."

"We feasted well that night," Odin said.

It all continued to blossom in my mind—bright and vibrant.

"Tyr got so drunk he lost his trousers and—" my words melted into laughter.

"Yes!" he said. "He lost his trousers, and when we found them first, we fed them to a herd of goats!"

"Don't you think that's a little mean-spirited?" Sigyn straightened the sleeves of her linen shirt.

I wiped tears from my eyes.

"Mean-spirited? We didn't make him pull off his own trousers and throw them in a tree," I said.

"But we did make him walk the entire way back to Asgard bare-assed," he said.

Another roll of laughter burst out from deep in our guts.

"We had good times then," I said.

I started to lay my hand on his shoulder—wait. What was I doing?

Did it seriously only take a single second of icky reminiscing to undo all my efforts in hating him? All these memories were supposed to be burned, and the ashes flung into the deepest pits of Muspelheim.

No. This was bullshit.

We were no longer brothers.

We were no longer friends.

We were no longer anything.

I put the knife back and snapped the case shut.

Odin frowned with an odd sort of disappointment. Disappointment concerning what, exactly, I couldn't care less.

"When can we start this wonderful venture?" I took a step away from him. Far away.

He rubbed his thumb over the garnet ring on his forefinger, and forced his expression back into ease and charm.

"Dawn approaches," he said. "I'd like to make it to the docks before the other gods wake."

Reasonable.

I grabbed a second set of knives—double-edged and pure steel with cut-outs along the handle. They weren't as precise, but at least they didn't come with memories.

I strapped one of the knives around my upper leg. I wedged another inside my boot.

Sigyn stood and tied back her curls with a bit of leather that matched her leather trousers. They showed off the shape of her legs quite nicely.

She pushed between Odin and me and pulled out a machete from the satchel.

"Which one of these will cut through the hide of a demon bear?" she said. "Although, I feel it will be more like Angrboda I need to arm myself against."

Again, she had a point.

I took the machete out of her hand and replaced it with a small axe.

"That should do the trick, for both."

She chuckled, but it died in the back of her throat. She turned and stared off into the shadows.

She scratched her collarbone again.

I reached out and touched the small of her back. My insides squirmed with how rigid her muscles felt beneath my fingertips. How cold, as if she had been standing in a blizzard for hours.

"What is it?" I said.

Her eyes remained locked—focused—on whoever she saw.

I didn't have to guess. Surtr.

"Leave me alone," she snapped at the wall. "You are wrong. They are helping me."

She scratched harder.

"Sigyn," I said, trying to snap her out of it.

Odin rushed behind her and seized her wrist, and spun her around. He clapped his hands on her cheeks, forcing her gaze away from the wall. She winced, trying to wrench her head free, trying to look back at Surtr.

"What are you doing?" I said, attempting to pry him off her.

He closed the remaining distance, shutting me out, digging his fingers deeper into her jaw, keeping her gaze on his.

"Don't look at Surtr, look at me," he said to Sigyn. "You cannot engage with this entity. You must disregard him at all costs."

"Why?" Sigyn pushed out, her gaze flicking to the wall and back to him.

"That's why." He motioned to her collarbone.

Faint black tendrils spread out from the spot on her skin. They had not been there before.

My mouth dried.

"The more you speak," he said. "The more you engage, the stronger Surtr grows and the less time we have."

He let his hands fall away from Sigyn's face now riddled with anxiety.

"What Surtr says makes me so angry..." She scratched. She stopped and curled her fingers into a fist and locked it by her side. "And that's what Surtr wants. He is trying to break me."

He nodded.

"Whatever Surtr says, whatever the darkness whispers in your ear, you must ignore," he said. "For your sake, and for ours."

She motioned understanding and tugged her shirt over the spot, hiding the charred skin.

He gathered our cloaks off the back of a chair and threw me a glance that clenched my insides.

It said everything I already knew.

We all teetered on the edge of being royally screwed.

7

BURY THE HATCHETT

Jotunheim

The Ironwood Forest

The smell of horse already permeated my clothes as we rode within Angrboda's lands in the Ironwood.

Pine forests marched towards the Gray Mountains, dark and thick and filled with whatever went bump in the night. And when the mists rolled in...You never forgot your first troll.

Took ages to remove the snot out of my hair when one sneezed on me. That was before it tried to bludgeon my skull in with a club full of nails.

Gods I missed this place.

However, while I enjoyed being back, I couldn't shake my annoyance that I'd already be at Angrboda's by now if it weren't for Odin. Apparently, flight, magic—*using my element*—was out of the question because of a billion reasons he explained in excruciating detail. Something dull about needing to preserve our power for what lay ahead? He always overreacted. Did he forget? I was chaos. My well did not empty easily. There was plenty to go around.

No. My time was better spent focusing on preparing myself for the true scourge awaiting me—enduring this entire journey on horseback, which meant days of dried venison, hardtack, and camping. Oh goody.

The trees groaned as cold wind gusted through the tight branches. What shards of light cut through the canopy danced across the narrow road, lumpy with muck.

Sigyn trotted ahead of us on her chestnut horse, mud caking the animal's legs up to its knees.

"You sent a raven with word of our arrival?" Odin said. "Angrboda is expecting us?"

A crow cawed somewhere lurking in the gloom.

"If I didn't know any better, I'd say you're scared."

He was a fool if he wasn't.

"I am not in the mood to be shot by an arrow." He wiped condensation off his brow with his sleeve.

"We are nearly there," I said. "I can just make out the impaling fields through the fog."

Her immense fortress of blackened limestone peeked over the packed pine on a hill. Turrets and towers and arrow slits. The keep loomed above the outer walls, as comforting and inviting as Angrboda herself.

This promised to be a lovely reunion. My mind ran with how to even start the conversation.

Long time no see. I know, pity Ragnarok didn't turn out. By the way, you wouldn't mind hiding Sigyn? Why? Oh, she just happens to be possessed by a very violent and dangerous element that is now manifesting itself into a talking being. No big deal.

Yes. I saw this going over like a cow in a catapult. Best to avoid the truth entirely.

But first...

I pulled back the reins and pushed into the saddle of my blue roan, making it stop.

"What are you doing?" Odin said.

He tugged on his reins, directing his black horse to stop and face me. We thought it prudent to leave Sleipnir in Asgard, so as not to draw attention to who we were.

"I think it best if you wait here," I said. "Your furs are so—majestic —and—well—if she'd invite us in for a bite, I couldn't live with myself if a servant accidentally spilled wine on them."

A twig snapped beneath Sigyn's horse and ricocheted off the tree trunks as she continued trotting down the path.

"You didn't tell her, did you?"

I clapped my hand over my heart, deeply offended.

"I'm trying to spare your clothes."

His face flattened into a straight line.

"Fine, no, I didn't," I said. "Is that what you wanted to hear?"

"Typical."

"I always find surprises are best when dealing with Angrboda," I said. "They run a much lower risk of getting oneself run through. As for you—regardless, she will kill on sight."

"He's right," a voice shot from the shadows. Her voice.

A knife zipped out of the darkness and lodged itself firmly into the tree directly behind Odin's head.

Angrboda followed, a storm of rage and vengeful delight.

She leapt and tackled him, toppling him off his horse and throwing him on his back into the mire. She pinned him between her legs and dug her fingers into his throat.

"How long I've waited for this," she said. Her black hair fell in front of her gray eyes filled with storms.

Odin clawed at her wrists. She crushed into his larynx harder, turning his face a cadaverous shade of blue.

"Stop!" I wrapped around her waist and wrestled her off him.

He heaved in a breath, choking and hacking.

She pulled back her arm and punched me across the cheek. White blinded my watering eyes. Iron coated my tongue.

"I will not miss my chance to watch Odin bleed out," she said. "After what he did. What he took…"

I wiped blood off the corner of my mouth. She remained absolutely breathtaking.

Odin rubbed his neck.

"Your children...are...are now free," he choked out.

"But they weren't," she said, the words deep and filled with anger. Pain. "Because of you. Because we believed you."

Still trying to catch his breath, Odin reached inside his cloak for his sword. Angrboda kicked him in the stomach, throwing him against a sap-riddled pine. She pressed her foot into his chest, keeping his back rigid against the trunk, and pulled out a small axe.

"He deserves a broken spine after what he did," I said. "But right now, I need you to set aside your anger for one blasted second. If Fenrir could walk away—"

"Don't you dare tell me to bury the hatchet," she spat. "Because the only way I'm doing that is if it's in his skull."

Odin croaked out curses at her. Each made her red lips stretch into a wider smile.

She swung back her axe, ready to hack it between his eyes.

"Let him go."

Angrboda turned and faced Sigyn riding towards us. She leapt off her horse and marched to Angrboda.

Angrboda kept her axe at eye-level.

"And who in Ymir's eyelashes are you?" She flicked her hair behind her shoulders.

Leather and wool covered her tall frame of sturdy muscle and contours. An exquisite rage brightened her long face and high cheekbones, making her simultaneously striking and cruel.

"If you kill him, you put all our lives at risk."

Sigyn held Angrboda's gaze.

Odin cursed louder, hurling out threats, each more vivid than the last.

"Lives at whisk? I cannot hear a damn word."

Angrboda holstered her axe and tugged off her boot. She slipped her knit sock down and off over her foot.

"*Risk!*" Sigyn yelled over a fresh flood of obscenities.

Angrboda folded her sock into a ball and stuffed it into Odin's mouth, stifling his grumbles.

"What risk?" Angrboda said, securing the gag with a bit of rope and tying it behind his head.

I wanted to enjoy Odin's humiliation, but Sigyn already said too much. Angrboda loved anything dire, but even she had her limits.

"No risk," I jumped in. "Nothing at all like that."

I gave her my biggest, most sincere smile.

Angrboda rolled her eyes and coiled the rope around Odin's wrists and yanked it tight, making him groan.

"So, you're being stupid, then?" she said to me. "Because I can't think of any other reason that you'd trespass into the Ironwood unless you were stupid."

"I was actually hoping for a favor."

She cackled.

"Those hamsters living inside your head must have eaten your brain entirely if that's the case."

Hold it together.

"I need you to watch over Sigyn," I said. "Odin and I have an errand to run—you wouldn't be interested—anyway, she can't come and I thought—"

"Why can't she go with you?"

"—and I thought it would be nice if she stayed with you while I'm away. The two of you can enjoy a spot of fishing, braiding each other's hair, throwing knives at traitors. That sort of thing."

She narrowed her eyes.

"You always find a new way to chap my ass."

"Is that a yes?"

"Will you let me kill Odin?"

She always played a hard game.

"Unfortunately, Odin is quite important to this errand, but I suppose after the errand is finished..."

Odin snapped his gaze to mine, burrowing daggers into me.

"Afraid that's off the table," I said.

She shoved her barefoot back into her boot.

"In that case...no."

"No?"

"First of all, I don't babysit, secondly...I don't babysit," she said. "And third...and third is I'm done with you bringing your Aesir drama to my lands."

My muscles tightened and my lips pressed together.

"This is in your best interests."

She pointed her finger into my chest, and something dark and pained flashed behind her eyes.

"The last time you asked me to do something in my best interests, you lost me everything."

I shrank, her words cutting me down. Forcing me to face the truth —that I was not blameless in what had happened to our children.

"Ang..."

She pointed west, back towards Asgard.

"Leave."

Sigyn stepped forward, the squelching mud pulling me out of black memories I struggled to pack away and heave into the abyss of my mind.

"Must you always evade?" Sigyn said to me. "For once, be honest and direct."

Honest? What was she?—

No. *Gods* no.

"Sigyn—"

"Look," she said to Angrboda. "I'd love nothing more than to not stay here with you, but the only way to stop Ragnarok was for me to take Surtr into my veins and...doing so left me with some side effects."

I curled my fingers into fists against my mouth, holding in a shriek.

Angrboda raised her right eyebrow.

"Side effects? Such as?"

"Sigyn," I said. "Why don't we talk about *not* this?"

"Loki, shut up." Angrboda said.

"But—"

Her face stiffened with a look I knew all too well.

I had three seconds until she gutted me with an iron hook.

Sigyn tugged back her shirt, ignoring me and showing Angrboda everything I wanted to keep from her. Angrboda's eyes widened at seeing the black spot on Sigyn's collarbone.

"Surtr is taking me over," she said. "If Loki and Odin can't pull this dark matter out of me in time...Everyone will be affected. Badly."

Sigyn covered the spot again. "Angrboda, I'm asking you to help give me my best chance. I need to be kept hidden while Loki and Odin find a way to end this."

"But why must you be hidden?"

"The gods," I said. "If she's discovered...If they find out what's happening..."

Angrboda stiffened, knowing the gravity of my words. What it all meant.

She turned away and walked to the knife still wedged in the pine tree beside Odin's head.

"I know what it is to lose children to the gods," Sigyn said. "Don't make me lose my own life to them as well."

Angrboda yanked the blade out and stared at the steel. I couldn't read her face, but I could feel the heaviness of her grief pulse out of her.

"The gods are cruel," Angrboda said. "They always think they own the place. Call all the shots."

She squeezed her grip on the blade.

She took in a breath and met Sigyn's gaze. Something I'd rarely seen glistened in her eyes. I believed it to be a soul.

"You can stay," she said. "If only because it will piss the other gods off."

I clapped my hands and rubbed them together.

"Wonderful," I said.

She wrapped her arm around Sigyn and pulled her in tight against her.

"Loki, bring her horse with her effects."

They started walking along the muddy path towards her fortress.

"And Odin?"

She looked back at him, still tied up and gagged and perfectly livid. She smiled.

"That rat bastard can wait here until you return," she said. "The mists won't roll in for another hour or two. He shouldn't be eaten by a troll until then."

Muffled grunts and swears followed. It took everything in me to keep my own lips from twisting into a smile.

I knew I shouldn't enjoy his situation as much as I did, but his misery was as sweet as brandied chestnuts covered in marzipan.

"Besides, he might spoil the reunion," she said.

"What reunion?" I said.

She chuckled from her chest.

"Let's just say you have a lot in common with my newest guest."

Somehow, knowing her, this unnerved me more than the trolls.

8

DOUBLE TROUBLE

I followed Ang and Sigyn down lime plaster halls decorated in rich paints and hanging tapestries. Through rooms crowded with oak tables, sideboards, and chairs—everything rough and dark and immense.

And every timber beam, every snap of my boots against the flagstones, tugged me deeper into memories of the life I once had here with Angrboda.

Passing a crackling stone hearth, Hel's laughter filled my ears as wood smoke filled my lungs. I scooped her up and balanced her on my knee as Fenrir and Jormungand sat crossed legged on furs, staring up at me, mouths open, as I told them dark stories of frost giants in the North.

Tell us the one about the dragon next, Papa!

We took a right down a corridor patterned with clay inlaid tiles, and I stepped into another memory.

Ang cradled Jormungand and sang a Jotun folk tune as I embraced them from behind, holding tight, holding on. Fenrir balanced on tip toes and clasped onto my arms to peek at his new baby brother. Even Hel smiled with affection, tender and true, as she combed a skeletal hand over Jormungand's fine hair.

"*Will he be a shifter like me?*" Fenrir said. "*We will be able to play the best of games together if he is.*"

My smile widened, remembering it all. How it had been.

Beautiful. Happy.

Loving.

And then thorns sprouted at how it all ended.

Laughter faded into tears when I told them I was leaving the Iron-wood for Asgard.

But he swore leaving would let me make the Nine Worlds better. For them.

Tears faded into cries when I had...

I swallowed bile.

...*When I had let the gods take them away from their home.*

That day I saw their love dissolve into hatred for me.

But he promised it was for their safety.

So many promises Odin made me.

And he broke every one.

Angrboda stopped us and pointed out a leaded window that overlooked the lake where Fenrir and I would go ice fishing in the winter.

That bile crept up the back of my throat again.

I turned away before the memory could fully blossom, needing it all to evaporate.

A shadow hurried into the sitting room.

What the—

I followed, leaving Sigyn and Angrboda locked in chatter, and walked into a chamber of red and white checkered frescoes and heavy furniture spread over a thick rug.

A man stood facing the stone fireplace ornately carved with boars, mountains, and figures that towered up to the wooden coffered ceiling.

Býleistr.

I stifled a sigh of indignation that *he* was her surprise guest.

She really crossed a line with letting him be here.

"Hello, Bly," I said. "I had hoped you'd be dead by now."

He turned and faced me, the firelight edging his tall and lean frame in yellow.

"I see you still haven't changed," he said. "*Brother.*"

I scowled. Did he have to rub it in?

A crooked smile cracked his sharp face—*my* face—making it even worse. Is that really how I looked when I was smug?

No, he had far more asshole in him than I did.

Býleistr wasn't just my brother, he was also, unfortunately, my twin.

That fact really boiled my turnips more than us sharing the same mother and father.

Especially with how he dressed.

His love of shoulder pads did nothing for our exquisite bone structure. Or how he kept his copper hair neatly tied back in a knot. Or how he still wore the same inferior leather jerkin he wore two millennia ago because, gods forbid, he spend two more coppers on a new one.

It was thoroughly depressing anytime someone confused us, one with the other. But what irked me most was that he was such an unfortunate cliché.

I plopped in a chair draped in sheepskins.

"You still wearing tassels?" I pointed at the monstrosities dangling on his boots. "Very brave."

He narrowed his green eyes. They might have been my same shade of green, but they did *not* have my same sparkle.

"Again with the tassels," he said. "It's always some quip. Some sarcastic remark with you. Did no one tell you how tiring your whole thing is?"

I leaned back into the wool and crossed my legs, savoring his outrage.

"Because your whining I've had to endure for centuries about me being Mother's favorite is any less tiring? Please."

Our mother loved us equally, but Bly never saw it that way. He only saw me as some kind of barrier to his happiness. His animosity worsened after her death, growing his anger as we grew up together, shoved from shack to shack across Jotunheim, scrounging, surviving —and I grew tired of him pulling at me. Blaming me. Until I was tired and old enough that I left him and went out on my own. Alone. He only blamed me more.

I languidly ran my fingers through the flame of a candle on the table beside me.

"Will you stop fingering the candlelight?"

"Why?"

I grabbed the flame, letting the light dance across my knuckles and settle in my palm before sending it cascading back through my fingers like a ribbon. I loved my element. My fire.

I knew I shouldn't use any magic, but Odin wasn't here.

"Because I hate it," he said.

I spread my fingertips, stretching the blaze into a web of flame.

"I know. That's the idea."

He had once tried to imitate me with this trick, to show Mother he could also play with fire. Took a month of aloe salves to heal the blisters.

He grabbed a silver goblet off a table and poured an arc of ale over my hand, extinguishing my fun.

"Before you set the whole place on fire," he snapped. "I won't have another room burnt to cinders because of you and your constant need for attention."

That wasn't a great loss. The wallpaper was horrid.

"You always were a sourpuss." I wiped my hand on a pillow.

The corners of his mouth tugged back, revealing the edges of his teeth.

"And you always think yourself so likable," he said. "Even after setting the worlds on fire, you truly believe yourself untouchable."

My breath hitched. How did he know about my involvement with Ragnarok? Surely Angrboda wouldn't have told him, especially as our own children had been embroiled in the whole mess.

Regardless of who spilled, I wouldn't give him the satisfaction of having burrowed beneath my skin like the worm he was.

"Did you miss the part where I also saved the worlds?" I said. "All has been forgiven."

There was no need to mention the banishment part.

He chuckled deep in his throat.

"*Forgiven*, yes, how could I forget?" he said. "But it doesn't change what you are."

"And what am I?"

He braced himself on the arms of my chair and leaned in until his overly woodsy cologne choked me.

"A liar."

Laughter burst out of me.

"How will I ever recover from that crushing blow?" I wiped tears from my eyes. "Explain to me how blackmail is more noble?"

He smiled, unfazed.

"I expose frauds and liars. I bring truth to light," he said. "And yes, I might make a little money off their sins from time to time, but either way, they are punished whether I lighten their purses or expose their dark deeds."

I rolled my eyes.

He always justified himself. He was nothing but a massive tattletale.

"Is that why you're here?" I said. "Is that what this menacing little tête-à-tête is about?"

"I'll give you until your return."

Oh, this was going to be good. He thought he had me. Like all those times before.

"Alright, I'll play your game. You'll give me until my return or what?"

"Either bring me what I want, or I'll test the theory of how likable you really are."

"What do you mean? Your riddles are too smart for me, Bly."

His pointed features tightened into a sneer.

"For starters, I'm curious. Do you think Sigyn would find you killing her brother likable, or unlikable?"

Cold trickled between my every vertebra.

"I haven't a clue what you're talking about," I said.

He laughed now.

Bly pushed off my chair and stepped back, reaching into his inner pocket. He pulled out a faded letter that iced my spine solid.

Crooked lines in Simon's cramped script ran across the parchment, my charm remaining strong after all these centuries disguising my hand beneath.

He cleared his throat and started reading the letter aloud.

"My dearest sister." His every word dripped with melodrama. "I've gone off to join the military and fight in Italy. But do not mourn for me, as I am content in my path and with God's good grace…" He snickered and peered over the letter at me. "Oh Loki, you really pulled the wool over that poor girl's eyes with this one, didn't you?"

I had.

And it would stay that way.

I launched out of my chair and marched to him. He hurried away from me until he struck the wall. He flung up his right arm, holding the letter above our heads, waving it this way and that, always out of my grasp.

"How did you get that?" I growled.

"Does it matter?"

I grazed the brittle paper and—it disappeared from his clawed fingers. Damn him. He was rubbish with all forms of magic, save for the vanishing charms he had learned from Mother. Those he was quite skilled in. It made sense for someone in his line of work.

I held his gaze that glowed with delightful spite.

"She won't believe you," I said, a hope pathetic and moth eaten.

"Are you willing to take that risk?"

"You're right," I said. "I've found two can keep a secret if one is dead."

I clutched into his jerkin and threw him onto the rug, his shoulders skidding against the rough fibers.

He laughed again.

I stepped into his sternum, turning his laughter into choking. He looked at me, that spite in his eyes burning fiercer. I wanted to snuff it out.

"We both know you won't kill me," he rasped. "More importantly, you know this isn't how this works. Punishment has come for all the wrongs you've done, and penance must be paid."

Rage exploded in my chest and my stomach roiled.

Because, for the first time, he had me cornered.

I wanted to kill him for that alone. Unfortunately...

Forcing in a breath, I lifted my foot and stepped back.

"What do you want?"

He pushed himself up and straightened his posture, rubbing out the imprint of my sole from his jerkin.

"Just a morsel," he said. "Something to keep my skin looking as pert as yours."

I tensed.

"You can't be serious."

"Unless you are a *god*." He spit out that last word. "One of Idunn's golden apples only lasts so long. I want to have my apple secured for when I am due for some maintenance."

I should have known.

Those who weren't a god needed a golden apple every ten millennia, give or take five thousand years, to keep on living—they weren't called the apples of immortality for nothing. And if you knew the right people to acquire one...

"This is impossible," I said. "There are no apples anywhere until the Autumn harvest, and even then—"

"This doesn't sound much like you," he said. "You always bragged how you could solve any problem that cropped up in Asgard for dear Odin. Or have you lost your touch?"

I wanted to strike him across the face and pound out his brains through his nostrils and eye sockets.

He knew what he asked of me. Something cruel.

Punishing.

"I can't control crops, Býleistr. Be reasonable."

"Bring me a golden apple, Loki," he spat. "Or I will take what you never should have been given—your happiness."

I swallowed sand.

Do you really think you can have a happily ever after? You don't deserve one.

"What will it be, Loki?" he asked.

The door hinges creaked, and Sigyn walked in.

I stepped in front of Bly to hide him from her view. I would rather be dead than have them meet.

"There you are," she said, relief in her voice. "Angrboda won't stop talking about how last night her lover begged her to fracture her spine and...can we go now?"

"Of course," I said, corralling her towards the door, away from Bly. Far away.

"You're not even going to introduce us?" he said.

Sigyn's gaze fell behind me onto Bly and her eyes widened.

Damn.

I shuffled her out of the room faster. She gripped the doorframe, pushing herself into my chest, forcing me back.

"Why are there two of you?" she said. "He isn't one of your illusions. Who—"

"No one of consequence," I assured.

She ground her heels into the floor as I gave her another shove, trying to budge her forward.

"Loki, what's the matter with you?"

She spun in my arms and slipped away from me.

Her eyes flashed between Bly and me, confusion knitting her brow tighter together with each glance.

"Explain what I am seeing," she said. "Because I am struggling to come up with any reason that isn't me having a stroke."

Bly's lips pulled into the most disgustingly charming smile as he stepped in front of her.

"I'm Býleistr Fárbautison, Loki's brother."

She looked at me, shock softening her features.

"Brother?" she repeated. "Don't you think having a brother is something you should have mentioned, especially the fact you have a twin?"

I shrugged.

"I choose to identify as an only child."

Her eyebrows shot towards her hairline.

"Loki," she said. "You're so lucky to still have family living and... and I can't believe you never told me."

Bly scoffed.

"Not telling you everything seems to be a trend with him, Sigyn," he said.

And we were done.

I grasped her wrist and tugged her towards the door again.

"Let's go get you settled," I said to her. "Odin won't forgive me if he gets gnawed on because I'm late."

I shoved her out of the chamber, following on her heels...until she was out of earshot.

I stopped beneath the doorframe, and bit the inside of my mouth and looked over my shoulder at Bly.

The fire snapped and licked the stone hearth behind him, casting his face in shadows that made him appear vicious. Merciless.

"I will bring you your apple," I said. "For your silence."

"I am glad to hear it," he said. "She seems like a good one. I'd hate to lose her for you."

I didn't believe him.

Nothing would give him greater pleasure.

9

THE WOLF AT THE DOOR

"You shouldn't hear the wolves too loudly in this room," Angrboda said. "If you aren't used to their howling, they keep you up all night."

She grasped the curtains of rich brocade that hung from iron rods and flung them open, throwing the bedchamber into streams of cold light.

"Did you hear that, Sigyn? Low wolf noise. How marvelous," I said, wanting to distract her from our encounter with Bly, and hopefully lessen the growing tension in her jaw.

"And when exactly were you going to tell me about Býleistr?" Sigyn said, marching inside.

Apparently, it wasn't working.

I rubbed my right eyebrow.

"I was saving that lovely morsel of my family history for the appropriate time," I said.

She eyed me.

"Alright. Never," I said.

"Seems about right." Sigyn plopped her satchel on the chest at the foot of the four-poster bed that was layered with good mattresses and wool blankets.

Angrboda straightened a vase on the mantel, while a servant girl, who seemed barely seventeen, struck steel against flint in the fireplace. A fire couldn't come fast enough to chase away these wretched drafts sweeping across the rugs.

"When Ingrid finishes lighting the fire, I'll have her bring up a pot of black tea with lemon slices and a plate of pickled herring," Angrboda said.

My mouth puckered already at the thought of soured fish, and more memories of *home* infused further into my bones as I sat on the edge of the heavy desk. Jotunheim remained the same. Drafts and cold and pickled herring.

Sigyn shook out her satchel, sending a shoe flying and landing on the floor in front of my toes. I shoved off the desk and picked it up off the wool pelt.

"What do you think, Sigyn?" I held the shoe out to her. "Doesn't pickled herring sound delectable?"

I swallowed down my gag reflex.

"What do I think?" She snatched the shoe from me. "I think you could have told me such a simple thing as you having a brother."

Sigyn gathered what few tunics she brought and crammed them into the wardrobe on the opposite side of the room.

She really wouldn't let this go.

"Are you well?" Angrboda asked Sigyn. "You seem irritated."

Sigyn shut the wardrobe doors and let her arms fall slack at her sides.

"I'm quite well, thank you," she said, her voice softening. "Please accept my apologies. I don't mean to be rude, as I'm very grateful for your generosity. I'm only dealing with something I should be used to by now."

Angrboda flashed her eyes at me.

"Ah. I know exactly the problem you're dealing with."

My skin itched as both of them stared into me.

Ingrid cursed, still struggling to light the fire.

"Let me help you, Ingrid." Sigyn walked towards the fireplace, allowing me a small reprieve from all the glaring.

She knelt beside Ingrid and smiled that soft, reassuring smile she always gave that made you know everything would turn out fine.

And I chilled thinking of that smile I so adored turning into hatred for me.

If Bly told Sigyn the truth about what I had done to Simon...

Angrboda walked away and towards the door. I hurried after her and pulled her hand off the latch.

"You could have mentioned Bly was here," I whispered, so low I wasn't even sure Angrboda could hear me.

"And ruin the surprise?" she said, twisting out of my grasp. "He only arrived a couple of hours before you. Seemed to expect you, actually. I was so close to getting my knife in that one-eyed bastard's temple thanks to his warning."

Expect?

I didn't like when people expected things they shouldn't know.

This entire Bly debacle was beginning to have the stench of rotten shark meat about it.

"Get rid of him," I said. "I don't want him around Sigyn. In fact, I don't want him within a hundred miles of the Ironwood."

"I don't answer to you." She kept her words beneath her breath. "He and I have a wonderfully twisted on-again-off-again thing going and—ah, I see..." She lowered her voice further. "Bly knows some skeleton of yours that might scare Sigyn off. Oh, this must be delicious gossip. Tell me everything."

Her eyes brightened, eager for me to spill all my dark adventures. As I used to do, recounting every wicked detail to her as I ate honey cakes, leaning back in my chair with my feet clopped on the table.

"Ang. Please." The earnestness in my voice surprised me.

It must have surprised her, too, as her mirth dissolved into seriousness.

She nodded stiffly.

"Fine," she said. "I will keep Bly away from her, only because I find Sigyn a dear—fantastic legs—but that's as far as I go."

"So that means you won't hang him by his thumbs in the dungeon until I'm back, because I was hoping—"

She scowled.

"No, you're right. Too much. Keeping them separated will be enough."

I wasn't so sure.

The crackle of fire filled the surrounding space, along with the shuffle of feet. Angrboda's eyes fell behind my shoulder. I turned and Ingrid walked towards me as Sigyn walked to a wash basin that stood on the side table.

"The mists are coming soon," Angrboda said, raising her voice. "If we are lucky, the trolls will have already ripped off all of Odin's limbs and stuffed them up their own nostrils before you get back to him."

Yes, what a great shame that would be.

She pulled open the door and left, Ingrid hurrying out behind her.

I shut the door.

Sigyn poured a pitcher of water into the basin and cleaned the soot off her knuckles.

"What were all those hushed tones about?" she said. "Discussing more of your secrets with her?"

She grasped a clean cloth and wiped her hands dry.

"Sigyn, please understand, I have my reasons for cutting him out of my life," I said. "He's someone I don't even think about, because he doesn't deserve a second thought."

"Why? What has he done?"

My throat slammed shut.

She sighed and her shoulders relaxed.

"It's not that you have a brother living and didn't think it important I know," she said. "It's that this isn't the first time you've kept things hidden from me. It seems a habit, one I don't like."

I breathed out, defeated. I detested how I shifted in my boots as I reached deep within me and yanked up the truth by the roots. Why did this have to be dredged up?

"Since we were children, Bly and I have shared a very *complicated* relationship," I said. "He hates me, and I hate him. That's the fact of it. And he finds no greater joy than in checking in on me from time to time and ruining everything I've built. He takes what he feels I don't deserve."

She tilted her head.

"What could he possibly feel you don't deserve? What could he take?"

I froze.

She took my hands and rubbed her thumbs over the tops of my knuckles.

"Loki, you can tell me anything," she said. "You know that, right?"

A yearning burned in my chest to tell her every wrong word I'd ever uttered, to unearth every secret, reveal each lie, but experience had taught me long ago that every love has a condition. Even ours.

I forced a smile, one I tried to make look as effortless and endearing as possible. I needed this discussion put to rest.

"Right now he is taking away what I hoped to be a very romantic goodbye," I said. "Let's not let him ruin what little time we have left."

Her gaze softened.

"I don't want that either."

I placed my hands on her hips and drew her in closer, wanting the distance destroyed. Wanting to ignore the fact that I was falling into a pit of vipers.

"Does this mean all is forgiven?" I said.

She smiled delicately.

"When you warned me you'd add some spice to my porridge, I expected a dusting of cinnamon, not you dumping out an entire bottle of cayenne pepper."

I chuckled and leaned in closer to her, nuzzling her cheek.

"Would you have me any other way?" I whispered, letting my lips graze her ear.

She squeezed my arms.

"Gods no."

I kissed her neck, loving how her skin prickled beneath my mouth as I trailed languidly down to her shoulder.

A wolf howled far away, high and sharp. Angrboda was right. It was more muffled on this side of the fortress.

"How long do we have until the mists?" Sigyn ran her hands up my back in that way that told me everything. Desire licked up my thighs.

I pulled back.

"I don't know if this is wise," I said, even though I ached for her. "You're not well."

"I'm well enough." She tugged at the collar of her tunic, hiding the infection. "If these are our last moments together..."

I caught her face in my hands, forcing her eyes on mine to reassure her, even though I think it was more to reassure myself.

"They won't be."

Sadness tugged at her features that filled with ghosts.

"You can't guarantee that," she said. "We must take what moments we are given."

Pain nicked my center at this truth.

"Sigyn..."

"We don't know what is coming, or what will happen. But what I do know is that we have now. And I want to spend now feeling your heart beat against my own. Again, tell me, how long do we have?"

I placed my finger beneath her chin and lifted her face closer to mine, our breaths thickening between us. My blood raced.

"Long enough."

Our lips met, and I melted in her kiss, in her taste, and warmth cascaded from my shoulders to my toes and back up again, every inch of me stitched with a longing that yearned to be fulfilled.

I slid my hands behind her waist and pressed her body against me, and warmth turned into a blaze. Our mouths moved slow and tender as we savored the other. Without realizing how we got there, we laid on the sheepskins on the floor, the wool warm from the fire. I deepened our kiss, exploring her mouth as I ran my hand up her side and...

Still dressed? Tsk. That would hardly do.

I broke our kiss, and sat back on my knees and held her gaze as I untied her trousers. She was beautiful doused in the firelight, and it took everything in me not to unravel right then and there seeing her coated in quivering golds.

I slipped my fingers beneath the waist of her trousers and slowly slid them down past her thighs, over her knees, her ankles, until I threw the wretched things behind me.

The fireplace popped and spit.

I grasped her right leg and bent her knee back and kissed her calf, inhaling the forest on her skin. My nerve endings lit as I ventured closer, wrapping my arm around her upper leg and kissing the inside of her knee.

I met Sigyn's gaze and something devilish quirked my lips as I spread her legs, opening her to me.

I slipped my finger into her, loving how she trembled as I worked her steadily.

"How does this feel?" I slipped in a second finger.

Her eyes darkened, and she opened her legs even wider.

"How long...do you plan...to tease me?"

I smiled.

"Until you beg."

I lowered my head between her thighs and closed my mouth around her, moving my fingers tenderly inside her. She arched her back as I loved her with my tongue, lost in the utter bliss of her taste. Sigyn wound her fingers tighter in my hair and soft moans spilled from her lips.

The fire crackled, and waves of warmth spread over us. She moved against my mouth, pleading for more. I was happy to oblige, loving how she shuddered as I tormented her with my tongue. She cried out, pushed over the edge.

And I throbbed harder in my trousers, my own desire skirting that same edge.

She panted as I crawled on top of her and kissed her, urgency pounding at the base of my spine. Sigyn slipped her thumbs into my trousers and slid them down, her hot palms skating over my backside, and with every inch of my naked skin she touched I thought myself flung into an abyss of flames.

I nestled between her legs and she held my gaze as I gripped her hips and lifted her slightly and thrust into her heat. She gasped, and I shivered at the shock of rich darkness surrounding me.

Gods she felt so good.

Sigyn wrapped her legs around my waist, and I moaned as she locked her ankles behind my back, taking me in deeper until I filled her completely.

Pleasure rolled through my core, sparking down my arms and legs to my fingertips and toes.

Sigyn pushed back my hair that stuck to the sweat on my temples, and stared into my eyes.

I slowed my movement within her until every stroke became agony. Everything in me hungered to go faster, to chase the precipice. I believed I might burn.

"Don't stop," she whispered.

Then burn I would.

I refused to hurry.

I just wanted to love her, to be one with her, for as long as I could last.

She kissed my neck. My cheek. My chin.

All she was, everything she meant to me, penetrated into my bones until I thought I'd evaporate.

My soul nearly wept that such a woman wanted me. Being wanted was not something I was used to, and I pushed away the terror of it, because the last time I believed I was wanted—no. None of that mattered anymore. She wasn't him.

Sigyn rescued me from an endless winter and pulled me into summer.

Winding my arms behind her back, I pressed her closer to me. Her breasts swelled against my chest with her every breath, and her racing pulse matched the same tempo of my own.

Waves of ecstasy crashed over me and pulled through me.

She moved beneath me, rocking me into her quicker. Needing me. And I made sure I worked that place in her that always made her whimper.

Passion took root, and we shared breath that deepened with the scent of the other. Our rhythm increased, and pleasure rushed and rippled along my spine, both of us chasing that slice of death awaiting us at the end.

When I was with her, in her, I was whole. I was safe.

Her skin cooled beneath my touch.

I can't lose her.

I can't lose love again.

Her skin cooled further.

We moved faster, and I careened towards the edge of letting go.

One heartbeat more and I'd fall into leagues of oblivion.

She screamed in pain.

Shock jolted me. I stopped and pulled out immediately.

Sigyn sat up and rubbed her collarbone, her face filled with worry and fear.

"Have I hurt you?" I said, placing my hand on her shoulder, trying to catch my breath.

She shook her head, her eyes rimmed in red. She tugged and twisted at her tunic.

"No, it wasn't you," she said. "Surtr shouted in my mind, and then a thousand knives sliced my body. The darkness was angry."

"Angry? But why?" I said.

"Because I was thinking how much I loved you," she said. "Surtr says I am a fool."

She wiped the tears from her eyes.

I gathered her to me and rocked her in my arms.

"I don't want this," she said.

Burying my face in her hair, I squeezed her tighter. I didn't want this either.

And Surtr could not have her.

I stood and gathered my trousers and boots and pulled them on. I had to leave for Svartalfheim.

Now.

"I will get Surtr out of you. I will fix this," I said, though I wasn't sure I could. "The price shouldn't be yours to pay for saving the worlds. For stopping what I unleashed—"

My hands shook as I fumbled, trying to straighten my tunic and put on my cloak. I was falling to pieces.

Sigyn embraced me and I thought I would break.

"I trust you, Loki," she said.

10

HAM IT UP

Asgard

(Technically...)

T he north lands of Asgard were as bleak as they were dull.
Clouds churned gray and thick in the sky. Wind gusted over cabbage fields that marched across endless hills, and every time you thought about how cold the wind blowing through your cloak was, it grew colder.

Gods, why did this have to be the quickest route to Svartalfheim? I just wanted Surtr out of her.

On top of that, there was only so much cabbage one could see in a day, and I had passed my limit five hours ago.

I braced myself against another lash of wind as I glided my finger over the engraved gold of the band of Sigyn's ring.

I trust you, Loki.

I clasped the ring tight in my hand. She wouldn't trust me anymore if Bly told her what I did to Simon.

But what choice did I have? She nearly lost her nose, ears, and eyes because of him, because the men hunting Simon wanted to teach him a lesson by mutilating his sister. And with their vengeance left unsatisfied, those same men returned and set her family's print shop ablaze.

Even after all this, still Sigyn refused to forsake her brother. She kept waiting for Simon to see the light, to come around, to repent and be the brother she once remembered.

She'd be dead before that day came, a knife meant for Simon in her stomach.

So, when Simon returned home that night to find her to demand the necklace she treasured most—his inheritance, he claimed—he found me instead.

I killed him to save her life.

She'd not see it that way.

I will take what you never should have been given—your happiness.

I clasped the ring tighter.

After I paid Bly off with that bloody golden apple, I'd hunt down whoever gave him that letter and rip out their—

"What are you constantly staring at?" Odin said, breaking my thoughts.

Again.

That man kept wriggling the thorn he was deeper into my side. The entire ride from the Ironwood he'd clear his throat or comment on the weather or eat his jerky. Could he chew any louder?

"None of your concern." I pocketed the ring.

He sighed.

"Are we to journey in silence for days, then?"

"I find silence lets one better enjoy the scenery."

I pointed at the surrounding miles of cabbage on either side of us.

I breathed in the damp air, savoring the rhythmic clop of horse hooves pounding the dirt road.

Savoring his existence fading away—

"I do find it ironic you living in Midgard, now," he said, interrupting my peace for the thousandth time in ten minutes. "Not that you had much choice."

I ground my teeth.

He was determined.

"What is the point of this conversation?" I snapped.

"To have conversation," he said. "To maybe—"

I put out my hand, stopping him from saying it.

To maybe heal old wounds.

I should have known.

"Let me make one thing clear before you get any ideas," I said. "This *thing* of us working together is just a rendezvous. When this is over, we are still done."

His lips flattened behind his short beard.

"Do you think that's what I'm doing? Trying to rekindle friendship?"

"Is it not?"

He rubbed his thumb into his leather reins.

He met and held my gaze.

A wash of memories I didn't want trickled down my shoulders.

How we had loved each other.

How he had promised me...

He promised.

It wasn't supposed to be like this.

He looked away.

I exhaled.

"We both know friendship doesn't work for us," he said.

Cabbages stretched to the horizon.

* * *

WE ENTERED GLEDIVIK, a lawless port town on the outskirts of Asgard populated entirely by thieves and sailors and adventurers who would quicker stab you in the face than shake your hand.

While slightly on the murdery side, Gledivik had a lot of heart.

Crooked, timber framed buildings lined the cobbled street we rode along. Men and women and people of all sorts screamed obscenities at each other between swigs of ale. A crow swooped off a windowsill and plucked an eyeball from the socket of a corpse hanging from makeshift gallows in front of the bakery.

My stomach rumbled at the thought of supper.

Odin agreed.

And the horses needed a rest.

We slid off our saddles and led the horses to a trough outside a tavern called *The Thirsty Kraken*, and tied their reins to a post.

We walked into a roar of dice and cards and the flash of daggers against throats. Bows hammered fiddle strings, cutting into the strum of guitars and whine of an accordion. Roasting meat mingled with ale and armpit.

I ducked as a wine bottle flew over my head and smashed against the wall behind me.

This place was delightful!

Squeezing between harlots leading their culls behind heavy curtains and up to the balcony, Odin and I took a table with the best view of the drunk patrons fighting with fists and chairs and potted plants. We ordered ale.

"What is your plan for getting Brokkr on our side?" I took a slug of ale, malt and earth filling my mouth. "As you kindly pointed out, I don't see him or his brother being receptive to our visit."

A group of rough women threw dice next to us, the clattering across the battered wood joining the ruckus of laughter and curses.

"Brokkr and Eitri will listen if we have something they want, which we do."

"Such as?"

That grin he always got when he did an especially naughty wrong crept across his lips, making my curiosity grow faster.

Odin glanced right and left, and opened his satchel inside his cloak.

I set my pint beside the candles melting into a mound of wax in the center of the table and leaned in to get a look at what he had and...I raised my eyebrows at a flash of something green, smooth and waxen.

Brokkr and Eitri would lose their minds over this.

He closed his satchel again.

"Please tell me you didn't take that from Falael," I said.

He chuckled and drained the last dregs of his drink.

"Took it the day I took that prophecy book," he said. "I thought it might be useful when I saw it sitting in his cabinet in Alfheim. While you reunited with Sigyn, I picked the lock and stashed it away, and good thing I did." He snapped his fingers at the server, ordering a second round. "Falael was a fool believing sticking me in that kitchen would keep his belongings safe."

I relaxed back into my chair, marveling at his genius move. He was so bad, and it made me smile, especially thinking of Falael's face if he knew what we were about to do with this Elven prize.

I smiled wider.

A server, all sweat and intimidation and shaven head, brought us two tankards, foam slipping down the pewter.

"You thieving bastard," I said.

Odin's laughter joined my own as we grabbed the fresh pints and struck them together in a toast.

We threw our heads back and gulped the ale down.

Odin's eye caught mine. A spark. A dare.

So, he still thought he could outdrink me? Please, the last time I sent him under the table, and still drank three more barrels of mead. The lovely gentleman who held back my hair as I hurled out my guts into a floor vase was very impressed.

I tilted my head back more. I'd show him and...

The ale turned acrid in my mouth.

No.

I put my tankard down.

I pushed it away.

Odin lowered his mug and chewed the inside of his mouth, disappointment tugging at his face. The same I had noticed when we were packing to set off on this venture.

Sniffing hard, he tapped his fingers on the table lacquered in centuries of spilled ale.

"The trick will be getting Brokkr and Eitri to even see the bloody thing before they set their dogs on us."

"Loki," a gruff voice whispered somewhere to my right.

I turned. A group of patrons gathered around a beam darted their gazes away from me and to the floor, and to the curtains, and to an iron chandelier. I believe one whistled some Vanir tune off key.

Dice clicked across the tables. Cards shuffled in hands. Another rush of cheers and threats and exploding glass swallowed their chatter.

"What is it?" Odin asked.

"I thought I heard..." I shrugged it off and faced Odin again. "I will take the lead with Brokkr and Eitri. Inspire a little common sense—"

Odin laughed. In my face. Gods I hated him.

"Common sense? Common sense was never their strong suit, and you blew up what speck remained. Only hatred awaits you with them, and that's why *I'll* take the lead and ensure your neck doesn't get sliced open."

I crushed my teeth together, but my imagining of pouring my ale in his lap was disrupted as my name burned my ears again.

I glanced over my shoulder. The group of seven was now fifteen. No, twenty. This time, they did not look away. Glares flared. Fingers pointed at me.

"Yes, hatred seems to be a continuing theme," I said, waving at them.

I went back to drinking my ale.

The crack of knuckles replaced the crackle of dice

A shadow fell over our table. A dozen more shadows followed.

"It really is you," a man with bulging eyes said. "Loki. The Trickster. The Sly God. The Lie-smith."

I sighed.

They always went straight to the lying thing.

"Sorry. Afraid you have me confused with another lie-smith," I said. "Now, if you'd kindly stop breathing on me. You could knock a buzzard off a shit wagon."

I took another sip.

The woman towering next to him stepped forward, her muscles glazed in grime.

"You turned my brother into a salamander," she said.

I crossed my arms and leaned back in my chair.

"Do you really expect me to remember everyone I've turned into a salamander?"

"*He* remembers," she said, fuming.

Grumbles bolted between the gathering crowd.

Odin stood, his chair legs scraping the floorboards.

"Come now," he said. "Let me buy you all a round of ale. There's no need to ruin the mood of your dice, cards, and fist fights."

Another man who sweat liver and onions from his pores pointed at my nose, which only intensified his stench.

"The mood is ruined by the presence of this fiend." Spittle sprayed my cheeks.

A rumble of agreement and *hear hears!* filled the tavern.

I wiped my face with my sleeve.

"I'm regretting that I couldn't turn you into a salamander like I did her brother," I said beneath my breath.

"I take it you know who I am?" Odin said, pushing back his cloak so the candlelight gleamed down the length of his sword.

"Gledivik doesn't care who you are," a woman with shorn hair said. "Only who you've crossed, and that louse crossed us when he killed Balder."

I groaned and shoved my face in my hands. Why was Balder always so damn popular? He really wasn't all that great.

The group closed in.

"Balder is back, if you haven't noticed," I said. "No harm done."

"No harm done?" A youth snapped, pulling out a mallet from their belt. "You took Balder from us, and then you tried to kill us all in Ragnarok."

Ragnarok? How did they know? They weren't supposed to know.

I bristled.

As did Odin, even more so than myself—which meant this news was let out by someone else. But who?

"Loki needs to pay for Ragnarok," one said.

Knives slid out of holsters.

"Hang him!"

They tread closer.

We inched back.

"Slice open his stomach and spill his bowels!"

Swords and axes appeared in their grips.

Several blades were Dwarven steel.

Now this was getting serious.

I pulled out my daggers.

"Ragnarok was *so* six months ago," I said. "Can't we let bygones be bygones?"

A muscular woman flipped the table, sending tankards crashing to the floor and rivers of ale racing towards the tips of my boots.

I took that as a no.

Good. Otherwise, I'd be incredibly disappointed. I deserved a spot of wholesome fun after enduring miles of cabbage.

Odin and I hit our backs against the wall.

He drew his sword.

She pointed her dagger at my chin, which sent a flush down my legs.

"You nearly took our lives," she said. "Now I will send you to Hel."

She lunged her blade towards my heart.

"Been there already, thanks."

I kicked her in the stomach, hurtling her over a table littered with mugs. Waves of ale sloshed the fronts of three patrons.

They stared and blinked, their beards and tunics soaked with ale.

The tavern erupted in a storm of screams and steel as dozens charged us.

A burly man cut his sword down at Odin, and Odin crossed his blade, raised up, and kicked the man in the groin.

I punched a lout across the face, enjoying the snap of cartilage crunching flat beneath my fist.

Half-eaten apples and chunks of stale bread shot through the air, as those without weapons grabbed whatever they could off their plates and tables.

A woman with webs of scars drove her sword at my leg. I caught her arm and circled her hand. A mug whizzed past my left ear. I seized her sword and flung it out of her hand, spinning the blade and cutting the cantaloupe hurtling for my head in half.

Men holding broken bottles and scabbards galloped towards Odin. He ran one through, turned, and shattered the teeth of another with the pommel of his sword and rammed his elbow back into the gut of a third.

More sped for him, shaking hammers and split turkey leg bones sharp enough to pierce skin.

A thug crept behind him and pulled out a knife of Dwarven steel.

I tugged out one of my knives from inside my boot and threw it into the man's chest, dropping him an inch before he drove his knife into Odin's back.

Odin turned.

Yes, quite right he thank me.

He pointed to my right, and I let my gaze follow—a splat of porridge plastered my face in wet slop.

Mush sloughed off my cheeks, and I rubbed the oats out of my eyes in time to enjoy the sight of a woman twice my size barreling at me with a Dwarven seax. Crossing my daggers, I blocked her blow. She growled, pressing down and showing me a set of crooked teeth.

"I'm going to kill you." Her face turned a deeper shade of red as she pressed harder into me.

My muscles shook. I held my ground, trying not to notice how my heels slipped backwards with another thrust.

"If you're to use that kind of talk, I prefer you buy me dinner first," I rasped.

I let up. She fell into me, and I tangled her in my arms, locking her in. A flash of shock lit her eyes. She struggled. The little tease. She wasn't going anywhere.

I tugged her down and struck her in her jaw with the pommel of her blade. She grunted, blood rushing out of her nostrils. I kicked her into a group holding daggers and honey cakes, enjoying their cries as she bowled them over.

And they kept falling, stumbling, knocking into chairs, breaking tables, chicken legs soaring over their heads, potted plants exploding on the floorboards at their feet, falling until a pyramid of barrels stopped them.

The barrels shivered. Quaked.

I stepped back.

The top barrel bounced down the sides of the others. The wood cracked against flagstone, and ale flooded between the splitting seams, gushing across the floor.

More barrels toppled to the ground and stampeded the crowd.

I vaulted over the barrel rattling towards me, planting myself in front of a man who slashed his sword across my chest, slicing through the wool of my tunic.

Now that wasn't very nice.

I locked blades with him, splashing through an inch of ale, dodging his thrusts and jabs. Each grazed my flesh.

Finally. Someone with a little gusto.

"Not bad," I said. "At least one of you knows what you're doing."

He narrowed his eyes. Barrels rolled and sprung and knocked people over behind him.

"I don't want your praise," he spat. "You don't deserve to have freedom. You don't deserve to get away with what you did. You don't deserve forgiveness."

I ground my teeth. He went too far.

Hooking his sword, I wrenched down and took his weapon, and skewered him in the liver.

He dropped to his knees and fell into the lake of ale.

A bottle smashed over my head, the sting radiating into my jaw. Had I been mortal, it would have dropped me.

But, being a god and all...

Turning, I flicked the shards of glass off my shoulders and smiled, facing a young ruffian rife with terror. Their eyes widened further as I stalked towards them, my daggers ready for their throat.

Odin crossed blades with a man and grabbed the end of their sword and pulled it down, slicing his own sword through the soft flesh between the man's shoulder and neck.

A scrawny youth to my right picked up a ham off a table and chucked it at Odin. I ducked, letting it fly over my head and strike the wall an inch behind Odin. The ham exploded into bits, and Odin laughed.

He stopped laughing when a second ham hit him square in the face.

Then I laughed.

Five more ruffians closed in on Odin. One struck him in the gut with a mallet. A second whacked him with a fiddle.

This was fantastic.

A rotten egg slapped my cheek, bursting sulfur and slime onto my chin and into my hair.

Alright. Now *that* crossed a line. I would not permit my hair getting soiled.

Time to go.

I looked for the exit. Dammit. The door stood clear across the other side of the food hurling throng. Of course.

Sliding over bits of cold ham, I ran towards Odin who fought beside a velvet curtain. Another egg cracked against my back and yolk ran down my backside.

Lovely.

A man blocked my path.

"You aren't going anywhere," he said.

He swung an axe over his beefy shoulder and started to chop it into my skull. Another woman came at me with a guitar, ready to smash it against my left side.

I jumped onto a table, narrowly missing both blade and instrument. I flung out my arms, keeping my balance as the table wobbled beneath me, lurching me left and right. The mob scrambled for me, hands reaching for my boots to pull me down. I kicked one in the chin. I stabbed a second in the eye. Hands tugged at my trousers. Fingers scratched my skin.

A man started to throw a third rotten egg at me.

I looked up and...

I couldn't believe I was about to do this.

It was such a terrible cliché.

I sprung and grabbed the iron chandelier and swung over the rabble. Someone shot an arrow at me, a searing line cutting across my calf. My palms sweat and I tightened my hold, not daring to slip off until the right moment...

Odin fought to my right, the swarm thickening around him.

Swinging the chandelier forward, I leapt off, landing on a man sitting at a table, smashing his face into a bowl of stew.

I ran next to Odin and blocked a mace and disarmed a sword.

"Finally decided to help?" he said, cutting one down.

"I don't know why you're making such a fuss." I tore a club out of a man's hand, a breath from striking my knee. "It's not that bad."

An egg erupted against my forehead, a fresh surge of putrid yolk sliding down my nose and between my lips.

"You were saying?" Odin huffed.

The horde grew. More flashes of Dwarven steel blades twinkled. They closed in.

We held out our weapons, backing against the curtain hanging from the wall and...

The wall moved.

"Oof!"

We fell through the curtain and landed on our backs in a room stuffed with cots, pillows, and people tangled in an assortment of precarious positions in a haze of incense.

Shrieks pierced my eardrums as naked patrons scurried around us, a sheen of sweat glistening on their skin in the soft lamplight.

"I do apologize." I stood and brushed feathers off my trousers. "Sorry to interrupt."

Light streamed in through a leaded window in the back. Finally a little luck. Odin and I made a break for it.

Someone tripped me.

I fell, planting my face into a perfumed rug. My daggers slipped out of my hands and spun beneath a low table strewn with unspeakable wooden artifacts.

Odin fought a gang armed with knives and swords, trying to work himself to the window.

I flipped over, greeted by three furious harlots glaring at me.

"You lost us business," one snapped, his sculpted muscles oiled to perfection.

I scrambled backwards and pulled out my last knife from inside my boot. They crept towards me. The tall woman on the left stomped her satin heel on my wrist. I yelped, releasing my knife onto the carpet.

The man grabbed my ankles, pulling me back, where the woman on the right waited to bash a brass bowl across my head.

I grasped the burgundy curtain and tugged, desperate to pull the heavy fabric over them and make an escape.

I yanked harder.

The curtain fell.

On me.

Well, this was going splendidly.

I wrestled with the heavy fabric, trying to throw it off. I only tangled myself further into the coiling velvet.

Pain exploded in my gut from a kick. A shot of white blinded me thanks to a well placed fist to my kidneys.

"A little...help here," I choked out at Odin. Steel struck steel between grunts.

"I'm rather busy," he said.

He was as useless as ever.

Someone landed on me, pounding all the air from my lungs. My ribs ached and my breaths burned. Kicks and strikes raised welts and dappled my skin in bruises.

I winced as they whacked something long and hard I imagined to be quite unseemly across my head.

Wriggling and wriggling, I grappled out of a split in the curtain and stumbled towards Odin, who kept slicing his blade into stomachs and across legs.

I was inches from him.

"Gah!"

A harlot leapt onto my back and slammed me onto the floor. Seriously?

My forehead bashed the rug and stars zoomed around the image of a woman with coal rimmed eyes as she flipped me onto my back. She clenched her thighs on either side of my chest, pinning me still, and held my own knife against my throat. The cheekiness.

Had this been another time...

She thrust it at my heart. I jerked left. It nestled between my chest and arm. Damn.

She drove it down again. I flinched. The deadly steel skated the delicate skin of my temple and sliced the top of my ear.

My heart hammered my ribs as she lifted it higher and lunged it towards my center.

I promised Odin to not use a drop of magic.

But what was the point of promises if not to break them? Besides, this was getting ridiculous.

I slapped my hand against the floor, feeling for something. Anything. I grasped a silk pillow, and sent a twirl of flame into the fibers. It burst into fire, and I threw it at her.

She screamed and jumped off me, tossing the flaming pillow directly into the curtain pooled in the middle of the room. Flames erupted, gorging on the dry material.

She and the other harlots started stomping on the fire, trying to smother it. Letting me get away.

I loved my chaos—*my fire*—it never failed in getting me out of a tight jam. It truly was the magic that was me.

The blaze grew, latching onto the sheer curtains and bed linens. Growls and grunts of fighting turned into screams of fleeing.

I let out more of my blaze. Gorging on its beauty. On its ability to consume.

A man leapt out the window, missing a tendril of flame I spun through the room. Glass scattered clear shards over the floor. More windows broke around us as the flames built, eating up the walls.

This was glorious.

The tavern filled with smoke.

Patrons hacked and coughed, pushing to get out of the doors at the front. Forgetting all about us.

We raced for the shattered window.

Hold on.

Laevateinn glinted next to a knocked over spittoon. I dashed and grabbed my dagger, trying not to think of what coated the handle as I holstered it at my hip and lunged out of the window on Odin's heels.

"I said no magic," Odin said, catching his breath and untying his horse. "Now look what you've done."

"I cannot be blamed for this," I said.

Another man flew out of the window, a stream of flame consuming his clothes, and landed in the trough. Smoke curled off his singed hair.

"I cannot be blamed for how flammable they made the building," I corrected. "I saved our necks back there, *thank-you-very-much*. Now let's go. We can't let my little magic slip disrupt our plans."

I jumped in the saddle of my horse.

"Disrupt our plans?" he said, mounting his horse. "Loki, someone has let out your role in Ragnarok, and that makes everything harder."

11

WHAT HAPPENS IN SAMSEY STAYS IN SAMSEY

SIGYN

You can't trust Loki.

Y ou can't trust Loki.
I pushed Surtr's words out of my mind and used my shoulder to force open a door with rusted hinges. My eyes watered, and I blinked away the sting of dust as I walked into a room of stone and damp. The insides of my nose prickled from mildew.

Water and soap sloshed over the rim of my bucket as I placed it on the flagstones beside a table covered in an inch of dust. Cobwebs stretched like nets between the vials of dried and shriveled things lining the walls on warped shelves.

Maybe three of the harshest bars of soap I ever found—they could scrub warts off pigs—weren't enough for this job?

You can only trust me.

I clamped my mouth shut, resisting the urge to answer. To tell Surtr off.

A squeaking sound peeped from beneath a cauldron in the fireplace on the far end of the room.

Please. No.

I gripped the handle of my broom and snuck towards it, careful to avoid the large glass distillery. I tapped the cauldron with the bristles.

A rat shot out and scurried across the floor, weaving between bits of papers and molding books.

Chasing it, I whacked the broom in front of its wriggling nose, blocking its path so it wouldn't vanish into the stack of crates. The rat reversed course, and I smiled as it zoomed towards the open door and...I frowned...and made a beeline for Kvasir's old desk, slipping beneath the toppled over chair.

I sighed.

How had Kvasir put up with this? Angrboda explained he had been a man of great wisdom and lived here eons back as their resident healer. I think the Jotnar only kept him as a kind of decoration. A talking piece. Jotnar harbored little patience for medicine or science, preferring spending their time with war games.

I found it a mean stereotype. But, when this morning I had to convince a young woman to endure six weeks of healing for her broken wrist rather than whacking off the offending hand...

That's when I knew how I could make use of my time here, while also keeping my mind occupied. Because if I stood any chance of beating Surtr, of not losing my sanity while I waited for Loki's return, I couldn't keep resting. I couldn't stay idle.

I had to stay busy.

I had to help.

And when Angrboda mentioned this room to me...

I sucked in a breath, a musty breath, and picked up the chair.

Springs popped out of the split velvet.

The rat raced over my toes and scrambled under a cabinet on the verge of collapse, safe from my reach.

For now.

I looked up, and a scream shot out of my throat. I swallowed my shock down.

Surtr stood next to the cabinet in the form of a man. Boredom hardened the sharp angles of his face, and masses of white hair as bright as flame brushed the tops of his broad shoulders. Layers of black robes raced down the elegant arch of his back, the sleek lines of his waist, his hips. A cruel beauty sharper than knives imbued his smile.

But his eyes.

Violet. Majestic.

Dangerous.

Surtr swiped his finger across the clouded glass of the cabinet doors. Slivers of white cotton peeked beneath his sleeves.

"I don't understand why you are making this so difficult," Surtr said. "I'm only offering you the ability to do exactly what you want. To help all the wretches with a snap of the fingers verses scrubbing them to the bone."

He rubbed his thumb over his fingertips, balling the dust clinging to his skin. A grimace tugged at Surtr's thin lips as he flicked the dirt away.

I did not have time for this. I had work to do.

Jiggling the iron latch of the cabinet door I jerked it open, the glass shuddering and wood screeching. I held in a sneeze as something acrid with a hint of wet dog shot into my sinuses. What did Kvasir keep in here?

"Gullveig didn't understand my full potential. She only wanted to use me for revenge. Cleanse the worlds and start again. How unoriginal. But you..." Surtr stepped behind me. His breath curled hot over the back of my neck. "You know the difference we can make. We can change things. We can make people's lives better."

My blood pumped harder.

Because I did know.

I rustled faster through the sticky and grime coated bottles and jars. Dragon's blood. Boar bile. Vanir viper flesh.

Mummy dust.

What century was it here in Jotunheim?

"This is a waste of your time," Surtr said. "Loki is a waste of your time. Of your talents."

My shoulders tensed.

Lies.

Always lies.

I turned away and collected the rotting books off the floor and stacked them on a wooden chest. They deserved better than to be tossed and left to disintegrate into the dirt. If I found some thread perhaps I could even mend the split binding of the top three. A heavy brick could flatten the pages of the other two and—

My breath wedged in my throat opening the cracked leather cover of a volume on astronomy.

Scribbled notes packed the margins in an elegant hand.

Loki's hand.

Warmth coated my chest as I flipped through the brittle pages, scanning his thoughts on constellations and moon phases. I ignored the lewd drawings. How long ago had he made these?

He rarely shared about his time in Jotunheim. In fact, he rarely shared much about himself at all, such as having a brother. That man, I swear. He kept his past locked away in a chest he threw into the sea.

What I'd pay to know who hurt Loki so completely so I could give them a black eye. He had so much to give.

He'd continually tell me how good I was.

And when I'd tell him the same, his lips would quirk because he did not believe me.

I just wished he liked himself more.

"Please don't say that Loki has a nugget of gold hiding somewhere deep in his center that makes this all worth it, or I may vomit," Surtr said. "He's three-day-old fish. Only fit for the bin."

I closed my eyes and brushed my finger over the fading ink strokes, concentrating on the indentations from his quill. Focusing on the truth, and not the lies.

Always lies.

"Loki used to spend hours down here with Kvasir chattering away over those tedious things," Angrboda said behind me.

I spun on my heel as Angrboda walked in and right through Surtr, who glared at her, absolutely offended at the nerve.

"Loki is the reason we kept Kvasir here." She picked up a book on herbs. "He thought we should listen to his wisdom and ideas. Bring some change to Jotunheim. Modernize. I told him too much wisdom only brings misery, as Kvasir proved."

"What happened to him?"

She smiled.

"Some Dwarves drained his blood into their mead after liking his ideas too strongly," she said. "Is this room to your satisfaction?"

I gripped my stomach.

"After a good scrubbing," I said. "I'd also like an assistant. Someone I can train. I'm determined to save what limbs I can."

"But what will we fish with?" she said.

My right eye twitched as playfulness twinkled in hers.

"That was a joke."

I exhaled.

Surtr stepped next to me and cold sweat coated the small of my back.

Angrboda walked to the table and looked from one stretch of the room to the other. As if looking at memories I could not see.

She picked up a bottle of powdered slugs.

"I actually find it quite noble what you're trying to do." She blew off the coating of dust. "Few care about us here, especially those connected to Asgard."

"And I find that abhorrent." I walked away from Surtr, shaking away his chill. "Everyone deserves care and kindness, enemies or not. Asgard is too snobby for its own good."

She smiled at this.

I pulled the sponge from the bucket and grabbed the bar of soap and worked it into the bumps and cracks, forming a lather. I slapped it on the table, a rush of water and foam flowing out of the sponge as I swabbed the grain. Rivers of gray ran through the grooves of the wood. I'd need gallons of linseed oil to bring the oak back to life.

Angrboda stepped to the far end of the table. Something flashed behind her eyes. Another memory, perhaps.

One that brought blood to her cheeks.

"I've not been in this room since Loki and I snuck down here when Kvasir was out fishing." She rapped her fingers on the wet wood. "We made good use out of this table. It's where I conceived Fenrir."

I stopped scrubbing.

"Excuse me?"

She grimaced.

"I've made you uncomfortable," she said. "I apologize. I figured you were past such human prudishness, especially being with Loki. There's not much wholesome left in a soul after he tells that story about when he and Odin were marooned three days on Samsey. The vegetation might never recover."

"What happened on Samsey?"

She tilted her head.

"Oh, he's not told you?" she said. "Pretend I never mentioned it."

I squeezed into the sponge's fibrous texture, the soap abrasive on my knuckles.

Naturally. Why would he tell me? Add it to the list. Loki was so frustrating. Or was infuriating the better word?

I resumed scrubbing the oak. Harder.

Angrboda shuffled over to the bookcase and scanned the collection of skulls—human, horse, ferret—lining the shelves.

And with each step farther away from me she took, the hotter a thousand questions burned the tip of my tongue.

But one burned the hottest.

And if anyone knew...

I dropped the sponge into the bucket and wiped my hands on my apron, ignoring how my heart leapt and crawled and spun within my ribcage.

I couldn't believe I was asking this. Why I cared. It didn't matter, but...

Odin had been an important part of his life. I just wanted to understand.

"Actually." I pushed the word past the lump in my throat. "Well... Loki rarely—*never*—speaks about Odin and—"

She raised her left eyebrow, and a smile pulled at the corners of her mouth.

"You're curious."

"Not about Samsey," I said. "Please spare me that tale, but...how did he end up with a man like Odin? Odin is—"

"An evil, glum clam?"

"Precisely."

She leaned against the wall and crossed her arms.

"I'm not surprised he's kept his lips sealed on that whole disaster," she said. "I'd also be embarrassed if I was with a man who nick-named himself Yggr, the *Terrible One*. I mean, really."

Surtr stood next to her with a hungry look, as if savoring her every word.

"Why would he be embarrassed?" I said. "We've all fallen in love with someone we shouldn't."

A storm of cackles burst out of Angrboda's gut.

"Love?" she said. "He really has told you nothing. This was far deeper than *love*."

"Oh, this is getting good," Surtr said. He sat on the chair next to Angrboda and leaned in, his violet eyes brimming with excitement.

My stomach twisted. I didn't want to ask more. I didn't want to know more.

"Deeper? How?"

Angrboda shrugged.

"It's their curse," she said. "They are ambition and chaos. Two elements driven together by what they can create and driven apart by what they are." She paused. "Loki was mesmerized by the tempest in Odin, and Odin...they both love to play with matches, and both were a match to the other. And black powder. And fuse."

I sighed.

Of course they were. Given this, I suppose it was understandable for Loki to not share this *detail* of their relationship with me. But it irked me all the same—especially with the two of them traveling alone together again—no. I wouldn't fall into this mind trap.

I trusted him.

"I wonder what else Loki hasn't told you?" Surtr said.

He smiled wider.

That spot on my collarbone itched into my bones. I kept my hand planted at my side.

Angrboda exhaled slowly.

"But in the end, it was what Odin offered him that made him leave Jotunheim."

"Godhood?"

"Opportunity."

A hush saturated with cruel *what ifs* hardened the space in the room. Her face stiffened and pain settled behind her gray eyes.

"He left with Odin and...and everything changed after that," she said. "I suppose I can't blame him fully. Loki and I didn't always have an easy time of it together—we both have strong personalities and cannot stand the thought of being wrong. I had him spend more nights than not outside in the forest, because I am never wrong. But I still catch myself sometimes wondering how it might have been different had I...no, as I said, too much wisdom brings misery."

She shivered as if waking herself from a dream churning with dark clouds.

"Sorry, I didn't come to bore you with dreariness," she said. "I actually came to invite you to a party. I thought you could use some relaxation. You seem stressed."

My eyebrows raised.

"Stressed? What would I possibly have to be stressed about?" I said, more sarcastically than I intended. "I'm only being possessed by Surtr while Loki is off with his former lover on a long journey full of longer nights. And now you've just informed me how both are walking heroin to the other. Spectacular!"

"Well, you did ask."

Touché.

"I'll put it bluntly," she said. "Bets have started as to the size of the stick up your ass after that very loud moratorium on amputations you gave earlier."

I pressed my lips tight together. Maybe I had been rather gruff this morning in the feast hall at breakfast. Apparently, it was difficult to make Jotnar cry, and I made three burst into tears after I confiscated their saws.

"While I appreciate your kind offer, I am quite busy stopping more rats from chewing through the plaster."

A second rat finished squeezing itself out of a hole in the wall and dashed across the room.

Not today vermin.

I brought down my broom, scooping the rat with the bristles, and gently swept the rodent out the door. Finally. One rat less.

For two seconds, I felt back in time when Simon and I caught the rats in the shed as children. I so loved the hunt! After rubbing our hands in sweet oils, Simon always insisted on sticking his hand into the straw first. He rather his fingers get bit than my own. Simon had been so kind. But he changed as he grew.

I wanted him to stop with his schemes and crooked deals. He forced me to live on a razor's edge, and one day—

Angrboda placed her hand on my shoulder, breaking me out of a past life.

"Listen," she said. "As I mentioned, we aren't used to outsiders taking an interest in us here. In fact, we view it with suspicion thanks to millennia of being betrayed by the Aesir and Vanir. If you want to help bring change to Jotunheim, if you want the Jotnar to trust you, it's good they get to know you. Because, anyone who meets you can't deny what you are."

"And what is that?"

Her mouth tugged into a soft grin.

"Hope," she said. "You have a rare kindness in you, especially for a goddess, and..." she stopped. "If Loki feels you love him, truly love him, he will do anything you ask. Odin knew this. And you know this, too."

I did. He would catch a shooting star if I told him it would make me smile. But what I loved about him wasn't that he would burn entire worlds for me—which I very much rather he didn't—but that, beneath his fragility, beneath layers of pain, remained a heart full of mercy. Of compassion.

I saw the good in him.

"But unlike Odin," she continued. "You don't use this knowledge to your advantage. You don't hurt him. Your fidelity, your kindness, is what Loki needs—what his *chaos* needs—and that's one thing Odin never could give him."

Surtr laughed.

"How *reassuring*," Surtr said, scorn dripping from each word. "I wonder what he and Odin are up to right now, without you, alone... Reminiscing old times, perhaps? Or re-enacting them? Let's speculate all night!"

The muscles in my neck stiffened as Surtr's gaze burrowed into me. Damnable creature.

My collarbone tingled again. I scratched my nails across the rough spot.

My breath caught. I stopped and made a fist. I had to keep strong.

"You know." A wicked smile twisted Surtr's perfect lips. "You can't trust Loki. You can only trust me."

Lies.

Always lies.

I forced my attention on Angrboda, focusing on the thick, black curl grazing her pointed cheek. On the cheer in her eyes. On how she could shank me faster than I could her.

Anything but Surtr grinning behind her.

"You're right," I said. "I think getting out will do me some good."

She clapped her hands and rubbed them together.

"Wonderful!" she said. "It will be a small affair. You don't have to join the midnight nude swim if you don't want."

12

IF IT AIN'T BROKKR

LOKI

Svartalfheim

"Shit, this is cold." I stepped into curtains of water surging over a ledge of jagged granite flecked with clumps of grass.

The waterfall beat my face and naked shoulders, washing away soot and grime and stinging my skin with iced needles.

Odin washed beside me within the pounding water threaded with white. Rivulets of old blood raced down his arms and stomach, packed with hard muscle.

"How did you talk me into this again?" I kneaded stiff globs of rotten egg out of my hair.

"We can't look like vomit collectors at a Bacchanalia." He rubbed bits of ham out of his beard. "You know what a stickler for respect Brokkr is. We only have one chance."

I sighed.

He was right, but I wouldn't give him the satisfaction of telling him.

Since the truth seemed *out* that I was the one responsible for

Ragnarok, we had no choice but to keep off the main roads. Bypass towns. We couldn't risk a repeat of *The Thirsty Kraken*.

If I was recognized a second time...

I really wanted to avoid being staked to the nearest tree with a Dwarven steel spike.

But what I wanted more was not letting Sigyn down. Not when she relied on me succeeding. When this had been all my fault.

Of course, roughing it on the back routes, coupled with the stench of blood and beef stew, would not make a good impression on Brokkr. The thickening flies around us confirmed it.

Now here I was. Bathing naked with Odin beneath a frigid waterfall so cold that it made your toes curl.

This day just kept getting better.

I turned, and a solid shiver cut into my bones as the water hammered my back.

His arms flexed as he massaged crusted ale out of his hair.

"I must admit," he said. "That scuffle at the *Kraken* reminded me of that one time we got into a brawl at that ale house in Vanaheim."

I smiled, the whole adventure blossoming in my mind like a rose garden.

"You hustled that card sharp to the point of tears."

He laughed, rich and joyful.

I forgot how much I loved it when he laughed. It was as if he'd never know sadness again, which, at one time, was all I had wanted for him. To chase away that lingering worry that always seemed to be with him.

"But nothing compares to Samsey," he said.

I grinned wider.

"What ever could?"

He glanced at me.

Water struck Odin's chest, and streams gorged with bubbles coursed along the lines of his stomach, over scars I had once spent hours tracing. I had memorized each. My fingertips tingled with the sensation of his hot skin.

I looked away at the rocks and froth and choked the memories back down.

They were nothing but a rose garden filled with thorns.

I scoured the last of the dirt from beneath my nails and waded through the clear water that reached my calves, needing to get away from him. Needing air.

I stepped out of the pool and onto a shore of slick pebbles and walked onto the grass, the thunder of the waterfall blending into the burble of the river racing to my left.

Opening my pack, I grabbed a clean linen shirt and pulled it over my head, following it with a tunic of thick wool.

Pine and spruce trees outlined the waterfall and shallow river. Clouds of breath escaped between my lips.

Odin joined me and dug through his own satchel, steam rising off his shoulders.

"Did I say something that upset you?" Confusion twisted his face as he slipped out a fresh shirt. "You always enjoyed talking about those stories...well...*before*."

Before.

"No," I said, shutting this conversation down. "I was just thinking about how disappointing it would have been to die at *The Thirsty Kraken*. You know I want to go out in grandeur style than taking a pitchfork to the gallbladder."

His expression relaxed, seemingly relieved by my answer.

"That is one thing I don't understand." He tugged on his tunic. "I gave orders for your role in Ragnarok to remain secret."

That wasn't the only secret let out...

My mind raced back to Bly and his threats. To what I still owed him to keep silent.

I pushed my legs into new trousers, pushing away the stress of finding a golden apple on top of everything else.

"Obviously the gods care about your orders." I pulled on my boots.

It was hard to narrow down who had it in for me. That list was quite long, and only growing longer.

"Balder," he whispered, pulling on his trousers.

"Is he still mad about me murdering him?"

"He's the only one with the most motive."

I sighed, buckling my belt around my waist.

"You'd think him human with how upset he gets over these minor things."

"It had to be him. Who else?"

He had a point. This had the stench of it being personal about it. I killed Balder, so he let everyone know I started the end of the worlds.

Still, this didn't seem his style.

This was artful and calculated. Two things Balder was not.

And it didn't explain who gave Bly that damned letter.

No, I sensed a larger hand stirring this pot.

But, if it was Balder manipulating all this to get in my way…Genius.

"We need to get going," Odin said. "This is nothing we can deal with right now. All we can do is get this job done and get back without any other incidents to slow us down or break our necks."

He stood on the riverbank and scanned the forest, curls of hot breath rolling out of his lungs, making him appear as if he belonged to the rock and the wind. Just like when we first met on the bank of the Ifingr.

When I…

When I had been a fool and trusted him.

I turned away and walked to my horse, hanging my satchel over the saddle. I didn't like how easily all these memories crept back into my mind. I didn't like sharing laughter with him again. I didn't like talking of good times.

We got on our horses and trotted along the rugged path, following the river bubbling over and around rocks, nothing but miles of pine and mountains stretching out before us.

I had no use for those times anymore.

I didn't.

I shouldn't.

* * *

THE AIR THINNED as we approached Brokkr and Eitri's mountain citadel, leaving the tree line hours behind us.

I hadn't stepped foot here since I acquired new hair for Sif eons back. Cutting her hair to the scalp was still worth it for the look on Thor's face. A harmless prank done in the name of a little mischief, and perhaps one too many bottles of wine.

It had been an exceedingly fun evening for me.

Until Thor threatened to crush my bones to powder unless I fixed what I'd done, requiring me to put my head on the chopping block for the gods—literally—to appease their weak sensibilities.

Brokkr should have known better when he accepted my deal. The serpents always hide in the details.

The wind swallowed my chuckle as I remembered all the shades of purple his face turned when he realized I'd tricked him.

Of course, me crawling back on my hands and knees to ask for his help tarnished that victory.

I was not a fan of groveling.

As I was not a fan of traveling along narrow, crumbling roads that twisted up sheer rock faces, one errant step away from a very bad day.

Odin and I crossed a stone bridge spanning a crevasse that plummeted below us. Watch towers and turrets shrouded in snow jutted out from the frosted granite of the mountain, as if carved out of the solid rock.

We rode into the bailey, and fires burned in iron baskets along the walls and on either side of the keep. A hollow wind howled through the valleys, flapping a wooden sign on squeaking hinges above the massive oak doors.

The Brothers Brokkr and Eitri
Blacksmiths. Goldsmiths. Gem Cutters.
Gods can bugger off.

Charming.

"They seem even more welcoming than last time." I dismounted my horse, along with Odin.

The frozen gravel crunched beneath his boots as he walked to the entrance and banged his fist against the doors, rattling the iron latches.

A small hatch—waist level— slid open with a *thunk*.

"What business do you bring?" a voice, deep and dry, asked in Dwarvish—a gruff and clipped language that made your tongue tired after ten minutes of speaking.

Brokkr.

Odin bent over, bracing his hands on his knees, and squinted into the darkness.

"Oh. It's one of *you*," Brokkr said.

The hatch snapped shut in Odin's face. I snickered.

Odin stood, squared his shoulders, and slammed his open palm against the door again.

"Open the door, Brokkr," Odin said, his Dwarvish comically guttural. "I've brought you a gift."

"Not interested," he replied through the thick oak.

"Not even if the gift is Loki?"

My snicker died in my throat.

"You bastard," I whispered. "What are you playing at?"

"Getting us in."

I was about to break his clavicle when the double doors creaked open. Wind blew harder over our heads and against our backs as it swept into the hall and over a man barely over four feet tall.

A heavy beard of brown mixed with braids and silver cuffs hid most of his square face. He still insisted on wearing his wool cap pulled so far down his forehead it skimmed his bushy eyebrows. Truth was, it worked for his whole crabby look. Brokkr was a Dwarf who existed entirely on spite and hot gas.

His gaze locked on mine and something I didn't quite like sparked behind his brown eyes that matched the sinister smile twisting his lips.

"Loki," he said.

"Brokkr."

The spark brightened.

"How long I've waited for this day when I can finally—"

"Odin? Loki?" a smoother voice said behind him. Footsteps clapped against stone.

Eitri.

He stepped next to his brother, an inch taller and with a kinder face wrapped in a beard braided past his waist and tied with a golden thread.

"Goodness!" He straightened his knit shawl around his shoulders. "This is quite the honor. Oh, ignore all that nasty sign stuff. I've told Brokkr to take it down, but you know how he is."

Brokkr crossed his arms over his leather jerkin and harrumphed.

"Come in, come in," Eitri said. "You must be cold after the journey up the mountain. How about a spot of tea? I've knitted some new teapot cozies I've been eager to show off."

"Yes," Brokkr said. "Come in for...*tea*." His smile stretched wider, the corners of his mouth meeting the corners of his eyes.

He extended his arm and held up his thumb and squinted at my head, as if gauging positions and angles.

I shook off the shiver of whatever brewed and cackled in that demented mind of his.

We followed Eitri and Brokkr down the hall, steel and metal filling my nose and the rhythmic thump of bellows my ears. Only the glow of blood reds and molten oranges of the forges in the back provided light, creating a sheen on the damp block and mortar walls.

We ventured deeper. The block smoothed into carved rock and everything dripped like a cavern.

Sweat slicked the small of my back at the thought of caves.

I am safe.

I am not in danger.

"So, when did you make the switch from mead to tea?" I asked, forcing down the taste of venom from my tongue. Needing to focus on something else. Anything. Even if it was on how badly my own

Dwarvish had become. I didn't use to trip over their umlauts. Now they waited for me like thorns.

"Made the switch two thousand years ago." Eitri's voice ricocheted off the stone. "The mead started giving Brokkr indigestion now he's getting older. He's been much more cheery ever since."

Brokkr grunted in reply, leading us into a sparsely furnished room. An oak table. Walls of Dwarven steel blades. Piles of jewels and gems and chests of treasure thrown about and spilling across half the floor.

Brokkr kicked a sapphire the size of an egg out of his way and plopped on a bench drenched in furs at a table that only reached our kneecaps. Odin and I sat cross-legged on the floor. Brokkr didn't offer us a single scrap of sheepskin as a barrier against the chilled stone on our backsides.

I hated how it made me grateful for Odin's body heat sinking into my skin as we huddled together for any smidgeon of warmth.

I hated more how Brokkr stared unblinkingly at my head and jawline.

I tightened my cloak around my neck.

"What brings you both here?" Eitri hung a cast-iron pot on an iron hook and swung it into a small fireplace red with coals.

Brokkr pulled out a steel protractor from his pocket and held it up, his eyes bouncing back and forth between my head and his device.

He whispered a string of measurements to himself.

"Business," Odin said.

Brokkr snapped his gaze to Odin and slammed the protractor on the table, the rows of gold coins in tidy stacks collapsing into a roar behind him.

"For any business, you know my price," he said. "The Trickster's head."

He unsheathed a small knife and jumped onto the table and bounded towards me.

I put out my hand and pressed into his chest, holding him back as he slashed his blade inches from my cheek.

"Please, we aren't still on about this?" I said.

"I won that head of yours fair and square." He swiped at my nose. "You cheated me."

"You should have been more specific," I said. "I kept my word. My head was yours, but it was hardly my fault you failed to mention anything about my neck."

I gave him a devious smile.

He tried to gash open my chin.

I jolted as Odin squeezed into my leg beneath the table to shut me up.

"Loki, now is not the time to antagonize..." Odin whispered tersely into my ear.

"Fine."

I removed my hand, letting Brokkr fall onto his face. More importantly, letting me rub out the prickling sensation where Odin had touched me.

Brokkr righted himself and—

"Oh, Brokkr. Shush and eat a biscuit." Eitri slid a plate of ginger biscuits into the middle of the table, which were really just misshapen lumps hard enough to crack a molar.

Brokkr's right eye twitched as he sheathed his blade. He grabbed a biscuit and sat back on his bench, staring into me as he rage chewed.

"Honestly, it's all he talks about," Eitri said. "I told him never to accept any job unless you receive the payment first. Lesson learned, I say."

"I quite agree," Odin said. "Which is why I have something that might smooth all this over."

He opened his satchel and pulled out the item he'd snatched from Falael and sat it in front of him.

Brokkr's mouth opened, unfortunately filled with chewed biscuit. Eitri pressed his fists against his lips and gave a high-pitched squeal.

"Is that?" Brokkr said.

Odin smiled.

"Yes."

He pushed it towards them, the dim light illuminating the supple green skin of a perfect, Elven pear.

Their eyes widened further.

Dwarves were suckers for two things: proving themselves the best and fruit—any fruit. A rare commodity in mountainous Svartalfheim, but the Elven pear? The grandest prize of all, thanks to Alfheim's continuing nine millennia long embargo.

Brokkr lifted it as if some holy relic.

"Is it genuine?" Eitri asked, leaning closer to Brokkr, stretching out his finger and grazing the peel.

Brokkr gave it a gentle squeeze. He brought it to his nose and inhaled deeply. He flicked the stem.

Stars filled his gaze.

"It's genuine."

"I only provide genuine," Odin said. "And it's been charmed, like the last time. It will remain forever."

Last time? What was he—

Brokkr and Eitri hurried to a cabinet with silver fittings and unlocked the doors. Eitri snatched an emerald the size of a baby swan off a velvet cushion and tossed it behind his shoulder, and Brokkr reverently lowered the pear in its place.

Something glinted on the shelf below between them. Something gold...

Something I desperately needed to put that nasty Simon business to rest.

No. It couldn't be so easy...

Could it?

My heart beat wildly in my chest. I shifted in my seat, trying to see over their shoulders, peer around their waists.

I had to be sure.

They closed the doors, and whatever it was behind them before I could tell.

I slumped.

"I realize all the bad blood that's happened between us," Odin said, silencing my racing mind. "But I come to you with this as a token of goodwill. Asgard wants to have a future with you again."

Brokkr returned to his bench. Eitri hurried to the hissing kettle and poured the steaming water into cups. Bitter mountain herbs infused the air.

"You must really need us," Brokkr said.

"I need the best," Odin said, holding his gaze.

Brokkr studied Odin, who remained unflinching, firm.

"We are the best," Brokkr said. "You're right. What is it you're wanting?"

Odin's body relaxed against mine. He had him.

He always could charm the fleas off a dog's back.

I cleared my throat. Now was my turn to seal the deal. "What we need is—"

Odin squeezed his fingers into my leg again, shutting me up.

"What we need," he continued, "is a vessel, an amulet, to trap an immense amount of energy."

"How immense?"

Odin kept calm and even.

"An element."

The cold deepened in the room, forcing Odin and I to nestle even tighter together. Gods. I did not sign up for this, even if his warmth was keeping me from frostbite.

Brokkr tangled his fingers within his beard, jingling the silver cuffs as he scratched the dense whiskers.

"An element?" he said. "Such an item will be difficult to make if you want it to hold that much power."

"Can you do it?" Odin said.

Eitri placed a tray with tea cups crammed around a ceramic teapot dressed in a miniature knit sweater—obviously the result of spending too much time in isolation.

"Yes," he said.

"I knew I could count on you—"

"Yes, I can make this amulet do what you wish," Brokkr said. "But I won't."

Odin's brow furrowed. He wet his lips and took in a breath as he always did when struggling to keep collected.

"What? Why?"

Brokkr pointed at me.

"The disrespect that *Trickster* has shown me..."

I rolled my eyes.

"Here we go again." I grabbed one of the tea cups and held it, only to feel the blood return to my fingers. I wasn't desperate enough to drink it. Dwarven Thistleberry made you pucker just smelling it.

"You doubted our ability," Brokkr spat. "We won that challenge."

"You did win," Odin said. "Which is why we are here, at the two greatest blacksmiths in Svartalfheim, and not at the Sons of Ivaldi."

"Quite right," Eitri piped. "They are hacks." He sipped his tea and gave a firm shiver. "How did they think *Skidbladnir* a suitable gift to Frey? What in the Nine Worlds does one do with a foldable ship? Now, a golden boar you can ride into battle...that's a gift truly befitting a god."

Brokkr's lip trembled.

"You think you can come here and dazzle me with a pear and sweet words. I stand by my sign—the bunch of you gods can go and burn in the fires of Muspelheim. You pit good Dwarves against the other like a game of chess. And that *thing*." He pointed at me. "Made fools out of me and my brother."

That *thing*?

I reached across the table and grabbed Brokkr by his jerkin, bowling over tea cups and knocking them to the floor where they burst into shards.

"You shithead." I pressed his nose against mine.

"See how he still treats me?" he mumbled.

I was going to throttle him until his eyes popped out and flew across the table.

I dug my fingers deeper into his jerkin.

I stopped.

No.

Pulling in a breath, I let him down.

A glimmer of surprise danced across his face as I scrubbed my own.

"This amulet isn't for us," I said. "It's...It's for someone else."

He scoffed, brushing the wrinkles out of his clothes.

"*Someone else*," he said, feigning my voice. "How convincing an argument."

"She is in trouble and—"

"And what?" he interrupted. "And have we *lost our touch*? Is our work *as good as Berling and Grer's*? Or *Andvari's*? Go ahead. You've told me all this before."

I had.

"Brokkr," I said. "I need your help."

He studied me, his face twisting with consideration, until it softened. And then coldness like the surrounding stone hardened it in seconds as he considered more.

"What is this sappy sad act?" he said. "You're still the same. Still scheming. Manipulating. You really know how to negotiate."

"Don't worry about him. Your dealings are with me alone," Odin said.

Brokkr laughed.

"Does that make this better?"

"Who is this 'someone else'?" Eitri asked, putting down his cup.

"Sigyn," I said, loving the warmth saying her name spread throughout my body. "She's in a bad way. Because of..." ...*because of me...* "Her life relies on you making this item."

Brokkr sneered.

Eitri clapped his hands over his heart, his cheeks flushing with a rosy glow.

"Is this for love?" he asked.

"Deeper," Odin answered, the word layered with meanings I couldn't dig out because I couldn't believe he had said it at all. He'd never uttered a positive breath about what Sigyn and I shared. Quite the opposite. Maybe he was finally accepting how things were now?

Eitri squealed louder than he had with the pear.

"How romantic!" Eitri said. "Brokkr, we must do this. It's for love!"

"You're getting snowed Brother. Again," Brokkr said. "You know he's just as bad as that other one."

Obviously, Odin was that *other one.*

"The lie-smith can't love," Brokkr said. "And even if he could, he doesn't deserve it."

My entire body clenched. Me not being deserving seemed to be a continuing theme, one I would remain relentless against.

"Brokkr..." Eitri said, his voice scolding.

"Perhaps had the *Sly One* shown a little respect...he made me a fool. He made all of us fools. And he doesn't care. Look at him! It looks like he bathed in a river before he showed up here. He only wants to take and take." Hurt filled his voice. "I won that bet. *I. Won.*"

Brokkr was immovable like the mountain.

And he was the only way.

I thought of Sigyn. What she'd say.

What she'd do.

That warmth rushed again through the chambers of my heart. It coursed through my veins and...

Oh.

I knew.

This would sting.

"Brokkr, look, I'm..." I swallowed bile. "I'm..."

He cocked his head.

"You're what?"

"I'm sor..." I gagged. "S..."

"Gods," Odin groaned, pulling his hands down his face.

"I'm sorry," I said. "There. I said it. I'm sorry. I'm sorry I cheated you. I'm sorry I tricked you for my own gain. You're right. I may not deserve your help, but Sigyn does."

Brokkr's mouth fell open.

"Brokkr, he apologized," Eitri said.

Brokkr took off his cap and combed his fingers through what hair remained, then replaced it by tugging it down his forehead.

He looked at me, a mixture of shock and appreciation.

Hope swelled in my chest.

"I feel sorry for the woman," he said. "Truly, but it's more complicated than a simple apology."

"Complicated how?" Odin said.

He stared at Odin as if Odin had asked if he'd like to invest in his new rat circus venture.

"If it got out that I helped the Destroyer, the Breaker of Worlds, the one that caused Ragnarok..."

My insides squirmed.

"You know about that, too? Of course. Who doesn't these days?" I groaned.

"My reputation as a Dwarf is at stake here," he said.

"Please," I said. "Don't damn her because of me."

I was doing a good enough job of that as it was myself.

Brokkr sighed, his arms falling slack at his sides.

"Fine," he said. "I will do this."

Eitri clapped.

"He has such a soft spot," Eitri said.

"Shut up and let me finish!" Brokkr yelled. "I will do this for a price."

Odin's jaw flexed beneath his beard.

"Price?" Odin said. "We've already paid."

A single laugh shot out of Brokkr's throat.

"That pear will hardly cut it," he said. "If I make your amulet, there are conditions. I have to keep up appearances. I'm breaking my own oath with my sign in helping you. I can't look like my rules are meaningless. Also, this way, if I'm asked, I can say that I had the gods do this for me. As a personal favor."

"What do you want?" I said.

He smiled.

"Brísingamen."

Odin choked.

My stomach fell into my bowels. I wanted to punch his smug face for requesting this of us. This was nothing but pure retaliation.

"Let me get this straight," I said. "You want Freya's necklace? *Freya.*"

"Is there a problem?"

"No, no, of course not. Why would there be a problem with you asking for the single most prized possession in all the Nine Worlds belonging to the fiercest woman in the worlds?"

"Why do you want Brísingamen?" Odin asked.

He took one of the unbroken teacups off the tray and took a slug, not giving a wince at the scalding liquid filling his cheeks.

"It's simple," he said, wiping the droplets clinging to the whiskers of his beard with his sleeve. "She stole it. We want it back."

"Stole?"

"She offered us a basket of Vanir lemons," Eitri said. "From her own groves in exchange for the necklace."

"They turned out to be all made of wax." Brokkr gripped his cup so tight I thought he'd crack the ceramic. "Again, you gods do nothing but cheat and steal from us. We want Brísingamen in exchange for the amulet."

"And how do you expect us to get it back from her?" I said. "You know how Freya is…What she is capable of. She is a goddess."

He shrugged.

"That's not my problem," he said. "You want something from me, and I'm telling you my price. Or are you afraid of getting scratched by kitty's claws?"

13

SNAKESKIN

SIGYN

Angrboda led me into the great hall and through a blanket of haze from candles and pipes that drifted below the vaulted ceilings, dulling the red plaster walls.

We walked between long tables crowded with Jotnar chattering loudly and shoveling baked salmon and beet stew into their mouths. Splits of laughter burst over the pulsing mandolins, panpipes, and crackle of spoons of a Jotun folk dance that vibrated through the flagstones and into the soles of my feet.

She took a seat in the middle of the head table and patted the bench to her right. I swung my leg over and sat beside her.

The spot on my collarbone tingled.

Not already.

"This is a pretty decent spread." Surtr stood on the other side of the table and gazed at bowls of fruit and piles of pork pies. "Although, I could do without the egg tower. Who thought that a good idea for a feast?"

I looked away from Surtr's upturned nose and moved my shoul-

ders, stretching within my heavy wool gown, trying to ignore the
tickle running up my neck and over my shoulder.

I tugged at my knit cowl. I didn't want anyone knowing my battle,
and especially not to see it.

Angrboda held out a drinking horn in front of my nose, concern
filling her eyes.

"Claret," she said over the music and banter. "This will help calm
you in two sips."

My heart cartwheeled. Thanks be to the gods for wine.

"Bless you." I took the horn from her, the wine inside nearly black
and the smell...oh. She may call it claret, but I found it more suitable
for stripping varnish.

She tilted back her head, chugged her horn dry, and smacked the
table with her fist, sniffing hard.

"See? That's how it's done in Jotunheim."

I leaned back and took a large gulp. I choked, the claret stinging
my nose and throat and all the way into my stomach.

She laughed, pouring herself a second and topping mine off,
sending me into a panic. I'd never get this down, even though I
desperately wanted every drop.

"You'll get used to it," she said. "Best for cold winter nights, which we
have plenty of here in Jotunheim. We believe it thickens the blood and—"

She explained to me the importance of hearty wine to the Jotnar.
Which led her into telling me how they only ate their dark bread
thickly spread with butter. How fishing was their favorite sport next
to sparring with swords. How they'd play Hnefatafl until dawn when
the snows were too deep to be outdoors.

The more she spoke, the more my shoulders relaxed. The less I
thought about Surtr until I didn't think of him at all. She told me
stories of the trolls she'd encountered in the woods, how big Fenrir
smiled when Loki would visit and bring them a basket of Asgardian
strawberries—she paused here—and changed the subject to the
variety of Jotnar goat cheeses.

I liked her very much, to the point I didn't know why I'd been worried about meeting her. Angrboda was quite kind, in her aggressive way.

The music screeched to a halt.

Angrboda's eyes trailed from mine to a burly man covered in sheepskins stumbling through the double doors. Her gaze fixed on his jerkin made entirely of snakeskin.

My mind raced to what Loki had told me about her bashing a man's face into the floor for wearing a wolf pelt.

Angrboda stood and straightened her posture, reaching her full height.

"You will remove your jerkin," she commanded.

The Jotnar at the tables stopped their feasting and stared at the man, who now took a swig of something from his flask. Obviously something he shouldn't have more of based on the redness of his face and how he swayed as if on a ship at sea.

Jeers followed.

"I don't have any other clothes—" he hiccuped "—I can't."

The other Jotnar started hurling out nastier insults at him.

"You know my one rule for staying here, Fyrnir. Take it off, or I will take it off for you."

He scratched behind his ear.

"I'm just passing through. Only staying the one night," he said. "I thought you'd be easy going about this. Can't you make an exception?"

The jeers turned into chortles.

"Excuse me, Sigyn." She pushed her sleeves past her elbows. "He's asked for an exception."

Fyrnir smiled. I feared he wouldn't for long.

She motioned to the musicians to resume playing as she marched towards him. Their spirited jig drowned out Fyrnir's howls as she pinched his ear and tugged him out of the doors, dragging him somewhere into the shadows.

On second thought, perhaps it was still best to practice caution around her.

With her empty seat beside me, I realized how alone I was here in this land. How out of place. Lonely.

Gods. I missed Loki so much my body ached. I just wanted him to walk through that damn door and pull me into an embrace. I just wanted us to go home.

Loki, where the hell are you? I need you here with me.

I tapped my finger against my drinking horn.

Was this our fate? Were we damned to spend our life apart from one another?

Wine. I needed wine. Now.

I shut my eyes and knocked back another gulp of claret, the sting already less than the first time.

I cracked open my eyelids to Hvalr, Rýgi, and Áma, pointing at me from their table in the back and snickering.

I sighed.

No doubt congratulating themselves on the new nickname they kindly gave me this afternoon.

The Iron Ball Crusher of Midgard.

I sighed again.

It was clever, really.

And, I suppose I earned the title when I scolded them for storing raw chicken next to the apples in the kitchens. I counted at least twenty eye-rolls as I explained the concept of food-born illness. Honestly, I'd never met more stubborn—no. I couldn't continue this way. Mutual frustration would get us nowhere.

Angrboda was right. If I wanted the Jotnar to trust me, they needed to see that I didn't have a stick up my backside.

I smiled at them and surprise lit their faces as they looked at each other.

I lifted my horn to them in a toast. Confusion melted into joy. Delight.

They poured their own horns full and lifted them in return. And they waited for me to go first.

I braced myself.

This time, I kept my eyes open.

I guzzled the claret. They chanted my name.

The fact it remained *The Iron Ball Crusher of Midgard* was no matter, as this time, they said it with endearment. At least for now. We would see what tomorrow would bring with what I had planned for them.

Eat it up, friends. Today we play, but tomorrow we work.

Draining the horn dry, I struck the table with my fist and sniffed hard, following Angrboda's demonstration. Cheers erupted as I wiped my mouth with my sleeve. They emptied their horns down their throats.

My head spun. The music swelled louder in my ears and the rhythmic clap of spoons and pluck of strings drummed down to my toes, which I couldn't help but tap.

Hvalr noticed. He got up and held out his calloused hand, which I took, and he spun me across the flagstones. I laughed as he led me in a type of reel, dancing faster.

He twirled me into Rýgi, who smiled behind his chestnut beard, and whirled us along with the waterfall of mandolin notes until he whirled me into Áma.

She and I giggled as we danced to the panpipes soaring into a crescendo, cheeks flushed with claret, with the rush of this place, ancient as stone. Wild as the wind racing down from the frozen North outside.

I wished Loki could be here to enjoy it with me.

I laughed as Áma spun me until I slipped out of her hand and flew across the stones and into arms that felt familiar.

"Sigyn?"

My breath stopped.

His voice.

I looked up at his face, the swirling images focusing into the one I most wanted to see.

Loki.

14

OH, BROTHER

This was impossible. He couldn't be back already.

His pointed face lit as his eyes met mine, green and sharp against the waves of his red hair that fell just past his shoulders.

My insides heated further.

Loki always could make me burn with only a gaze.

I wrapped my arms around his waist and drew him against me, burying my face in the crook of his neck. Home.

Why didn't he smell like pepper and cardamom?

The unfamiliar salted pine rising off his skin made me pull back.

"While I'm deeply flattered, I believe I'm not who you think I am," he said. "I'm not *him*."

Of course.

Býleistr.

My racing heart slammed into a boulder.

"I'm afraid it was wishful thinking on my part." I massaged my thumb over the bones of my wrist at my mistake.

His lips pulled into a reassuring smile, one that would have made Loki's eyes light with laughter. Býleistr's remained focused, like the rest of him—steady, calm.

Off.

"Don't worry yourself, I'm quite used to it," he said.

"The exact resemblance is uncanny." I trailed my gaze down their same lean frame, their same beautiful hands and long fingers.

"I'm alright with sharing the looks," he said. "But may a frost giant strike me dead if I share anything else with *The Terror*."

"The Terror?"

"It was his nickname growing up. Everyone called him that. I don't understand how anyone can put up with him and his insuffer-able—oh...I've insulted you already."

How very perceptive of him. Did he also perceive my desire to stomp on his foot?

"I should leave," I said, my tone frosted. "I don't think this is something we will *share* an opinion on."

He smiled weakly.

"Forgive me for speaking out of turn," he said. "I'm afraid there is still a lot of bitterness between Loki and me. I hope I've not made things awkward between us. It was not my intention."

I tried to squeeze past him and the row of Jotnar sitting on the benches, feasting away.

He reached between two men and grabbed a bunch of grapes from a wooden bowl on the table, blocking my escape.

"It really sticks in my craw how Loki is, anytime I'm around—I'm sure you noticed the tension wedged between us?"

"I—"

He held out his arm to me, offering me a cluster of grapes.

Býleistr also seemed to share all of Loki's aggravation, but without the benefit of the charm that took off the edge.

I pressed my mouth together and exhaled deeply.

He frowned, retracting his hand.

"And I *have* made things awkward," he said. "Again, I apologize. We don't know each other at all and here I am chatting away like we are old friends when I'm sure Loki has already done excellent work pitting you against me."

He tore a grape off its stem and popped it into his mouth.

"Loki likes to pretend I'm some kind of fiend," he said through his chewing.

"And are you?"

He smiled and stepped back and leaned against the wall, leaving my path clear. Thank gods.

"I've only ever tried to mend our broken bridges," he said. "But you know how he can be. Once you cross him, there is no forgiveness."

That much was true, and Loki nearly ended the worlds because of it.

I wanted to walk away. Really, I did.

My feet grew roots into the flagstones instead. *Dammit.*

"And what happened between you two to cause no forgiveness?"

"Are you trying to see if I'm the one to blame?" he said.

"If the shoe fits."

"If I hold any blame, it was simply in my stupidity of thinking that if I loved Loki hard enough, he would be the good brother I always wanted." His hands tightened into fists at his sides. He seemed to catch himself and relaxed them, spreading his fingers and wiping them on his trousers. "I suppose you and I have this in common—Loki hurts us until we break."

The roots keeping me planted twisted deeper into the floor and my every muscle hardened into stone.

I considered stomping on his foot again. Hard.

"We do not have this in common."

"Don't we?" he said. "He's a man of a thousand tricks he wields to confuse us and twist us and turn us inside out, so we remain under his spell—"

"That's untrue—"

"—A spell I see you are still under."

The pine on his clothes strengthened as he leaned in.

"You really don't know who Loki is, do you?" he whispered. "What he is capable of?"

Irritation flushed through my veins.

"He's capable of more than anyone gives him credit for." I glared at him. "I believe in him because he is capable of good."

He snorted.

"The good he does is only to use as a balm for the bruises he gives us." He exhaled softly and gave me a pitying grimace I absolutely hated. "I had hoped to avoid all this nastiness."

"Then why do I get the feeling that this is exactly what you wanted to discuss?"

Sincerity deepened within his gaze that I searched for any glint of deception.

"I don't say this to be unkind, but, in the grand scheme of things, you and Loki have not spent that much time together. And—forgive me—you are only five hundred years old and he's—well—*far* older. He's lived thousands of lifetimes and has accrued a collection of skeletons to prove it."

"I don't care if it's a crypt."

I kept my eyes firm on his, searching for a flicker of a lie, a crack in his game I could catch.

His concern remained annoyingly genuine.

Real.

The bastard.

"Your fidelity, your blind faith, in such a man is actually deeply inspiring. I remember when I felt the same."

"What are you implying?"

"You know he keeps everything shoved beneath the bed like some sort of hobgoblin."

My stomach churned at that barbed truth.

"Your point being?"

"Loki is a trickster," he said. "Do you really believe that the God of Lies is honest with you?"

He tread too far.

"I trust him," I said.

"But he doesn't trust you," he said. "Ever consider that? It's why he hides things. Keeps things. He knows you'd leave him if you found out..."

He stopped and compressed his lips into a flat line. The same as Loki did when he realized he said too much.

"Found out what?" I hissed.

Býleistr shifted in his boots. He rubbed the back of his neck.

"Loki made me promise to keep my mouth shut." He cursed beneath his breath. "Alright. Look, I'm giving up an awful lot by telling you this, but...this is wrong and you don't deserve to be kept in the dark. You deserve to know the truth of what he did."

"You keep hinting, but never say," I said. "It's making me think you have nothing worth telling at all."

The corners of his mouth quirked for a heartbeat.

"I have plenty to tell," he said. "For example, that night you received that letter from your brother—"

"—Simon? How do you—"

"Bly, remember what we discussed?" Angrboda interrupted, tapping her foot.

He turned to her and smiled, my ears still burning from his words I didn't want to hear but craved all the same like some depraved animal.

"I got lonely being stashed away and thought I'd enjoy a bit of the festivities," he said. "Everything else was a coincidence."

Her nostrils flared and her eyes narrowed.

"I'm sure." She took my arm in hers and whisked me between the tables, leaving Býleistr behind within the layers of candle and pipe smoke.

"Where are you taking me?" I tugged back. "He knows about Simon and—"

"I've no doubt," she pressed out, clamping tighter on my arm. "Leave Bly to his spite and shadows. Whatever he claims to know will not bring any joy."

"But—"

"Remember what I told you about too much wisdom? Some things are better left buried."

Her grip turned into steel, pulling me towards the doors. I wanted to fight her, but I knew she'd probably find enjoyment in the bruises I'd give her.

"I suppose I should be more like you and smash men's faces into floors because of their clothing? Some things are better shown mercy."

She raised her eyebrow.

"You can scratch when you want, can't you? As it so happens, I was merciful and gave Fyrnir the exception he asked for. I threw him naked into the lake instead of splitting his lip with my fist."

"How generous of you."

Her shoulders dropped.

"You think me cruel," she said. "I only have one rule here— nothing made from wolves or serpents. Everyone knows it, yet they continually defy me. They feel I'm extreme. *Me.*"

"You just threw a man into a lake."

I twisted out of her grip as we walked out of the great hall and into the stillness of flickering candles of a hallway. We faced a portrait of Angrboda surrounded by her three children. Fenrir I recognized, with his kind eyes, a stark contrast to Jormungand's stern expression beside him. The woman sitting between them, half her face decayed, the other half severe, I knew must be Hel. They all had Loki's green eyes.

An ugly black blob hovered beside Angrboda, where I imagined Loki had once stood before he was aggressively painted out. I hope she didn't notice me frown.

"I cannot abide thinking of my children hunted for their pelts or made into trophies that hang in rooms of yellow silk," she said. "I lived so much of my life in fear for their lives, even still." Her breath shuddered. "It's why I allowed...I trusted Loki. I trusted the gods. I believed I was giving my children safety..." Her voice cracked. "I still hate myself for how stupid I was."

My irritation cooled.

I was the stupid one. How could I not realize?

I reached out and touched her arm, reassuring her. The same as I did for Loki, when his own ghosts spontaneously rose and haunted him about their children.

And our own.

"You weren't stupid," I said. "You were trying to give them their best chance. No one can fault you for that."

She turned away from the portrait to me and held my hand, her skin cool like Loki's when he touched my arm or traced my jawline.

That ache of missing him returned and shredded me.

But something else shredded me deeper. Something frigid and stifling that filled my ears with wool.

The room wobbled.

I blinked and tried to focus on her face that wouldn't steady.

"You really do bring hope to one's soul." She squeezed me gently and let me go. "I've lost track of the time and it's nearly midnight. Let's go jump in the fountains. It will chap your tits, but it's incredibly refreshing."

"As tempting as that sounds, I have—"

My body felt light while simultaneously weighing as much as a rhinoceros. And I was going somewhere. Where was I going? Why did sulfur sting my sinuses?

You can't keep ignoring me, Sigyn. Surtr's voice spoke in the darkness, smooth as silk. *What is Loki hiding from you? What does Bly know that Loki doesn't want you to discover?*

"Sigyn!"

The right side of my face sparked with pain.

I creaked open my eyelids and Angrboda's face stared into mine as she patted my cheek.

"What happened?" she said. "Are you alright?"

I winced and slowly sat up, angered at having succumbed to another episode.

"Nothing, just a dizzy spell. They strike me from time to time."

She grimaced and pulled me to my feet. The floor heaved beneath me and my knees trembled. I hated this.

"There is no one to impress here, Sigyn," she said. "You don't have to be strong all the time. How can I help you? Sigyn?"

Couldn't she see? I had no choice but to be strong. And it was slowly killing me.

"Just...Get me to my room. I need to lie down."

She nodded and kept me steady as we walked through the hall. I focused on keeping my breaths even and every step grounded, even though my guts twisted in knots with Surtr's words still running through my head, and with Býleistr's that followed.

Loki made me promise to keep my mouth shut.

What would Loki not want him divulging? No. Angrboda was right. Whatever he had to tell was all drivel. Utter drivel.

My stomach lurched, and the room tilted again.

"Is it drivel, though?" Surtr said.

Angrboda hurried our pace towards my room, through halls of orange tiles and rugs. Surtr kept pace following us, his black robes making him appear like a shade against the whitewashed walls.

"As I've been saying, Loki's hiding something, and it looks like I was right. Otherwise, he wouldn't have burdened poor Býleistr with this secret. I am eager to discover what it is. I hope something dastardly!"

Angrboda pulled on the brass handle and walked me inside and sat me in a sturdy chair.

"I'll be back with some tea and whiskey," she said.

She closed the door behind her, and Surtr walked right through the inch of oak as if vapor.

Why wouldn't he leave me alone?

I stood, teetered, and walked across the rugs and braced myself on the desk and breathed out, the wooziness lessening. I concentrated on the heat from the fireplace. On the howl of the wolves outside the leaded window.

On anything but the darkness and my racing thoughts and—

I laughed.

All this angst clawing at me was stupid. Loki and Simon never even met. Really, why was I even wasting thoughts on this nonsense? All of it was nonsense.

"Because you're doubting," Surtr said. "You know you can't trust

Loki. Look what happened to Angrboda. She trusted him, and she lost everything."

Surtr stepped behind me. I hardened my grip on the edges of the desk, resisting the prickle on my collarbone needling into my marrow, begging me...

"And worse." His voice rippled down my spine. "Loki doesn't even trust *you*. The burn of that irony."

My stomach clamped.

I couldn't accept that, even though it explained everything.

Because that thought terrified me the most.

I turned and faced Surtr.

Surtr's violet eyes glimmered behind wisps of his white hair. Daring me...

I put my finger out to Surtr and opened my lips to tell him to go to Hel, or to Muspelheim, or back to wherever he bloody came from.

A smile cracked Surtr's sensuous face as that burning, violet gaze of his dropped to my neck.

The prickle on my collarbone turned into a blaze.

I drew back my hand and raced to the mirror and tugged off the knit cowl from around my neck and threw it to the floor. Staring at my reflection, my breath left my body.

The spot grew, tendrils of black stretching like a web over my chest and up my neck and over my right shoulder.

No.

I stumbled back and grasped the bed post and sank into the layers of blankets and mattresses.

I cannot succumb.

I will not succumb.

My lungs burned as I forced breath in through my nose and exhaled slowly through my lips, determined to remain calm. Unshaken.

Strong.

Loki is relying on me to stay strong.

Surtr's laughter filled my ears, bewitching and lethal, mixing with the rush of my blood.

"Let me get this straight," Surtr said. "You're enduring all this suffering because Loki is *relying* on you when you can't even rely on Loki? Look at yourself. What he's ground you into." Surtr brushed a lock of my hair away from the sweat slicking my brow. "It's as Býleistr said. Loki hurts. He's hurting you. Once. Twice. A hundred times over. He's left you. Abandoned you. And I don't even need to mention Ragnarok...It's why you know you can't rely on him, Sigyn. You can only rely on me. On us."

Lies.

Always lies.

I hated that my words weren't as strong as before.

15

DIAMONDS ARE A GODDESS'S BEST FRIEND

LOKI

Vanaheim

C yprus trees lined the dirt road Odin and I walked along, unfortunately providing no shade from the Vanir sun broiling our skin.

The scent of olive and lemon from the groves covering the hills of Leira mixed with the salt of the sea pounding the rocky beach below Freya's palace. When not attending to business in Asgard, she spent what time she could in her homeland of Vanaheim. She claimed the superior Vanir water gave her hair that certain bounce.

"There are a hundred ways this can go sour," I said over the scream of cicadas.

Small lizards darted across the path and scurried under stones.

"Don't tell me you're scared," Odin said, teasing in his voice.

I stopped, the gravel popping beneath my boots. I didn't like how the dry air parched my throat further. How my insides spun.

This was such a terrible, terrible idea.

"Wait, you are," he said. "But you're never scared."

Admittedly, this was very unlike me. Few could unravel my laces, but...I knew better than to underestimate her. Freya was powerful, a warrior, with magic equal in strength even to my own. Even to Odin's.

"This isn't some skull crushing Draugr or frost giant," I said. "This is *Freya*."

His lips thinned behind his beard.

"Plus," I squared my shoulders, "If we should fail, I don't want to lose my—*well*—you know her fondness for ripping off—"

Odin put out his hand, stopping me from saying the grisly bit.

"I was trying to forget about that particular risk." He squeezed his legs together. "But, there is only one way to do this if we stand a chance."

I crossed my arms.

"You still want me to shift our forms, then? Because I thought you said *no magic under any circumstances*," I said. "Or is this one of those moratoriums able to be lifted only at your convenience? Because I may have an opinion on that."

He sank his face into his hands and released something that straddled being a breath and a groan between his fingers.

"Do you have to choose now to be difficult? We could be spotted."

I smiled.

"Now look who is scared," I mocked.

He dropped his hands back at his sides and the sun blinding his eye made him squint at me. My own eyes burned from the surrounding glare reflecting off the gravel and bright stone.

"We discussed this. If Freya sees you have broken your banishment. That I have allowed it..." He inhaled sharply. His nerves were finally working on him as well. "If we want this to work, she cannot know who we are and—"

I groaned and stepped over clumps of brush and stood beneath the pitiful shade of an olive tree for a little reprieve. I blinked the burn of sunlight away.

"Yes, yes," I said, growing bored.

Unfortunately for Odin, he was not as creative at shapeshifting as myself, and Freya recognized all of his forms. Given it would take too long for him to devise a new disguise, the task fell upon me to cast an illusion over him.

"But after this, we cannot use magic again." He stepped next to me beneath the tree, a web of shadow and light covering his face and shoulders.

"I think you're making a bigger deal about this no magic thing than is necessary. It's causing an immense waste of time. Highly inconvenient."

"What will be inconvenient is if..."

"If what?"

He remained tight lipped.

"We must reserve everything we can for what's coming with pulling Surtr out of Sigyn."

I didn't like the chill in his words, but I shook it off. He always overreacted.

"So, what form do you want?" I cracked my knuckles. "Strapping youth with large hands? Demure milk-maid? Oh. I could see you as a blushing virgin oracle, although that may be a stretch even for me to pull off."

"Loki..."

"Fine. The boring option. Got it."

"And don't make my forehead so high this time."

"Wouldn't dream of it."

I waved my hands, casting an illusion over him, narrowing his waist and widening his hips. His dark russet hair lightened into a blonde one shade away from white, and fell in a thick braid down his back that I clothed in the rich silks worn by high-bred Vanir women.

My lips quirked as I finished smoothing his cheekbones, making his nose a touch too large for his face.

I couldn't help myself.

Odin spun in his gown of blues and teals, and admired the rings of gold stacked on his boney fingers.

"How do I look?" Odin asked, the eye filling his missing right socket rolling slightly to the left.

I held in a snicker.

"You are a beauty beyond words," I lied, expanding myself as I shifted into a man of hardened muscle with a strong jaw.

While some days I felt like a good set of breasts, other days...*well*. I loved being a shapeshifter. It made things much easier to match my appearance, should I so wish, to when I was man, woman, neither, or all.

I finished broadening my shoulders and bulking my usual lean physique into something more rugged that complimented my now square face that said *I wear flannel and chop wood in the forest.*

In other words, the perfect, dashing Vanir nobleman with an unfortunately plain wife, the ideal couple for the post of Palace Guardian.

I know.

It was quite odd for a goddess to entrust her estate to another, but since she could not move her cats—*precisely one thousand cats*—back and forth between Vanaheim and Asgard—*she said the long journey made them irritable*—she had no choice but to leave them behind in the care of her nobles. Servants could hardly be trusted to not upset the routines of her beloved felines, after all.

Freya boasted how her courtiers viewed being chosen as her Palace Guardian a great honor.

The truth was, no one wanted the job, and the Vanir nobles all drew straws over who would have to next apply for the position. Which meant, lucky for us, we could easily throw our name into the pot and acquire an audience with her.

"This plan better work." I smoothed the wrinkles out of my purple robes. I loved feeling silk against my skin again.

"It will," Odin said. "You know how Freya gets after three glasses of wine."

"More importantly, I know how she gets after two," I grumbled beneath my breath.

She got a bit amorous.

No. A *lot* amorous.

I rubbed my inner thighs at the memory of the first and only night I ever spent with her. She liked to use her teeth in places teeth should never nibble.

"There's nothing to worry about," Odin said. "Frey is here. She won't do anything with her brother around."

I wish I shared his confidence.

* * *

A SERVANT who appeared to have swallowed a spoonful of vinegar commanded us to remove our shoes at the door—and proceeded to watch us with a glare sharper than most knives as we put on the provided slippers that would not scuff the inlaid wooden floors. After she gave us an approving sniff, she finally allowed us inside, as long as we promised to follow her and not touch the sconces, or anything else for that matter.

No problem.

The warm breeze skittered through the palm trees outside the open archways and swept through rooms of frescoed limestone in reds, yellows, and greens.

I was grateful for the airy spaces. It lessened the cat smell permeating my every breath.

Cats stretched on silk pillows. Sat on gilded tables. Licked themselves on plush velvet settees. Stared at us from the tops of armoires and curios.

I preferred their icy glares to the leering cats frozen in oil paint on Freya's lap in the portraits lining the lavish halls we walked along.

An usher opened the door, permitting the servant to lead us into an elegant room filled with more cats lounging on delicate furniture, and...

I held in the biggest of sighs.

Freya stood on a dais, wearing absolutely nothing except the Brísingamen necklace. Links of gold and diamonds woven so thickly together covered her entire décolletage. She rested her manicured fingers on the glittering chains holding a pose as the painter on her left caught the glow of her cheeks in acrylics, while the sculptor on her right preserved her perfect breasts in Carrara marble.

"Make sure you get my waist correct," she snapped at the artists. "I've not eaten only trout and steamed spinach for three weeks solid to have you not capture my hourglass figure."

"Yes, my lady," both replied, a trace of a shiver in their voices.

Freya's dark brown eyes rimmed with black kohl spotted us. She shoved her hair of blackest brown behind her naked shoulders, away from her face of soft arcs, radiating beauty like the sun—minus the warmth.

"Gyda, who are these *people* blocking my light?" she said to the servant in the Vanir tongue—a language sounding simultaneously harsh and lyrical and ancient.

The servant, all perfect cat-eye and spite, took two steps closer.

"They are Lord Halvar and Lady Jorunn of the noble house of Torvalderson, my lady," she said. "For the Palace Guardian post?"

Freya raised her right eyebrow.

"And?"

Gyda stood silent for a breath, as if tossed into a den of cobras.

"You...you requested their presence for a private audience?" Gyda whispered.

Freya's pink painted lips twisted into a smile.

"Ah, yes! Why didn't you say that in the beginning? The incompetence Gyda, really. I expect more from you."

I pressed my smirk flat at Gyda's reddening cheeks until cold water doused my enjoyment as Freya fixed her eyes harder on Odin and I.

They flashed with something I didn't quite like.

Freya stepped off the dais and walked towards us, her necklace reflecting every bit of light in the room, throwing stars across the frescoed walls of birds and exotic fruit.

"Their jaw lines aren't bad, I suppose." She circled us, inspecting us up and down. "Nice figures. Good breeding and a strong Vanir name. Although..." She leaned in and sniffed the air next to my ear. "Curious."

My skin prickled.

Perfect. Just what I hoped to avoid.

"What is curious?" I said in Vanir, stepping in front of Odin and pulling the illusion coating him tighter. I deepened my magic around myself as well.

She moved her nose to the crook of my neck and pulled in a larger breath, as if savoring a fine perfume.

While my element of chaos allowed me to sense when someone lied, Freya's element allowed her to sense—

"The immense heartbreak between you two," she said. "It's as ripe as brown bananas left out in the sun."

Odin shifted behind me and I hoped she didn't notice me bristle.

She stepped back, her eyes narrowing, scrutinizing us as she hunted for some seam or crack in my form and the illusion disguising Odin.

"This scent is familiar to me. In fact..."

She breathed in again.

I hardened the magic further, my temples pounding from my concentration. Had it only been me needing to stay shifted, it wouldn't have been a problem, but with two of us...I stretched my magic to its limits with Odin's illusion. I couldn't risk one ripple. It was the most exquisite magic I'd performed in eons.

"...In fact, I think I've met this devotion before," she said.

Devotion? Alright, maybe she wasn't as formidable as I remembered. I harbored nothing but hatred for Odin. Anything else was preposterous.

It had to be.

It better be.

I coughed, ridding the stupid wriggling sensations from my throat.

"Afraid you're picking up on the sardines we had for lunch," I said. "One may have been off."

"What my husband means, my lady," Odin said, peeking over my shoulder. "Is that we have excellent references."

He pushed me aside and pulled out a folded letter from his skirts and held it out to her. She slipped the letter from his fingers, glanced at it for two seconds, and tossed it to the ground. She laughed.

"References? You amuse me." She planted her hands on her naked hips. "I need more than *references* for this post. I need to see if you have what it takes. That certain *je ne sais quoi*."

I tilted my head.

"To feed your cats?" I said.

Her face hardened and sweat broke out across the small of my back. I recognized that look.

"Oblige me," she said.

Odin looked at me, as if he had stepped in a fresh pile of manure. Please. It was stupidly clear what she wanted. Flattery and adoration.

"Go on," I encouraged through a forced smile. "*Oblige her.*"

"In that case." Odin blinked, as if trying to figure out what to say next. "Allow me to...Ah, allow me to recite a poem in your honor."

My shoulders dropped.

A poem? Really? That was the best he could do?

I was about to slap some sense into him, but stopped when he spoke.

Verses from Asgardian sagas fell from his lips, all about adventure and magic swords and rival families. And even though his voice was a woman's, it kept that even tone of his. That familiar softness that had warmed my insides on those cold winter nights when he'd read to me the same tales in our bed.

I remembered how in those gentle moments the world had slipped away, and it was only us.

He promised me he would always—

I never should have trusted him.

I rubbed my chest, trying to smother whatever emotions gnawed inside my ribs.

Freya yawned.

"And amusement has turned into boredom," she said. "You are so sedate. You might as well speak about the weather or other dull things." She sighed. "I had such high hopes...Such excellent cheekbones. What a waste."

She turned and stepped back onto the dais and snapped her fingers. The painter and sculptor jumped to attention, and furiously painted and chiseled again as Freya struck her pose.

Odin's brow furrowed.

"What about a sonnet?" Odin said. "There's a good one about a shepherd."

I dragged my hands down my cheeks.

No sonnets. My gods. He had all the charm of a constipated slug.

I never should have agreed to this.

I pushed in front of Odin because it was obviously up to me to save our hides.

I gave a warm laugh, as if everything had all been an intentional joke.

"You must forgive my wife," I said. "I'm afraid she is a bit tongue tied around such perfection as yourself."

Freya scoffed, holding perfectly still.

"Gyda, remove these disappointments from my presence," she said. "Their tediousness will give me frown lines, and that I cannot allow. Oh, don't you *dare* use salmon pink for my lips when they are rose, Birger."

The painter nodded with a tremble.

Gyda started to escort us out. No. It couldn't end like this.

"Wait, wait." I pulled Gyda's iron grip off my arm. "I must know, or else my entire journey home will be nothing but me crying fat, mournful tears. Please."

"What?" Freya snapped.

"Tell me, what is it like being the most beautiful goddess in all the Nine Worlds? I feel it must be a terrible burden being so alluring... and...and ravishing."

She perked, a small smile tugging at her mouth.

"It can be trying some days." She combed her fingers through her hair. "No one appreciates how much time I spend bathing in donkey's milk and rose petals. You don't get this complexion without diligence."

"No wonder your skin is smoother than the marble." I smacked

Gyda's hand off my shoulder. "Your hard work shows."

Freya blushed.

"You really think so?"

She snapped for Gyda to stop her attack.

"Indeed," I said. "In fact, I think you are quite naughty setting such an impossible task for these artists. Nothing can capture your most sublime allure."

She giggled and coiled her hair around her finger. Her eyes flashed hotter making my stomach twist.

I recognized that look, too. I liked it the least of all.

Thank goodness Frey was here.

Somewhere.

She tapped her chin with her manicured finger, considering.

"Maybe you would be a good fit for this position after all," she said.

I smiled, making sure it was filled to the brim with devils and charm.

"Wonderful, because I can imagine several positions I'd be a good fit for."

Her face brightened, and she laughed again.

"You naughty rogue," she said.

She stepped off the dais again, and walked to me. The painter and sculptor slumped and laid back in their chairs, wiping the sweat from their brows.

"Let me personally show you around and give you the house rules." She ran her hand down my arm and my skin raised in goose-flesh. "As long as you keep with those little funnies of yours."

"That can be arranged."

She giggled.

"Let me first change into something more titillating."

She marched past us, maneuvering around sleeping and saun-tering cats, and disappeared behind a folding screen.

Odin gripped my wrist.

"What are you doing? We agreed this part was mine," Odin whispered.

"And you're doing a bang-up job," I said. "Poems, really? She has no patience for nuance. We were seconds from her turning us out. She's the goddess of sex and war. She has to be finessed. Excited. Not read *sonnets*."

Even on the battlefield she was a tease with the enemy and enjoyed toying with them, just as a cat batted at a mouse before breaking its neck.

Odin looked offended.

"I don't understand," he said. "She didn't find my poetry *sedate* that time we spent a week together in the Southern Isles."

"Only because she wanted you to share your runes and charms with her."

"That's not true. She was deeply intrigued by the Midgardian Sagas particularly."

I cocked my head and pressed my lips together. Really?

"Was she dazzled by everything you said?" I said. "Did she hang on your every word as you spoke lengthy epitaphs on dueling families and farmers and kings?"

"I'll have you know she grew deeply aroused and...*oh*. She was only using me."

And he finally got it.

"Exactly. We need her too—"

She stepped around the screen, her silk skirts split up her right leg to the top of her thigh, and the top split to her belly button. Brísingamen glimmered around her throat and chest.

Say what you will about Freya, but she knew how to wear a gown to the point of making me envious.

"Let's keep this tour quick," she said. "I'm having my pussy cast in plaster at noon and I cannot be late." She picked up the white cat with a smooshed face walking beside her and scratched behind its ear. "It will need to be stroked at least twenty minutes until it is willing."

Odin and I shared a look.

"Is she referring to the cat?" I asked.

"Gods, I hope so."

16

HOUSE RULES

We followed her through halls and rooms and courtyards full of sun and lavender and fountains. Courtiers bowed as she glided past them, casting their eyes to the floor not out of reverence, but out of necessity lest Brísingamen blind them as it flashed with her every high-heeled step.

I studied the clasps bolting it together behind her neck, a veritable mess of locks and hooks and inevitable cursing when the time came to unfasten the damn thing without her severing us in two.

"While you tend to the cats—feeding, brushing, administering Mr. Ragnar's medication for his rectal prolapse—you must also keep a watch on the sun."

"The sun?"

"Of course the sun, are you stupid?" she said. "I won't have its rays bleach my floral printed cotton armchairs. The curtains must be closed following the sun's path as it moves obnoxiously across the sky. And as I'm on the subject of what's obnoxious—water spots. I detest those garish flecks. If I see so much as one blotch on my gold faucets...They must be wiped clean after each use. Got it? For that matter—"

She continued on and on, about not touching the silk wallpaper, eating no foods that made crumbs, wearing no dark clothing that may leech color and stain her white cushions that also had to be rotated regularly. I'm surprised we were even permitted to breathe.

"And finally, my pride and joy."

Freya stopped us in front of a walnut curio filled with a collection of porcelain boars, some dancing, some holding violins, others promising a dark curse on you and all who you love if you looked into its eyes too long.

"If you chip one of my porcelain boars—" her voice deepened "—I will destroy you. Let me show you the gardens!"

"Wonderful," I said. "It will give me a better chance to admire your figure as you walk."

She laughed, her eyes sparkling with mirth.

"You are a scoundrel." She booped my nose. "Don't stop."

Freya winked at me and disappeared through a split in the sheer curtains.

I exhaled, letting my shoulders relax.

"Where is Frey?" I whispered in Odin's ear. "I don't know how much longer I can keep this up. You saw that look she gave me when she showed us the proper way to fluff the pillows? They are usually inseparable and I've not seen one hint of him."

We walked towards the curtains and gardens behind them. Gods. Their whole thing was disgusting. But it was the Vanir way.

"Stop fretting," he said. "Frey is here. He's always here. Probably out hunting with Gullinbursti. You know how much he loves that damn boar."

True.

I swiped at the curtains, trying to find the split.

"I don't care. We're getting in too deep," I said. The curtains billowed, tangling me within perfumed silk. "I will not endure bite marks on my thighs a second time. I had to use a whole jar of healing ointment—where is the bloody opening?"

"You are acting like a coward," Odin said under his breath.

Coward?

"Now look here—"

He pulled the curtain back and pushed me through. I gulped as Freya faced us, leaning against the stone railing on the veranda. She ran her fingers along the embroidered edges of her gown and over her breasts that threatened to fall out.

"You know, Halvar," she said. "If those robes get too hot and confining, I have something else you can *slip* into."

I forced my most charming smile, though everything in me wanted to shed tears.

"You are all generosity," I said.

Courtiers walked through hedges of rosemary, careful to weave between the cats sunbathing on the gravel paths and the lawn.

Freya shoved off the railing and forced herself between me and Odin, causing him to stumble a step backwards.

"Do you mind if I have a feel?" She reached out and touched my arm. "I'm curious what kind of handsome stallion I have here."

Freya squeezed my upper arm, a little gasp escaping between her lips. Freya ran her hand down my chest, nudging closer to me, her eyes darkening as they followed her hand's descent towards my stomach.

Her necklace glinted and temptation swept through me to uncoil the latches and swipe it off her neck right here and now...but I'd be dead before I took a single step.

"Oh!" she said, stopping at my belt I had buckled tighter than usual. I wasn't risking anything. "You are strapped in there, aren't you? Poor dear. Let me help you loosen that..."

She shifted my belt, tugging on the leather and buckle.

I glared at Odin over her shoulder, mouthing at him to get on with it and move us out of this entr'acte and into the main event.

He put his fist against his mouth and started coughing, producing a marvelously disgusting roll of phlegm.

Freya retracted her hand seconds from unbuckling my belt.

Again, I exhaled.

"Ew." She scowled at Odin. "Are you sick, Jorunn?"

I frowned.

"Must be from that rain storm we got caught in on the way here," I told her. "Poor, poor Jorunn."

I turned to Odin.

"I told you to drink something warm to prevent this from happening, my sweetness. But you're always refusing my advice."

Odin sneezed over a Terra Cotta pot full of herbs and Freya shrieked.

"Do not goober up my tarragon!"

Odin wiped his nose on his sleeve and wobbled over to a stone bench. He sat beside a gray cat with flat ears that stretched in the shade beneath an olive tree.

"Apologies." Odin hacked and sniffed again. "I feel a little faint. I think...I think I need to go back to our rooms we let in town and rest."

Freya's lips twisted into a smile.

"Of course, my dearest Jorunn," I said. "If you excuse us, my Lady Freya, we must depart this instant for Leira."

Freya's smile vanished.

I helped lift him to his feet and brushed off his gown and started walking him away.

She stood in our path.

"Go? But surely there's no need for *you* to go as well. She seems perfectly capable of getting home on her own."

Odin moaned and swooned in my arms. I held him up.

"I'm afraid I can't allow that in her state," I said, taking his hand in mine. "I am her husband, after all."

She crossed her arms and tapped her foot.

"This is very inconvenient, Halvar," she said.

"I know," I said. "And we were having such a lovely time."

We walked past her, and with each step farther away we took, the more my lungs burned as I'd stopped breathing.

Everything rested on her response.

"How about..." she said.

I stopped and without thought, I squeezed Odin's hand, feeling it as slick with sweat as my own.

"Yes?" I turned and faced her.

"What if you both stayed here for the night?" she said. "That way, Jorunn can rest, and *we* don't lose the fun we were just beginning to have."

Breath returned in my lungs.

"I wouldn't dream of inconveniencing you," I said.

"Nonsense," she said. "If you are to stay here as my Palace Guardian, I might as well give you a trial run, anyway. Make sure you've remembered all I've told you. Make sure you can *perform* up to standard."

Her eyes sparked as if already imagining us tangled in a hundred different positions, each more bone-breaking than the last.

"Then how can I refuse?"

I hid my smile. Now, all we had to do was wait until—

"Dinner will be served precisely at six," she said.

My stomach curdled.

"Dinner?" Odin and I said in unison.

I melted my surprise into a chuckle.

"I believe what my wife is trying to say is, that it would be best we keep to our rooms."

Freya smiled and brushed the side of my cheek with the back of her fingers. Her eyes burned hotter and she wet her lips with her tongue.

"If you don't attend dinner, then that would be very rude of you, and I do not tolerate rudeness," she said. "And we will have a very different discussion."

I gulped.

"Then I guess that's settled," I said.

She went to a lemon tree and picked a lemon from the branch, yellow and plump.

"Perfect," she said, brushing her thumb over the smooth peel. "Your company will be a blessing. I've been quite lonely with Frey not being here."

Wait.

"Lord Frey is—" I shuddered. "—gone?"

She dug her nails into the skin, gripping the fruit tighter.

"Returned to Asgard yesterday," she said. "Afraid it's just me and all this sexual frustration that has been building inside me since our separation. It's like I've been a caged tiger yearning to leap out and run through the jungle. I am about to burst!"

She crushed the lemon, and juice and seeds squirted out of the broken rind and ran down her arm. Sour bits flew into my face.

"How incredibly vivid." I wiped the lemon juice from my chin.

"And if things go how I intend," she said. "We can enjoy all the wilds the jungle has to offer together."

I swallowed again. Harder this time.

"Now," she said. "If you excuse me, I have a pussy to plaster."

She clapped her hands, and a servant started to usher us away as Freya walked back inside.

"Maybe we are in too deep," Odin whispered beneath his breath.

No shit.

17

CUSTARD

Ocean waves struck rock, and white froth exploded over the jagged coastline. I leaned my elbows on the stone railing of our veranda and stared at Sigyn's ring that I squeezed between my thumb and forefinger. I missed her. I missed her touch. I missed her calm that told me I had finally found home. That I finally was safe.

Warm pinks and reds tinted the gold as the sun slipped towards the horizon, awakening the crickets in the shrubs and lemon groves.

Funny. Not five days before, I had held her ring just like this, looking out over the Pacific, imagining our future together.

Bitterness filled my mouth.

Our future.

Until I got that bloody necklace from Freya, until we stripped Surtr from her insides, our future remained a house of cards.

And then there was still the golden apple needing to be paid...

I clasped the ring tight between my palms and leaned my forehead against my folded hands, as if in prayer.

I was in prayer.

To deliver Sigyn from the darkness. To deliver me from the catastrophe waiting for me in everything I touched.

Do you really think you can have a happily ever after? You don't deserve one.

Those words ricocheted inside my head.

I hunched further, crushed the ring tighter, crushed my eyes closed. Pleading.

"Please. I love her," I whispered, my words swallowed by the wind, swallowed by the answering laughter.

Every love you've ever known has ended in disaster. What makes you think this will be any different?

"Loki? Are you alright?"

Odin's voice jolted me out of the storm clouds, forcing me back to the chirr of crickets and the blink of stars filling the darkening night sky. I pocketed the ring as he walked over and stood next to me.

"I just want her to be free of all this mess," I said.

He grimaced, now returned to his usual form. I needed to rest what I could before I had to shift myself back and cast him in an illusion again. The magic was prickly to wield and maintain for us around Freya, not that I minded the challenge. But it left me with a splitting headache, which made everything about my mood worse.

"I know," he said. "We all do."

He braced himself on the railing and stared out at the sea. The breeze, full of citrus and olive, skated his dark hair over his eyepatch.

I couldn't believe he was here. I couldn't believe that *I* was here with him, alone, just as it used to be back when I had trusted him. Trusted him until he reminded me it was far safer to be an island.

I couldn't survive my heart broken a second time. If Sigyn would...

My eyes stung and my chest seized.

"I can't lose Sigyn." My voice broke. "I can't."

I scraped my nails against the stone railing.

"We will make it back in time for her."

"You don't know that."

"I do."

He gripped my hands and turned me until I faced him.

"She will survive this darkness. Look at me."

I held his gaze through the water blurring my vision, needing him to tell me it would be fine. That it would all work out.

"But what if—"

He squeezed my knuckles.

"She will survive Surtr. I will make sure of it," he said. "I want her to be safe the same as you."

He squeezed harder, branding his reassurance into me.

And for that heartbeat, I believed him.

Until I remembered, I could never believe him.

I pulled out of his hold and cleared the emotion from my throat, sprouting claws. My head throbbed.

"Stop this pretending act." I wiped my hands on my trousers, wanting to remove any residue of him.

His face stitched with confusion.

"Pretending? How am I pretending?"

I scoffed.

He was always an excellent actor.

"Because you don't actually care about Sigyn," I said. "You never have. You've only ever seen her as a stone in your shoe."

"You're upset. Please. I want to help you—"

"Help me? You're only here to protect your own skin from Surtr, not because of any goodness in that black rock you call a heart."

He stiffened.

"That's not true," he said. "Yes, my skin may be in this game, but I'd help you, regardless. As I always have."

I laughed.

"Have you?" I said.

He sighed and his shoulders dropped.

"Give me a chance to fix things," he said. "Allow me to prove to you that maybe we can..." his voice trailed off into the thunder of the sea.

"That maybe we can *what*?"

He searched me, as if drowning in the words he wanted to say.

"Nothing," he said.

"Nothing is right, because *nothing* is all you'll ever be to me."

His features threaded with pain as if I'd struck him, and I regretted my words immediately.

Why did I regret them? I should want to wound him even deeper. Drive a stake through his heart and hammer it through until I impaled him to the ground. He deserved every sting. Every cut.

"You know no one else would stand here with you now, especially tonight when we face Freya." He kept his gaze locked on mine. "Think of my motives as you will, but I'm here by your side fighting this darkness with you, and that counts for something."

Silence settled between us, disturbed only by the rustle of palm trees.

Odin turned and walked back towards our room.

Guilt chewed harder at my ribs because he was right.

He could have refused me. He could have let me confront this tragedy alone. He could have let me flounder. If it wasn't for him, Sigyn would already be lost.

"Odin," I called.

He stopped and looked at me over his shoulder.

Could I give him another chance?

Should I give him another chance?

"Do you think Freya will sing at dinner?" I said instead of what I should say. Instead of telling him *I'm sorry*.

A small smile cracked his face.

"I suggest preparing your soul," he said. "It's inevitable."

* * *

It was in the second hour of Freya's opera seria that I started to contemplate carving out her voice box with my dinner knife and feeding it to her cats.

The felines sauntered between platters of fish, salads, and exotic fruits on tables packed with agitated courtiers. They drained goblet after goblet of white wine between sighs and frowns, while servants sweat through their silk robes in the mad scramble to keep those goblets refilled, one spill away from an all out revolt.

A fresh set of trills and vibrato erupted out of Freya's lungs, the force of the notes shaking the chandelier over our heads.

This did nothing for my nerves. Especially as they already frayed with keeping the magic disguising Odin and myself wrapped tight around us.

It wasn't that Freya's voice was bad, it was actually beautiful, but there was simply so much opera one could take in an evening. Plus, I knew what she could do with that voice if provoked...

What she could make people do with its power...

While I wasn't a coward, that particular butchery was an experience that just wasn't very me, and I owed it to myself to respect that.

Freya flew out of the recitative and immediately into the ninth aria, all about love and couples with enough angst and pining to turn one's stomach.

When would these torments end?

I snatched my table knife and squeezed the silver handle, my knuckles pulsing white.

"Don't you dare make this worse," Odin hissed beneath his breath. He chased a cherry tomato across his plate with his fork, dragging the sleeve of his teal gown into a puddle of balsamic vinegar that the silk immediately soaked up. "Dammit. Every time."

I frowned and nodded slowly. All that beautiful embroidery— ruined. He was always hopeless when it came to wearing gowns properly. They never lasted more than one meal before he spilled half of his dinner on them.

"How could it possibly be worse?" I said. "If I jam this in her larynx, they will all hail me a hero. It's a mercy, really."

He closed his eyes and sharply inhaled, trying to leech away the stain on his sleeve with his napkin.

"Eat your damn fish." His voice sank into the depths of despair. "As if I need more noise bashing my skull with this tantrum you're having. We're all miserable."

"Tantrum?" I slammed my knife back on the table beside my plate of snapper slathered in butter and slices of lemon. "You know what? I'm sorry. You're right. I'd absolutely love to eat my fish. Oh, look, it's delightfully covered in cat hair. Don't you just love that added texture?"

Odin groaned and massaged the middle of his forehead, making his pearl drop earrings jiggle against his rouged cheeks.

"Shut up and pick it out."

Fine.

I spat out a colorful insult I made sure he heard as I plucked three white hairs off the fish's eye that stared back at me. I suppose I'd have to make the best of it. On the bright side, my velvet robes remained pristine, and my nose the correct size for my square face.

Yes, I could get through this evening.

A tabby cat plopped down beside my plate, hiked up one leg, and licked its—I shoved my plate away and filled my goblet with more wine instead.

Applause filled the room and Freya took a bow, Brísingamen casting points of shivering light across the frescoes of gardens and birds—and into my eyes, blinding me for a solid five seconds.

I inhaled slowly and imagined my rage as a cloud, floating higher and higher away into a perfectly blue sky.

Freya walked towards our table that stood in the middle of the room, her lavender gown brushing the black and white tiled floor. She was all curves and arcs with the elegance and grace of a flower in bloom, if that flower was belladonna.

"Remember what we have to do." Odin grabbed a carafe of wine and filled a silver goblet to the brim. "Three glasses will put her out, and then...My! How incredibly enchanting your performance was, Lady Freya."

She smiled, her lips coated in red paint. Beads of gold were woven into the braids of her hair. Jasmine and vanilla radiated off her skin.

"It was divine, wasn't it?" Freya wedged herself between us, ramming her elbow into my stomach and punching the air from my lungs as she grabbed the purple pillow beside me.

She crammed the cushion beneath her armpit and stretched on her left side and faced me. She tossed her dark curls and braids behind her back, smacking Odin in the face. While I wanted to enjoy him clawing the hairs off his mouth and chin, I couldn't stop staring at Brísingamen glistening in the candle light, begging me to rip it off her neck.

It would be so easy.

It would get you castrated in three seconds or less.

"And what did you think?" She nestled closer against me and pressed her finger into my chest, thankfully rousing me out of that unhappy thought.

"I never knew such sounds were achievable by the throat," I said. "You must be absolutely parched after that performance."

I reached over Freya and grasped the prepared goblet out of Odin's hand and presented it to her as if it were an offering.

"Allow me to quench your thirst."

Her lips pulled into a smile as she lifted the cup from me, her red painted fingernails filed into rounded points. I shivered at the thought of those fingernails scratching my skin if this went wrong.

Freya tossed back her head and guzzled the wine, her neck pulsating with every swallow.

That's right, Freya. Bottoms up.

If Odin and I stood any chance at getting that bloody necklace off her neck, she'd have to be asleep. Easy enough. She always passed out cold after her third glass of wine, even though she always denied it. Of course, getting her to drink that third cup is what would be a bitch, especially because of—

Freya wiped her wine stained lips with the back of her hand and locked eyes with me. With a hiccup, she slipped her thumb beneath her left shoulder strap and pushed it down, revealing a patch of bare skin.

"Oops. How did that happen?" she said.

I swallowed.

—because of this. Alcohol never ceased to heighten her arousal, shooting it into the atmosphere.

This plan had better work, because there were some things I was not willing to do, and Freya was one of them.

"I'm rather a big deal in Jotunheim, you know," she said. "They love my singing there."

"No doubt." Odin poured an arc of wine into a fresh goblet.

"I once even sang for Thrym, a Jotun war lord," she said. "He never got over me. Demanded my hand in marriage so he could hear me sing every day."

She fiddled with the lace edging her bodice.

"Who wouldn't love a woman with such marvelously healthy lungs?" I said.

She laughed and ran her fingers across the clusters of jewels of Brísingamen, each stone more precious than the last. It was worth entire kingdoms.

"I wouldn't mind giving you a private performance later." She traced the veins on the top of my hand, the light tingle switching into a bite the deeper she scratched those sharp nails of hers.

"I can't hardly wait. More wine?" I directed her gaze to Odin behind her, who held the newly filled goblet out to her.

"My, so attentive," she said. "I hope you're this attentive in all matters?"

I forced a smile and tugged at the collar of my robes. I hoped I wasn't sweating through the layers of silk already.

She twisted and plucked the cup from Odin and brought it to her lips. My heart pounded into my throat, wanting this all wrapped up and done with.

She stopped. Her eyebrows contorted. She lowered the goblet, and with it fell my heart to the floor.

Freya turned onto her stomach and looked at Odin.

"Wait. Aren't you sick?" she said. "I don't want your illness."

She stretched forward and banged the goblet on the table, a wave of wine splashing over the rim and splattering the white fur of a sleeping cat.

"No, no, she's all better." I picked up the cup and handed it back to her. "It was only her allergies acting up again."

Freya tilted her head. As did Odin.

"Allergies?" she said.

"Yes! My poorest, dearest Jorunn is frightfully allergic to…to sunlight. Yes. Sneezing fits and dying every time—but you were telling us about the Jotnar and their adoration of you. I want to hear everything."

I really didn't.

She perked and kicked her sandaled feet like a thirteen-year-old girl chatting with her friends over who was the cutest in the mead hall.

"Yes, the Jotnar are always longing for me." She took the goblet from me, her hot fingers grazing mine. "It's all very flattering, but can you imagine my complexion in Jotunheim? The harsh winds would chap my lips, not to mention I refuse to smell like forest."

She had a point. Everyone smelled like pine and beets and cabbage.

She lifted the goblet to her mouth.

That's right. Keep going.

She stopped.

Dammit.

"But having Jotnar continually fight over me isn't always roses. The duels got boring three millennia ago," she said. "Especially when they only see me as an object to be won, and not as a woman with my own set of needs."

She drained the second goblet, and I flashed a glance at Odin, who furiously poured the third. He extended his arm out to me, and I reached for the cup…

"Oopf!"

Freya pounced on me and straddled my hips, shoving me further into the silk cushions. I gasped for air.

That second glass hit her faster than I recalled.

She raised her arms and lifted her dark hair and let it spill over her shoulders.

"What I really need is someone who understands me." She slid her hands across her chest. "Sees me for me, and not just my perfect breasts."

Freya grasped her bodice and ripped the laces apart, shooting buttons and crystals over my head and freeing her breasts.

"Oh my gods, and there they are," I said.

I scrambled out from beneath her, knocking her over into the cushions, and snatched the goblet from Odin.

She crawled out of the pillows and clasped my face between her hands, smooshing my cheeks and lips.

"Oh, you are feisty," she said. "I like that."

Freya lowered her mouth, racing towards my puckered one. I thrust the goblet between us, blocking her kiss.

"How aboot another drnk," I mumbled.

She released my face and extracted the cup from my fingers. I massaged the sensation of her sweaty grip away.

Odin just blinked as it all happened to me.

"You know what I want to do to you?" she said.

She leaned in and flicked my earlobe with her tongue, returning the goblet to the table. No. I tried to reach for it. She forced me back into the cushions and whispered her plans for the rest of the evening into my ear.

I choked.

"My, that's incredibly graphic," I said. "You forget I do have a wife, so I will have to pass on that kind offer. Although, I doubt you'd find that amount of custard at this hour."

She glanced back at Odin and smiled. Odin swallowed.

"She can come, too." Freya turned her gaze back to mine. "The more the merrier."

She grasped my robes and tore them open, revealing my chest and flat stomach. Her breath smelled of olive and parsley, and for a heartbeat, I believed she was going to swing me over her shoulder and carry me to her bedroom.

I needed to throw cold water on this situation.

"Dearest," I said to Odin. "Tell her more about poetry. She seemed so entranced by the subject earlier today. Explain to her the difference between fornyrðislag and galdralag meters. No. Something more bewitching. Explain to her the structure of a sonnet."

I struggled, trying to reach for the goblet in Odin's hand.

"Which structure?" Odin said, holding out the goblet to me. "Iambic pentameter? Couplets? Quatrains? Although, that depends if you're wanting English or Spenserian, and that's just Midgardian verse, otherwise—"

"This is the hottest nonsense I've ever heard," Freya said, standing.

She took the cup out of Odin's hand, downed it, and grabbed us both by the wrists and tugged us to our feet.

She swayed, but dug her nails deeper into us.

Please. Please. Please.

Freya took a wobbly step.

"Let's go..." She hiccuped. "Let's go...Let us go..."

She stared at us and blinked, as if trying to decide on which of us to focus on.

"Is everything alright?" I said.

"Perfec—tly," she slurred.

Freya wavered.

And fell across the table, arms and legs splayed out and her face planted in a platter of raw oysters.

Odin and I shared a glance.

"Freya?" Odin poked her arm.

I held my breath.

Deafening snores rattled out of her mouth.

I exhaled.

Thank gods.

Her lady's maids hoisted her up. Oysters stuck to her right cheek and forehead. The women slipped their hands beneath her arms and dragged her away across the tiled floor, the heels of her sandals filling the room with screeches.

Now for the hard part.

18

THE LEECH

SIGYN

"This is a new low." Surtr stood on the bank and crossed his arms. "Look at you. Three feet deep in muck. Leeches gnawing at your legs. Disgusting."

I choked down a choice word I wanted to hurl at him.

I hiked my skirts higher and squelched through the mire and waded farther into the pond, stirring the layer of duckweed on the surface. Cold cut through me as the water rose past my knees, soaking the edges of my petticoats. My feet sank into the silt and I agitated the mud further, encouraging more leeches to latch onto my skin.

Irritatingly, Surtr wasn't wrong about this being unappealing work. But it was the quickest way to catch leeches, which I needed to help heal Kyrmir's black eye and Litr's bruised chest. And that was before the brawl broke out. Good gods. Children. All of them.

Who would ever believe that an afternoon of fishing would result in three dislocated shoulders and a host of split lips and swollen jaws.

The leech suckling on my upper leg detached itself, and I caught it before it tumbled back into the water. I slipped it into my ceramic container along with twelve others, all twitching and fat on my blood. Not a bad number, but I needed more.

Surtr sighed and sat on the grass. Angrboda's fortress stood behind him on the hill like a stern giant, the stone blackened with moss and mildew.

"I guess this blood sucking parasitic parade you're insisting on makes sense." Surtr leaned back, planting his hands behind him in the grass. "You've always seemed to have a thing for leeches. I mean, you can't find a bigger leech than Loki. At least these can't talk."

The black veins stretching over my chest and shoulder and up my neck prickled and pulsed with each word that fell from Surtr's lips. That familiar sickly chill trickled along my skin.

Shit. Not again.

I took in a steadying breath, wanting to keep the wooziness tingling my vision from taking hold. I refused to have one more blasted spell.

Another wave of needles.

And another breath. This one deeper.

The world focused. Sharpened.

The barbs needling my skin soothed.

Good.

I adjusted my cowl, ensuring the infection remained hidden, and waded out farther into the water.

I hissed as another leech pierced my calf. A second leech chomped on my ankle.

"You'll be bled dry by those wriggling, disgusting things before the Jotnar appreciate what you're doing for them," Surtr said.

Three days ago I'd agree, but since the night of the feast, something marvelous happened. The Jotnar started to trust me.

Instead of rolling their eyes when I mentioned bacteria, they asked me questions. They asked me for my advice. Rýgi, Hvalr, and Áma even helped me collect nettles and dandelions from the surrounding meadow for teas between the mists.

We spent afternoons in Kvasir's healing room that slowly started to look like something proper, and I taught them how to make salves of plantain and calendula for burns. Afterwards, they took me into the heart of the Ironwood and taught me how to recognize troll caves, and what to do if you accidentally touched the slime coating the deadly Weeping Mushroom.

Apparently, the answer was to pray that death claimed you before your face melted. Yes. That filled me with great confidence.

Grass crinkled beneath quick footsteps. Áma must already be finished with bundling the lavender to dry.

I looked up, smiling, expecting her dark hazel eyes and solid frame marching towards me.

My smile flattened.

Býleistr stood beside Surtr on the bank, his copper hair pulled back and neatly tied into a ponytail. Surtr smoothed his own waves of white hair and grinned up at Býleistr, as if eager for some kind of delicious drama.

"Whatever are you doing in there?" Býleistr's sharp face scrunched with confusion.

Spending time with some of your friends is what I wanted to say.

"Collecting leeches," I said instead, cursing my politeness. There were times I truly wished for Loki's disregard of tact.

"Ah. For Bylgja's broken thumb, I take it?"

"No, for Hyrm's."

He nodded.

"Both were asking for it from what I heard," he said. "You don't cast off and cross the fishing lines of others, especially Gripnir the Devourer's. They're lucky to still have thumbs at all."

True.

I buried my toes deeper into the mud, stirring more silt and scum, hoping he'd get the message and leave me alone to my work. I winced with several more zings as more leeches sank their miniature fangs into my skin.

"Do you enjoy fishing?" he said. "If you haven't already gathered, it's a popular pastime here. We take it very seriously."

I held in a groan. He was determined.

"Why are you here?" I wiped sweat off my brow with the back of my wrist. "You don't strike me as a man who just wants idle talk about fishing."

A smile cracked his expression and even glinted through his green eyes. Gods, he looked just like Loki, but cold and worn. How had his life differed from his brother's?

Behind Loki's laughter and smiles existed a sorrow, a sadness that never failed to reach into my heart and squeeze. Looking at Býleistr, I saw that same sorrow, but it was far harsher and barbed with resentment.

"I wanted to know if I'd done something wrong to upset you," he said. "I feel like you've been avoiding me since the feast."

Perceptive.

I had.

I listened to Angrboda's advice and left Býleistr to his shadows, even though his words kept clawing at me.

Loki made me promise to keep my mouth shut.

What did Loki promise him not to tell?

It didn't matter. Angrboda was right. Some things were best left unknown. I trusted Loki, and that was enough.

"Offending you was never my intention," he said. "I only wanted to bring to light certain aspects of Loki's character I felt you were owed."

"Aspects based on your own disdain?"

He raised his right eyebrow.

"Everything I said was kindly meant."

I smiled at him, ensuring sarcasm beamed through.

"I'm sure it was," I said.

Mud squished between my toes as I plodded through the water and stepped back onto the shore. Grit, duckweed, and a dozen leeches clung to my legs.

Surtr's lips recoiled, and he shook his head at my state.

I plopped on the grass and slid my fingernail beneath a leech's head and separated its mouth from my skin. I tossed it into the container. It was best to wait until they were full and released themselves, but I couldn't stay here that long. I had to get away from him. From both of them.

"It's just..." Býleistr's face turned shades of green, watching my blood stream along my calves from the Y shaped marks the leeches left. "...isn't truth, *trust*, important in a relationship?"

"I quite agree with Býleistr. If there's no trust, what point is there?" Surtr said, his voice smooth and every syllable caressing.

I nodded slowly as it all started to become clear. I knew this game.

A game Býleistr would not win.

"Stop trying to put a wedge between us," I said. "It won't work."

I gently twisted off another leech, a gush of blood coating the pads of my fingers. Býleistr put his hand on his stomach and swallowed.

I tried not to enjoy his obvious suffering as much as I did.

"I'm not putting any wedge between you that Loki hasn't already put there himself." He gulped again and sucked in a breath. "I told you. You deserve to know the truth about what he did."

A cold wind rippled the pond and fluttered the reeds, tugging at the locks of my hair escaping the kerchief tied around my head.

Why couldn't he understand?

"I don't care what he did."

"Liar," Surtr said, a cackle running beneath the word.

Enough of this nonsense.

I stood, grabbed my ceramic container, and marched up the hill towards the fortress. I needed to get these leeches on those breaks and bruises. Then I would help Áma hang the lavender from the rafters. Yes, that would keep me busy and my mind off—

"What did Loki tell you happened to Simon?" Býleistr called after me.

Keep walking away.

I stopped, turned slowly, and faced him. My body woke with knives that burrowed into my organs and stirred.

"How do you even know about Simon?"

Býleistr's grin twisted tighter with each step I took closer to him. I tried to ignore how Surtr beamed stars.

Býleistr's face relaxed into ease and pleasantness.

"Just answer the question," he said. "What did Loki tell you happened?"

Another gust of wind filled with mountain air and specks of rain pricked my cheeks.

"Loki said nothing," I said. "He only handed me Simon's letter that night my father..." All these years and still I choked mentioning my father's death. "Simon explained everything inside. He left Basel to become—"

"To become a mercenary for the Hapsburgs for their land war in Italy," he finished. "Loki always could make a garden out of a swamp."

I scoffed.

"Swamp? It's a fact. I read Simon's letter with my own eyes."

"Are you sure Simon wrote that letter? Think who you're dealing with."

"Right now? Because right now I think I'm dealing with a cad."

Pain imbued his features as if I had struck him. Good.

"I am not a cad," he stated. "Unlike my brother. Don't you see? It's all a trick. An illusion. Loki never could have you discover what fate he gave your brother that night."

"And what fate is that?"

He grimaced.

"Death."

Laughter bubbled out of my throat, and then from out of my gut as I laughed louder. Býleistr's eyebrows shot to his hairline.

"You find this news funny?" he said.

"Yes," I said. "I find it absurd. And clearly you're insane if you expect me to believe this rubbish. Don't come near me again."

I turned on my heel and started to walk away. He grabbed my wrist, stopping me.

"Hey—"

"Loki killed him," he said. "He murdered Simon in cold blood. You must believe me."

"Let me go."

I tried tearing out of his grasp, but the more I wriggled, the harder he gripped, desperation bleeding from his eyes. What madness was this? Was he truly insane?

"Sigyn, please," he said. "It's what happened. I have no stake in any of this other than to bring you out of the web Loki has trapped you within. He wanted you to stay blind. To stay a fool. It's why he made me promise never to tell you."

Loki made me promise to keep my mouth shut.

My veins iced, colder than the seriousness hardening the lines of his face.

I didn't like how he looked at me. Because it was sincere.

He was sincere.

What if...

"I don't believe you," I said, the words more hollow than I liked.

Býleistr let me go and shook his head.

And I stayed. Gods, I hated that I stayed though I wanted to run, because those roots that secured me to the ground once before with him grew again out of my soles and planted me rigid.

"Was there ever any trace of Simon after you received that letter?" he said. "Any hint of where he ended up? Did he just *vanish*?"

"People vanish all the time with war."

He chuckled.

"And I'm sure Simon spoke often about joining the military?"

"Well, no," I said. "I was actually surprised he took the initiative. It wasn't like him..."

My breath caught.

It wasn't like Simon at all. My brother didn't have an initiative bone in his body.

"Loki would never betray me like that," I said. Why did my words falter?

Býleistr closed in and I held his gaze that filled with pity for me.

"I'm sorry, Sigyn. But you know he's betrayed others," he said. "What makes you think he'd not do the same to you?"

Surtr clapped.

"Finally someone speaking a little common sense," Surtr said.

Lies.

Always lies.

"This is malicious slander," I said, staring into him, searching...

"It's not," he said. "*This* is the man you love, Sigyn. This is what he's done. This is what he's capable of—causing pain. Hurting those who love him." His voice hitched. "Hurting you."

A glint of something finally broke through that thick mask of *honesty* he wore.

And it all made sense now.

What this was really about. I wanted to laugh having caught him. At realizing just how vile and petty he truly was.

"You hate Loki, don't you?" I said.

He searched my gaze, offense knitting his brow.

"I'm trying to help you."

Oh, I was sure of that. Just like all those times Simon said he was *helping* me.

"Help. This isn't about helping me," I said. "This is about punishing your brother."

He kept staring into me, continuing to hold up the pretense, until his lips pulled into a smile that revealed everything. His shoulders relaxed, and that meanness I had detected filled his eyes further until it took them over.

He cocked his head.

"I see why he loves you," he said.

"Why are you doing this, Býleistr?"

"It's quite plain," he said. "Loki shouldn't be given happiness. He doesn't deserve any kind of peace when his crimes are so high."

My cheeks heated. He was detestable.

"And so this is your method to take it all away? Some contrived kind of blackmail?"

"Blackmail is such a dirty word," he said. "What I practice is much more refined. I punish those who hurt others by letting them feel the sting of their transgressions. An eye for an eye and all that. More importantly, I help people—people like you —so that they can see the light before they are swallowed whole."

I wanted to throttle Býleistr. If he thought he could hurt Loki with me standing by his side now...

"And what has Loki done that's deserving of such punishment?"

He looked dumbfounded.

"Are you serious?" he said. "You can't consider any possible reason? He really has you warped and twisted."

"What did he do?" I demanded. "Tell me. Make me understand, if that's truly your goal."

He leaned in to me, as if I offered him the challenge he wished for most of all.

"Why should Loki get praised for saving everyone at Ragnarok, when he caused it to begin with?" he said.

My throat dried.

"He was willing to kill everyone in the entire Nine Worlds," he continued. "Jotnar, Elves, Dwarves, Vanir, Aesir, Humans...all the people you claim you want to help. He made us all his sacrificial lamb, and you think *that* isn't worthy of punishment? And now he is just forgiven? Allowed to have a happily ever after?"

I swallowed what felt like hot sand.

"Yes," I said. "That was wrong, and he stopped Ragnarok because he knew what he'd unleashed was unspeakable. In his heart, he's a decent man and he's trying. He's—"

He rolled his eyes.

"Complicated? Misunderstood?" he mocked. "Tell me all about that good mischief he does. Please, I've heard it all before. Always forgiven. Always excused. Always given second chances. When is it enough?"

"Wasn't five hundred years of torture in that cave enough?" I spat.

His face lit as if I granted him the final key to get me.

"And what did Loki do first when he broke out of his bindings and tasted freedom?" he said. "You say he stopped Ragnarok because he realized what he'd done was vile, but deep down you know. He only stopped Ragnarok because of you. Otherwise, we'd all be dead."

My stomach fell into my bowels as if I swallowed a stone.

"He lost his mind from the horror," I said. "Unceasing darkness and unending venom searing your body will do that to any person. He wouldn't have gone through with it."

The fact was, I'd never truly know, and I didn't want to know.

"Another excuse."

I stiffened, and I hated how much I wished to slice him open. Anything to stop him from speaking.

"Aren't you tired of it all?" Býleistr asked. "He only hurts and maims and kills. He breaks our worlds and breaks us over and over again."

"Stop this."

"You can't tell me your life wouldn't be easier if he was never in it. If you had been spared from all the pain he causes. Your brother would have lived. Your children—"

"Shut up!"

"Loki should have stayed in that cave."

Red filled my vision. Blazed.

I lifted my hand to strike him across the cheek. I forced it back at my side, my ears filled with my pounding blood.

I would not become a beast like him.

"You will never make me lose my trust in Loki," I seethed.

He laughed, the tone cold as ice.

"Deny any way you want, Sigyn," he said. "Find any excuse you will, but the truth remains."

He dug into his satchel and pulled out an old letter and held it out to me, kicking me back in time to that night when Loki held out the same letter to me.

Sweat trickled down my back, turning my skin clammy.

"How did you get that?" I snatched it from him.

I gently opened the brittle paper, the edges disintegrating and jagged with age. I traced my brother's familiar cramped letters preserved in faded ink. A moment frozen in time. All genuine. Real.

Simon.

I had a piece of him back after centuries of nothing. Nothing to remember him by. Nothing at all. Only a thousand questions that clawed at me, scratching my curiosity to know. To consider.

What if.

Loki was capable...

But my faith in him was stronger.

I folded the letter and held it back out to Býleistr. He put his hands behind his back, refusing.

"This letter proves nothing," I said. "If anything, it proves the opposite of your story."

"And here I thought you were clever," he said. "It's charmed. An exquisite illusion only my brother could make, and only he can remove—"

"Then I guess that's the end of everything."

"—only he can remove, if you didn't have a touch of his chaos in you," he said.

"Meaning?"

He smiled and walked away, leaving me with the letter still tight between my rigid fingers.

"I'm sure you'll figure it out," he said, walking up the hill. "Once you decide to accept what you already know. You can't trust him, and he certainly doesn't trust you."

19

A CAT-ASTROPHE

LOKI

I inserted bent wire into the keyhole of Freya's door and rooted inside the lock.

"Can you hurry before we're spotted?" Odin said. He looked down a hall alive with shadows from the quivering light of his candle.

Catching the lever, I pushed it up, and I held it in place as I slid in a second wire.

"Sorry I don't have three hands," I snapped, fishing for the bolt. "I almost have it…"

The lever slipped, and the lock remained bolted. Damn.

"This would be a lot faster if we could use magic," I said, starting the entire bloody process over. Again. "You seem to forget who I am. What my chaos is capable of. There's always some to spare."

Of course, I wouldn't tell him about the tiredness nipping at my body.

Finally getting to shift back to my usual form and drop the illusion concealing Odin was like taking a breath after holding it underwater. The headache had thankfully already abated. But, the remaining fatigue...No. The fatigue would leave soon enough, as well. It always did after a stiff drink and a good night's sleep. Not that I had a chance for either the last weeks on this journey.

"And you seem to forget what's ahead of us with Surtr," he said. "Getting the darkest, most powerful element in existence untangled from Sigyn's body is immense in itself, but getting Surtr into that amulet...It will take more than a snap of the fingers."

I slowed turning the wire. The creeping shadows seemed to grow, as if grim omens that wanted to feast on my bones.

Another wave of that irritating weariness flushed down my spine.

Maybe it was for the best I abstain from magic. But not because Odin said so. Only because I felt like doing something novel for me— practice caution.

And what better time than now when facing a goddess who was sorcery and death? Yes. I saw no issue whatsoever.

"And if the worst should happen with Freya?" I said. "If she sings...I don't want her to feed my mangled corpse to her cats like she did Ivar."

His features hardened.

"We just have to hope these work." He stuffed globs of beeswax into his ears.

Lovely. What I wanted to put my faith in.

Click.

Odin blew out the candle as I twisted the handle and opened the door to Freya's bedroom. A rush of gravely snores filled the hall with saws.

Gods.

I crammed the wax Odin handed me as deep as I could into my ear canals, muffling Freya's snores into a dull roar. I wish I could have given the same blessing to my nostrils to help lessen the stench of cat and rosewater.

He pressed his finger against his lips and we slunk inside a room drowning in moonlight. We tiptoed past a vanity and divans of satin sandwiched between massive birds of paradise and monstera. And cats. At least fifty cats sleeping on velvet pillows and feather cushions scattered across the parquet.

Freya slept drenched in pink silk sheets beneath a painted ceiling of herself reclining on clouds being attended on by an army of ugly, flying babies.

She laid on her stomach, left arm dangling off the side of the bed. A lovely puddle of drool soaked into her pillow.

I gently lifted the sheets covering her shoulders and pulled them back.

A white cat curled at the end of her bed, roused from slumber, arched its spine, and promptly fell back asleep. Good.

Odin gathered Freya's thick hair and held it above her head, exposing her neck and Brísingamen. Even doused in silver from the open archways, the jewels sparkled brighter than the stars in the night sky.

I squinted at the mess of locks and hooks that secured the neck-lace—three box clasps, each with its own set of miniature safeties and promised irritations. Now how best to untangle this damned bowl of noodles?

Cursing my being blessed with nimble fingers, I touched the top clasp of Brísingamen, the gold as warm as Freya's skin I grazed.

A hundred yellow eyes snapped open. The cats stirred and stretched on their pillows, their gazes fixed on Odin and I.

Did it seriously ever stop?

Chewing the inside of my mouth, I caught one of the miniature latches on the side of the clasp with my fingernail, trying to ignore the herd of cats padding towards us, their eyes glowing red in the dim light like monsters spat out of Muspelheim.

The safeties unhooked, I pushed a small button of sorts forward. The tongue slid out, releasing the first clasp.

Odin shifted, still holding Freya's hair. I looked over my shoulder. A dozen cats leapt onto Freya's bed, a dozen more slunk between our legs.

A gray cat nuzzled the length of Freya's side, another's whiskers grazed Freya's chin. A third cat flexed its paws on the blanket covering her legs.

Freya twisted beneath the sheets, her face scrunching.

I retracted my hands and everything in me seized.

She stilled, and a fresh spill of drool ran between her lips.

Odin motioned for me to hurry. As if I didn't know.

I started on the second clasp.

Another wave of cats jumped onto the bed.

They sniffed my knuckles as I unhooked the delicate gold latches. They prodded my hands with their foreheads, making my fingers slip as I pushed in the button.

Odin swatted two cats away from nudging Freya's cheeks.

Come on!

I jiggled the mechanism. The clasp released, and the tongue slid out.

I exhaled.

One clasp left.

I fingered the fragile loops...

Freya stirred again, extended her arm and flopped onto her back, pulling her hair out of Odin's hold and smacking me in the nose with her fist. My eyes watered and I stifled a cry.

I took a second to collect myself, rubbing the sting from my nose.

Odin and I nodded at each other. It was the only way, although I didn't like it at all.

We bent over Freya and grabbed the sheet beneath her. A cat opened its mouth, I assume hissing at us, though I heard nothing except the throbbing silence from the plugs of beeswax lodged in my ears.

We lifted the silk, forcing Freya to roll over onto her side, exposing that final clasp I desperately needed. If Sigyn's life depended on me extracting this mess of gold and jewels from a violent woman, then I would do it.

Sweat rolled off Odin's forehead as he held her steady, letting me undo the latches and...these damned buttons!

The swarming cats all sat still, as if at attention, their eyes no longer on us, but on their mistress.

I tugged at the clasp, trying to tear the tongue out and...

Freya looked over her shoulder, meeting my gaze.

I flashed my most charming smile at her.

"This is a dream," I said. "Just a funny dream. Go back to sleep."

She cocked her head and sat up, the necklace hanging on by one single clasp. My heart stopped beating as her eyes, still glazed with sleep, trailed languidly from mine to Odin.

My lungs refused to take in a breath.

Freya's chest convulsed with what I believed to be laughter, the wax keeping whatever cackles bubbled out of her throat a low thrum.

Odin lunged for the necklace, his fingertips brushing her collarbone—Freya grasped his wrist, crushing into his bones. He squirmed in her hold, trying to tug back, and it only brightened that glint in her eyes I did not like.

She spoke a noiseless word.

The cats bolted off her bed and leapt off the floor and charged. Freya released Odin as the monsters mauled us, latching onto our legs and torsos, sinking their claws into our flesh. Pricks of heat seared my muscles with their every scratch and bite.

I gripped the scruff of a gray cat, and a yelp tore out of me as I ripped its teeth out of my thigh. I flung the beast across the room and yanked the spotted calico off my elbow next.

Three more cats fastened onto my arms, and a sharp chomp sizzled deep into my side from a fourth and a fifth. I knew I screamed, but I heard nothing but muffled whimpers.

Odin flailed beside me, struggling to free himself from the felines clawing and scratching his face and chest and hands. He'd toss one aside and five more would take the animal's place.

Freya stood off the bed and marched towards me, a wicked smile curling the corners of her lips. Brísingamen shimmered around her neck, one clasp away from being mine.

A hundred miniature razor blades lacerated my calves, my

cheeks, my back, as cat nails punctured and scraped deeper into my skin.

But I refused to leave without that bloody necklace.

I tugged the cats off me, cursing with every split and sting of my flesh. Warmth trickled between my shoulder blades as my blood soaked into my tunic. I rushed Freya. I extended my arm and reached behind her neck, feeling for the clasp.

Just one good yank.

Freya grasped my shoulders and struck her knee into my groin, shooting entire constellations of stars across my vision.

I sucked in a breath and forced my stance straight, locking my eyes on Freya's that danced with unbridled enjoyment.

"Now you're..." I huffed. "...now you're really starting to piss me off."

I lunged and grappled Freya to the floor. Satisfaction rolled in me feeling the crackle of her cartilage and ribs compress beneath my weight. I tried to grab her wrists, wanting to pin her down long enough for me to snatch Brísingamen away. Every time I got close, she wriggled out of my hold and clawed at my face, scratching the bridge of my nose and cutting my chin with those pointed nails of hers.

We wrestled across the parquet, each trying to gain the upper hand, until my actual hand got nearly trampled by Odin as he flung cats off his torso left and right.

I latched onto Brísingamen and tugged, ready to break the damn thing into a million pieces if necessa—Freya bit my knuckles and I screeched, my blood coursing between my fingers. I pulled back and curled my bleeding hand into a fist and punched her across the jaw. She struck me in the stomach, forcing all the air out of my body. Gasping, I reached for Brísingamen again. She blocked my reach and struck me a second time between my legs, the stars even brighter than before in the shuddering darkness of agony.

She really was the worst.

Freya stood, straightened her gown, and kicked me as hard as she could in the small of my back. My lungs clamped shut at the second explosion of pain. I rolled over and laid on my stomach, wheezing for breath between spitting up blood and choking on blood.

A faint, far away scream burst out behind me.

Odin.

I turned. He struggled as cats shredded their claws through his tunic, but what shot concern to my toes was how they bit and tore at his ears, as if commanded to dislodge the wax plugs for their mistress.

I crawled towards Odin, gathering my strength to peel the creatures off him myself.

Hands grabbed my ankles and dragged me back, my palms skidding across the parquet that I dug my nails into. Freya picked me up by my tunic and catapulted me into a wardrobe, the wood splitting and cracking into splinters. My head smacked the back of the cabinet hard, and an avalanche of gowns piled on top of me.

My head stuffed with cotton and ringing bells, I grappled out of the rubble and tangle of fine silks.

Odin tugged off one cat from his head. I squinted, the room refusing to still, but that didn't matter. I could see enough to make my breath hitch.

Blood trailed out of Odin's right ear and ran down his cheek and into his beard. The beeswax plug was missing.

Freya marched towards him, a cruel smile cracking her face, and he did not notice.

No.

Freya's eyes glowed pale pink.

She opened her mouth, heaved in a deep breath, and sang what I knew was her favorite tune.

A lullaby.

An enchantment.

And once under her control...

With a few simple notes of the spell, Freya could make you do whatever she wished.

I forced myself to stand, and I ran towards him, though the room shifted and spun. Freya's chest kept rising and falling as she belted out the enchantment.

If I could reach him before the end...

She closed her mouth and smiled.

It was too late.

The cats leapt off him, and Odin stood rigid, his gaze vacant. He was hers.

My blood frosted. And grew colder when Freya snapped her gaze onto mine, her element shining through her eyes. She'd have me next.

She opened her mouth, and her chest convulsed with the same song trying to trap me.

I pushed the wax plugs deeper into my ears and ran towards her.

Her eyes narrowed and she sang louder. At least, it appeared that way. I heard only the thrash of my blood.

I was inches from knocking her down.

Freya's eyes widened and the pink glow sucked back into herself as she realized I was impervious to her enchantment. At least, for now.

She spoke another word.

Cats sprung and latched onto me again. I stumbled back, yelping with every puncture and scratch.

Bloody monsters! This would have all been a lot easier had I been able to use magic.

As it were, I saw one option.

I flailed my way to a fountain of Freya squeezing her breasts, water pouring out of her nipples into a marble basin carved into the shape of a shell.

I careened into the pool, dousing myself utterly as waves slopped over the rim and splattered across the floor. The cats retracted their claws from my flesh and leapt off my chest and legs and scurried away, trails of water dripping off their soaked fur.

One problem solved.

Two arcs of cold water cascaded out of Freya's breasts and pelted my forehead. I blinked and rubbed the wet out of my eyes in time to see the real Freya stalking towards me.

And one problem still to go.

Water sloshed around me as I gripped the sides of the shell and made to stand, only to slip and fall.

Freya drew closer, her eyes flashing pink once again. This wasn't great.

Odin remained motionless behind her, still trapped within her spell. Typical Odin. Utterly useless when you needed him most.

I gripped the marble again and hoisted myself upright and stepped out of the basin, my wet socks squelching in my boots. Water rained out of my clothes, the wool fibers bloated from my impromptu swim.

Freya spoke quickly, her face reddening further with fury. I wasn't sure which enraged her more. The fact we were trying to steal Brísingamen, or the growing pool of water at my feet staining the parquet.

She lunged for me, arm outstretched as if preparing to thrust her hand into my chest and rip out my beating heart. Not if I got hers first.

I unsheathed my daggers at my hips and stabbed my right blade towards her side. She blocked my blow with her arm and snapped at my nose, missing it by a hair.

I slashed again. She gripped my wrist and twisted, disarming my dagger.

No matter, I had a second—she kicked me square in the stomach, hurtling me onto my back. She followed, a storm of fury and rage and violence.

It was definitely the parquet.

Mounting me, she squeezed my torso between her thighs, crushing my ribcage. Her eyes glowed brighter with her element as she clawed at my ears. I thrashed and wriggled. She squeezed tighter, making my every breath agony as she compressed the remaining air out of my lungs.

For two seconds, her element sank through my skin, and I believed myself falling into an opening rose.

I was beautiful.

I was loved.

I was hers.

And it was all a lie.

Because nothing but thorns waited to split me open and spill my bowels.

I hardened my grip on my hilt and stabbed my blade into her calf. Her element extinguished as she relaxed her hold on me and pulled out my dagger from her leg. I gasped in full breaths. She tossed the blade away and dug her fingers into my tunic. Freya jerked me towards her face, bit my ear and wrenched her head back.

I took my chance, grinding my teeth through the pain sparking across my scalp and down my neck.

A small price to pay for her not to notice.

Reaching behind her neck, I unfastened the last clasp of Brísingamen and ripped it off her neck. I unsheathed a knife from inside my boot and sliced her forearm from elbow to wrist.

She released my ear and screamed as I scrambled to my feet and raced towards Odin. A quick shake and I'd get him out of her enchantment, and we could leap out of the archways and escape through the gardens.

Sigyn was safe.

We were all safe.

My heart pounded, my fingertips inches from grazing Odin's shoulder.

"You dare break your banishment to steal from me, Lie-Smith?" Freya said.

I stopped.

How was I hearing her? I shouldn't be hearing her. I clapped my hand over my still throbbing ear.

The wax plug was missing.

20

CAT AND MOUSE

I turned, and my stomach roiled. She held the wax in her hand, a dangerous smile tugging at the corners of her lipstick smeared mouth.

She took two steps towards me, the trickle of blood dripping out of the slice in her arm lessening as the wound mended. Same with the hole I had put in her leg. Her cats hissed and growled behind her, their eyes unflinching.

"You can't steal what was already stolen," I said, holding my ground.

Her smile widened, and she rubbed away sweat and streaks of black eye kohl that ran down her cheeks.

"I knew I recognized that stench of angst from somewhere when you first showed up here. You and Odin remain a pathetic pair."

I laughed.

"Pathetic?" I said. "At least I don't collapse onto a tray of oysters after three glasses of wine."

Her shoulders tensed.

"Shut up," she snapped. "You're lucky the gods allow you to breathe at all after Ragnarok, and this is how you repay our kindness?"

I sneered at that.

Kindness.

I gathered my sopping hair and wrung out the water, smiling at the deluge splashing against her prized floor. Freya's shoulders tensed harder.

"Yes. Tell me more about how very, very kind the gods have been to me. How exceedingly merciful."

Her anger melted into amusement. This was bad.

"Why are you here, Lie-Smith? Wait. Please don't say it. That this entire ill-planned lark concerns some new disaster involving that woman you destroyed your blood oath to Odin over—your only protection—and then tossed yourself into that pit," she said. "That's the only reason you'd risk facing me, choosing, once again, the stupidest course of action."

I hated how her words made that scar linking me to Odin burn. Tightening my grip on Freya's necklace, I swallowed several insults I wanted so badly to hurl at her.

"I lost a bet to my cousin Hymir is all. You know how serious us Jotnar take our wagers."

She cackled as if I'd told her the greatest of secrets.

"Oh, it *is* the woman. I see it in your gaze," she said. "Along with a thousand thoughts racing through your eyes, plotting your next ten steps. But I've already won. You're soaked, and your magic is worthless. You're no threat to me, as if you ever were. All I have to do is sing, and you'll be just like your boyfriend."

She pointed at Odin, who remained rigid to my right, still trapped by her spell.

My muscles hardened.

"He's not my boyfriend."

She laughed harder, and took two more steps closer to me, her cats swishing their tails as they trailed behind her. Blood soaked her silk nightgown.

"This will be glorious."

Freya flicked her wrist and Odin pulled out a small knife from his belt, the Dwarven steel flashing in the moonlight. His face showed all the emotion of stone, but that didn't stop beads of sweat from beading at his temples.

Just as my own temples slicked with sweat.

"What are you doing?" I said.

She pursed her lips and sauntered to Odin.

"Let's play a game." She stood in front of Odin and sneered. "Because a game is always more fun in these situations, wouldn't you agree Trickster?"

Odin pressed the edge of the blade against the thrashing pulse in his throat. She gasped with delight and turned and met my gaze.

My mouth soured, but I refused to give her the satisfaction of having got me.

"If you're proposing what I think, you're saving me the aggravation of me killing him later."

Her mouth formed a mocking kind of grin.

"And again, your eyes bleed."

Odin squeezed the knife harder into his throat, splitting the delicate skin. Drops of his blood fell and soaked into his tunic.

I forced my body not to wince. Not to cave.

Freya combed her fingers through the tangles in her hair as she watched Odin sever his skin, waiting me out.

Odin cut the knife deeper. More blood came.

"Stop!"

She flashed her gaze away from Odin and back to me and walked towards me.

"After all this time." She shook her head and tutted. "Still this twisted romance between you two. Good. Otherwise this game wouldn't be as interesting, because I want to know."

"Know what?"

My back hit the rounded marble edge of the fireplace, the warmth of the embers heating my legs. She drew closer, her scent of rose water saturating the air.

"Which love you will choose, of course," she said. "The new, or the old."

Freya always was cruel, like her cats playing with a mouse.

I was the mouse.

"The rules are simple. Choose Sigyn and keep Brísingamen, or you can return my property to me, *which is my suggestion*, and save Odin's life. Although, I'm sure you'd be doing him a favor by having him slit his own throat here and now. I don't envy him his return to Asgard. Once Frigg finds out what he's done, how he allowed you to break your banishment—"

"And if I decide not to play?"

Her eyes narrowed and flickered with the faintest hue of pink. The ashen logs in the fireplace collapsed and another rush of heat sank into my feet.

"Then whatever ridiculousness you were planning ends tonight with a swan song."

I looked at Odin, his right shoulder now stained with his blood seeping out of the gash in his throat.

I looked at Brísingamen clutched in my hand, each jewel catching the faint glow of the embers in the fireplace. It appeared as if burning.

I tightened my grip on the necklace. On Sigyn's salvation. I had it. All I had to do was walk away.

Leave Odin to Freya.

Have a glass of wine and forget.

It would be easy.

It's what I wanted to do.

I raised my eyes to Odin again. Something pleaded within the blue of his iris. Telling me to run. To go.

And I knew the choice I had to make.

I just hoped it was a choice I wouldn't regret later. This was going to be a bitch to accomplish with being wet. Not to mention the fallout with me breaking Odin's rule, but no magic my ass.

I slid my left hand behind my back and hunted the ash and coal and cinders in the fireplace for something, anything, that I could latch onto. My chaos may momentarily be smothered, but that didn't mean I couldn't control what fire surrounded me.

"You know what, Freya? Your games are as dreadful as your dinner parties."

I fastened onto an ember and begged the ember to grow. To heat. To burn.

Smoldering warmth rolled out of the fireplace, more whimper than I liked. I strained, forcing my power to breathe into the cracks of the ashy wood. Into the bits of glowing coal.

Come alive. Please.

"Do you really think antagonizing me a good idea when I'm in the position I'm in, and you're in the position you're in?"

My muscles burned, struggling to build the fire behind me, every pop dwindling back into ash.

I hoped she didn't notice me chew the inside of my mouth.

The coal and embers boiled, each breath I gave strengthening the smoke to turn into flame.

I tasted iron, bidding the embers to ignite. To heed my command.

"Probably not." My hand trembled, fighting through the wet still smothering the fire inside of me. "But, I quite enjoy seeing your eye twitch."

Faint yellows finally spilled across the parquet and the light built behind me, lengthening our shadows.

"Enough! Make your choice, or you both die right here, right now."

A spark! And a second, and a third...

Everything rode on this. I gathered every bit of strength in my body and fanned the flames in the fireplace like a bellow, battling against the damp of my skin, the wet of my clothes, my hair.

My body shook.

I pushed myself further. Dove deep into myself. Then deeper.

The remaining wood crackled now as flames rose from the coal.

"Make your choice, Loki. Or, I will make it for you in three seconds."

I hooked onto the flames and smiled and stashed Brísingamenn in my satchel.

"Don't worry, I'm making it."

I exploded the fire out of the fireplace and raced the flames towards Freya. She jumped out of the way, but she wasn't fast enough. Arms of flame skimmed her sides, catching her skirts alight.

I sent another tangle of burning ropes at her, just to make my point clearer.

Cats screeched with a roar of hisses and bolted out of the doors and leapt out of the open archways to safety. I spiraled the flaming cords, twisting them around the room, loving how the flames fastened on pillows, blankets, and paintings and feasted.

Freya stomped out the fire from her gown and locked her gaze on mine, and growled. Her eyes turned bright pink, glowing as bright as the flames licking up the walls behind her.

I knew what would follow.

She opened her mouth.

And sound came out, a lullaby more ethereal than song.

Small snares of enchantment worked on seizing me rigid. On making me hers. I couldn't become hers.

I screamed and latched onto more fire, my body already aching with fatigue, and wielded the blaze to grow. To consume.

She sang louder, and my every cell wanted to fall to my knees and worship her.

The room flooded in crackling golds and yellows and oranges. Explosions of heat prickled my cheeks as the fire fed on potted plants and tapestries and clothing.

Smoke and cinders filled the room, thickening the air, making every breath suffocating.

The song ceased, replaced by Freya coughing and wheezing.

Her spell uncoiled from around me, and I rejoiced, cracking the bones in my neck, fully free of her.

"What?" I said. "A little smoke bad for the lungs?"

She hacked harder. Soot stained her forehead. Her chest.

"Fine, I might not get you under my spell, but Odin remains mine."

She straightened her spine and set her eyes on Odin. Fingers of fire ate the murals on the ceiling, charing her portrait into ash.

"Do not touch him, or I swear I will—"

"Will what?" Phlegm made her words rough and strained "You got a good shot in, I'll give you that." She coughed. "But you're still wet and your chaos remains smothered inside of you. You can only do so much with what fire is in that fireplace."

Unfortunately, she was right. If I wanted to win, I had to get the fire in me lit again.

She flicked her wrist. Odin crushed the knife deeper into his neck, a hair from severing his artery.

I raced her, the room pressing down on my shoulders, hot and boiling and stifling. And I absorbed every spark, gobbled every cinder, fanning the flames inside of me despite my soaked clothes. Struggle didn't even begin to describe the torment I endured trying to light what was essentially damp firewood.

I must.

I consumed more. Needing every particle of energy to accomplish what I wanted.

I can.

Sparks snapped in my chest.

Embers crushed between my fingers.

I grunted and cried out and thrived in the scorching heat drying my clothes, and my hair, and running through me and out of me.

I grasped her wrist, stopping her from finishing Odin off. She screamed.

And I hardened my grip, and cinders crackled in my smile as I felt her skin sizzle beneath my palm as I broiled her.

And still more I stirred my core, and fought, and struggled to trigger my chaos, to fuel my element into fire.

Her eyes met mine, a mixture of fear and shock, and I saw the fire in my own eyes reflect at me in her gaze.

"No," she whispered.

They always doubted.

My hair moved again, as wild as the flames dancing around me, as my chaos fully ignited.

I laughed as her skin blistered beneath my palm. And I seared her deeper with all of my rage, sinking my chaos into her bones, wanting to boil her marrow.

Something between a croak and a cry spilled out of her throat. She tugged, trying to free herself from my hold.

"You see Freya, you always underestimate me."

Wood snapped and burst as wardrobes and divans and her massive bed collapsed into flames.

Her nostrils flared and the wonder in her eyes toughened into venomous hatred.

"You will pay dearly for what you've done here," she wheezed.

"The only one paying will be you."

She plucked out a short knife from her bodice and raced it at my heart.

I released her and called up all of my fire and blasted her back. She hurtled through the air and knocked into a marble statue of herself, striking her head on an elbow. Blood ran down the side of her face as she slumped to the floor.

Finally. Now to wake Odin and leave this party.

Guards burst in through the doors and hacked on the acrid stench of peeling paintings and smoke. Several went to Freya and dragged her out of the room. Three other soldiers set soot irritated eyes on me and took chase.

Could I really not have one bloody second to enjoy my victory?

I ran to Odin's side and rose my hands, grunting as I called on more of my fire, reaching deep into my core and pulling it up, pushing it out. White flames turned into blue. I needed it hotter.

The guards drew their swords, steps from us.

My insides ground raw as I forced all I was out of me, shooting a wall of fire between us and them. My heart pounded as I whirled the flames higher towards the ceiling, screaming as I twirled the surrounding fire into a vortex that rivaled the fire pits in Muspelheim.

My entire strength, my entire power, spun around us, and I kept pushing out more heat, more fire, more...

I fell to one knee and caught my breath, my muscles crying out to collapse completely from all the fire and energy I'd exerted.

I really would need a stiff drink to recover after using all of this magic, but I'd worry about that later.

Right now, we had to run.

I staggered towards Odin and gripped his shoulders and shook him.

The firestorm spit and popped, spinning faster around us. Wind filled with sparks tore through our hair, lashing it around our eyes and cheeks.

He kept staring straight ahead.

Dammit, how deep in her spell had he fallen?

I slapped him across the face. A deep shiver cut through him and he woke free of her hold.

Odin looked down at the knife still in his hand, edged in his blood, and tossed it away as if it were cursed. The wound on his throat mended itself immediately.

Then his gaze fell on the absolute inferno engulfing us, and horror took root in him.

He knew how much power I had to muster to produce so much fire.

"What did you do?" His hair whipped around his face coated in golds and oranges, reminding me of that time we were marooned on Samsey so long ago.

"I saved us, is what I did," I said, opening one side of the vortex so we had a clear path to the balcony and to freedom.

Guards shouted and hacked and coughed.

Odin kept staring at the fire. At the storm of flames consuming everything around us.

"But the magic you used...this is immense..."

The flames spiraled faster. Hotter.

"I can't believe—"

"You would have died!" I shouted. "You were going to split open your own throat."

I gripped his wrist and forced him to stare into my eyes. He had to understand. There was no other choice.

"It was this, or complete failure," I said. "We have the necklace. At least now we still have a chance."

His cheeks hollowed.

He nodded.

"Let's get out of here," he said.

21

IN THE COLD LIGHT OF DAY

Freya's entire palace actively burning to the ground thankfully kept her guards rather occupied in trying to salvage what they could of the estate. Freya left unconscious was a bonus. But she would wake, she would recover, and when she did, she would want our suffering.

However, she already achieved *my* suffering in the guise of the horse I stole from her stables.

Not wanting to risk losing our head start, we had no choice but to abandon our horses with all our supplies on the opposite side of Leira, where we had left them with an annoyingly chatty tavern owner. At least they would be in good care with him, even if they had to endure his babbling on about the only proper way of brewing Vanir ale.

Odin and I saddled the first horses we reached, he an affectionate brindle whose name on the stable door read "Eira," and me, a rose gray named "Ylva," who snapped at my fingers when I slipped the bit into her mouth. Apparently, she was highly offended to be woken before her breakfast of organic grains, and was determined to hurt me for it.

For three miles Ylva bucked and spun until she finally relented with the increasingly rough terrain the deeper we fled into Vanaheim.

Night marched on until cool blues faded into the dusty oranges of dawn, coloring the low mountains full of scrub vegetation ahead of us black.

"Let's stop here," Odin said. "The horses will need rest before we can continue on into the mountains."

My aching backside rejoiced at the word rest.

I'd lost track of how many hours we'd been following the wide path of scree at the bottom of a gorge, with nothing worth seeing except scraggly pine trees, rock, and grass clinging to the crags towering on either side of us.

And then that trick I pulled at Freya's and all the magic I spent... My shoulders weighed a thousand pounds.

Yes. Rest sounded a treat.

At least now we were safe from Freya's reach. Even her most expert trackers would never find us lost in the Vanaheim wilderness.

We dismounted our horses and led them to a shallow creek flowing along the center of the gorge. Eira nuzzled Odin's chest in thanks and lowered her head to drink.

He took the reins and fastened them to the same tree I tied my horse—I cursed at the top of my lungs, the unwholesome word echoing through the gorge.

Ylva stepped harder onto my foot. I met her gaze, a thousand voice choir of death and vengeance burning within her eyes as she ground her hoof deeper into my bones.

Odin grabbed her reins and led her away, relief flooding my throbbing foot.

"I swear," I growled at the horse. "When we get back, I'm turning you into glue."

Ylva snorted and drank beside Eira, as if my threat carried all the bite of a flea.

"And you always bragged how you could charm any horse." Odin gave the knot a final tug, securing the animal to the tree.

"That's because this isn't a horse." I shook the ache from my foot. "It's a demon."

My heels slipped on the loose shards of stone as I walked to the edge of the creek, the water prattling louder than the doves cooed. Crouching, I submerged my hands into the stream and splashed water on my face, cleaning the soot from my skin.

Cold.

Naturally.

What I would give for a hot bath and food that wasn't only the two clumps of crumbled hardtack at the bottom of my satchel.

Odin's knees popped as he squatted next to me, his joints as fatigued as my own, and washed the smoke off his hands. The fine lines around his eye seemed deeper than I remembered.

He was tired. Hungry.

Miserable.

Like me.

And it made me happy.

Not because I lived for his hardship, but because this time, I wasn't having to be wretched and depressed alone.

I owed him for being here with me, because he could have let me go on this isolating journey by myself. But he didn't, and appreciation spun inside of me.

I was grateful to him.

I furrowed my brow at that thought. What an odd turn of events.

"Damn that's frigid." He splashed water on his forehead.

His gaze met mine.

"What?"

I looked away and pushed my sleeves to my elbows and washed my arms.

"Freya will want our blood after Brísingamen," I said.

"As long as we stay off the main roads we will be safe."

He removed his eyepatch and cleaned his eyelid and around his empty socket. He often complained how the patch rubbed against his face, but he refused to let anyone see him without it. Which is why I insisted he burn the damn thing when we were alone. Embarrassment had no place between us back then.

"That's not what I meant." I slowed, scrubbing my wrists and hands. "She will tell your wife. Frigg will learn that you've been *assisting* me, even though I'm banished. I can't see this going well for you when you return to Asgard."

He stilled and stared at the water burbling over the smoothed pebbles worn by the current. The same as he'd worn Frigg's patience for millennia—since he brought me to Asgard. Even before, when he rejected falling into the peg she desired for him. Odin stood on thin ice with her, and I wasn't sure how much longer until it cracked.

"Is this concern?"

"Hardly." I quickened, massaging smears of dirt from my wrists. "I'm just trying to decide which flower arrangement to send for your funeral. This will be difficult for Frigg to forgive."

He laughed softly, but the laughter grew darker in the back of his throat.

"You seem to forget that Frigg never forgives me. Like everyone else I've ever..." His words trailed away. "What does it matter?"

He stood and replaced the eyepatch in a fluid movement and squared his shoulders.

"Now," he said. "Let's see Brísingamen. I want to enjoy our spoils at least a minute before we consider the vipers."

Fair point.

Standing, I wiped my hands dry on my tunic and pulled Brísingamen out of my satchel. The braids of jewels and gold gleamed in the morning light.

He reached out and ran his fingers along the diamonds and rubies and sapphires and delicate settings.

"Beautiful," he said.

That's really all that could be said about Brísingamen—beautiful.

And it was ours. Absolute joy filled my heart knowing soon Brísingamen would get us the amulet I desperately wanted for Sigyn.

Knowing soon she would be free from Surtr.

"And Brokkr thought he set us an impossible task." I stashed the necklace safely back in my satchel. "Taking Brísingamen off Freya wasn't as bad as I expected."

He gave me a look.

"I remember holding a knife against my own neck."

I shrugged.

"Maybe it got a little hairy at the end."

He smiled and shook his head and walked back to his horse and unbuckled the girth of the saddle.

I pulled out my flask from my pocket, untwisted the cap, and took a large swig of mead. I chased it down with a second. Finally, this morning was looking up.

"Thank you, by the way," he said. "For back there. For saving my life."

He gripped the pommel and back of the saddle and lifted it off the horse's back.

"Don't get too excited," I said. "It's just because you're no use to me dead."

He chuckled, placing the saddle on the ground, tipping it onto its front.

"That's what I suspected," he said. "I appreciate the sentiment all the same."

Odin started unbuckling the saddle from *The Beast*, the rising sun turning the surrounding rock into burnt umber. A gust of wind tousled his hair as he worked.

I took another sip of the crisp honey and orange. Heat from the alcohol warmed my body, relaxing my stiff muscles.

He dropped the saddle beside the other and sat on the stones, staring down the length of the canyon.

And I knew how I could repay him for the risk he took in joining me on this venture.

I walked next to him.

"But," I said. "Even if I didn't need you...no one deserves to die like that. Not even you."

He twisted and looked up, meeting my gaze. I tapped his shoulder with my flask, offering it to him, and surprise filled his features.

"What's all this about?" he said.

"Perhaps I've been unfair to you."

He cocked his head, still not moving. Unsure.

"What's caused this sudden magnanimity?"

I smiled gently.

"You were right," I said. "No one else would help me. They would have all let me flounder. But you...you didn't. You are here. And...and that means a lot to not do this by myself. Thank you."

He took the flask from me, careful not to graze my fingers. He knocked back a slug.

"Maybe you do deserve a chance," I said.

His shoulders relaxed, and he placed the flask on the stones beside him and stood. He stepped closer.

He extended his hand to me, and a sincere warmth lit his face.

"A chance is all I want," he said, as if making a wish.

His hand remained hovering, waiting for me to accept or refuse.

I don't know if it was the thrill from the victory, the high of renewed hope for Sigyn, or the blur of mead, but I grasped his hand, and pulled him into an embrace as I had a thousand times before, back when the monsters that always seemed to claw at our door could not touch us.

We relaxed into each other and the sage on his skin filled my lungs.

"I've missed this," he said. "I've missed our friendship."

I held him tighter. Because, in that flickering moment, I think I missed our friendship, too.

"And I can't deny it anymore," he said. "I'm still..."

His words melted into silence as if he fought with himself about what to say next.

"Still what?" I whispered.

He inhaled sharply, pressing me closer to him.

"I'm still in love with you."

Everything in me froze. Cracked.

I stepped back, away, out of his arms, and walked to the row of trees. I braced myself against a pine and faced a wall of rock.

"Loki?" he said.

I gripped the trunk harder, not caring that the bark scratched my palm.

"What am I supposed to say to that?" I said. "What am I supposed to do?"

Gravel crunched behind me as his footsteps drew closer, each grating me down further.

"I've struggled," he said. "It can't be helped. I've tried to obliterate you from my heart. I have. And then this journey...Gods. Loki, why can't we move on? Be how we were?"

I faced him, his gaze full of pleading.

"And what?" I spat. "Forget the betrayals? The pain?"

"Yes."

Rage cracked white through my chest.

He said it so simply, as if it were the easiest thing in the worlds. As if...

I marched back to the shore of the creek and crossed my arms and stared at the water gurgling along its path through the shade. Couldn't he leave me alone?

"This is what we are now," I said. "Accept it."

A second passed. Two.

"And that's all the reply I'm to get? 'Accept it'?"

"I don't even know why you'd tell me any of this at all after—"

"I know our past," he interrupted. "But Loki, we don't have to be locked in this battle forever. We can have it all back and be together. We can be us again."

I looked over my shoulder at him, his face open and imploring, and it made my stomach churn.

"Us? Are you so demented? You think I'd leave Sigyn for you?"

He trudged towards me, the pebbles snapping and clicking beneath his boots.

"You don't have to leave her at all," he said. "You know that. It would be how it always was between you and me."

"I don't want that," I said.

He shrunk, as if I had cut him down with an axe.

"How could you not?" he said. "After all this?"

"Because." I paused. "Because I'm happy now. I survived you after you broke me into pieces. I suffered over you."

He scoffed.

"And you don't think I continue to suffer?" he said. "You carry such hatred for me that I don't feel for you. Gods know I've earned it. Gods know I should hate you equally after Ragnarok, after the positions you've put me in, but I don't." He pulled in a breath. "I want to hate you, but all I can hate is how I can't stop loving you. How I'm lost without you." His voice faltered. "I'm lost."

He was rich.

"You were the one that chose to walk away," I said. "You threw our love to the wolves. You—"

A pain I thought killed bubbled awake, alive and hungry and gnawed my organs, eating me inside out.

I had begged him not to go through with what he wanted so long ago. To stop the bloodshed, to spare the boy...

I had given him a choice.

And he had made it.

Odin opened his mouth as if he actually had some defense to say. Some excuse to make.

He immediately shut it. He knew better.

"That's right," I said. "Don't speak to me of love again. You ensured there is none to be found in my heart for you anymore."

I stomped across the scuttling stones following the creek, needing distance. Needing to be away from him.

"Then why did you save me?" he called after me.

I stopped and turned to him marching to me.

"You always act like you want my throat slit," he said. "Well, you had your chance last night to anoint your anger with my blood."

"This is ridiculous."

I started to walk away. He grabbed my wrist and tugged me back.

"You know you could have found another way without me," he said. "You had Brísingamen. You didn't have to save my life, but you put everything on the line. Risked it all. Even Sigyn, because..." He released me. "Your actions prove what you won't admit. If you truly felt nothing for me, you would have let Freya finish me."

That truth cut my insides like a razor.

I had wanted to let him die. But I couldn't do it.

I cursed whatever part of him still existed in my chambers, whatever residue of caring remained, that prevented me from abandoning him. Tossing him into the darkness of gnashing teeth as he had done to me time and time again.

"I don't know what I expected." He shook his head, pushing his fingers through his hair. "Why I believed taking this journey with you would let us..."

"Would let us what?"

He blinked, standing taller.

I dared him to say it.

"That perhaps it would let us start over."

I chuckled darkly.

Give me a chance, he asked.

And I did.

And again, he made me a fool, because again, I believed him.

I pushed into his chest and shoved him back.

"You've been conning me since the first day we set off."

"No. It's not like that—"

I shoved him again.

"Your help never was genuine."

"That's not true. It is real..."

"Every old memory you recalled—taking Utgard, out-drinking each other, that brawl in Vanaheim, *Samsey*...It was all to awaken sentiment in me?"

"Yes, that I did do. I just thought—"

"You just thought that perhaps enough time had passed that stupid Loki would forget everything you did? That I'd forgive you? That I'd fall into your arms and we'd go back to fucking each other senseless?"

"Stop!"

His eye misted with red.

"I admit I saw an added benefit," he said. "Is it so wrong to take it? You want me to pretend as if we had nothing. That we shared nothing. But we lived so much life together. I thought if you remembered that maybe..." His voice broke. "I wanted you to remember."

"Remember what? The screaming? The tears?"

"The beauty."

He reached out and placed his hand on my shoulder and squeezed. Wind stirred our hair and rustled the pine trees alive with the cooing of doves.

"Remember when we mixed our blood in Jotunheim and swore our oath?" He opened his element to me and I sucked in air as rivers of his ambition streamed into me, submerging me in ice.

My eyes shut despite myself, despite everything.

He stepped closer until the heat of his breath skimmed my cheeks.

"Remember when you kissed me during that storm on Samsey?" His lips brushed mine and my skin prickled.

His element crawled through my veins, flowed into my nose. Darkness crashed over me and pulled me out into a vast ocean.

He slid his hand along my arm, burning every inch he caressed.

He leaned into my ear.

"Remember how you always shivered when I touched you here?" He circled the inside of my wrist with his thumb.

Another rush of cold.

My eyes flashed open and he moved even closer.

He slid his hand over my trousers, trailing lust up my thighs.

"And here."

Odin held my gaze as he slowly knelt at my feet with all the reverence of a man kneeling before his master, bringing back rare memories of those times he'd submit to me.

He pulled one of the knotted cords of my trousers free, and wove his fingers within the tangle of the others, loosening the threads, eager to unfasten me.

I braced for that wicked pleasure of his mouth.

No.

I seized his wrist, stopping him from untying me further. I yanked him to his feet, forcing myself awake. Forcing myself back into the morning light and the incessant songs of doves.

And a madness descended over me. An uncontrollable rage I could see nothing through.

Gripping into his tunic I tugged him against me, our breath mixing hot between us.

"Funny," I rasped. "And I thought you said we weren't to use our elements? But then, you always said a lot of things to me. Vowed. Promised."

I threw him to the ground, and he gasped as his back struck the pebbles, knocking the air from his lungs. I straddled his waist, pinning him beneath me.

He looked up at me, burning his gaze into mine.

"Is this what you're begging for?" I drove tendrils of my chaos blazing through him. "Is this what you're asking of me?"

I dug my nails harder into his skin. I wanted him to scream.

I thrust all of my chaos into his sinew. He cried out as I burnt his chambers to coal. Seared his bones. I stormed my chaos into his marrow, burning and branding and broiling.

My lungs clamped shut as he forced out his ambition into me, flooding me, surging up my nostrils, spilling down my throat until I choked on frigid black.

Our energies met in a maelstrom. Fierce. Brutal. I gagged on the deluge of his full element and scorched his insides with my fire, draining myself into him, refusing to succumb.

He writhed between my legs and his pulse pounded against my palms, each an echo of our past.

As much as I tried to stomp the memories back into their graves, they rose around me as Odin and I fought next to the creek. Of everything we were. Had been. All laid bare and open beneath the morning sky.

Tender. Violent. Healing. Bruising.

We shared breath as we wrestled on that bank, the stream

coursing over rock, the constant murmur the same tone as the Ifingr river where we had first met.

More memories woke.

How he tasted, how he felt. How we would kiss until our lips ached. How soft touches became scratches, a frenzy, clawing, tearing at the edges where he ended and I began, until we bled and still it was not enough of the other.

It was never enough.

And I remembered.

I had spent millennia stitching the thousand gashes he'd cut into me over and over again, and now they all split open. Tore. And my heart I wanted to remain steel, turned into glass.

I loosened my hold on him and a wave of his ambition battered my chest and pulled through my veins and grasped my ankles and pulled me under.

I drowned in him.

Falling deeper.

Suffocating.

And I remembered...

Trusting him.

Loving him.

Being one with him.

He was my religion.

As I was his.

And I remembered...

That's what angered me most. Because he was right. It had been beautiful.

"You promised me that you'd always choose our love!" I screamed.

I fell onto his chest and hot tears streamed down my cheeks as I spilled my guts, unable to stop the centuries of grief and pain and regret bleeding out of me.

"You promised me..." My voice cracked. "You promised you'd choose us...and I trusted you...and you just gave us away."

"Loki."

He stilled and clasped my face between his hands and pressed our foreheads together, letting my tears mix with his.

We held each other. And we were broken. A moment. A heartbeat. Just holding on before the current swept us apart again, as it always did.

"When can I be free of you?" I said.

I shoved off him and stood and walked away into the gorge.

"I ask myself that same question," he called after me.

22

DEVIL IN THE DETAILS

SIGYN

I shoved the letter Býleistr handed me deep in my pocket.

The note was just a memento of my brother, nothing more.

It didn't prove Loki's guilt.

It didn't prove anything.

"Please, that message proves everything," Surtr said. "And you know it. Otherwise, you would have tossed the letter in the lake as the rubbish you claim it to be."

Lies.

Always lies.

But whose, I wasn't sure anymore...

23

THISTLEBERRY TEA

LOKI

Svartalfheim

We neared the tree line of the mountain and the road—well, it was more twisting roots and boulders than road —grew steeper and the air thinner.

Odin gave a piercing whistle behind me that cut into my back. I looked over my shoulder, careful not to meet his gaze. He stared out into the forest of pine and spruce for the same reason. For three days we traveled like this. Speaking only when absolutely necessary, anything else was a mix of grunts and rude hand gestures.

He motioned with two fingers to take a right at the fork, into a lovely patch of fog thicker than most stews.

I nodded.

I didn't know how much longer I could endure these awkward exchanges, but there was no way of putting the guts we had spilled that morning back inside of us.

It was all out in the open now.

And I'd been so stupid.

We both had.

It all replayed in my head over and over.

What we had done.

My mind raced with a fresh wave of chatter, every bit of it chastising me for letting my emotions get the better of me. Gods. I couldn't remember the last time I felt so drained. So exhausted. My body wanted to slump forward in my saddle. To close my eyes for a little to rest. To let my element recover...

Sigyn needs you, and this is what you do? Waste your chaos because you can't ever control your anger? Because you can't walk away?

I never intended...

No, of course not. You never do.

I forced my back straight and my shoulders square.

What was done was done.

There was only moving forward. It would be fine. Totally fine. I just needed a decent night's sleep without some hooting owl, a meal that wasn't rat-on-a-stick, and by the time I returned to the Ironwood I'd be right as rain, my chaos bright and burning as ever, ready to go for what came next.

It would be *fine.*

Damn.

And I still had Bly to deal with.

I groaned.

Between Odin, the exhaustion, and Bly's bloody apple, a dozen fires burned around me needing put out.

Maybe fine was too optimistic a word.

At least in another two hours we'd arrive at Brokkr and Eitri's citadel. I'd give them Brísingamen, I'd get the amulet, and I'd be one fire less.

And if what I'd seen in their cabinet was what I hoped...two fires.

Ylva stopped abruptly, jolting me forward, my nose crunching against the back of her head, making my eyes water.

What now?

I peered between her flicking ears, assessing the important

problem that must have caused this reaction, because it must have been important to have made it worth almost breaking my face.

A gurgling stream, one foot wide and one inch deep, cut across the road.

You've got to be kidding me.

Eira clopped across with Odin without complaint.

I kicked my heels into Ylva's sides, demanding her to follow. She snorted and shook her head and backed up three feet, refusing her hooves to get wet.

I grunted.

Odin turned and sighed.

I rocked in my saddle, urging her forward over the trickle of water.

"Kick her harder," he said, the first string of words I heard from him in days.

"What does it look like I'm doing?" I said.

"Failing."

I held my tongue.

"Show her one of those nuts I know you've been hiding from me and tempt her across," I said.

Odin rolled his eye and slipped off his horse and stepped over the stream. He took off his belt.

"What are you doing...no...don't you dare," I said.

He slapped the horse on its backside. Ylva whinnied, reared and jumped two feet in the air and popped over the stream, while I slid off her back and landed in the creek with a splash.

Delightfully cold water soaked my trousers and seeped up my back.

"Great help," I said. "Fantastic."

Odin exhaled sharply and stuck out his hand, offering to pull me to my feet.

"Let's get on with it," he said.

Our gazes met for a second. He looked at his boots, and I looked past his shoulder at no spot in particular.

I smacked Odin's hand out of my way, not wanting any

repeats, and pushed myself up. My hand slipped on the slime coating the rocks. I fell again, water leeching between my thighs.

Laughter erupted to our right.

We were not alone.

Perfect.

I stood, a deluge of water raining off my trousers as Brokkr stepped out of the fog, Eitri beside him, a small wicker basket hanging from the crook of his elbow.

Brokkr buckled over and cackled louder.

"It looks like you pissed yourself, Loki," Brokkr slapped his knee, another rumble of laughter bursting out of his lungs.

Pity softened Eitri's face, and he patted his tunic and pulled out his kerchief, and held the stained rag out to me. Lightly used. How generous.

"To dab up the wet," he said.

Not wanting to offend, I took the kerchief from him, touching the cotton as little as possible.

"What are you doing down here?" Odin handed me a clean kerchief from his satchel.

I turned away from him and blotted the wet on my pants with Eitri's, doing my best to not grimace at the blotches of mysterious origin.

"Picking thistleberries," Eitri said. "We ran out of tea and—"

"What are *we* doing down here?" Brokkr cut in. "What are *you* doing down here trespassing—again—on our lands? I thought we made it clear—"

"Clear, that if we returned with Brísingamen, you'd make us our amulet? Yes. Crystal," I said.

He chuckled.

"But you didn't actually get Brísingamen," Brokkr said.

Odin and I stared at him.

"Wait...you actually got it?"

They always doubted.

I flipped open my satchel and dug Brísingamen out of the leather, allowing the jewels to unravel, so the necklace dangled in front of his nose.

"As requested," I said.

Brokkr's mouth fell open, thunderstruck. Eitri dropped his basket, ruby thistleberries scattering across the moss and pine duff.

"But how?" Brokkr said.

"And here I thought the thing with my neck would have been enough for you to know to never underestimate me, Brokkr," I said.

He narrowed his eyes.

Eitri stepped in front of him, Brísingamen casting his beaming face in a thousand constellations.

"Look how the little diamonds are twinkling!" he said. "Just as I remember! She's finally returned home."

I smiled.

"I believe you owe us one amulet," I said. "We'll take it to go, if it isn't too much trouble."

Brokkr and Eitri shared a glance and gave a nod.

"A deal is a deal," Brokkr said. "Now, hand it over, and we will head to the forge."

He extended his arm and opened his hand, motioning for me to drop it in his sweaty palm.

I coiled the necklace in my hand and locked it in my fist.

"Make our amulet, and then you'll get Brísingamen," I replied.

"Give me Brísingamen, and then you'll get your amulet. Or don't you trust me?"

I snorted.

"I wouldn't trust you as far as I could kick you."

Brokkr ground his teeth behind his beard, the silver baubles tied within his whiskers shaking from his rage.

"Loki, stop antagonizing Brokkr," Odin snapped. "You're being cranky."

My face contorted into an expression of irate wonder.

"Cranky?" I repeated. "I'm wet. I'm cold. I'm hungry. Sorry if that makes me a little *cranky*."

Odin sighed.

"Here we go again. Can you ever just—"

Brokkr and Eitri's gazes bounced between Odin and I, as if watching a tennis match as our argument heated into accusations of who set the bed on fire that one Midsummer.

"Are you both alright?" Brokkr said.

"We're good," I said.

"We're fine," Odin added.

They blinked at us and the rolls of hot breath curling out of our heaving lungs.

Eitri tapped his fingers together, considering.

"Maybe we should discuss this over a bracing cup of tea," Eitri said. "To help cut the tension."

Brokkr held his hand out farther to me.

"But first," Brokkr said. "Out of the two of us, who has actually lied?"

"Well..."

"Exactly," he said. "I've kept my word, so my word will be the one honored."

"He is right," Odin said. "Let him have it."

Damn.

I clapped Brísingamen into his hand and gripped hard. He tugged back. I hardened my grip until he whimpered, happy that the diamonds bit into his flesh as they bit into mine. I wanted him to understand.

"You cross me, and I'll kill you," I said.

He tilted his head and smirked.

"You cross *me*, and *I'll* kill you."

24

AS GOOD AS GOLD

We walked into the cramped smithy, and iron, steel, and fire tingled my sinuses.

Brokkr unhooked a poker from the rows of hammers and tools covering the walls, and thrust it into the brick forge, crackling the coals as he shuffled and stirred. The small fire quivering inside the hearth washed him in dim reds and oranges.

I had to hold back tears of joy at having secured the amulet for Sigyn. But another monster remained needing put to rest before I could finally relax into peace.

"How long will this take, Brokkr?" Odin removed a mallet from the bench shoved against the back. He brushed away iron filings and dirt and sat, lacing his fingers in his lap. "I might try to catch up on some rest while we wait."

I grinned at that.

"Yes," I said. "How much time do you think, Brokkr? One hour? Two hours?"

How much time do I have without your penetrating gaze to spy on me?

Brokkr had made it awfully difficult for me to nosey about that cabinet when we all drank tea as Eitri explained their plans for creating the amulet—setting a round, amber stone in gold imbued with runes and magic. This promised to be their most ambitious project yet, and they couldn't wait to rub their creation in the noses of the Sons of Ivaldi.

Every time I drew close to the cabinet, trying to inspect the fittings, the lock—I just needed a peek inside—Brokkr growled in the back of his throat and I stepped away, pretending a spider or some other sort of arachnid had garnered my attention.

"Typical gods. Always in a hurry." Brokkr picked through the collection of tongs hanging below the forge. "Art takes time. And art mixed with magic, even longer."

He removed a long pair of tongs and placed them on the massive anvil in the center of the shop. An amber stone, deep as cognac, lay on a velvet pillow on a table next to Eitri who inspected the stack of small gold bars on the opposite side. He roved his finger along the thin blocks. He stopped, his lips pulling into a smile alive with wonder.

"This one sings louder than the rest. It's the sister of the stone."

He lifted the bar, and lovingly cradled it in both hands, his fingers stacked with rings and jewels.

"Pure gold is tricky to forge," he said. "But only pure gold will do for what is needed to set the stone."

He looked at Brokkr, who removed his cap as if out of respect for the metal.

"You will have to be meticulous, Brother." He picked up the tongs off the anvil. "Too much, or too little, and the gold will be ruined."

"You're fussier than the bellows." Brokkr replaced his hat and tugged it to the tops of his ears. "I know what to do."

My grin widened.

As did I.

I knew an opportune moment when it hiked its skirt and flashed its ankle at me.

"Seems you've got everything under control," I said. "If you need me, I'll be not here."

I walked towards the door, passing Odin who leaned against the granite wall, arms crossed, and eye closed, and slouched into slumber. Jealousy flashed through my aching body wishing I could do the same, but I had an errand to run.

"Don't you even think about leaving this room," Brokkr barked.

I skidded to a stop.

"I'm only popping out for a stroll. Stretch the ol' legs. Won't be a tick," I said.

His gaze burned into me, the whites of his eyes reflecting the molten oranges from the forge.

"You will stay where I can see you," he snapped. "Something about the last time you were flitting about unobserved...Now, sit down and shut up."

I cursed and sat next to Odin, brushing his arm. I scooted away from him to the far end of the bench.

I tapped my fingers against my knee.

No this wouldn't do at all.

I stood.

"I'd really prefer—"

Brokkr grabbed the handle of the bellows to the left of the forge and forced it down, a wave of heat exploding from the hearth as the fire swelled and ate the coals.

Eitri faced the forge, bathed in searing yellows and seriousness hardened his always kind expression.

Clamping the gold bar with his tongs, Eitri placed the bar on a firebrick beside the flame as Brokkr pumped the bellows in a steady rhythm, like a heartbeat. Like a breath.

It was a breath.

With each pulse, he breathed a soul into the metal.

And the gold woke with life, glowing hot and beautiful.

Eitri pulled the gold out of the forge and placed it on the anvil behind him. He grabbed a hammer, swung back his arm, and struck the gold. He whispered words, incantations, each an intention he beat into the metal with every strike of his hammer.

He plunged the gold back into the forge to fire again, repeating the process.

My heart swelled witnessing their good work, knowing the treasure they created would save Sigyn.

Each clap of the hammer gave me hope.

For our happiness.

For our future.

Sigyn's face lit in my mind, smiling, happy, and filled with love.

And I wouldn't see this love dissolve into hatred for me like every other love before it.

Not this time.

Not again.

I needed to get out of this room and to that cabinet where I hoped...*gods let it be true.*

I coughed, ridding the smoke from my trachea.

"Sorry to interrupt," I said.

Eitri pounded the gold flatter.

"I thought I told you to shut up, Trickster?" Brokkr said, the light from the forge reflecting off the sheen of sweat on his brow.

"Afraid it can't be helped. A bit of an emergency." I scratched behind my ear.

"Emergency?" Brokkr kept the bellows at a steady pulse. *Thwump. Thwump. Thwump.*

"I didn't realize this would take so long, otherwise I would have seen to certain functions beforehand."

He eyed me.

"Functions?"

"Well, you know." I fidgeted. "You kept pouring me all that tea. I've been holding it so long I'm enduring my third sweat."

Odin yawned and shifted and arched his back, keeping his eye closed.

"What are you going on about?" he whispered. "You emptied each cup into that vase behind you."

I started to shush him, but he drifted away back into sleep before I got the chance, his snores mixing with Eitri's hammering.

Brokkr groaned, pumping the handle of the bellows.

"You can use that over there to relieve yourself."

I turned to where his gaze fell—a bucket in the corner with a dirty rag flopped over the rim.

My shoulders sank.

"Hey."

Eitri removed the thinned gold from the forge and placed it back on the anvil.

"Oh Brokkr, let him go," he said. "All this tension..." *Whack!* "...is making it difficult..." *Whack!* "...for me to concentrate." *Whack!*

He struck the gold harder.

"I don't trust where I can't see him."

"Well, neither of us can leave to escort—watch the bellows!"

Brokkr growled, another whoosh of broiling heat bursting out of the forge. *Thwump. Thwump. Thwump.*

"Fine," he said. "The loo is down the hall and to the right. But if you're not back in five minutes, I stop these bellows and you can go home empty handed. Got it?"

My jaw wanted to clamp shut, imagining his spine between my teeth. I forced a smile instead.

"Naturally."

I walked out the door and turned right...for three steps. I peered back into the smithy. Brokkr and Eitri's eyes remained fixed on their work. Odin remained asleep.

I spun on my heel and marched the opposite direction down the dark hall towards the sitting room with the cabinet. Any of the heat from the forges died and cold nipped at my cheeks and fingertips. The hammering and bellows echoed and bounced off the cavern walls and vaults and chambers.

My pulse quickened.

Why did they have to live in a stone labyrinth?

Water dripped somewhere.

No matter.

Sweat broke out on the small of my back.

The hall tilted.

I am safe.

I am not in danger.

Venom filled my mouth.

I stopped and took a second to collect myself. To recenter.

I am safe.

I am not in danger.

The hall leveled, and I quickened my steps to my destination.

I slipped into the sitting room and maneuvered around piles of gems and treasure. Around the oak table still strewn with our tea cups. I hurried past the fire that remained perpetual embers and stepped in front of what I desired most.

The cabinet that held within it a golden apple.

At least, that's what I wished. I only caught a glimpse, a flash, when Eitri had opened the door to put in the Elven pear we had given them on our first arrival.

A glimpse was enough to give me hope.

Bitting my bottom lip, I jiggled the latch.

The thwack of Eitri's hammer ricocheted around me, stifling the creaks and groans of the wood as I tried to pry the pine door open. The thump of the bellows drowned out the jingle of the iron fittings further.

The door gave.

I jerked the thing open, the door skidding each inch and—

My heart somersaulted.

There it sat on a velvet cushion. A perfect, golden apple.

My perfect salvation.

So, this is what Odin had charmed for them to stay preserved forever? At least he'd done something useful for once, because now I could pay Bly the price for his silence, and Sigyn would never know about the part I played in that whole nasty Simon business.

The high pitched ping of more delicate tools replaced the whack of Eitri's hammer. Time ran thin.

Thwump. Thwump. Thwump.

I reached for the apple, my future with Sigyn, my everything I wanted most.

I stopped, my hand hovering over the fruit.

Could I really take this apple? Could I really destroy the new relations Odin had built with Svartalfheim just to pay off Bly to keep my secret?

I laughed.

I grabbed the apple and stashed it in my satchel with a whistle.

With a turn of my heel, I sauntered to the door.

My whistle died.

My skin itched.

My throat tightened.

Was this guilt?

My stomach roiled at that thought. Or was that just more guilt?

I sighed.

Sigyn's little chats about honesty and doing the "right thing" were really making life complicated for me.

But, if this apple was all that stood between me and my happiness, I would not lose my chance because of some light villainy.

Besides, this was for love, and could there be any more noble reason?

I took another step.

My throat tightened further.

My scalp prickled.

My chest burned.

Dammit.

Fine. I got it. If this is how my conscience wanted to play it...

I scrambled for something to write on, grumbling as I tore a scrap of paper from a cookbook and scribbled out a note promising an explanation and replacement once the harvest came in. Folding the paper, I placed it on the empty cushion where the apple had been and gave a satisfied nod at my good deed. How could it be wrong if I made it right later? Yes, the note made this all incredibly moral.

The constant rumble of hammers and bellows ceased, and the room fell into a hush.

Silence pressed heavy on my shoulders.

Shit.

I ran for the hall and tugged at the buckles on my satchel, locking the apple safely inside.

* * *

I BURST INTO THE SMITHY, doing my best to keep my ragged breaths tame. I smoothed my hair and Brokkr gave a disappointed huff as I slowed my pace and ambled across the room, rubbing the seconds I had left to spare in his scrunched-up face.

I'd done it. Truly done it.

I had the apple, and I had the amulet.

I wouldn't lose her.

I wouldn't lose love again.

For the first time in days, I could breathe. And more importantly, I could rest.

Rest. How beautiful a word.

I flopped on the bench beside Odin, the wood popping beneath my weight, and stretched my legs. He stirred a second or two and fell back into slumber, which I found a smashing idea.

Brokkr and Eitri huddled around a vice, filing away at the gold clamped between its jaws, while I wrapped my arms around my chest and relaxed against the wall. I closed my eyes and exhaled, settling in for a long, *long* nap.

For once, everything was working out and coming up roses.

My body twitched with the beginning bites of sleep, my element overjoyed finally having the chance to recharge. I unwound further into absolute bliss.

I hoped to dream of Sigyn...

"It's finished!" Eitri said.

My eyes shot open and my every muscle and fiber and cell screamed.

Odin woke with a snort and stood, stretching his back. He yawned and walked to Brokkr and Eitri, who stood in front of the anvil, googily-eyed over something I could not make out.

I counted to three and heaved myself up and followed, dragging my feet.

"Well, let's see it." Odin rubbed his hands together.

Eitri held the amulet out to him, and Odin's face softened as he took it. He caressed the smooth amber with his thumb, the crackles in the round stone a collage of honeys, bloods, and bronzes. Delicate runes, each a spell, a charm, etched the edges of the setting—a thick disc of gold.

I thought I'd never breathe again.

"Remarkable." Odin turned the amulet over and upside down, admiring the exquisite craftsmanship. The perfection. "As always."

Brokkr's shoulders relaxed for a blink from the compliment, and then he bristled, reminding himself he didn't like us and our compliments meant as much to him as a canister of rocks.

"Obviously, the amulet is remarkable," Brokkr said. "Because the Brothers Brokkr and Eitri made it, and we only make the best, and this time, don't you forget it."

Odin smiled at him in that calming way of his that made you feel so assured, confident, even though you should be anything but.

"Of course we won't," Odin said. He smiled wider.

Odin handed the amulet to me, and the stone and the gold breathed beneath my touch, vibrations of magic pulsing in its center like a heartbeat. This was not a piece of jewelry, this was a living thing, and it starved.

"The stone is hungry," I said, staring into the depths of the amber. It whispered. Or did it hum?

Eitri chuckled.

"Hungry enough to consume Surtr to the dregs," Eitri said. "Your friend will be free of the element possessing her."

My features lifted at the thought of Sigyn finally being unchained from the darkness eating her alive.

"Excellent," Odin said. "Then I suppose this is farewell. We have a lot of ground to travel if we want to make it back in time."

"Eh..." Eitri rubbed the back of his neck.

I lifted my gaze off the amulet and on to his.

"Is there something else?" I said.

A malicious glint flashed in Brokkr's small eyes. He smiled, the edges of his teeth showing beneath his beard.

"Let me tell him, please," Brokkr said.

Eitri smacked Brokkr upside the head.

"Brokkr! That's not nice," Eitri scolded. "You shouldn't enjoy their coming difficulty—"

"Difficulty?" Odin said.

Eitri gave a sheepish grin and rocked back on his heels and forward again onto the balls of his feet. He clasped his hands behind his back.

"There is a condition for the amulet to work as you wish," Eitri said. "Once Surtr is in the stone, well…"

"Well, what?" I pressed.

"The stone must be encased in the gold," Brokkr said, a snicker rolling within his tone.

Odin's neck stiffened.

"Encased?" Odin said. "But we have no forge where we are headed to melt the gold."

"And that's our problem how?" Brokkr said. "We've done what you asked. This will do what you want. We've upheld our bargain, now it's up to you to get it to work."

Odin's eye twitched.

"You could have mentioned this caveat earlier," Odin said through gritted teeth.

"And ruin the surprise?" Brokkr said.

Eitri slapped Brokkr's shoulder.

"Hush, Brokkr," Eitri said. "Look, after Surtr is extracted from Sigyn and fed to the stone, every drop of energy merged into the amber…" Eitri turned from Odin to me. "…the setting must be melted and you must seal the stone within the gold. Only when the stone is sealed completely in the metal, will Surtr remain inside, the dark matter trapped within the amulet forever."

That didn't seem so bad.

Brokkr's cackles said otherwise.

"You didn't really believe you'd say a few charms and pop Surtr inside and tuck the amulet away lickety-split?" Brokkr said.

Odin's lips thinned and he rubbed his forehead.

"No, I suspected there would be further requirements. There always is."

"Since we will be forge-less, I guess the melting part of the job falls to me," I said. "I think I can supply a little fire."

Eitri shrieked. Brokkr cackled louder.

"A *little* fire? To melt Dwarven gold? To melt *magic* Dwarven gold?" Eitri shivered. "This will require an immense amount of your chaos to encase Surtr inside the stone. I hope you're well rested, because the amulet will be uncompromising in what it needs to finish the job."

Rested.

My pulse increased as I stared at the amulet. At all it promised. At all it would require.

Odin stepped next to me and gave me a look that cut me cold.

"This is why we saved our magic—our elements," Odin said. "What we must do will push us both to our breaking points. If not break us completely."

I squeezed the amulet, and I hated the weakness of my grip. The ache of exhaustion riddling me with holes. The sinking feeling that all the magic I had used, wasted, needed...I wasn't sure I'd have enough power left in me to give.

"Why the worried face, Loki?" Brokkr mocked. "You always love to brag about how you are the *God of Chaos*. Or is providing the necessary fire going to be a problem for you?"

25

_____

BETWEEN THE LINES

SIGYN

"I t's time for you to accept your new role now that only shreds of your *fidelity*—" Surtr gagged on the word, "—remain. You'll be vastly happier once you stop fighting me."

I read the opening line of my book for the fifth time. Something about great Jotnar families. Or was it over Jotun flora?

"Stupid Býleistr," I grumbled beneath my breath. "All nonsense."

"Did you hear a word I said?" Surtr sat on my bed across from me, sinking into the layers of blankets.

I curled tighter in the wingback chair, more spring than cushion, resolute to get Býleistr out of my head and simply enjoy my book. Dragging my fingertip across the text, I read each word with determination.

I would make it through this chapter, so help me.

My shoulders relaxed, and I settled deeper into my chair.

You can't trust him, and he certainly doesn't trust you, Býleistr's voice broke through.

I groaned to myself.

"Ridiculous," I breathed, dropping the book to my lap.

The window panes rattled with a gust of wind, and the low moan of a wolf ran beneath the jingle.

Surtr stood and leaned against the banister, crossing his arms over his flat and firm chest. The waves of his white hair glowed in the candlelight, and his black robes pooled on the floor at his feet.

"I thought this Loki-murdered-Simon drama would be helpful in removing the clog that Loki is from your pipes, but all it's done is clog you further," he said. "Sigyn? I'm trying to have a heart-to-heart here."

I chewed my fingernail. Did Býleistr really expect me to believe that Loki killed Simon?

Laughter burst out from my stomach.

Tripe. All of it tripe—

He's dangerous to you, Sigyn, Loki's words pulsed in my ears, along with another screech of wind. The piercing howls of wolves followed.

Loki detested Simon.

He thought he would cost me my life because of the dangerous rogues he cheated, but...

I picked up the book, attempting to read the paragraph again, forcing my eyes to focus on each word.

Why couldn't Loki understand? To him, turning Simon out on the streets was an easy decision. The only decision.

I knew Simon was dangerous to me.

I did.

But I couldn't forsake my brother.

He's a man whose exploits will rip you apart, Loki's words erupted again, scalding and irritating. Like him, some days.

My teeth ached, and I relaxed my jaw, not realizing I'd been clenching. The last thing I needed was to crack a molar.

I slumped in the chair and tossed the book on the table beside me, clattering the bowl of cold beet stew I had no appetite for.

"Right," Surtr said. "I guess it will be up to me to flush him out. Look, you know how Loki deals with his bugbears. He removes them from the equation. He was willing to burn entire worlds with Ragnarok."

I picked at the skin around my thumbnail.

Loki always jumped straight to the extreme. He had a true talent for acting before reason had a chance to set in.

"Simon was nothing but an ant beneath his boot. An ant he deemed a threat and squashed."

Before I noticed, before I stopped myself, I slid Simon's letter out of my pocket. The paper crinkled and decay weakened every crease as I unfolded the note, careful not to crumble the broken wax seal. I lifted it to my nose, shocked how the scent of my old home remained infused within the paper—wood smoke and lavender.

I remembered when Loki had handed the letter to me that night, and the joy its message had brought to Father and I.

And now, as I read Simon's words, my eyes stung seeing his familiar scrunched hand again, each ink stroke a link to the past, to him.

I forced myself to take in a breath through the emotion, even though it burned.

Something shimmered over the letters. Waved.

I tilted the paper. The letters stilled.

I held the paper near the candle to illuminate the note from behind. The quivering returned.

I squinted.

I didn't like how my insides squirmed and laced with fire.

"*Finally*," Surtr said. "Let's get this all out of the way, then we can move on to the fun things, like exploring your new nature of Surtr, and all the powers that come along with being dark matter. There's nothing that compares to making your own planet."

I tried to ignore the tingle of the paper. The itch on the pads of my fingers.

Was Býleistr right about the illusion?

"Do you think Loki used a knife?" Surtr said. "He loves knives. Ooo! No. His hands. I bet that's what he did. Less messy that way. He wouldn't want to stain that beautiful hardwood flooring you used to have."

My insides knotted with images of Loki strangling Simon, windpipe crushing, eyes bulging and weakening into a blank stare.

No.

Loki wouldn't trick me.

I trusted him. And he trusted me. He would have told me the truth.

Surtr sighed louder this time.

"Can you please piss or get off the pot?" he said. "Come on, why this constant struggle with you?"

I folded the letter and stuffed the note into the book and snapped it shut. I tossed the damned thing into the shadows beneath the bed where it belonged.

Lies.

Always lies.

Surtr laughed, his violet eyes flashing with amusement and malice.

"Please don't tell me you actually believe Simon died on some battlefield in the Italian countryside, a prayer on his lips?"

No. I always hoped he had found a family. That he had found happiness. I only wanted him to be happy, as I remembered him being before Mother passed. He was only fifteen, and then he turned into someone I didn't recognize.

Surtr buried his face in his hands and moaned through his slender fingers.

"This is pathetic to watch," he said. "I've given you everything, and still you insist on torturing yourself, and me, I might add, which is incredibly rude."

Loki wouldn't have taken my brother from me. He wouldn't have taken his life.

He wouldn't lie to me. Not about this.

Surtr dropped his hands to his sides and cackled, tears streaming down his angled cheeks.

"Wouldn't he? Loki took *your* life from you," he said. "That night he made you a goddess, he stripped you of all you knew, and hurled you into a world you did not ask for, nor want."

I wrapped my arms around my knees and hugged them against my chest as specters bit at my ankles. My skin grew clammy as cold sweat soaked into my chemise.

Wolves yipped and howled and wailed outside.

"You're remembering those lonely nights, aren't you?" Surtr said. "The first weeks were the worst after what happened in that cave. How many times did you wake yourself screaming?"

A chill trickled down my back. Sweat collected along the lines of my palms. Across my forehead.

Those early nights were hell. A thousand faces. A thousand voices crying. Screaming. Loki. Myself. Our children.

My babies. Narfi and Nari. I never even got the chance to tell them goodbye.

And Loki...

He was bound and I could not help him. I could not rescue him from the torture. I had tried to save him, even though it was impossible. I had even fled Alfheim and made it to the edges of Vanaheim, determined to get back to Loki. Determined to get him out of that cave.

Until I was found. As if my escape had been expected before I even began. And I learned then that I was trapped in a snare set for me from the start.

Tears burned my eyes.

I gasped in air and looked at the candle flickering on the table beside me, forcing myself back into the room alive with the cry of wolves. I pulled the blanket tighter around my shoulders, as Simon had done for me when I was a child, when nightmares had woken me. He always lit a candle, telling me it would frighten away the ghosts.

But there were so many ghosts now.

If Loki had seen that side of Simon, he would have understood. He would have understood why I waited, why if I could just reach out, I could have pulled him out of the darkness he had fallen into and...

...and he'd come home.

I just wanted Simon to have a chance.

A chance Loki never would give him.

Loki always could be so cold.

"Cold, cruel, unforgiving," Surtr said. "You do know him, don't you?"

My gaze fell from the flame to the book beneath the bed, and to the letter still lodged within its pages.

Mournful yells filled the room. Wind squealed.

The spot on my neck prickled. I winced, my fingernails slicing into my skin before I even registered I had scratched at all. And I scratched harder.

Blood crammed beneath my nails.

Sulfur filled my nose.

"You know he is capable. You know he did it."

Lies.

Always lies.

"Stop resisting what can bring you peace," Surtr said. "Of finally being free of Loki and the pain he causes you."

I locked my gaze onto Surtr's, the thread holding me together snapping.

"I see that got your attention," he said. "My, you are staring daggers into me. You...ah, you're burning to tell me that I'm wrong. That he doesn't hurt you. That you and he have trust. Well then, prove it."

I would prove it.

Because we did have trust. How could we not after all we'd been through together?

The tingle traveled down my shoulder. Crossed my chest. I stopped flaying myself open and stood, the cold air stinging the thin cuts.

I walked across the cold flagstones and grabbed the book, and ripped out the letter.

The paper crinkled between my shaking fingers as I unfolded the note again. Blood stained my fingertips.

Pins and needles flushed my skin.

Simon's slanted cursive glistened with something, or was it my tired eyes? I deepened my concentration, asking the letter to break free of whatever charm coated the parchment. If anything coated it at all other than the smear of blood from my thumbprint.

Please. Don't change.

The text wiggled.

Please.

I exhaled, the letter being as stubborn as Loki when I begged him to just once think before he spoke and said something regrettable.

This entire letter was a hoax.

Please.

I focused everything, my every intention, on asking the letter to reveal its truth.

It remained.

And then my guts heaved and dropped to my feet.

I read Simon's letter over and over, a dozen times, a hundred, and each time the writing was not in Simon's hand. My chest clamped tight and everything I thought I knew, believed, shriveled into dust because the handwriting was Loki's.

The same handwriting I had found in his old book in the healer's room that had brought me such joy, now brought me nothing but cold realization.

"And after everything, this is what I have with Loki," I said.

"Tell me," Surtr said, his voice soft as candlelight.

I faced him, my breaths quick and burning.

"Lies," I answered. "Always lies."

Surtr smiled and stepped closer.

I smelled sulfur and brimstone and a thousand worlds breaking and building.

I grunted as my skin cracked and split down my neck and over my shoulder, the infection spreading quicker, deeper, further...

"Yes," he said. "Lies is all you have with him. Lies is all he will ever give you. And now that you've learned the truth, the last connection you have with him is finally severed. You are free. You can finally become what you are."

I fractured. Shattered. Rage and betrayal and hurt boiled in my gut, all mixing together and oozing through my veins, demanding change. Offering promises. Truth.

I clung to the last piece of myself. *I had to hold on.* But I didn't know if I could. If I even wanted to.

There had to be an explanation as to why he'd do this.

How could he do this?

Surtr stood and braced himself on the arms of my chair, his hair slipping over his strong shoulders.

"End your torment, Sigyn. Finish it." Surtr leaned in. "Put your last shred of fidelity Loki has dealt the death blow out of its misery. Accept what you are. Darkness. Power. All."

I couldn't let go. But it would be so satisfying to let go...

I saw it all before me in flashes and pulses.

A beautiful world. A new world. No hurt. No lies. No suffering.

I could make Loki be honest with me, grovel, and beg my forgiveness and make his promises true.

I could do it in a word.

How lovely it would be.

How peaceful. Ordered.

The tip of my tongue burned with the words.

"Just say it, and it will all be yours."

My lips parted.

26

RUST

LOKI

Ylva snapped, and I yanked my hand back, my fingers missing the crushing splendor of her teeth by a hair. She struck the grass with her hoof, furious. I understood. This was day three of my outwitting her with removing her bridle, and she grew thoroughly displeased with underestimating my dexterity.

"Thought you had me, didn't you?" I tied her to the tree beside Eira. "Maybe next time you'll be faster if you want a taste of my skin again."

Ylva gave a snort imbued with rage.

I drew in a satisfied breath for a job well done and walked away. Hot pain burst down my legs and up my back as she kicked me in my ass, jolting me forward. I fell, my palms skidding against the grass, the aroma of dirt and earthworm surging up my nose.

Grumbling, I craned back my neck and spit out a clump of grass and stared up at her. Ylva whinnied and did a small dance, pounding her hooves into the ground.

Grumbling louder, I pushed myself upright and limped to our

campsite, unmoved by the picturesque grassy knolls and fields of sunflowers surrounding our hill.

Odin sat on a log by the fire and held a long stick over the flames, roasting a squirrel. I groaned.

Thank gods this was our last night on the road. I didn't know how much more I could endure.

"Squirrel again?" I said. "I'm so sick of squirrel."

I stretched the kink from my spine and plopped in the grass, hating the involuntary *oof* I made. Why did the ground have to be so far down?

"You can always spend another hour or two trying to catch a rabbit, otherwise squirrel is the only thing on the menu."

Sighing, I collapsed onto my back and looked out at a thousand stars blinking in a black sky, wanting to think of better things than squirrel. Of better things than Odin critiquing my poaching methods.

Of better things than what I still had to do to remove Surtr from Sigyn's veins.

I pressed the butt of my hands against my eyes that burned, wanting the smallest sliver of rest.

How was I going to fuse Surtr into the amulet in this state? It would be difficult and...

A fresh wave of exhaustion rolled through my body, weighing me down further into the grass, deepening the ache in my bones.

Uncompromising the amulet may be, but so was I.

Especially for Sigyn. Especially when I was the reason for this mess in the first place.

I caused it. I would fix it.

"Don't tell her," I said.

I removed my hands from my eyes and relaxed them on top of my chest, keeping my sight fixed on the blooms of blues and purples of the milky way stretching from one side of the sky to the other.

"Don't tell Sigyn how the amulet works," I said. "That I must play a part. At least, not until the time comes."

"Why not?"

A breeze rustled the leaves of a few nearby oak trees.

"Because if Sigyn thinks this is beyond my chaos...beyond my capabilities..." I said. "She will want to figure something else out. Find some other way. I can't let that happen. It must be finished."

Odin considered my words.

"And is this beyond your chaos, Loki?" he said. "I know you're tired. Exhausted like me. But you must be certain you can do this before we proceed."

"There you go, sounding just like her—"

"Just answer the question," he said, shutting me up. "I know you. You wouldn't talk like this unless some anxiety is troubling you. Now tell me. Is this task beyond your capabilities or not?"

Fatigue nibbled at my edges.

I locked my gaze on his.

"If you ever ask me that again Odin, you will wake up a head shorter."

He nodded slowly.

"Very well. Then we continue as planned. Now eat. You look like death warmed over."

"Such compliments."

Odin held out the stick to me, the impaled squirrel shriveled into an appetizing mummy with massive teeth.

I covered my mouth and belched, my stomach protesting with cartwheels.

"Stop being stubborn," he said. "You must eat to gain what strength you can before we perform the ritual. We both do."

I sat up and crossed my legs, snatching the squirrel from him. I forced a bite—nutty, sweet, stringy—and swallowed, sending a prayer with it that it would stay down.

Odin poked the fire, cinders popped and wood collapsed into embers and white ash. He stared into the flames, his pensive expression glazed in quivering yellows and shadow.

"The silence we've been in since that *morning* has given me time to reflect, and—"

Gods.

"Not interested in hearing any of it," I interrupted. "We've already exceeded our allotted conversation for the day."

He cast his gaze to the ground.

"Don't worry. I won't repeat any of those sentiments you found so revolting," he said. "It's just...I always hoped that I gave you an easy life in Asgard. But it wasn't easy at all, was it?"

I slowed chewing.

"Let me see," I said. "You lured me from Jotunheim and my family with promises you broke one by one. You fed me fables with silver spoons until I choked. You tossed me into a world where I was hated, because how could the gods not hate me knowing what I was?" I pulled in a breath. "You damned me to a solitary life dependent only on you, and then...I survived the life you gave me. So no, it was not easy."

He nodded stiffly.

"I just wished that when I brought you back with me the gods would have shown you mercy," he said. "I tried to get them to understand, but...we have no mercy in our bones. Especially to *The Destroyer*. I believe they thought you'd burn us all to the ground with one sneeze."

Now this was a grave misfortune. If only I'd known how much they actually feared me rather than reviled me. All the missed opportunities. One remark, and I could have enjoyed watching Thor scrub his chamber pot with his hairbrush.

I frowned at never having had the pleasure.

"I suppose it all makes sense now why the gods got anxious anytime we had one of our spats and I said how this time I was leaving you for good."

His brow furrowed.

"Spats? You threw a hatchet at my head."

I shrugged.

"Only because you threw it first."

We both had wicked tempers, which was unfortunate for anything breakable laying within reach. Of course, the fire of our anger only stoked the passion that usually followed. Sometimes I'd wake his rage on purpose just for that exquisite explosion to result in vigorous apologizing in tangled sheets and sweat.

"But every time you left, you always came back," he said. "You always came back to me until..." his voice trailed away and then the crackle of the fire swallowed it completely.

Until that night that ended us, he meant.

"You shouldn't have underestimated my resolve when I gave you my ultimatum," I said. "I told you we would be done if you went through with what you wanted."

He grabbed a log and threw it onto the fire. A burst of sparks curled into the air.

"No," he said.

"No?"

"It wasn't your resolve I underestimated," he said. "It was myself with how far I had pushed you."

Pushed you.

How nicely phrased. Spoken like a true diplomat.

"You mean you didn't notice you were slowly killing me? I drenched my hands in blood to satisfy you."

He hoarded the souls of the slain for Valhalla like a dragon hoarded treasure. At the time, I thought it only a grisly eccentricity, a brutal fixation, but I later learned the true reason—he was gathering an army for Ragnarok.

The worst part was I helped him. Sourcing, retrieving, ensuring...Whatever he wished, because I would do anything for him. I would shatter myself into pieces if it meant his happiness, and he knew it.

And when he set his eyes on King Aun's ten sons...Again, I did as he asked. I kept returning to the king to tell him another sacrifice to Odin was needed to lift the famine cursing his lands. Nine times I went to that man to tell him to hang another son and spill their blood.

Until it came to the final son. A child.

I refused Odin. I would not see a child slaughtered to fulfill some twisted necessity. I gave him a choice, one that should have been the simplest for him to make because he had promised me to always choose our love. *I trusted him.*

It was the boy, or me.

Memories kicked me back, and my kneecaps prickled where they had struck the flagstones when I had collapsed, watching him walk away and out the door. Choosing. *Wasn't I enough?* My own words echoed in my ears, screaming how I hated him and begging him to come back. *Please come back. Let me be enough.* I just wanted him to come back. He would come back. There was still hope he might change his mind...

He promised me.

The snap of the boy's neck rang through that field. Telling me what I always knew.

I was not enough.

But the choice was made.

The thing was done.

And so were we.

"You just stood there and watched me burn into ashes," I whispered. "I loved you, Odin. And still...you just let me burn."

I stared out into the darkness, over the field of sunflowers rippling like waves on a lake.

He remained silent.

Good. I wanted him to hear every word.

"You were the first person I allowed myself to trust in eons. Even when everyone warned me not to trust you. Warned me that one day I'd be left with scars on my back from your knife. I told them they were wrong. Because I had what they didn't. I had your love."

He swallowed and seemed to grow smaller.

"You say the gods have no mercy," I said. "And maybe that's the reason I never fit in with the rest of you, because I do. I have a heart, and I knew if I returned to you after you took that small life, my heart would have become as black as all of yours."

Odin met my eyes and my insides smoldered with all his betrayals. With all of the hopes we once shared.

"Please understand," he said.

I scoffed.

"What is there to understand?" I said. "I believed you when you told me that if I came with you to Asgard we would make a better world together. I never wanted a world built on taking innocent lives."

"I couldn't let you ever know the true reason why I needed them all for Valhalla," he said. "I couldn't..."

"You could have kept your promise to me, Odin," I said. "You could have kept it! Instead all you did was teach me what I should have known all along. That trust is for children."

"I...I..." He exhaled and nodded. "Gods, I regret that day."

"And I regret that day we met on the bank of the Ifingr," I snapped. "Knowing what you knew, you should have left me in Jotunheim. Then, I never would have ended up bound in that cave. Ragnarok wouldn't have happened with that sludge consuming Sigyn. And we both wouldn't be here now hating each other."

He pressed his hands against his brow.

"I gave my body to save you from that cave," he said. "I gave my body to have a life with you. I loved you more than I ever loved anyone, and instead...All this horror is my fault."

He slid his right hand down the side of his face and rubbed the red band of twisted flesh circling his throat—the scar he had told me was from a fight with a frost giant in the North.

I remembered when he had returned to me in Jotunheim with that ring of red lesions and bruises around his neck. How my stomach had dropped to my feet at the sight of him, battered and mutilated. How I had reached out and gently touched the puncture wound on his right side, blood soaking his tunic.

My throat dried.

I later learned that the scar was from the noose he had swung from for nine days on Yggdrasil's branches. The wound from his own spear. All this suffering to have a life with me.

"I often imagined killing that frost giant," I said. "I wanted to break their spine for what they did to you. If only you had told me the truth, maybe we could have spared ourselves all this heartache?"

He rubbed his hands together, squeezing his thumbs, his palms, his knuckles.

"Told you what? About your destiny? You know that wasn't possible." He gripped his side where the spear had entered. "The tree promised me a solution—our blood oath. I still remember how cold I was as my life drained out of me, as my life trickled from my wound and sank into Yggdrasil's roots as a sacrifice. My lungs burned from suffocation. I was so thirsty. But..."

"But?"

He met my gaze again, his eye piercing and blue and vivid.

"I thought only of you."

My throat tightened and I massaged my arm where the scar of that blood oath we made still remained cut into my skin. The oath Yggdrasil told him to make to avoid our fates. The oath Yggdrasil told him to make so we could have our love.

He kept holding my gaze, and after all this time, there was still something profound in the way he looked at me—something searching and riddled with worry. And after all this time, I still wanted to chase that worry away, and let him know it would be alright.

I felt myself slacken, as if my entire body sighed and relaxed into the raw tragedy of it all.

The fire spit and cinders spiraled into the inky black.

An owl hooted within the whispers of oak leaves fluttering on the trees.

"You were right," he said. "About what you said to me in the stables before we left on this journey. I did break far more to you and far earlier than you ever did our blood oath. And if I had one wish to make..." His voice lowered, almost as soft as the chirr of crickets. "I'd wish I wasn't a coward."

My shoulders slumped further. I shook my head.

"Coward?" I said. "You aren't a coward. The battles I've seen you fight..."

He snorted and looked back into the fire, the lines of his face stiffening.

"I offered up myself to Yggdrasil so we could be together, only to break the promise I made you in the end," he spat. "All because I was terrified of my fate in Ragnarok—of true death. I did whatever it took to push off my end a little longer. Plucked out my own eye. Sacrificed a child." His voice cracked. "Don't you see? My fear of death was greater than my love for you, and I hate myself for it."

That owl hooted again, the tone eerie and sharp, as if confirming all of Odin's dread.

"But you," he said. "You accepted a fate worse than death for Sigyn without a second thought. And when that snake was placed over your head, you didn't look away, you didn't beg. You stared into its eyes, into your destiny, and you laughed, and...I could never be that brave."

Odin looked out over the field of sunflowers, and his jaw firmed as if seeing some terrible vision he'd give anything to look away from.

"I've tried so hard to be strong for you," he said. "But my fear always wins, and I hate who my fear has made me become. I don't want to be this monster, and..." He sneered and scorn hardened his expression. "And traitors like me never win. My cowardice lost me everything. I lost you. *Gods*. I tried to love you as you needed, Loki. I tried. I just wanted..."

He crumpled in on himself and laid his face in his hands and wept bitterly.

"I just wanted to be yours."

I remained still, silent, watching him fall to pieces. I wanted to desert him to the night, to walk away and let him break alone as he had let me break alone in that room, forsaken. Beaten. It would only be fair.

But whatever shifted in me wouldn't allow it.

He had been my friend, and my entire life, after I left Jotunheim.

I stood slowly and walked to him. He pressed his face harder in his hands as I knelt before him and dragged him down with me, having his knees sink into the grass.

Gently, I grasped his wrists and pulled them away from his face. He tried to turn away, but I wouldn't let him.

"Look at me," I said.

He obeyed and peered into my eyes as tears streamed down his face. A thousand lifetimes, some good, more bad, bled from him. Odin was a man in his prime, rugged and beautiful, but here in the darkness, defeated by truth, I saw how ancient and withered he truly was. How very old.

I shoved my thumb beneath the strap of his eyepatch and slid it off his head and tossed it aside. His good eye was red with tears, and the other...

I took a clean cloth.

"No," he said.

"Let me do this."

I softly pressed the cloth against his skin. An invisible hand gripped my heart and squeezed as I blotted the wet away from around the empty socket. What pain had he suffered when he had gouged it out and gave it to Golda to learn of Ragnarok? How many sacrifices had he made to stop his fate, and my own?

"A coward wouldn't sacrifice their own body for a chance at love."

"Loki..."

"A coward wouldn't try at all."

"I'm sorry for breaking my promise to you," he said. "I'm sorry I chose to give us away...I wanted forever with you, and...I'm sorry. For all of it."

I stared into his gaze, into the man who I had once loved. The man who had given everything for me, all for a love we had both wanted. All for a love he had turned into rust until there was no salvaging the remnants from the decay.

We were never meant to have forever.

"Loki, I'm so sorry."

I slid my hands behind his neck, wanting him to calm.

Wanting him to know it would be alright.

I bent forward and kissed his forehead, the salt from his skin filling my breath. He placed his hands on my shoulders, barely touching me. Maybe not touching me at all.

"I'm so sorry," he whispered.

I gathered him in my arms and pressed him against my chest, cradling him as he shuddered with each breath he took. With each cry he let out. I laid my chin on the top of his head and squeezed him tighter.

I just wanted him to know it would be alright.

"I'm sorry, too."

27

TURN BACK THE CLOCK

Jotunheim

The Ironwood Forest

I caught only glimpses of Angrboda's fortress through the twisting branches of the pine trees blanketing the hills. The branches thickened and tangled tighter together the farther we rode.

"The dungeons should offer the strongest protection for you to perform your spell to strip Surtr from Sigyn," I said. "And then I'll entomb that sludge into the amulet."

My heart burned having Sigyn's name fall from my lips again. Another mile through this mud and forest and I'd get to hold her, kiss her, and remove Surtr from her veins so we could start our life together.

We were going to save her, and I'd finally have the future with her I always wanted.

Odin coughed in his way that made my shoulders drop. Droplets of dew clung to his hair and beard from the delightful mixture of damp and cold. Typical Jotunheim.

"What?" I shoved arms of pine packed with needles out of my way. I grimaced at the sap left sticking to my fingers.

"I can't perform a spell like that here."

I wiped the sap off on my trousers, although the pads of my fingers remained tacky. Great. Forests were always a delight.

"Quite right. Much too musty and blood stained. You feel the impaling fields a better choice? The crisp air could be nice and—"

He ducked beneath a branch crooked with knots and lumps and bark ragged enough to scrape skin.

"You realize where this must happen."

Don't say it.

"As Vigridr is still heaped with corpses from Ragnarok, Yggdrasil is the only other realm that can withstand the exposure of such raw power."

Damn.

I tightened my grip on my reins.

"But men don't survive who visit the tree's branches," I said.

"You think I don't know that?" A hint of panic tightened his words, and he rubbed his neck.

No, of course he knew. More than anyone. At that moment, I was struck by his willingness to go to Yggdrasil at all. He understood from the start this is where our journey would end, and still he agreed to come.

"Thankfully." He cleared his throat. "We won't be needing to use Yggdrasil's branches, but it won't make what we are about to do any less treacherous. I'm not eager to return, but it's our only option."

Yggdrasil stood outside of space and time, on the edge of a universe while simultaneously a universe of its own. One could lose themselves staring at its leaves for eons, or take one errant step and fall between pockets of dimensions and...I really wasn't in the mood for the possibility of being exploded into a million pieces and scattered over the surface of a million suns.

No, Yggdrasil was a place best avoided unless absolutely necessary.

I suppose this was just one of those times.

"You could have dropped this delightful nugget of information earlier," I said.

He snorted.

"And deal with your sour mood the entire trip because of it? I spared myself that joy."

Fair.

A tall man walked towards us along the muddy path, his hands shoved in a long coat that billowed around his legs. The coiling branches behind him made him appear like a spider in a web. I squinted to make him out.

His red hair stuck to his sharp cheekbones, wet with mist.

My every muscle stiffened with recognition.

"You." Odin stopped his horse.

I tugged back my reins and pushed into the saddle, forcing Ylva to a halt, although I wanted to kick her into a gallop and crush Býleistr beneath her hooves. I smiled, imagining the *pop* of his skull cracking.

"Why is that always what people say when they first see me?" Bly said. "And here I thought you and I got along so well. Did that last job I do for you mean so little?"

I snapped my gaze onto Odin, who shifted in his saddle.

"What job?" I crossed my arms.

"Nothing."

My expression flattened.

"You mean you engaged his services when I expressly told you how much I hate him?"

Odin pinched the bridge of his nose and sighed.

"You were in one of your moods," he said. "And Býleistr is the best when it comes to digging up dirt. How else was I supposed to get the Elvish ambassador to negotiate with Asgard? That tentacle thing was indispensable knowledge."

Bly's laughter broke through our bickering.

"You always were a fine pair," Bly said. "Eternally squawking like a couple of old hags."

How quickly could I cram a glob of sap into his hair?

I groaned and swung my leg over my saddle and dismounted my

horse, hating how my bones creaked as my feet struck the ground. I slid in the mud as I walked to him.

His nose wrinkled.

"You look like shit," he said. "Ugh. Smell like it, too."

My left eye twitched.

"What are you doing out here, Bly?" I said, forcing away thoughts of rubbing the sap still on my fingers onto his face.

He shrugged, keeping his hands jammed inside his pockets.

"Just walking the grounds," he said. "Angrboda keeps saying the fresh air will do my health good, or some excuse like that to keep me away from Sigyn."

A small part of me relaxed. Good. She did what she promised me. I'd have to thank her later.

"Loki, hurry this up, we need to go." Clouds of hot breath rolled out of Odin's mouth.

Bly stepped aside and opened his arm out towards the fortress.

"Walk back with me to the house?" he said. "And maybe we can tie up loose ends?"

His green eyes lit with mocking laughter.

And the tension that had gripped my every muscle since leaving Jotunheim returned.

"Loose ends?" Odin asked.

"Wait here with the horses." I adjusted my satchel where the golden apple remained inside.

"By the way, Odin," Bly said. "If I could make a recommendation. Instead of waiting around for gods know what reason, I'd scurry on back home to Asgard. Or else things are only going to get worse for you there, from what whispers I hear."

Odin's brow knit together.

"And what whispers are these?" Odin said.

"Hugin and Munin must really be falling down on the job if you don't know what's being planned," he said.

Hugin and Munin had been oddly absent. But I couldn't give a rat's ass. Not now.

"Come on," I snapped at Bly, hiking towards the fortress.

"Ta!" Bly waved to Odin with a token smile that turned my stomach. Gods. I hated if that's how I really looked when I was too pleased with myself.

The clouds darkened above the tree canopy and the scent of rain saturated the air, making every breath heavy and damp.

Bly removed his hands from his pockets and held them behind his back as we walked down the road in silence, dodging puddles and squelching through the sludge.

I couldn't shake the sensation of walking towards the gallows.

"Do you have it?" His voice dripped honey.

We were feet from the entrance of the house.

I bounced my gaze across the grounds, making sure no one sauntered about. I didn't want anyone to see what they would try to steal. The prospect of immortality brought out the worst in a soul, and more than one god had been cut down by those wanting to take such a precious item.

I opened my satchel and shoved my hand inside and pulled out the apple. Bly's eyes widened, scanning the gold skin that gleamed in the gray light as I pressed it into his hand.

"I don't want to see you for another five millennia," I said.

He chuckled and met my eyes and stepped closer to me, studying my face.

"Your pallor," he said. "I've never seen you without that signature sparkle of yours. How tired you look. How beaten." He tossed the apple into the air and caught it again. "This must have been grueling to get."

He squeezed the peel.

Grueling didn't even begin to describe it.

"As a matter of fact—"

The flesh split and he crushed the apple in his fist. Juice streamed down his fingers and pieces fell into the mud at our feet.

I thought he reached into my gut and tore out my intestines.

"What have you done?" I fell to my knees and tried to gather the broken apple. My fingers trembled.

"Finishing what I was paid to do," he said.

He ground the rest of the fruit into pulp with his heel.

I looked up at him, into his face ripe with glee and retribution.

"We had a deal!"

He laughed and flung the juice off his fingers, splatting it into my eyes and across my face.

"But see, there's the rub. My deal isn't with you. It never was." He wiped the remaining juice from his hands onto his trousers. "I was hired to punish you by, well...my benefactor wanted me to hurt you deep. For me to take everything you shouldn't have been given, and now..."

His lips twisted into a smile. My entire body shook as I rubbed the sting of the juice out of my eyes.

I saw now.

There had never been a chance.

"This entire thing has been you torturing me from the beginning?" I said.

"Pretty much," he said. "It was more fun than I thought, in fact—"

I stood and grabbed him by his coat and shoved his face against mine.

"Oh, you are angry!" he rasped.

"Who hired you to do this? Tell me."

His smile only unrolled further, barbed with demons.

"It was admirable how Sigyn tried to defend you. Admirable, but disgusting. You really have her twisted around your finger to have her trust you," he said. "But, once I showed her the letter—"

Letter.

Sigyn.

The world spun, reeled. Or was it fragmenting beneath my feet?

"Did she remove the illusion?" I shouted.

"I'll never understand how you can sleep at night."

"Did she remove it?"

"You don't deserve to be loved."

I punched him across the face, cartilage smacking against my knuckles, and pain shooting up my fist, radiating through every fine bone.

He kept his footing, that wicked smile remaining frozen on his face, even though blood coated his teeth. He spat out blood onto the ground and wiped his mouth with his sleeve.

"You'll have to find out, won't you?" he said.

I stepped back, and I ran.

I ran through the oak doors.

I ran down whitewashed halls.

I ran past crackling hearths, along corridors of inlaid tiles, rooms, and rooms, and rooms, and...

I burst through the door of Sigyn's quarters.

Warm.

Bright.

Empty.

My breaths quickened as I hurried across the patchwork of sheepskin rugs. Where was that infernal letter?

My heart hammered against my ribs as I tore off the layers of bedding, searched the wardrobe, riffled through scattered papers on her desk.

The apple was supposed to be enough.

My breath stuck in my throat. On a chair in the corner by the fireplace laid the letter.

Warm relief coursed between my shoulders. I snatched the letter, and I held it for seconds, minutes, hours, I don't know, as a thousand choices swarmed in my head.

No.

One choice.

I turned and faced the fireplace, the fire licking between the logs offering me an escape.

A solution.

I walked to the fireplace and knelt by the crackling embers, each snap a way out. A way to keep her.

Stretching out my arm, I held the letter over the spitting flames.

I can't lose her.

The top edge of the paper seared, and a molten line browned the paper in a curl as flames ate the letter and every incriminating stroke of ink and...

My heart, my entire body, seized into stone. I couldn't breathe.

The handwriting wasn't Simon's, it was mine.

Sigyn had already removed the illusion. It was too late.

You already have lost her.

The door hinges creaked behind me and someone entered the room.

"It's true then," Sigyn said.

28

INTO ASHES

"I 've been considering what could have possibly caused you to take Simon's life," Sigyn said, her voice slow and measured.

My blood chilled until I thought it froze.

Removing the letter from the fire, I stood and faced her. She shut the door behind her. I clutched the letter tighter, crumpling the paper in my grip.

"I know who my brother was. A cheat and a cutthroat. And I know who you are—or, at least I thought I did," she said. "I trusted something had to have motivated you to have done such a horrifying thing. Maybe he threatened you. Maybe he attacked you. Simon would have done that. I gave you the benefit of the doubt, and that you'd tell me the reason when you returned. I was sure of it."

Her gaze fell to the half burnt letter crushed in my hands. She scoffed and peeled the letter out of my fingers and stared at the destruction. At the evidence that I had no intention of ever telling her.

"But why would you tell me, when you've not once told me anything beneath the surface?" she said. "Not about Býleistr's existence. Not about your deeper connection with Odin. You will always keep everything hidden from me, won't you?" She pushed her words through the start of tears. "You will always force my head under water and watch me suffocate as I drown in your lies."

"Sigyn...I..."

My voice died in my mouth as she walked to the leaded window and stared out, holding the note at her hip. Rain clicked against the glass, and gray light washed out the greens of her wool skirts and fingerless knit gloves she kept pulled to her elbows.

She fiddled with the paper and I cocked my head slightly noticing the black crescent moons of the infection beneath her nails—Surtr.

But I didn't dare move towards her.

I didn't dare draw in a breath even though I wanted to ask her how much more the infection had spread in my absence.

"I keep seeing your face and his, over and over," she said. "I see you standing over his body. His blood on your hands. Gods I could scream and tear you in two. Why did you do it?"

Her calm wavered and my back broke out in a sweat.

She scratched at the thick cowl wrapped around her neck, and the scent of sulfur mingled with the rosemary in her hair she wore fastened back with bone pins. Stronger than when I had left her, as if Surtr was gaining the upper hand within her.

She turned and met my gaze, and the pain and anger bleeding from her eyes nearly destroyed me.

"Tell me why," she said.

My panic spiked.

I wanted to fall to my knees and beg her forgiveness, but this was a brick wall I couldn't scramble over or around. I couldn't escape. There was only facing the fact of what was.

"I...I never meant..."

A crack of dry laughter.

"What? You never meant for me to know? Isn't *that* what you mean to say?"

I parted my lips to speak and pressed them closed again as anything worth speaking turned as hollow as brittle bones.

"So that's it, then?" she said. "No exquisite defense? No intricate apologies for taking my brother's life? No explanations?"

Silence thickened between us, suffocating and damning. Final.

Sigyn smacked the letter onto the side table and marched to me and grasped my arm.

"You bastard!" She dug her fingers into me. "Say something!"

"And what would you have me say? Your mind is obviously made."

I wrenched free.

She grabbed me again and tugged me against her, keeping her gaze burrowing into mine.

"Be honest with me for once in your damn life and tell me why you killed Simon?"

I pushed her off me and tried to get some distance. She blocked my path. She walked towards me, each step forcing me to take a step back until my back hit the wall.

Or perhaps her mind was not made.

"Alright," I said. "Let me explain…"

She hit my shoulder.

"You betrayed me in the worst possible way." She struck my chest.

"Please stop. Let me speak."

Locks of her hair fell out of her pins and flew wild around her face with each strike.

"Simon did not deserve your judgement!" she said. "He deserved to be given a chance, and you took that chance from him."

He deserved?

My anger lit now, burning away the panic.

"Sigyn. No. You don't understand."

"He could have changed," she continued to shout. "He could have become more, had you allowed him—"

That cracked something even deeper inside of me. This was one accusation I would not permit.

"Had I allowed him?" I pushed her away.

Heat filled my chest and blood pounded in my temples.

I swung at a vase sitting on top of a table, sending it crashing to the ground. Porcelain exploded and shards and water and wild-flowers burst across the floorboards.

"HAD I ALLOWED HIM?"

She shook her head and looked at me as if I were a beast. Perhaps, because I was.

"I'm done with you," she whispered.

She walked towards the door and opened the latch. I slapped my palm against the woodgrain and shut the door with a bang and grabbed her upper arm. She wasn't going anywhere. She would get her honesty.

"You want me to be honest?" I pulled her against my chest, forcing her to face me. "How can I be honest when you aren't even honest with yourself about your precious Simon? You once even admitted to me long ago he was a fraud and a con. But I see accepting he didn't care for you is still one truth too far? You keep living in lies."

She tried to yank back while still continuing to glare daggers sharper than needles into me.

"The only lies are yours." Her breath hit my face, hot and quick.

Both our tempers wanted to claw the other to shreds.

Fine. She wanted me to tell her why. And so I would.

I drew her in even closer.

"You dare—" she pressed through tight teeth.

"Quiet! Now you will listen to me speak. Yes. Simon came home the night of your father's passing," I said. "He was looking for you. He found me first. He wanted money."

"And?" She shoved me off her. "He always asked for money. I would have given him a few francs and sent him on his way, but you—"

She shoved me back again.

And again, I caught hold of her arm and made her face me. I wouldn't let her turn away.

"He didn't come for a few francs," I said. "He spoke to me of his mounting debts. Of dangerous men trying to find him. He came to take your mother's necklace from you to sell and pay off what he owed."

Her muscles tightened beneath my grip.

"He what? Mother's necklace?" she barely whispered.

She traced small circles on her chest where the necklace her mother had given her had always rested. It had meant everything to Sigyn.

"Simon was going to use the money to pay off some cur who was worse than Bertolf. Remember him? The man who tried to cut off your nose and ears and then gouge out your eyes?" My throat burned thinking of how close that had come to happening. "The man who burned your print shop all because of your brother."

Her breaths deepened and her face reddened with outrage, as if she wanted nothing more than to lance me with spears.

"And you killed Simon over this?" she said. "You could have found another way."

She twisted out of my grasp.

"I did try to find another way," I said. "And I gave him that chance you claim I took from him."

She moved her face even closer to mine. Our noses grazed.

"I told him to leave Basel," I said. "To leave you alone and take his troubles with him to Italy. That's the chance I gave him, Sigyn. Freedom. A fresh start. Deliverance. And he ground it all beneath his boot heel in what he replied to me."

"And what did he reply?" She looked into my eyes. Daring me.

I held her gaze, refusing to back down. Refusing to give one inch.

"He said he was going to force you to go with him to Naples," I said. "He was going to force you to sell your father's print shop. He was going to force you into chains and exploit you and all you had, even if it meant costing you your life. Simon would see you strung up on a tree as long as it benefitted him. He had no worry for your well being, and my decision was made."

"Rubbish," she said. "Simon loved me. He...I was his sister. He wouldn't have forced me to do anything and..." She exhaled. "And had he known what Bertolf did, he wouldn't have stood for it."

My heart broke for her.

"But Simon did know."

"That's impossible. How—"

"Because I told him," I said. "I told him what Bertolf had attempted with mutilating your face."

"Well, then. I'm sure you saw how much that shook him—"

I hated telling her this.

"No, Sigyn. He didn't care," I said. "He said it was your choice to protect him. *Better her than me.* He took none of the blame for the jeopardy he placed you within. He took no responsibility. Do you understand? He abused you. He would see you hurt or dead."

Her gaze softened for a second. Maybe two.

"He said that? That it was my choice?"

My muscles relaxed and I was back in that room with Simon. I had pinched his nose shut and clapped my hand over his mouth, strangling the air out of him. It was a decision I didn't want to make, but there was no other recourse. Why couldn't she understand? This wasn't easy for me, either. But I did it to save her life.

"He was willing to sacrifice you, Sigyn. To let others come after you. To lose you everything, including your life," I said. "You were expendable to him. And I saw, then. There was no choice but one, because you weren't expendable to me. Simon didn't love you, but I did and I wouldn't let you die at his hands."

I truly hadn't wanted to kill him. I had taken many lives, but his was one of the few that I remembered. That stuck with me in vivid detail. I hated how I felt his windpipe crush in the crook of my elbow. How he had wheezed, clawed, and thrashed. How he had fought for his life. He wanted to live. To survive. And I had squeezed tighter.

Sigyn sat on the bed and sank into the layers of mattresses as realization imbued in her features along with sorrow.

"But he might still have changed." She spoke the words softly, as if each were a prayer.

He might have, which was the tragedy.

"You'd be dead before that day came," I said, which was the truth.

"My sins are great and many Sigyn, but killing your brother is one decision I stand by," I said. "I take no pleasure in the pain I've caused you. I take no pleasure in having taken his life, but don't you see? It was your survival, or his."

Her shoulders dropped and her fists uncurled.

She hunched over and laid her face into her hands. Her body shuddered with grief and all I could do was watch. We remained locked in this way, lost in the brutal torment of it all for minutes that seemed to march on without end.

She lifted her face from her hands, pain and heartache flushing her cheeks.

"I know," she said. "I know he would have brought harm to me. He already had, more than once, but he was still my brother. I wished so greatly for him. I wished...I was always wishing. And I'm tired of constantly wishing."

She looked at me, searching me like I was someone who couldn't see their own nose.

"When I learned what you did..." She tugged again at her cowl, and a fresh wave of sulfur filled the air. "I'm ashamed of myself now, but I was so full of anger and hurt and...I almost gave into the darkness. Into Surtr."

She stood off the bed and unraveled her cowl and slipped it over her head.

And with it another wave of sulfur, and I knew.

And my guts twisted into knots.

I stepped towards her and hovered my hand over her chest, now half charred and pulsing with the infection. The black spread up the right side of her neck, small veins curling beneath her jawline, and drenched her right shoulder in coal.

Pins jabbed the back of my throat.

"I opened my mouth to finish it and..." She exhaled. "I don't want this."

"I know."

She stared into my eyes.

"No," she said. "No, you don't know. I don't want *us*. This is about honesty. And I don't want a relationship that lacks trust. The reason I didn't give into Surtr was because of one single hope I still clung to—

that if you had done this, and you knew Bly had that letter, that you would tell me the truth when you returned." She rubbed her mouth. "I believed in you, and you poisoned my belief when you put that letter in the fire."

Fractures split into my heart. My eyes burned with tears and my vision blurred.

"You would have left me."

"Is that really what you think? After all we've been through. All the hurt. All the love. Do you really feel I'd give all we have away?" she said. "I can understand the truth. I am capable of that, Loki."

"I couldn't take any chance of losing you," I rasped. "I couldn't bear to see you turn on your heel and leave like everyone else I've ever...*please*."

Tears coursed down my cheeks, the same as hers that fell from eyes coated in quivering wet.

"You burning that letter was you walking out on our relationship, not me," she said.

I reached out for her, needing to touch her, to beg her to take me back. *Please take me back.* My heart split deep into my roots, into a dark place I never wanted to feel again.

She stepped away, leaving my hand hovering.

She wiped her eyes and wrapped her cowl around her neck, positioning it so it hid any spot of blackened purple. She walked to the door and placed her hand on the latch.

I remained planted. Incapable of moving. Incapable of anything but pleading and wishing and enduring watching all of my hopes disintegrate into ash.

"I'd sacrifice anything to keep you. Please. Don't—" Emotion choked my words as I drowned in the fiercest fight for my life. "—don't go."

"I know you would sacrifice anything," she said. "Because you sacrificed my faith in you by choosing to keep me in the dark. You don't trust me. And after this, I can't ever trust you."

Those words skinned me alive.

She pressed the latch open and walked out, leaving me alone in that room, the cold and the bitterness and the inability to take it all back leaving me in fragments.

I sat on the sheepskin rug. Or did I collapse? What did it matter? I pressed my face, wet and hot with tears, into my palms.

We were over.

And this time...this time I had no one to blame but myself. I broke us.

Sigyn was right about me. I didn't trust her, no matter how much I lied to myself that I did.

I felt something slip out of my pocket. A delicate *clink* and roll of metal against wood stirred me from the beasts and monsters cutting me into ribbons in my head. I lifted my gaze from my hands.

Sigyn's gold ring rolled across the floorboards and twirled until it fell flat and still and silent.

I blinked through the sear of my tears and reached out, picking the ring up from the floor.

Our future.

Did you really think you could have a happily ever after? You don't deserve one.

For the first time, I believed it.

29

LOVE IS

SIGYN

"Didn't I tell you?" Surtr said. "Loki is three-day-old fish, only fit for the bin. Now maybe you'll finally believe me."

I scratched my burning skin and tugged at my cowl as I stormed down the stairs towards the healer's room. Flinging open the door, I banged it closed behind me, and marched across the flagstones, nearly tangling myself in the bundles of lavender hanging to dry from the rafters.

Stopping in the middle of the room, I shut my eyes.

And I screamed.

Screamed from the betrayal shredding my insides.

Screamed from the loss of my brother.

Screamed from the loss of Loki, and the life we were supposed to have together. All because he chose to destroy any chance of us making it.

I believed the castle we had built together was made from rock. But all this time, it was only ever a castle made from sand on a shore battered by waves.

That was the cruelest trick of all. I loved him more than the air in my lungs, and I could not be with him, because every promise would only ever be an illusion.

Surtr groaned.

"Feel better now?" Surtr said. "I never thought you were the melodramatic type."

My stomach heaved as I pulled out a chair and sat. I propped my elbows on the table and cradled my head in my hands and wept, letting my tears splash and bead on the freshly oiled wood grain.

I didn't want to cry. I didn't want to be so broken into pieces.

I didn't want any of this constant battle.

Surtr sauntered behind me like a phantom, a looming shadow hungering to envelope me in an embrace.

"I was disappointed when you refused to accept your new role last time we chatted," he said. "But now I see you needed this closure. It's understandable. At least you will leave Loki now. I mean, how can you not?"

Every breath stung, and I hated how I shivered trying to stay knit together, though everything in me wanted to unravel and liquify and sink into the earth.

My mind raced through my thoughts. Through images and clips and words.

How can I be honest when you aren't even honest with yourself about your precious Simon?

I pressed my hands against my ears, wanting Loki's voice to stop blaring in my mind. Wanting him to shut up so I could remain righteous in my anger.

Simon may have changed someday.

You'd be dead before that day came.

His words kept pulsing in my mind, and I knew the truth they carried in my marrow I wished I could scratch out.

No. Surely Simon cared for me. Deep down. Somewhere. He had to. He was my brother...

I leaned back in the chair, the wood popping, and I traced the spot on my chest where my mother's necklace used to hang. I never took it off and...and the print shop. My life in Basel. Simon was going to take it all from me.

Simon was going to take everything.

My mind continued to toss back and forth as I argued with myself.

No. He wouldn't. He wouldn't have done that. When it came to it, he would have done the right thing. He would have chosen me...

I laughed through my tears and it rolled through the phlegm in the back of my throat.

No, he'd never choose me. And I knew it, in the depths of my core, in a place I rarely visited...I knew.

Simon would have chosen himself. He always did. Because he was a snake.

A snake who always depended on his "reliable little sister," as he had called me, to give him what he wanted. To provide what he needed.

My dear, reliable little sister, always looking out for me.

My dear, reliable little sister, always keeping those bastards guessing.

My dear, reliable little sister, always who I can count on in a pinch.

Always and always and always. Needing me, *using* me, one minute and throwing me beneath a wagon wheel the next to break.

He had already taken so much from me before. Why would this time have been any different?

A consensus waited for me on the horizon. One I couldn't believe I was reaching with myself.

"Wait, you are leaving Loki, aren't you?" Surtr said. "Because I can't imagine you'd do something so stupid as stay with him after this. You can't trust Loki. You never could. This proves it."

That letter from Simon saying he was joining the military had given me hope. The same hope that sparked in me any time he told me he was finally getting his life together. That he had entered a new profession he claimed legitimate.

They always sounded legitimate in the beginning.

But deep down, it was always me wishing rather than believing him sincere.

I wept harder. Uncontrollably.

It was true.

Simon wouldn't have blinked twice in taking it all away from me. He would have taken everything, and he would have let me die in the process.

And in the end...

Complete realization came.

It all fell on me like bricks.

The blunt, painful, horrid truth.

Simon didn't care about me.

He didn't love me as I loved him.

Simon had made his choice. And his choice was himself. As it always was, and always would have been.

And if Loki hadn't protected me...

I shuddered, searching myself.

Loki was right. I would have died, letting out my last breath for Simon, while still hoping...

Forever hoping.

Because I couldn't turn my back on my brother. I couldn't turn my back on my brother, even though he saw me as nothing but dispensable.

Surtr groaned and walked next to me.

"Enough of this mewling," he said. "You are really trying my patience, Sigyn."

Surtr laid his hand on my shoulder and squeezed. My flesh sizzled, and I jumped. I turned and met his violet eyes and smile edged with razors.

Eagerness lit Surtr's entire expression.

"I'm sure the fact you can feel me touch you now is a shock," he said. "I'm growing stronger, and you're growing weaker, you see. You keep acting like there's something else. Something left. But there's nothing for you anymore except me. Nothing but the darkness."

I chilled to my bones.

The hinges of the door creaked.

Surtr's hand vanished from my shoulder as I turned and faced Angrboda walking in through the door.

My muscles turned rigid, everything in me wishing she'd just go. I couldn't take much more.

"You are going to chip a tooth if you keep grinding them like that," Angrboda said.

"I really want to be alone." I wiped my eyes and tried to suck my emotion back in and cram it down into my depths.

She ignored me and strolled about the room, gazing at the newly filled bottles of herbs and jars of ointments in the cabinet. She ran a finger along one of the cleaned shelves lined with books and minerals.

"No more dust," she said. "No more rats. No more cobwebs. Marvelous! I never thought I'd see it brought back to life."

I nodded stiffly, reminding myself my anger was at Loki and not at her. But I still wanted her to go. The last thing I needed was a brawl with her when I inevitably lost it. I did not want to top this day with scratch marks and knife wounds.

Another wave of emotion tingled the length of my spine, my throat, my eyes.

"Thank you, now if you excuse me—" I stood, the chair scraping the flagstones.

"Loki is a frustrating being to understand." She picked up a vial of oregano oil from the desk and sloshed it gently.

Gods.

I saw where this was headed. The last thing I needed was relationship advice. Especially from her.

"I don't know what you're talking about." I wiped away the emotion running out of my nose.

She rolled her eyes and placed the vial back with the others.

"Please, I heard everything with all that screaming," she said. "That was my mother's three thousand year old porcelain vase that got shattered."

Embarrassment flushed my cheeks.

"I'm sorry," I said.

She waved my worry away and walked to the end of the table, and uncorked a bottle of claret.

"It's quite alright," she said, pouring an arc of wine into a pewter goblet. "Although, I would have preferred if it had been smashed against Loki's head rather than the floor."

I nodded. I would have preferred that, too.

She handed me the goblet, and I sat back in my chair.

"I think you need that."

I think she was right. I took a large swig and swallowed, the heat immediately prickling through my body and into my fingertips. I hoped she had a second bottle nearby. Because I'd require that as well.

"Since you heard, then you know why I need some time to myself." I took a second large swallow. "To consider...To process—it's over between us, you see."

"Over?"

She refilled the goblet. I knew I liked her. This was the sort of care I needed from a person.

"How can we possibly go on after this? After—"

She put the bottle on the table and sat in the chair opposite me. The chair creaked as she leaned forward and laced her fingers together on the table. The usual fierceness in her gray eyes that always warned you to stay ten feet away melted into concern. Understanding.

"Don't you think you're being a little unfair to him?"

I choked on the claret, wine burning inside my nostrils.

"Unfair?" I wiped my mouth on my sleeve. "I don't feel I'm overreacting to finding out he killed my own blood, and then not trusting me to understand all that surrounded it."

She chuckled and reclined in her chair. She grasped the claret and took a slug directly out of the bottle.

"You are still so human, aren't you?" she said. "If I stopped talking to everyone who killed one of my kin, I'd have no one left to gossip with."

I stared at the wood, tracing the ripples in the grain with my fingernail. I shook my head.

"You don't understand. I sometimes feel like Loki and I are two people driven together that never stood a chance. Look at us. Chaos and fidelity. We were made to fall apart."

She sighed and leaned forward again. She grasped my hands and squeezed. Heartache bit the back of my throat again. Tears welled in my eyes.

"Look at me," she said.

I obeyed, despising every tear that slipped over the edges of my eyelids.

"You are valid to feel hurt and betrayed by what he did, and his usual lack of trust, but..."

"But what?"

She smiled softly and pressed her thumbs into the top of my hands.

"You expect the world from a mouse."

I scoffed and pulled out of her grasp.

"I can't believe you are defending him."

She tapped her nails on the table, and her eyes grew distant, as if she stared off into that place I dared not ask her about.

"Loki wasn't always the God of Lies," she said. "Mischief? Sure. Chaos? Definitely. But, the lies...the lies came later to protect a broken heart that repeatedly got ground into pulp. And then Odin chewed up and spit out what remained of him."

Angrboda paused for a heartbeat, only the crackle of the fire filling the silence.

"Loki is a delicate soul," she whispered. "And to stop the pain, he buried himself behind walls of stone."

I hated that twinge of pity I felt in the roots of my heart for him, when all I wanted to feel was resentment. His face came alive in my mind along with those green eyes of his—always full of laughter that never could hide all the sorrow beneath.

"I just wish he'd let me in," I said. "But he won't. How can we go on if he keeps me locked out? We have no trust."

She pulled in a breath, as if pulling herself back into the room, and met my gaze. A sad smile crept across her lips.

"No," she said. "You don't. Neither did we. That doesn't mean you won't one day—if you want to fight for it. The decision to fall back together is entirely up to you."

"I can't force him," I said. "I won't force him into anything he doesn't want, or can't give. That would only cause misery for us both. I don't want that. And I don't want that for him."

She squeezed my hands harder, as if wanting me to understand. To find the strongest part of myself.

"Who said anything about forcing?" she said. "You're the *Goddess of Fidelity*, aren't you? You are hope. Give him that hope and show him how to trust again. Show him he *can* trust again. Let him know it is safe to tear down his walls."

"What do you mean?"

"Love is struggle," she said. "If you wish to help Loki, love him as he is now, and not who you want him to be. If anyone can help him, it's you, but you have to know if you're willing to try. No one would fault you for walking away. No one. Just make sure that whichever path you choose, that it is the right one for *you* and what *you* want. I didn't want that path, but you're not me."

She stood, her chair screeching across the flagstones, and walked towards the door.

"Why do you think I'm so different from you concerning this?" I said.

She smiled softly.

"You're far more patient than I am, and patience is what he needs —and what I couldn't give him. Wouldn't. And that's what I still find myself wondering, more days than I care to admit. How everything might have been different had I been patient with him. But choices were made, by all of us. And now, you must make yours."

Angrboda opened the latch and left while I remained frozen, my mind storming with doubt and possibility and fear.

Choice. My choice.

Could I stay with Loki, knowing all that came with him? Saying you want to help mend someone is different than actually sewing them back together. Loki was chaos, and loving chaos meant loving something as changing and unpredictable as the sea.

And while I could not condone Simon's death, I could understand Loki's reasoning, as much as I didn't want to.

He had saved my life.

Loki saved me from myself.

Was I looking at everything in black and white, when I needed to see in blazing color?

Surtr pushed off the wall and picked up the wine bottle. That hadn't been possible before...Since when could he hold solid objects?

"Are you seriously *considering* staying with that trash god?" he turned the bottle upside down and frowned when only a single drop slid over the rim. "After what Loki's done? You have no faith remaining in your bones."

I curled my fingers into my gown. Closing myself. Shutting Surtr out. Wanting all this uncertainty gone. Just wanting to know what to do.

"Sigyn?"

Surtr smashed the wine bottle on the ground, and an explosion of green glass twirled across the stone floor and over my shoes.

I jolted and stared at him, his eyes burning, wanting to turn me into ash. My blood iced.

"Stop shutting me out," Surtr said.

I stood and inched away from him. Surtr followed.

"Stop this constant denial."

The flames of the candles in the wall sconces exploded, raged, consuming the candlesticks inch by inch.

"Stop running."

Heat seared my cheeks. Wax slid down the sides of the candles and spilled to the floor, where it pooled and boiled and bubbled.

What was happening?

I ran for the door.

Surtr stood in my path and marched towards me, and my skin

crawled. Needles sank into my bones as the infection spread further. Deeper.

Everything wobbled and hazed. Nausea gripped my stomach and squeezed.

I had to get out.

I darted around him and stumbled out the door. Why was the hallway full of screams chanting for a fight? Who was fighting?

"End them. Help them. Do what you will, but do not doubt what you are now," he seethed behind me, chasing me. "You are darkness, Sigyn. You are mine."

30

AU REVOIR

LOKI

Still reeling in the aftermath of my fight with Sigyn, I collected myself as best I could and searched for her in every room and every corridor. I had to find her and get her to Odin and the horses.

I had to get her to Yggdrasil and remove bloody Surtr from her veins.

My nerves frayed, and then they burst and everything collapsed into red violence when I caught Býleistr still walking the grounds through a window.

The entire Nine Worlds melted around me, leaving only a consuming craving that his blood alone on my fist would satisfy.

I marched outside.

I punched him in the jaw and sent him sprawling onto his back.

He sprung and went for my throat.

Rain started.

"I knew Sigyn couldn't resist removing that charm," he said.

We circled each other through the driving rain that drenched our clothes and made them stick to our cold skin. Clouds of hot breath curled out of our lungs and the lungs of the throng that packed in tighter around us.

I swung at his head.

He jumped back into a puddle, splattering mud across the tunics and jeering faces of the gathering crowd as they chanted louder for violence and guts and gore.

"You worm eating prick!" I shouted over the howls and hoots.

"What was her expression like?" He shoved his wet hair away from his eyes. "Crushed? Betrayed? Filled with the knowing of who you really are?"

"I'm going to gut you like a pig." I sloshed through the sludge, gauging whether to strike him in his kidney or break his femur.

Bets started. The weather never stopped any Jotun from enjoying a good fight.

"Your threats are as disappointing as soured milk." Bly held my gaze, unflinching even with the rivulets of rain running off his forehead.

"I did what you asked," I said. "I brought you that fucking apple. Why did you do this?"

His smile was as sharp as knives, and his green eyes sparked with enjoyment. With unbridled glee.

He relished in my suffering.

"Because you've always been allowed to be untouchable," he said. "Finally, you're paying for all the wrong you've done to the worlds. For all the wrong you've done to me."

Ah. And there it was. After all this time, he remained bitter and petty. This wasn't about punishing me for Ragnarok, so much as punishing me for his own created offenses he continually accused me of committing.

"Bust open his head, Býleistr!" a woman shouted.

"Break his jaw, Loki!" a man yelled, along with a dozen others all calling for blood.

Water streamed down my back and plastered my hair flat to my skull. A cold wind pommeled us, and rain beat and pricked my cheeks.

"You are such an immense cry baby," I said. "When will I have paid enough for all your imagined wounds to be satisfied? Or are you mad because you know I wouldn't piss in your eye if your brain was on fire?"

His fingers curled into fists at his sides.

"Imagined?" he said. "You always treated me like some kind of toy, something to poke and prod, so you could enjoy a good laugh. That is hardly imagined."

My lips twisted into a smile, perhaps more cruel than I should have allowed. But he deserved cruelty after what he did to me.

"It's hardly my fault your reactions were always hilarious," I said. "You shouldn't have been so easy to bait."

"Easy to bait? Is that all you think of me?"

"Actually I don't think of you at all, Bly."

His face melted into that of a boy. The boy I remembered getting riled up over a little harmless jabbing. Getting testy over a decent joke. In two seconds, it was back to that of a man, a man wanting me dead.

"You could have been kind to me," he said. "Just once, you could have been a true brother, and I'd have been on your side forever."

Gods. He was always whining.

He punched me across the nose. A crunch filled my vision with flickering green and yellow dots. Pain sprouted and throbbed, and blood rushed out of my nostrils.

"That's the thing I hate about you most." He shook out his bloodied fist. "I wanted you to like me. I wanted to be friends—but you always hurt me instead. And now, I have finally hurt you."

I spat out a mouthful of blood onto the ground.

Hurt him? He was insane with what tales he dug up, going all the way back to the cradle.

"Everything you're telling me makes me like my decision more in choosing to scrape you off my shoe like the white dog shit you are."

I lunged at him, tackling him. He wrapped his arms around my torso, clawing into my sides, my back.

We fell into the mud and he pinned me beneath him and

pounded my chest with his fists. I lifted my arms and smeared sludge in his face, trying to grind it up his nose, into his mouth, into his eyes.

The cheers thundered around us.

"*Get it in his eyes! Two silvers on Loki blinding the bastard.*"

"*Bite off his ear! Put me down for five coppers on Býleistr tearing it off.*"

"*Grab him by the balls! I bet twenty gold coins if either go for the balls.*"

Bly yanked back my hair and I grunted, pain exploding over my scalp. I tried to pry him off.

"You always got everything," he said. "Mother always made excuses for you. That I had to be *understanding*...Understanding of what? You were a terror."

"Because you were so endearing what with all your screaming and tantrums if I got a spoon more porridge than you? Yes. I can see how traumatic your childhood was for you."

He clamped his fingers around my neck and squeezed, his face growing even more livid. Dirt speckled his cheeks. His chin.

"I obeyed Mother," he said. "I did what was right. All you ever did was trick and prank. And still, all my goodness was never enough to be treated equally. You always had to be the special one."

He crushed his thumbs deeper into my windpipe. I struggled for breath, writhing beneath him and tearing at his fingers to release me. The world darkened.

I kicked him off me and he skidded through the mud.

I gasped for breath, the air prickling my starved lungs.

"Pranks? Are you still not over that frog I put in your stew?" I rasped, rubbing away the burn around my throat.

"You know I hate frogs!"

I wheezed out laughter despite the pain. His irrational fear was a beautiful prize I had cherished, and I took every opportunity to collect the harmless creatures and leave them around to leap out at him.

My lips flattened.

Perhaps it had been rather mean of me...

Wait. Was this empathy?

I shuddered at the thought. I was really letting myself down.

"At least Father knew what you were," he said, wiping blood away from the corner of his mouth.

Father.

That tore me out of such a disgusting sentiment as a thousand serrated images and words sawed through me. Memories I tried to keep buried deeper than any of the rest.

I pulled out my knife and pointed it at his heart.

"Don't you dare mention that man to me."

He cackled.

"Still soft about him, are we? I still remember when he broke that shovel handle on your back. And you say I'm easy to bait."

He really wanted to die today.

I slashed across his chest, but he was faster, kneeing me in the groin to the loud cheer of the spectator with the twenty gold coin bet.

I doubled over, the world darkening a second time. I panted, trying to swallow the pain bursting between my legs.

"Frigg was right," Bly said.

I flung back my hair and winced, forcing myself to stand tall, and wiped the mud out of my eyes. Pinching my broken nose, I held my breath and snapped it back in place. Damn. Relief flooded immediately as the bones knitted together as my body healed itself.

"What does that...frigid bitch have to...to do with any of this?" I ground out.

He laughed.

"You really never guessed? She's who hired me," he said. "Odin isn't the only one with eyes watching you. Once Frigg learned that you broke your banishment, she came to me. She gave me that letter. Told me where to find you in the Ironwood. Told me where to hit you hardest. To do whatever it took to break you. To punish you. And, if the rumors I hear are correct, I suspect Odin will have his own punishment waiting for him when he returns to Asgard for helping the god that started Ragnarok."

It all made sense now. So, Balder was innocent after all. Mildly disappointing.

But his mother...Frigg knew exactly how to strike me like the scorpion that she was.

I hated thinking of her face filled with glee when she learned that I stepped foot off Midgard. Me breaking my exile was a beautiful gift to her, because then she could finally tell everyone that I had started Ragnarok.

That's how everyone on this entire journey knew.

That I was going to end them all in fire for my revenge.

My own self-serving desires.

I shook an odd sinking feeling from my gut.

I kicked his leg, making him fall on his stomach. I straddled him and twisted his right arm behind him until he screamed. His pulse thrashed beneath my fingers.

"Which bone do you want me to break first?" I said. "Loser's choice."

He cried out as I bent his arm back farther, stretching his tendons to the point of tearing.

"The radius? No, the humerus. Oh. I know. I'll just rip your arm out of its socket."

"That's right," he hissed. "Prove my point further. Break me like you always break me. Like you break everyone. All you do is cause pain."

All you do is cause pain.

I caused pain.

I caused everyone pain.

Something seized me in that breath. Something I didn't like.

I believe it was myself.

"And this is your opinion of me?" I said. "That I always cause pain?"

"Do it!"

I wanted to do it. Gods I wanted nothing more.

I loosened my grip on him. I let him go.

I meant what I had told Sigyn. I was trying to be better.

"No," I said.

Boos erupted from the crowd while coins exchanged hands.

I stood off him, the rain washing rivers of blood and dirt away from my skin and clothes.

Bly pushed himself upright, surprise filling his face. I was a bit surprised myself. It appeared I'd grown quite controlled.

"I'm sorry I hurt you, Bly. I'm sorry you feel I deserve this. Truth is, you're right. I do deserve this, because I do cause pain."

Rolls of hot breath spilled out of his nose and mouth as his face swam in confusion.

"I'm sorry," I repeated.

I held his gaze a second more, turned on my heel, and walked away.

"You're sorry?" he roared over the din of the crowd. "That's it?"

I ignored him.

I was tired.

Really tired. If I could sleep for a hundred years, I would.

My muscles ached as I stretched and—

"Loki?"

Sigyn's voice.

I looked up.

Sigyn pushed through the throng of Jotnar still exchanging money. The rain soaked her skirts and coated her cheeks in a sheen of water.

"Loki, I've been looking for you. I need to tell you—your nose! Your face!"

She scanned my cuts and lesions I already felt knitting together across the bridge of my nose and my cheeks. Always the doctor, even when she despised me.

"I'm fine." I choked in large breaths.

She wavered and her cheeks hollowed. Her breaths deepened, as if she tried to anchor herself.

She decidedly was not fine.

I reached out to help steady her.

She put out her hands to me.

"I'm alright. No. No, I'm not…"

"What's wrong?"

"Now you know who he really is, Sigyn," Bly spoke over us. "He's nothing but a liar."

Sigyn shut her eyes and released a sharp sigh.

"Will you please shut up for once, Býleistr?" she said.

She straightened her posture, standing tall, and pushed past me and walked to Bly, wavering only once.

"I'm glad you could see what he does first hand." He pointed at me. "Now you understand how I was helping rescue you from a mercurial fiend and—"

She punched him across the face.

He spun and collapsed into the mud. The Jotnar cheered and started clapping, chanting the *Iron Ball Crusher of Midgard*.

The *what*?

Sigyn wavered again, as if she had pressed her last dregs of power into that strike. She took a step.

She collapsed to the ground, bracing her upper body with her palms.

I raced to her, and she grunted, pushing herself back and standing on her feet. She wobbled for a heartbeat and looked at her hands.

"Sigyn...what's happening—"

My breath hitched.

Dark purple bordering on pitch spread from the tips of her fingers and over her knuckles.

She locked her gaze onto mine, terror filling her eyes.

It matched the fear flowing cold in my veins.

"That's what I wanted to tell you," she said. "I think Surtr is winning."

31

VENOM

We raced our horses out of the Ironwood and traveled south towards the Asgardian Sea. My body wanted to sink into itself the harder we pushed, keeping up the grueling pace through forests and mountain valleys trying to make it to Yggdrasil before Surtr finished possessing Sigyn completely.

We had to make it. Surrender was not an option.

The rain stopped somewhere between the stone roofed villages of Kret and Hilna. A minor blessing, as Sigyn continually tugged at her cloak and layers of wool and knit scarves wrapped around her.

My stomach burned each time I glimpsed at the midnight purple covering Sigyn's hands that now reached her wrists. She suffered trying not to lose herself to Surtr. And what did I do? I made it worse because I couldn't be honest. Because I'd shut everyone out for so long I couldn't trust Sigyn enough to let her in.

And I wanted to let her in...

Bitterness filled my mouth. No matter how much I tried, how much I wanted, I couldn't seem to change.

Knowing who I was, I never should have believed we could have been happy together. Every love I'd ever known had ended in disaster. Why did I think ours would have been any different?

Sigyn rode with Odin, insisting it would be best for us both. Fine. It didn't make it any easier watching her sit in front of him, leaning her back against his chest with his arms on either side of her as he held the reins of his horse.

I caught bits of their muffled conversation on the wind that grew colder the closer we trekked to the edge of Jotunheim.

He explained the spell to her. How the ritual would be performed. What sensations would be experienced. What pain to brace for.

He didn't mention the part where I had to be the one to melt the gold and encase Surtr within the stone. Odin and I neither had a chance to fully recharge as we had hoped, the ramifications of which I refused to consider.

The hooves of the horses clacked across the rocky beach, and surf pounded the shore. Froth scuttled through the stones, sweeping in and pulling out, and in the distance the sun set, outlining the clouds collecting on the horizon in red.

Veins of lightning blazed and struck the churning water. Thunder rumbled like a low growl far away.

This wasn't ominous at all.

We dismounted the horses, and wind beat our clothes, dampening the clack of pebbles beneath our every step as we walked towards the low cliffs topped with vegetation.

"Now what?" I said.

Hair whipped across Odin's forehead and he pointed at a black slice in the sloping limestone. A cave.

My skin chilled.

"Great," I said. "Just what I thought we needed. Another cave."

"Do we have to?" Sigyn stepped over a large piece of driftwood and faltered for two seconds. She steadied herself and kept walking forward.

Odin glanced at me and frowned.

"I'm sorry. I know." The wind ate his words. Or, was it my rushing blood suppressing everything into a dull roar? "But the cliffs are the closest entrance to Yggdrasil, and we can't wait."

Sweat slicked my palms. Slicked the small of my back.

I am safe.

I am not in danger.

"It's fine." I dragged in a breath. "Let's just get this over with."

If Odin could face Yggdrasil again, I could face my own demons.

I marched towards the cave, though my muscles wanted to go rigid. Everything inside of me wanted to run the other way.

I am safe.

I am not in danger.

I refused to be stopped by some stupid hole in the ground, especially if it was the only route we had to Yggdrasil and saving Sigyn.

My heart thundered harder as we approached the opening. Chilled air rushed out of the cave mouth, filling my lungs with cold and must and stone and—the world tilted.

Cold and must and stone.

I had smelled that for five hundred years. Cold and must and stone.

Pain snapped at my nerve endings.

Adrenaline rushed through my veins. What if I became trapped again?

I tasted venom on my tongue.

I gagged.

I can't be trapped. Don't trap me. *Let me out.*

I took in a breath.

There is an opening. There is an exit. There are ways out. I can get out. I am free.

Odin held a small candle he had lit and entered the cave first.

I am safe.

I am not in danger.

I breathed deeper.

I took a step inside the cavern. And another. Moisture suffocated the air.

There is an opening. There is an exit. There are ways out. I can get out. I am free.

I took a third and fourth step.

Shadows grew as the space filled with yellow hues from the candlelight.

Every shadow turned into serpents.

Screams filled my ears. Cries. Narfi and Nari.

I had failed them as I had failed everyone.

I am safe.

I am not in danger.

I froze.

Darkness spilled over me. Swallowed me whole.

Always darkness...

My skin burned. Everything burned.

I choked as venom drowned me.

I rubbed my wrists, having to erase the sting of my bonds digging into my flesh. I had to remove them. I can't have them touch me. Why can't I remove them?

Please. Let them go. Let my family live.

A hand squeezed my shoulder, forcing me back to the present, out of the past I wasn't sure I'd ever fully escape.

Sigyn slid her hand down my upper arm and gave me a small tug forward.

"Look at me," she said.

I locked onto her eyes. Sweat coated my entire back. My chest. My forehead.

"You are safe," she said. "You are not in danger."

Another step forward. I lost count how many steps I took the deeper we traveled.

She had taught me this mantra for when these episodes struck me. The worse was waking from nightmares, soaked through with sweat, nearly as soaked as I was now. But she was always there to calm me. To tell me I was safe.

I am safe.

I am not in danger.

She always let me know I was safe.

And here she was, helping me, when I should be the one to help her. She looked so ill.

I followed her farther into the cold, into echoing footsteps and trickling water and looming shadows.

I am safe.

I am not in danger.

We squeezed through the tight passageway, and I stayed focused on her eyes, her touch, anytime I brushed the damp rock or a drop of water splashed onto my head and it seared my skin.

Fangs hung over my head. The snake...

I am safe.

I am not in danger.

Sigyn squeezed me again and my pulse calmed. Steadied. But I didn't fool myself to believe what she did for me meant forgiveness.

It was only a kindness, because she was so good even though I deserved no such consideration.

"Here," Odin said, the candle light flickering from his breath.

He walked towards a door. Well, it was more a chiseled outline of a door than an actual door. He sat the candle on the ground, and the entire cavern quivered with silhouettes and shapes.

I concentrated on my breath. Even. Deep.

"Remember to practice caution once we cross over," he said. "Especially with *you-know-who.*"

Damn. I had almost forgotten about him.

I wiped the sweat off my forehead with my sleeve.

"Who?" Sigyn asked, her voice holding a weariness to it I didn't like.

How to explain him...no. It was better to leave him as a surprise.

"You'll see soon enough," I said. "Come on."

We huddled and Odin grasped Sigyn's wrist and pressed her open palm against the rock. I reached out to do the same. I hesitated a heartbeat.

I breathed sharply and slapped my hand on the rock and concentrated on the rosemary in Sigyn's hair instead of the wet slicking the stone I squeezed my palm harder against.

I am safe.

I am not in danger.

The door shifted. Actually, we all shifted.

The world closed in on itself, folding and folding, a hundred different realities collapsing in on one another and pulling taut.

I didn't totally despise the tickling sensation running up and down my legs, but the massive pressure building in my head I could do without.

The damp vanished.

I smelled clarity. Color.

I heard worlds growing and expanding.

Everything breathed.

And we stepped out of Jotunheim and into another realm unlike any of the rest.

32

A PROMISE

An ash tree stood on the edge of a cliff, branches twisting and stretching into a sky filled with a thousand stars and purples and blues. Fireflies floated between the waxy leaves as large as a head and drifted lazily around us as we walked through the field.

But for all this realm's beauty, it was not a friendly place. It took before it gave and demanded a price most could not pay. My mouth dried, thinking of Odin and what he had paid—for us. And now, he stood here again, for me and for Sigyn.

He stood rigid, his head bent back and staring at the tangle of branches where he had hung from for nine days. Thirsting. Dying. And I knew. His own demons attacked him now, as mine had in the cave we just left.

I laid my hand on his shoulder.

Gray mist coated him, raging and wild like a summer storm. Relentless. Another oddity of this realm—our elements shined through our skin, visible and naked.

"Are you alright?" I said.

He fidgeted with the hem of his sleeve.

"I'm fine." Odin rubbed his neck.

Clearly.

I nodded, letting my arm fall back to my side.

Entranced, Sigyn stepped towards Yggdrasil and a thousand universes reflected in her eyes. I grabbed her wrist and pulled her back before she stepped into the clear pool, swimming with goldfish.

My chaos rippled over my knuckles as a fiery sheen, coating her skin in golds.

Sigyn's fidelity radiated beneath her skin, flowing from her pores and shooting out of her fingertips, reminding me of when I first caught sight of her all those centuries ago. And it's why my heart sank deeper, seeing ropes of black ink coiling tighter around her element, choking her hope like weeds in a wheat field.

Time ran thinner than we thought.

"Step in that pool and you'll slip into another dimension and become a cube," I said.

She grimaced, and I released her.

Odin nodded.

"Keep to the grass only," Odin said. "And whatever you do, don't tread on the mushrooms, especially the red ones."

Alarm flooded her expression.

"What happens if you do?" she said.

He scratched his beard.

I rubbed behind my ear. Apparently, it had been a terrible mess after Sven exploded.

"Don't worry about it," I said.

We passed through tall grass teeming with fireflies. Through the points of light swirling around us, that melted seamlessly into a night sky flooded with constellations.

We walked around flowers that were planets and galaxies.

We reached the base of the tree, and the bark pulsed, singing a song without words. Yggdrasil stretched over our heads, endless and dangerous and terrifying.

I chilled, unable to free myself from the image of Odin's limp body swinging back and forth, a spear in his side.

What awaited us would be no less pleasant.

"Where do we do this?" I said.

"We must acquire his permission to use what we need first."

I groaned.

"I don't understand why we always have to grovel to that tattle-tale rat—oh, hello Ratatoskr! How lovely to see you again," I said.

A squirrel scurried down the bark to us, his red fur puffed on the tips of his ears. His white stomach always begged for a tickle, but I wouldn't dare lest he bite me with his overly large yellow teeth.

"Tattle-tale?" he said. "I prefer *well informed.*"

He gripped his claws into the bark and flicked his bushy tail in quick snaps.

Sigyn's mouth fell open. Understandable, to be honest. It was hard to see a talking squirrel and not be slightly alarmed.

He scampered an inch to the right.

"Why are you here?" he asked Odin. "Oh, I do hope it's not to kill yourself again. You were such miserable company. All that moaning. And I was so looking forward to the gossip you promised me."

Ratatoskr scampered an inch to the left. He snapped his tail again.

"Speaking of gossip," Ratatoskr said. "You wouldn't believe what the eagle at the top of the tree said about the dragon below in the roots—"

"Ratatoskr..." Odin said, trying to get a word in.

"—and then the thing the dragon said about the eagle!"

"Ratatoskr, I..."

I tapped my foot and forced down a million curses from spilling out.

Did this squirrel ever stop talking and take a breath?"

"Of course, when I told them both what the other had said and—"

"Ratatoskr!" Odin screamed.

"Alright, alright, what?"

"I need to use Yggdrasil—again," Odin said, combing his fingers through his hair.

Ratatoskr tilted his head and blinked his round, black eyes. His nose and whiskers wriggled.

"What do I get in return?" He dashed up the tree three feet. He gnawed at the bark.

"You get to hide something special away," Odin said. "Hide it so deep that no one can ever find it again."

"And what's that?"

Odin smiled and reached into his satchel and rustled through.

"A kind of *nut*."

Odin pulled out the amulet, the amber stone vibrant against the gold.

Ratatoskr clicked and squeaked.

He scurried back down.

Say what you will, but a squirrel is always a squirrel, no matter how magical.

Ratatoskr sniffed around the gold disc, his whiskers twitching. He sniffed the amber.

He sneezed.

"Quite pretty." He stared at the amulet. He sniffed the stone again. "What will be inside? Will it be something that would make the eagle and dragon jealous?"

Odin flipped open his satchel and dropped the amulet back inside.

"This will be pure power." He patted his satchel. "I know how you love to hide anything of value, and this will be the most valuable of all."

He always was good at laying it on thick.

Ratatoskr chirped.

"Oooh!" he said. "Sounds boring."

Odin's shoulders dropped. "What?"

"Sorry, but we will have to discuss this later. I have a bunch of acorns I just dug up sitting on my table, and the dragon was going to tell me what really irks him about the eagle in twenty minutes."

Odin sighed.

Sigyn wobbled. I steadied her, hating how she trembled. How cold she felt...

"I'm quite well," she said, twisting out of my hold. "I can do this. I can make it."

She was not well.

And this was going on long enough.

I glared at Ratatoskr.

"We are rather pressed for time," I pushed between my clenched teeth.

"And when the eagle finds out—" Ratatoskr continued on and on.

I mulled over how to catch him and hurl him into one of the dozen moons. But I'd tried that once before. It didn't work.

"Can't you consider having this gossip-fest later?" I raised my voice over his chatter.

Ratatoskr gasped and swished his tail faster.

"You want me to do *what*?" Each word screamed horror. "Later? I will never consider such an outrageous suggestion."

He scampered to the left, towards a small hole in the bark above a branch. He scratched the side of his face with his back foot, thumping the tree trunk.

"But I suppose..." Ratatoskr stilled. "If you happened to have some new gossip from Asgard, you can keep me entertained until my chat with the dragon."

Odin's lips pulled into a grin, a touch on the dastardly side. He waved Ratatoskr back over and he scurried down, his ears perked.

"I hear..." Odin leaned in and whispered something to Ratatoskr.

Ratatoskr squeaked in response and thrashed his tail. *Snip-snap!*

"Oh! They found Heimdall with *how* many pineapples? Now see, this is tea you must spill. The dragon will love hearing these juicy tidbits, and the eagle will hate that Fafnir heard them first. And then...*if* time remains...then we can discuss if you can use my tree, and I suppose hide away this underwhelming nut."

Fafnir. Now there was a name I'd not heard in eons, nor did I care to again. That dragon was nothing but a problem.

Ratatoskr whirled around three times and leapt up and away into a hole in the tree trunk. We followed him.

Sigyn stopped and stiffened.

"What's wrong?" Odin said.

The stench of rotten egg rose from her skin—burning sulfur. Brimstone. My eyes watered and my nose wanted to refuse any further breath.

"Sigyn?" I said.

Her eyes fixed on something behind me and her face dropped, the corners of her mouth pulling into a frown. I turned to see what caught her attention.

There was nothing.

"Surtr," she said. "He is laughing at me. He says I will never escape him. That it's too late. That...that I'm already his."

"You will never be his."

Purple and black ribbons coiled around her fidelity, choking her element with torment until her energy barely pulsed. Only thin shudders of calm and peace radiated from her now, and each whisper of what remained of her filled me with rage at Surtr. That Surtr thought she belonged to the darkness. That Surtr wanted to kill her fidelity I loved.

She locked her eyes on mine and my insides twisted. Her eyes flashed black.

They were only black.

She croaked out laughter. Horrible laughter. The kind that clawed down your spine and made your hair stand on end.

Sigyn collapsed to the grass and convulsed, her fingers curling and uncurling.

I knelt beside her, careful to avoid the leaf that would have turned me inside out and plunged me into a river of fire.

I took her rigid hand, her arm jerking. Her entire body spasmed harder.

"Sigyn!"

She cackled louder. Her neck twisted. Her eyelids fluttered.

"Sigyn isn't here," the voice said. "It's just little ol' me. Best get used to the idea."

Odin grasped her cheeks between his hands, trying to still her. She snapped her gaze onto his.

"You think you can get rid of me, Odin? Allfather?" She spat in his face. "You think your power greater than mine? Than pure dark matter?"

Sigyn inhaled sharply and gasped for air and coughed. Her eyes flickered and returned to brown.

"What happened?" she said. "The world vanished. There was nothing."

The infection reached her elbows. The fidelity in her chest burned less brightly, the black cords squeezing her element tighter, while others wove inside and twitched like parasitic worms.

"It will be fine," I said. Hoped. Hoped even though I wasn't sure.

I wasn't sure at all.

I looked up at Odin.

He wasn't sure either.

"Stay here with her," Odin said. "I'll go with Ratatoskr and make this quick."

"You better." I helped Sigyn sit up, and she winced, pressing her hand against her stomach.

He nodded stiffly and left.

* * *

SIGYN LAID her face into her hands and her body shuddered. All I could do was stare at her. Stare and wish and be utterly useless.

She sniffed hard and lifted her face from her hands and looked out at a sky alive with pink shooting stars. Purple light bathed us both.

"This is bad, isn't it?" she said.

I wanted to lie and tell her no.

"Yes." I said, telling her the truth, even though the truth gutted me.

She shut her eyes for a second. Maybe three.

"I need you to do something for me." She rubbed the insides of her fingers with her thumbs.

"Anything." I crossed my legs and sat on the grass and faced her.

"If the worst should happen." She swallowed hard. "If this goes wrong...you must destroy me."

I felt the air kicked from my lungs at such a statement. That proposal was unacceptable.

"Sigyn, don't talk like this."

She met my gaze and my throat burned.

Tears streaked her cheeks. They were blood.

My chest tightened further. Twisted. Cracked.

"Promise me," she said. "If you don't destroy me, I will destroy everyone."

"That won't happen," I said.

She shook her head.

"You know there are too many variables."

I reached out to touch her cheek and...and I stopped myself. She was no longer mine to touch in that way. We were no longer lovers.

I grasped her hand instead. As a friend.

"I won't let you fall to the darkness," I promised, even though I had no right to make such a promise, knowing what needed to be done with the amulet, knowing I wasn't so sure I could.

I forced a breath to chase away the fatigue from my bones.

She smiled weakly. A drop of blood fell from her nose.

A second followed.

"I know you mean this," she said. "But good intentions help no one. Loki. Tell me you'll do this for me. Swear it."

She leaned forward onto her knees and put my hand on *Laevateinn*'s hilt at my hip. She squeezed into my knuckles, forcing my fingers into the leather.

Blood trickled out of her left nostril.

"Use *Laevateinn*," she said. "Trap Surtr within my heart and cut it out like your mother cut out Gullveig's. Do whatever you must to end this."

Blood trickled out of the right and seeped between her lips.

"Sigyn..."

She dug her nails into my skin and I grunted from the bites of pain. She ground my palm harder into the hilt, wanting me to understand.

More blood streamed down her cheeks from her eyes as she cried, mixing with the blood coursing out of her nose.

She was losing her battle in front of me.

"Swear it!"

I nodded, and I wanted to scream.

"Alright," I said. "I promise."

I hated her in that breath.

I hated her because she was right. I hated her because it was the only other way. I hated her because I loved her so much it felt like I ripped out my guts agreeing.

She released me.

"This is my fault," I said, fracturing. "What's happening to you is all my fault."

"No. It's not."

My vision blurred.

"I'm sorry, Sigyn. For all of it." I gripped her shoulders and cherished the feel of her. "I'm sorry I started Ragnarok. I'm sorry that I took your brother's life. I'm sorry that I betrayed your trust so many times. I never wanted to hurt you. I never..." Tears ran down my cheeks. "But I have. And...and I'm so sorry."

Pity welled in her bloodshot eyes, every fine vessel bursting and bleeding.

"Loki..."

I caressed my thumbs into her wool sleeves. My element coated her skin in light, making her glow gold.

"Every time I have a chance at happiness, it turns into sand and slips through my fingers," I said. "And every time I have a chance at love, it either dies or I kill it."

"Please don't say such things," she said. "That's not true."

"But it is true. I killed us. I never wanted to lose you, and that's exactly what I've done," I said. "Because it's who I am. It's my destiny to lose everything and everyone."

She gripped my upper arms and squeezed. I believed I burned.

"Lose? Loki—I needed time to consider. To...to understand. I've made a choice about us, and I think you should know—"

I smiled softly. Accepting.

"You don't need to say it. I know we are done."

Her brow knit together and her fidelity sputtered in her chest, as if trying to break free of the bonds I bound her element within.

"Loki I—"

Grass crinkled in the distance. Odin walked over the hill towards us.

"Ratatoskr has given his permission," he said. "Thank gods for Heimdall and his *ingenuity*."

I pushed myself off the grass and hoisted Sigyn to her feet. She coughed and teetered and gripped into the bones of my hand, trying to stabilize herself.

I tensed as another wave of sulfur burrowed into my sinuses.

She squeezed my hand harder. Blood stained her teeth red and trickled down her chin.

"Remember what you promised me you'd do." Her voice rasped. "If the amulet doesn't work..." she gasped in a breath. "You cut out my heart and end me however you can."

She cried out and gripped her stomach, buckling forward.

She choked.

She vomited blood.

33

BLOOD

"I can't stop the bleeding." I draped Sigyn's arm over my shoulder, keeping her upright as we walked behind Yggdrasil. Droplets of her blood splashed over the clover. Her every step faltered. "What's happening to her?"

Odin skated his hand along Yggdrasil's trunk, searching for some spot he needed.

"Surtr is expelling Sigyn's blood."

"Surtr is *what*? Why?"

Fireflies buzzed and hovered around us in the air. He brushed his fingers over the bark faster. The bark shivered.

"Surtr is finishing the transformation and is forcing Sigyn's blood out of her body," he said. "Surtr won't require blood anymore with the life-force of the darkness running through her veins."

Panic ripped through me as we stepped over the exposed roots of the tree, each contorting and buckling through the topsoil like a web.

So that was it then. I'd have to watch her bleed out before my eyes.

"How long?"

He paused his movements for a heartbeat, considering.

"Minutes," he said. "If we are lucky."

More blood gurgled out of her throat and spilled down her chin. "Hurry," I said.

"I'm going as fast as I—" Odin stopped on a knot in the wood and pushed into Yggdrasil, and Yggdrasil responded.

The tree growled and my ears filled with the roar of monsters and beasts and life and rebirth. The ground rumbled beneath my boots as Yggdrasil stretched and opened like a yawn, and there was only terrifying beauty as the tree swallowed us inside of itself.

Earth and mildew filled my nose.

Odin lit a candle, chasing away the darkness and illuminating walls of dirt packed between twisting roots and wiggling grubs and earthworms.

Sigyn weakened further in my arms, and the blood staining her mouth and chin gleamed in the dim light. Her breaths turned rasped and labored as I lowered her to the ground and leaned her against the wall of roots, fibrous and creeping.

The roots trembled. The entire room creaked like a battered ship at sea.

Odin and I shared a glance as dirt rained from above and dusted our heads. Most likely due to the dragon chewing the roots deep in the Below.

But you never knew with Yggdrasil.

The rumble stilled. I exhaled and Odin knelt on the ground of trodden earth and opened his satchel and pulled out a bundle of mugwort, horehound, and a small vial of crushed malachite.

My throat tightened as I recognized each—and their dangers.

Sigyn heaved and choked and spit up a fresh surge of blood. My insides turned raw.

"Anytime would be good." I rubbed her hand. Why was it so clammy with sweat? So waxen?

"You must stay calm," he said, though his fingers trembled as he unsheathed a knife and placed it next to the row of herbs.

Sigyn wheezed, and I pressed my fingers against her forehead. Her cheeks. I thought I touched a cadaver.

I hoped she didn't notice my grimace.

Odin took out a wooden bowl and set it in front of his knees. And I wiped the blood from Sigyn's nose with the hem of my tunic. I tried to keep her clean as best I could. I tried to stop the blood from rushing out of her. But the blood kept rushing. Rushing out of her eyes. Out of her ears. Blood soaked her clothes. My clothes.

He chopped mugwort and bruised the leaves of the horehound, every movement calculated and intentional and fluid. Could he not speed this terrible process up? No. He couldn't if we wanted this to have any chance of the ritual working.

Odin dropped eight silver coins into the bowl and emptied the vial of powdered malachite. He picked up the ninth silver coin and stood before Sigyn.

She was so cold.

He looked into her eyes that bled.

"I need your hand," he said. "This won't be pleasant."

"How...could it be...any worse?" She reached out to him.

If only she knew how much worse it could be. This was dark magic he performed. I braced myself on her behalf.

Odin cradled her hand in his and spread open her fingers. He pressed the piece into her palm.

She cried out in pain.

Her skin hissed beneath the silver as the coin scorched and branded her.

She tugged back. He firmed his grip on her, refusing to let her go. I wrapped my arms around her shoulders, keeping her as still as I could, though she writhed in my hold. I hated this, but a link had to be forged between her and the spell and—

An arc of blood spouted out of her mouth and splattered Odin's face and his chest.

He pressed the coin harder into her skin, continuing through the horror.

She screamed. I held her tighter and shut my eyes, forcing myself to stay together.

Odin removed the coin in a swift movement and wiped her blood from his face with his sleeve.

He looked me in the eyes.

"Surtr will fight us." He dropped the coin into the bowl with the other ingredients. "Get the amulet ready."

I nodded and pulled out the amulet from his satchel. The runes glowed within the gold and the amber stone pulsed with hunger, wanting to feed. I tried to ignore the sweat trickling down my back.

You always love to brag about how you are the God of Chaos. *Or is providing the necessary fire going to be a problem for you?* Brokkr's voice stormed in my head.

Before all the fire I expelled at Freya's, I wouldn't have thought twice, but now...

Fatigue gnawed my insides, telling me I didn't have a chance.

No. I didn't care how exhausted I was. How bone tired. I would melt the gold around the stone and encase Surtr inside of the amulet. I would finish this no matter what.

"I will tell you when it's time." Odin scattered the herbs in the bowl.

The amulet vibrated stronger beneath my fingers, alive with magic. Whispers escaped through the stone.

Sigyn grasped my hand harder, smearing blood across my wrist.

"What part..." she wheezed. "What part must you play in this?"

Her eyes flickered. Brown, black, brown. And blood. So much blood. A lake of crimson spread out from her towards Odin who drew runes in the dirt with his forefinger.

"Odin, please," I said.

"Quiet! I'm nearly done, dammit."

He pricked his thumb with the knife and squeezed until a bead rose to the surface. He flicked it into the bowl.

Sigyn gripped into my arms. Holding on to me as if she'd lose me. She struggled for breath.

"Loki." She gasped air. "I...I don't see this...ending..." She gulped a breath. "...well. You must do what you promised me."

"I—"

Odin lit a reed and dropped the flame into the bowl. The ingredients snapped and crackled, a purple flame fluttering out of the basin casting everything in lavenders for a flash and died into embers.

Thick smoke twisted out of the bowl.

Odin closed his eye and hovered his hands over the white smoke, letting it curl around his fingers and gold rings. His eye flashed open, white and glowing with power.

He started to chant.

The air sucked out of my lungs as he recited ancient words—dark rites teeming with the forbidden.

The spell filled the room, sinking into the earth and into Yggdrasil's roots.

Each word struck me like a drum beat, pounding into my bones. Into a place inside of me I did not know, but knew I possessed all the same.

He spoke faster, finding a rhythm as he ventured deeper into the magic.

And Surtr began to respond.

Sigyn winced and twitched as the black threads constricting her fidelity in her chest coiled tighter, as if trying to keep their claim. Her fingers stretched straight out, rigid and shaking, then retracted— curling tight against her palms.

Odin hardened his words and the tones of his voice fell octaves into something guttural and primordial.

One of the black cords squeezing her fidelity snapped in half.

Sigyn spasmed and cried out. While one would think being freed would be a relief, this was purging, and purging felt like being cut open and having your organs spilled.

No relief would exist until the thing was out of the body completely.

She thrashed and screamed as another rope split from her element. She shook. More threads severed.

Odin spoke louder over her wailing. Over her pleading for mercy.

And then she fell silent, and an eerie hush flooded the room.

Wha—?

Sigyn blasted me back three feet.

The tree trembled and groaned, and wind spun around us, tearing through our hair. I blinked away the sting of dust from my eyes.

Sigyn slowly stood, one shoulder hunched. Blood poured out of her nose and flowed down her chest. Her red curls waved behind her.

"You think this is enough to stop the transformation?" Surtr said through Sigyn.

She stretched her neck and took one step towards Odin, her fingers stiff like claws.

Odin's brow knit closer together and sweat collected at his temples. He pushed more of his voice, more of his power, into the incantation, wrestling with the darkness.

Sigyn faltered and growled, as if struck by an arrow as another cord splintered.

"Stop this nonsense." Sigyn took another step. "Or else I'm going to be *very* angry."

Three more cords formed, taking its place, clawing into her element, not letting go.

The amount of power Odin emitted trying to get Surtr to obey him was tremendous.

A dozen cords released.

A dozen more reattached.

I got back to my feet and Sigyn turned her head steadily and locked eyes on mine. And she smiled, coy and damning, and my veins froze.

"You won't get her back," Surtr said. "I'd stop while you're ahead. While I still allow you to live."

My jaw clenched.

"Don't be so sure," I said.

She cackled, blood rushing over her lips. She turned back towards Odin.

"Any minute now, and it will be complete. It will be finished," she said.

Sigyn straightened and marched to Odin, her skirts swirling

behind her in the wind. Odin's voice roughened, and he quickened his words and—

Her smile dropped.

The blood stopped pouring out of her nose.

Black smoke slipped out of her nostrils instead. She lifted her hand and touched beneath her nose, and shock widened her eyes that followed the trails of vapor.

Hope sparked in my chest.

Odin was succeeding.

"I told you not to be so sure," I said.

She gagged and rose into the air, her toes lifting an inch above the ground. Her arms spread straight out at her sides, leaving her chest open and exposed.

Dust and dirt hurtled through the wind gusting around us.

The black threads suffocating her element slackened, and a hundred cords dropped limp from her fidelity all at once.

Surtr flooded out of Sigyn's mouth. Her ears. Her pores. The smoke twisted and writhed and thickened, turning into tendrils of thick tar and out of the tar stepped the figure of a man. A man with masses of white hair that framed an angled face of points and shadows. He radiated a lethal allure and his mouth begged to be kissed, even though nothing but poison waited for you on his lips.

Surtr's eyes set on mine—violet and burning and promising.

And then he rolled them at me.

Rage lit in me more from the absolute nerve.

"You two are really beginning to piss me off," Surtr said. "This possession was supposed to be easy. But, I suppose if you want something done right..."

He extended his arm and ribbons of black sludge ran out of his palm, manifesting into a sword with serrated edges.

Surtr grinned and flipped back his hair as he stalked to Odin, his knuckles pulsing as his grip hardened on the hilt. A mess of buttons and belts and ties fastened his black robes that waved behind him like water.

Sigyn levitated higher, more slime oozing out of her.

I unsheathed my daggers at my hips, loving the rush of steel against leather, and stepped in Surtr's path, blocking him from reaching Odin.

This was extremely ill advised, but what choice did I have? Odin could not have his concentration broken now in the thick of the spell. I had to buy what seconds I could.

"I've been waiting for the chance to bury my blade between your eyes." My pulse pounded against my hilts.

Surtr tilted his head, looked me up and down, and laughed.

"Bless you." Amusement saturated his voice that sounded like a caress. "You and I both know such weapons are useless against me. I'm—oh, what's the word? Ethereal. Non-corporal. *Sublime.*"

I sneered and flipped my dagger in my right hand, and squeezed into the leather wrapped around my hilt.

"Oh, I know this is thoroughly useless," I said. "But it won't make stabbing you feel any less satisfying."

Grunting, I thrust my dagger into Surtr's chest and I vibrated with delight, feeling the steel slide straight in with no resistance.

Surtr laughed harder, his chest convulsing around the steel nestled deep in his non-flesh.

"Feel better?" Surtr said.

"You know, actually a little—"

Any speck of mirth vanished, and Surtr grabbed me by the throat and hoisted me off the ground, filling me with a thousand regrets. While his body was shadowy, his grip certainly was not.

Surtr lifted me closer to his face, his long fingers crunching deeper into my neck like iron clamps.

"Now that the games are over..." His breath stunk of brimstone. "...I have an Allfather to skewer."

Surtr launched me backwards, and I flailed through the air and struck the far wall that twisted with roots. Pain burst through my entire body from the impact. Dirt and grubs rained over my throbbing head and aching back.

Alright, new plan.

Surtr straightened his robes and flicked an earthworm off his shoulder and marched towards Odin who didn't lose a beat of the rhythm of the spell. Sigyn continued to hover, and the slurry kept pouring out. Gods, how long would this take to finish?

Surtr stepped before Odin and stopped. His face lit as if considering something magnificent.

I pressed into the packed earth and pushed myself up and stumbled towards Odin.

"Unless..." Surtr lowered his sword and tapped his pointed chin. "Tell you what, Odin. I'll make you a deal. Instead of impaling your liver, I'll let you complete this spell...*if* you take me in yourself. I'll forget about little Sigyn. What with your power and my everything else, we would be unstoppable together."

Sweat ran down Odin's forehead and temples, his face skewed with concentration as he chanted through Surtr's strengthening words. His promises.

"This sounds like the deal of the desperate," I said, staggering towards Surtr. I pulled out another knife from inside of my boot— Dwarven and double-edged.

A grin cracked Surtr's beautiful face.

"Not desperate," he said. "Just power recognizing power. You wouldn't understand—you're so...*basic*."

Alright, I really would have to find a way to cause this asshole pain.

Another dozen threads snapped away from Sigyn's element. Odin's muscles corded in his neck and his body shook as he kept chanting. Blood ran out of his own nose now from the exertion. The excruciating struggle.

Any other god would have crumbled by now.

Even me, which I hated admitting.

"Wouldn't that be nice, Odin?" Surtr said. "I can give you all you want. I can allow you to escape what you fear most. Invite me in, and you'll escape death."

Odin kept chanting.

I threw my knife at Surtr's stomach, eager to draw blood. Surtr snatched the blade out of mid-flight.

Bollocks.

He gazed adoringly at the steel reflecting the light in his hand and chuckled.

"You should know it is rude to interrupt," he said.

He spun and flung the knife back at me. Shit.

I tried to jump out of the way—the blade lodged deep in my left side and I cried out from the punch of white heat. I had to choose the double-edged one.

Surtr walked towards me, sword drawn.

"Do you know how annoying you are? How perfectly irritating?" he said. "I busted my backside trying to break Sigyn free of you. I needed her faith in you broken. I needed her hope killed for her to succumb to me. You were all that stood in my way of succeeding."

I grunted and ripped the blade out of my flesh and tossed it aside. I pressed my hand against the stinging wound to stop the bleeding as best I could until my skin stitched itself back together. My blood ran through my fingers, hot and sticky, and soaked my tunic.

"Well, sometimes we aren't as alluring as we think ourselves to be," I rasped. "I'm sure you'll recover from this crushing blow."

I breathed easier, feeling the sinew knitting back together, although slower than I liked. Damn this fatigue.

Surtr held out his sword to me. My throat dried.

"I'm sure I will, but you won't."

Before I could react, Surtr drove his sword into my right shoulder. Pain splintered deep into my sinew as the steel scraped below my clavicle and shredded my muscle and tendons. The blade felt like nothing made by any Dwarf or Elf.

This was like having a thousand sharp teeth eating you alive from the inside.

"You absolute waste of a god. You belong in a pit with the rest of the rubbish. Yet she kept believing in you, and your love kept her from surrendering to me."

Surtr clutched the hilt and twisted the blade, driving it deeper into me. I screamed and saw black for three shuddering seconds as the blade tore my nerves that burned with fire. The sword punched through the back of my shoulder as Surtr ran me through and pinned me to the dirt wall.

My body shook from the agony ripping into my marrow.

Surtr released the sword and stepped back and pulled in a calming breath. He wiped his hands together, removing clouds of dirt from his palms.

"But it doesn't matter anymore," he said. "Because thanks to what you did to Simon and burning that letter, Sigyn has no hope left. She doesn't believe in you anymore. I knew I just had to wait it out. Because your ending is always the same. You always reveal who you truly are to anyone who knows you. And now Sigyn knows that all her faith in you was for nothing, and the transformation can finally be complete...well, unless Odin doesn't want to do a little trade. This could go either way honestly."

Surtr left me spiked to the wall and manifested a second sword in his hand and marched back to Odin, dragging the blade behind him, the tip scraping the ground.

34

FIRE FIRE

With my right arm hanging limp and useless from my injury, I grabbed the hilt of the sword impaling me with my left hand and tugged. I screamed louder as the serrated edge of Surtr's blade chewed my flesh and scraped my bones as it slid out only an inch. I thought I pulled out a million razors and hooks from my body.

There had to be an easier way to keep Surtr from breaking Odin's concentration.

Surtr stood in front of Odin.

"How about it, Odin? Last chance."

Odin kept chanting.

Surtr tapped his foot and huffed.

"Fine, if you won't take my deal, you leave me no choice," Surtr said. "Pity. I really hate to destroy such a magnificent being."

I jerked the blade harder, fighting the sweat and blood slicking my grip to get it out of me. My face scrunched with blinding agony.

Dammit!

Surtr's eyes livened with glee as he cut his sword directly at Odin's head.

Odin snapped his gaze on Surtr's and caught the blade between his hands, stopping the sword from severing his skull in two by a hair. And he kept speaking the spell.

His words wobbled as he strained, keeping the spell driving forward, and pushing back against Surtr who pressed the blade harder towards Odin's skull.

I wasn't sure how long Odin could keep up.

Surtr bared his teeth and yanked back on his sword, ripping it out of Odin's hold and brought it back down, striking Odin's forehead with the hilt of the blade instead.

Odin collapsed to his knees, his hands smacking the earth floor. He tried to keep going, to keep speaking, even though his words stilted.

Then his words silenced.

The spell stopped.

And all that black sludge swept back into Sigyn, flowing into her mouth and into her nostrils.

Surtr surveyed the carnage and laughed at the sight of us, Odin on his knees, and I impaled to the wall as he slowly returned into Sigyn's levitating body.

"I told you this was all a waste of everyone's time and energy," Surtr said. "Don't you feel silly now? I know I would."

I yelped through the blazing white pain, finally pulling the sword out of my shoulder. Blood gushed from my jagged flesh, and I clapped my left hand over the wound. I pulled in a breath. A second breath. My sinew and muscle knit together, healing and stopping my blood from running out of me.

A third breath. I stood taller and flexed my grip with my right hand, hating how it wasn't as strong as before Surtr drove his sword into my shoulder. My shoulder kept healing, but slowly, as if every stitch required power I no longer possessed.

I was so tired. And this made it all worse.

Surtr walked towards Sigyn.

I hobbled to her and stood between them and held out Surtr's sword to him. I pointed the lethal tip over where his heart rested. Well, had he had one.

Surtr's shoulders slumped, and he groaned, thoroughly annoyed.

"Really?" Surtr said. "You continue to be the most pathetic of all."

Surtr flicked his wrist, and the sword vanished from my hold. Cold coated my vertebrae.

He grabbed me by my tunic and hoisted me off the ground.

I let my gaze flash a second behind Surtr's head.

Odin struggled to stand and pressed his hand over the gash cut across his forehead. Blood trickled down his cheek and into the whiskers of his beard.

"Tell me why," I wheezed.

Keep talking...

"Because you're a spoiled brat."

"I'd hardly call having high standards being a brat."

Surtr's eyebrows shot to his hairline, and laughter burst out from deep inside his gut.

"You threw a tantrum because some gods were mean to you, and in recompense you decided Ragnarok the sane choice."

I ground my teeth.

"The only reason I'm standing before you now is because you released me from Gullveig's heart, *World Breaker*."

"I never asked for any of this."

He pouted and made puppy eyes.

"No. Of course not," he cooed. "Because all the choices you made are everyone else's fault. You child. You never take responsibility. You never control yourself. You could have greatness with your chaos, you know? But you only ever use your chaos to hurt others."

My heart fell leagues into my bowels as his words jabbed needles beneath my fingernails.

"Fuck you."

Surtr's face brightened.

"The inarticulate retort of one who knows when they've been beaten," he said. "You know you are undeserving of love. You know you are undeserving of forgiveness. You know you deserve *nothing*."

I glared daggers into Surtr, wanting to split into his sternum and carve him into sections and fragments.

"And neither do you," I spat.

Surtr smiled.

"You can't stop me from taking Sigyn."

Odin stood, his knees shaking, and met my gaze and nodded softly. He was alright. And hope flooded my body that we still had a chance.

"No, I can't," I said. "But Odin can."

Odin chanted again.

Surtr looked behind his shoulder at Odin and shrieked. Smoke and tar spilled out of Sigyn's mouth and ears, emptied out of her pores.

Surtr threw me, my still healing shoulder pounding into the ground. Fresh pain split through my still mending tendons and the amulet flung out of my pocket, skidding across the room.

No.

Odin's voice croaked through his parched throat, but the spell continued to flood out of him even stronger and more forcefully than before. Odin locked his gaze with Surtr who manifested another blade. He rose it over his head.

The tendrils of tar grew thinner as the last dregs emptied from Sigyn.

Almost...

Odin spoke faster as Surtr neared him, and with each step, Surtr grew less steady. With each stiff step, Surtr's face grew more livid.

Wind surrounded Surtr, flapping his robes around his legs, whipping his hair over his eyes. Odin's chanting built and filled the room with thunder.

Surtr grunted, as if punched by each incantation Odin hurled at him. He forced his way through the wind beating his body and robes.

Odin spoke harder.

Surtr roared through Odin's rumbling baritone, cutting the blade towards his neck.

The last threads of black slipped out of Sigyn.

The blade and Surtr liquified into a cloud of twitching sludge, a breath away from severing Odin's head from his shoulders.

Sigyn fell to the ground. Her eyes fluttered open, and she gasped in air. Free.

Odin had done it and my chest swelled with respect and veneration. This is why Odin was the most powerful of the gods.

This is why I went to him for help.

Only he could free Sigyn from this monstrosity.

And now came my part to make sure it stayed that way.

The sludge buzzed like swarming flies, bouncing off the walls, writhing and furious, trying to break through any crevice in the tangled roots.

Surtr screamed, the voice like a drowning demon as the darkness tried to escape the confines of Yggdrasil.

The wriggling tar twitched to the left, inches from smacking into the roots and sped towards Sigyn, who rubbed her forehead with the butt of her hand. Drying blood caked her face.

I forced myself to stand though my shoulder screamed, and scrambled towards Sigyn. Surtr barreled faster, screeching until I thought my ears pierced with knives.

Odin put out his hands and spoke another spell. Surtr howled as Odin trapped the element in an enchantment. The sludge boiled.

"The amulet." Odin kept his eye locked on Surtr, moving his hands to keep the roiling tar contained. Surtr screeched and wailed.

"I'm fine," Sigyn panted. "Go."

She grabbed hold of the roots and hoisted herself up, straining every inch. She waved me away.

Dammit.

I ran for the amulet, even though everything in me wanted to embrace Sigyn and check if she was alright. My fingers grazed the metal—a force kicked me in the chest, knocking the air from my lungs. Pain burned in my sternum.

The black tendrils of tar wrapped around my ankle and yanked me back.

Odin crunched his face harder, and moved his hands, uncoiling Surtr from my calf. I slipped free from the element and crawled on my stomach towards the amulet, digging my nails into the dirt.

"Any time would be great," Odin said.

"I hear you!"

I clutched the amulet and spoke a litany of runes until the engravings along the edges of the gold glowed.

The amber purred, ready to feast.

And feast it would.

I laid it before Odin's feet and nodded at him. He moved Surtr over the amulet and spoke another set of runes, darker runes. Runes only he'd ever dare to speak.

He forced his hands down, forcing Surtr down with them, jamming Surtr into the amulet, stuffing the sludge inside the stone. Screeching pierced my eardrums as Surtr flailed and snapped and writhed as the stone caught one tendril and started to suck Surtr into its center.

The amber drank faster, guzzling the grease, drinking Surtr down like a ravenous beast lapped blood. The amulet swallowed the last drops of the element, and a black haze swirled in the stone's center.

The amulet popped and flipped on the ground, Surtr raging within, trying to break free of the prison.

I grasped the amulet and hated how weak my grip was on the damn thing.

But I wouldn't let that stop me from encasing the darkness within the gold.

After all, it was time for the show.

I could do this.

I swallowed a lump in my throat.

I shut my eyes and called up my fire.

My element smoldered in my core and seared through my chest and out of my hand. And I cranked up the heat, turning my insides molten and surging it through my palm and into the gold.

The amulet glowed orange. I squeezed harder.

Sigyn braced herself against the wall, grasping onto the roots, trying to stand. She was already looking better, stronger, as her powers healed her and replenished her blood.

"Loki, what are you doing?" Sigyn said, somewhere behind the rush of blood in my ears. Behind the crackle of cinders crushing between my fingers.

My breaths deepened as I urged more of my fire out, pushing more of my chaos through the fatigue weighing my bones. Flames coursed over my knuckles, dousing the amulet in flame.

My knees weakened.

The gold softened beneath my fingers.

I fell to my knees.

I kept going.

Embers cracked and popped between my palm and the amulet. I burrowed deep into my center, deeper into my roots, and touched the very ends of my core, and scooped up all I could, and cried out, forcing all of my fire into the amulet.

The gold turned molten as I burned through the runes, liquifying the spells, and sweat ran down my face and my heart pounded as I coated the stone with the metal, every inch taking all my strength. All my concentration.

Surtr continued to shriek and fight, trying to punch through the amber I slowly encased in gold. I would not let the darkness win.

I screamed, shoving more of my element out into the gold. The amulet tugged at my insides, needing more fire, needing more chaos, needing all of me.

My throat burned.

My ears throbbed.

The metal slipped over the stone, coating the amber in gold, encasing Surtr in a gilded prison. And still the amulet tore at a million strings attached to my every cell and yanked and tore. I shook.

It needed more.

And I gave it more.

I gave and I gave until I thought I'd rip in half.

But I kept going. *I had to keep going until it was finished.*

The amulet burned red as the gold thickened around the stone. I felt my chaos empty completely as I sealed Surtr fully within the gold

Surtr's shrieks ceased.

I collapsed.

It was done.

The amulet fell out of my grip and dropped to the ground. The roots and dirt hissed and snapped beneath the searing gold. Smoke curled around the glowing edges.

I heaved in a breath and brushed the soot off my hands onto my trousers.

"That wasn't so bad," I panted, sitting up. "Although, I think I'll really pay for this in the morning."

Sigyn hobbled to my side and slipped her arms around me and helped me stand. I hated how I wobbled. I hated how my body wanted to pull me back to the ground. I hated how I wanted to collapse in on myself.

I was so tired.

Drained.

Empty.

But it was done.

"What did you do?" she asked. She wiped the blood away from her mouth. Her chin. Her entire bodice and skirts were soaked with blood.

But her element...her fidelity...it shined bright and clear and free. *She was free.*

I could have died happy in that moment.

Odin walked to us, his own breaths ragged and blood splattered across his chest. He looked tired, too.

We all were tired.

"Surtr had to be encased within the metal," Odin said. "And only Loki could melt the gold."

My mouth was so dry. If I could just drink something...

And my shoulder. Every movement made it ache.

"It's done now. That's all that matters," I said, feeling my lips crack with each word. "You're free, Sigyn."

"I'm free," she repeated. She smiled, and I never wanted to see any other sight. All of my pain. All of my struggle. It was all worth these seconds.

And for those seconds, I forgot the cold reality.

I'd not see that smile again once we left Yggdrasil.

I turned to Odin.

"Odin, thank you."

He smiled gently.

"I said I'd help, and I did. But, when you get back to Midgard, I really must insist—"

And my thanks quickly melted into annoyance.

I put out my hand to him, stopping him.

"Please. I beg you. No lengthy speeches until I've had a drink and slept for a week. No. A month."

He chuckled.

"I think I can manage that."

I took a step. I winced and gripped my shoulder that still mended itself.

"Your shoulder," she said, her eyes latching onto mine.

I stretched my arm and stretched my hand and fingers. I exhaled with relief. Already more limber. Nearly there.

"A breath or two more and it will be all back to normal. You forget I'm rather good at surviving."

Sigyn kept staring into me, and something welled behind her eyes. Something I desperately wanted to be true...but how could it?

The amulet flipped. Jumped.

Odin stepped closer. I didn't like how his muscles stiffened.

The amulet shook.

"Something is wrong," he said.

Cracks split across the gold in deep veins.

Shit.

It wasn't done.

35

HAVE A HEART

Fractures raced across the gold, splintering branches that multiplied into a dozen more.

"I thought I used enough chaos to encase the stone," I said, unable to take my eyes off the cracks that kept forming and splitting and tearing.

Surtr raged inside the stone, battering the gold to break free. A fresh storm of branches cleaved through the gold and split off from one another like rivers.

"I don't understand." I raked my fingers through my hair, and my fingers trembled, and my every movement ached and creaked. I was so exhausted...

Odin turned gaunt with that same haggard look he wore when he stepped on Vigridr at Ragnarok—when he believed he faced his own death.

"The gold is still too thin. Too weak," Odin said. "We need a little more of your fire. A little more and it will be enough to strengthen the gold and fuse the cracks together. Then it will finally be finished."

A little more...

Those words struck me like spears that stirred my bowels. Burned deeper than Surtr's blade had punched through my shoulder.

Only dregs of my power remained, but they were in a place even I could not reach. My element had never been so depleted. So hollow. I'd siphoned off everything I could already.

A little more was a problem.

"I have no more chaos to give." Cold sweat broke out across my back saying those words. Admitting them as if admitting a heinous crime.

Sigyn's shoulders dropped.

"You're the god of chaos. Surely you have a spark left. Just one..." Sigyn said.

I scoffed.

"Unless you rip me open and tear my element out of me, I...I can't do it."

My stomach clenched.

I can't do it.

Odin's muscles went rigid and his mouth flattened into a thin line. He understood what I said.

What it meant.

We had failed.

I failed.

The amulet would be uncompromising in what it required to finish the job, and I didn't have enough chaos, enough fire, left in me.

The amulet popped and spun on the ground, new fissures bolting across the gold as Surtr pounded within the cage. Purple glowed between the cracks that grew. Spread.

"Then this was all for nothing," Odin whispered. "Surtr will break free, and the darkness will return inside Sigyn, and we will all be finished. The worlds will be finished."

Sigyn nodded and looked at me and her face firmed with a determination that cut me cold.

"No, that won't happen." Sigyn marched towards me, her every step gaining strength as her body healed.

She stood and faced me and slid *Laevateinn* out of the sheath at my hip and forced the dagger into my hand. I wanted to break.

"Loki, you know what you must do to end it now." She wrapped my fingers around the hilt and my breaths burned. My body burned.

I wanted to scream.

"Sigyn..." I said, my voice hoarse.

She tore open the laces of her bodice and exposed her chest. She grasped my hand with the dagger and jerked me closer, pointing the blade at her heart.

Her eyes remained firm on mine that filled with water.

"You promised me you would do this," she said, her voice low and thick with resolve.

"Loki, what did you promise her you'd do?" Odin said.

I held her gaze and choked on pins and needles. On my stupidity this entire journey. Had I listened and saved my magic, my element, instead of frittering it away. Had I controlled myself for once in my damned life...

I had let her down...again.

And now here we were.

And I promised her.

She squeezed the steel tighter against her skin.

"When Surtr breaks out, let the darkness take me," Sigyn said. "Trap Surtr in my heart, and then you cut it out of me. Destroy me."

I shook and my eyes seared with tears.

Odin inhaled sharply as understanding fell on him. But he didn't stop me.

Why didn't he stop me?

Would someone please stop me?

"Loki, don't break your promise," Sigyn said. "You swore."

I did, and the world hazed as I moved the tip of *Laevateinn* between her breasts above where her heart beat. Sweat slicked my palm, and my stomach churned with sick.

But there was no alternative.

Unless you rip me open and tear my element out of me...

I rotated the dagger and turned the blade onto myself.

Grasping her wrist I forced her right hand on the hilt. She tugged back. I clapped my other hand over hers so she could not pull away.

I had told Odin all those weeks ago that *Laevateinn* was more than a simple dagger. *Laevateinn* held magical properties like a wand, and because of that, the steel was capable of channeling magic.

Or channeling an element...my chaos.

"No," I said. "I won't take your heart when you can take my element instead."

Her brow furrowed and panic stiffened her features.

"What are you saying?" she said.

"Take my chaos. All of it. It will seal the amulet forever."

She shook her head.

"Loki, no." She tugged back again. I tightened my hold on her, forcing her to stay where she stood.

"You heard Odin. We only need a spark or two more," I said. "The amulet is uncompromising in what it needs, but this way...Strip me of my element. Take what's left from deep inside me. The dredge. The residue. Then the gold around the stone will be strong enough."

Her face sunk into despair.

"Loki," Odin said. "If you do this, you'll be..."

"Mortal?" I said. "Yes. I know."

"Mortal," Odin repeated. "You remember what that means? If you go through with this...your chances of surviving are slim."

Death was not something I thought much about. Best to avoid that subject entirely. Truth was, I didn't know where I'd go, to Hel or some other place. But it didn't matter.

"But Sigyn will live," I said. "You will live. Everyone will live. Don't you see?"

I stared into Sigyn's eyes that rimmed in red.

"I don't deserve my chaos anymore," I said. "But you do."

Tears streamed down her cheeks as she searched me.

"Don't deserve? Why do you say such a thing?"

I choked on my tears.

"I could have said no to revenge. I could have listened and saved my magic. I could have been honest with you. I always make the wrong choice, and for once, I want to make the right one."

"What are you talking about?"

"Surtr was right," I said. "Bly was right. I've only used my chaos to hurt people. I started Ragnarok. I released Surtr. I was going to kill everyone because of my anger...and now, because of that, I've hurt everyone. I've hurt you. I won't let you pay for my sins. This is my price to pay. Let me pay it."

Surtr roared in the amulet, and more fissures ruptured in the gold. Tar seeped through the deepening crevices.

"Time is running out," Odin said.

"No, I won't do it." Sigyn yanked back on the dagger. I kept her firmly in position. "I won't let you sacrifice yourself again when I can be the one. What you've already given...The cave..."

I smiled softly, and my lips trembled and tasted of salt and blood and dirt.

I pulled her in closer, the tip of the blade crushed against my chest.

"What I gave was for you to be free, and I won't have you in chains again because of my choice. Let me end this nightmare I alone started. The responsibility is mine. I must have it."

"Loki..."

Tears ran down my cheeks and I squeezed into her knuckles, wanting her to understand. To accept.

"Sigyn, please. Let me atone."

A battle raged behind her gaze, a war screaming with refusal and objection. I squeezed her harder. She shut her eyes for two seconds and nodded, slumping into silent surrender.

"Just promise me we will have our future together," she said, resting her left hand on my cheek. "Promise me you will survive."

My breath hitched.

"Together? I thought we were done."

She smiled through the emotion choking her.

"I know. We were done," she said. "But I've decided to forgive you. I forgive you, Loki."

I searched her gaze that misted further in red, wanting to hold onto each word like a life preserver. This wasn't possible. I wasn't worthy of forgiveness.

"But why? How? After what I did. All I've done. I broke our trust."

"Forgiveness is how we repair our trust. That's what I had to understand. I had to understand what it means to love someone. Especially what it means to love you. And I've chosen to love you, Loki, and all that comes with it. You are enough."

Tears fell onto her cheeks, normal and crystal clear, because she was free.

"Are you sure?" I said. "Are you sure you want me? I can't ever give you peace."

"Yes, I'm sure," she said. "I want the mess. I want the tears. I want you, Loki. I love you. All of you, as you are."

She stroked her thumb through my tears, and I pressed my cheek into her palm.

"Gods, Sigyn. You're my salvation and..." My heart ached. "And I wish we had more time."

I slid her hand away from my cheek and rested it on top of her other hand that gripped *Laevateinn's* hilt.

"My shoulder is still too weak. You'll have to do this."

She shook her head. I clasped both her hands harder around the dagger.

"No. I can't."

"You know where to strike to kill or not kill," I said. "Stab *Laevateinn* into my chest, into my element, and I will transfer my chaos into the blade. Then you can take my element and finish encasing the stone in the gold."

"But I'm afraid I will miss"

I smiled.

"I trust you," I said.

Sludge pooled around the amulet as Surtr oozed from the veins of split gold.

Odin started chanting again, forcing the slime back into the stone. Surtr fought him, small tentacles lashing out of crevices and grooves.

Time ran thin.

"I promise you, Sigyn. We will have our future together. But you must do this. Now."

Sigyn raised her head to mine and kissed me and I thought I'd shatter into a thousand pieces. Our mouths moved together with longing, and the rosemary in her hair filled my breaths.

I breathed her in deeper. Tasted the salt on her lips.

And in her kiss, in her love, I had my happiness.

I was happy.

Sigyn thrust *Laevateinn* between my ribs.

A punch of steel. A flash of white heat tearing muscle.

Our kiss broke.

"I didn't want to do this," she said.

I know.

But that didn't make this any easier.

She tried to pull back. I forced *Laevateinn* in deeper into the web of my element. I forced her to stay. I bore down and raced inward, to the very edge of myself, and cut the threads of my chaos free. I grunted with each slice, and I screamed as I drove my chaos into the blade.

I was tearing. Splitting. My vision flashed in bursts of greens and blues and whites and my every cell cried out for me to stop.

I drove more of myself into the metal. Heat built. Pressure.

My head throbbed.

My grip on her weakened.

I pushed harder. I forced all of my element into the blade, transferring my chaos, my fire, into the steel. And *Laevateinn* drank and sucked me dry, siphoning my last drops of energy, making my fingers and toes curl as I emptied all of me into the blade.

Blood spilled inside me, flowed warm over my stomach, filled my chambers and empty spaces.

The last drop of my element sank into the metal.

I tasted copper on my tongue. Hot silk coated my lips and trickled down my chin.

I released Sigyn's hold, and she yanked out the blade, her skin taut over her rigid knuckles.

Pain followed, deep and searing and splitting.

The world shifted and blurred. I reached out to her.

I wavered. My knees buckled.

I fell.

My head struck hard earth, forcing dirt and rot and damp into my nose that burned with the blood coursing out my nostrils.

I choked on iron and stretched my fingers towards Odin standing over me, a tangle of roots and shadow behind him.

Help me.

But that wasn't how this worked.

His mouth moved quickly, chanting a guttural and ancient language brimming with dark magic.

His words drowned in the ringing that battered my eardrums.

Cold raced through me as fast as my blood raced out of me.

I crushed my hand against the jagged gash in my flesh, trying to stop my blood from emptying. Trying to stitch my torn sinew back together. Trying to survive.

I must survive. I promised.

Sweat coated my skin.

The wound wasn't healing itself.

Damn.

I'd already forgotten.

Of course it wasn't healing itself.

I wasn't a god anymore.

I was mortal.

I dragged in thin breaths that kept growing thinner.

So, this was dying.

I glared at the amulet that jerked and hopped. Five tendrils of black sludge stretched out of the cracks and whipped and snapped. Odin's spell took hold, and they withered back into the amulet, only for Surtr to throw out ten more.

"Go," I rasped to her. No, whispered.

Sigyn grasped *Laevateinn* and raced to the amulet. Odin's voice rose higher and Surtr growled within the gold, entire fragments bursting off and—Sigyn touched the tip of the dagger to the amulet.

The room exploded with light.

Arcs of fire blazed in a spiral out of *Laevateinn* and doused the amulet in flame.

Wind stormed around us, broiling our faces and tearing at our hair. The amulet pulsed with an eerie glow as my fire—all my fire—melted the gold into molten scarlets.

The amulet lifted off the ground, levitating into the air. White flared between the branches of fractures and cracks, burning like rivers of lava.

Sigyn struggled pouring my element from the dagger into the amulet, flames cascading off the steel and plating the amulet further with chaos.

The wind beat at our clothes. The ground rumbled beneath us.

The gold bubbled and popped as the cracks filled in with the thickening metal encasing the stone.

The last ribbon of flame slipped off the blade and sank into the amulet. More fractures melted together, strengthening the gold around the amber.

Surtr screeched as a sheet of flame coated the amulet that shook and hissed. The gold burned brighter. Scalding.

The final split fused solid.

Light radiated from the amulet. An explosion of power burst from the gold, blowing Sigyn and Odin back, and punching me further into the ground.

The amulet fell to the earth, whirled three times, and collapsed heavily to the ground with a reverberating *thud*.

The glowing reds cooled into pale golds.

A hush fell over the room.

It was done.

And, I feared, so was I.

"Enjoy your prison," I forced out, wincing and clutching my chest. I tasted iron.

Sigyn and Odin both raced to my side, their faces filled with worry. Sigyn ripped open my tunic and inspected the puncture in my flesh. Blood flowed out of the wound and seeped down my side and pooled beside me.

"Loki, stay with me," Sigyn said. "You promised me you'd survive."

She ripped strips of cloth from her skirts and applied pressure to the gash, trying to stop the blood that kept gushing out of me, trying to save me.

But I knew.

"I want...I...I don't know if I can...Sigyn I—I'm sorry."

Her gaze met mine and a thousand wishes and hopes lived behind her eyes.

"Don't say it," she breathed. "Don't you dare say goodbye to me Loki Laufeyjarson."

I tried to smile.

"Then let me just tell you...I...I love you."

Her lips trembled harder, and she wiped tears from her eyes.

"I'm not letting you go. I won't," she said.

She kept working to save me.

Couldn't she see?

A darkness grew along the edges of my vision.

Pain lanced each breath that turned threadlike.

"What are his chances?" Odin asked Sigyn.

Sigyn gave him a grim look.

Odin took my hand and squeezed into my knuckles and fingers as she continued to try and keep me. But I had another place to be.

And, I think I was supposed to be there soon.

I hoped they understood.

"He's so cold," he said.

She tore more cloth. Applied more pressure.

"You can't go," he said to me. "Not yet. Please."

My eyelids grew heavy, and his image fell in and out of focus.

A peace fell over me. Like a warm blanket tucking me in on a cold night. How lovely.

Odin laid his hand on my abdomen and spoke runes and spells.

"I know...I would have liked to have stayed," I said.

"You are staying," Sigyn said. Stated.

Always so hopeful.

I smiled at her, somewhere.

Sigyn.

36

MAYBE

Midgard

Los Angeles, California

Beep. *Beep. Beep.*
> I cracked open my eyelids.
> Fluorescent lighting burned my retinas.

I winced and shifted in layers of cool cotton sheets. I hissed at the deep ache in my shoulder, having made the mistake of moving. Slowly, carefully, I turned my gaze to the right, sliding the back of my head against a pillow. I blinked at a monitor with a black screen and bouncing green lines and numbers and other hieroglyphics.

What the f—

A jungle of wires were hooked to my chest, and thin plastic tubes were taped to my arms. Other tubes were lodged in places tubes should never be. *Oh gods.*

How did I get in this bowl of spaghetti?

I patted myself and grimaced at the thin hospital gown clothing me. Hospital. Why was I in a hospital?

It all rushed back in a shock and the bouncing green lines on the monitor sprung quicker and closer together.

The tree. The amulet.

Sigyn.

I scanned the room—a linoleum nightmare—and the beeps of the machine softened again as I found her. Sigyn slept curled in a reclining chair in the corner, her clean face resting in the crook of her elbow. Her hair draped over her shoulders and she looked so snug in her chunky camel sweater and black slacks. Slacks?

Where had her blood stained Jotun clothes gone?

How long had I been in this bed?

I shifted, trying to sit up, wanting to go to her. A searing heat cut into my chest, and the gash from the blade pounded bright and sharp and forced me back against the mattress—which had the happy side effect of slicing the stinging already throbbing in my shoulder even deeper.

My entire body felt broken. Was I broken?

But I survived. I—

The door on the left swung open and Odin walked in holding a porcelain mug, a yellow paper tag attached to a string dangling over the rim. Tea. *Tea*? He didn't drink tea—

His gaze met mine and for a second he seemed stunned, and then he smiled behind his beard that was no longer caked in blood. He wore a brown leather jacket that matched his lace-up boots. A gray plaid shirt was tucked into a pair of jeans. Everything about him looked rugged and long-lasting.

"You're awake," he said. "Took you damn long enough. It's been three days."

Three days?

"To be perfectly honest, I'm not sure if I'd prefer to remain unconscious." I winced again, a fresh wave of stings and pricks biting my shoulder and chest. "Is Sigyn alright?"

He sat the mug of tea on the table next to Sigyn. Steam curled from the hot liquid and diffused into the air.

"She's fine, just exhausted, which is why I thought some

chamomile tea might help her. I'm glad to see she's finally fallen asleep," he said. "She's been non-stop double checking every nurse and doctor that walks in here. She can be *assertive*."

One of her best qualities.

"I'm sorry to have missed that. I love it when she yells and commands people about. It's deeply erotic."

He sighed.

"Well, while she monitored each fluid and medication being shoved into your veins, I calmed the questions of the staff as to our clothes and general horrifying state. The screams."

"That I do not envy you."

"I explained we were re-enactors from a far away medieval fair, and that you suffered a jousting accident. You're unfortunately very clumsy with lances and swords. You really shouldn't have insisted on forgoing your shield, but you're so stubborn..."

My brow and mouth flattened.

"How kind of you," I said.

"Thankfully the staff bought it, and let us clean ourselves and I found us new clothing."

Stole, from one of the other patients, he meant.

"I see," I said, my mind racing trying to take it all in. "I remember the tree and then...and then...and then it's all dark. But what happened in between there and here?"

"You almost died," he said. "That's what happened."

Died?

More rushed back to me as I searched through the fog.

I pressed my hands against my eyes, the wires dangling off the sides of my arms.

"That's so embarrassing," I said. "Did they use the paddles? Please say no."

"They used them three times."

I groaned and dragged my hands down my face that hurt. Why did my face hurt? Why did everything hurt?

He walked closer to my bed and stood next to the monitor and a steel pole crowded with plastic bags full of clear liquids hanging from hooks.

"You lost an incredible amount of blood," he said. "It's actually a miracle you're alive at all—" His voice cracked. "But, Sigyn and I combined our efforts, and together, we somehow managed to save you long enough to get you here."

My ears filled with the memory of him chanting over me—and then Sigyn. She had pressed and pressed into my chest, breathed into my mouth. The memory fractured into bits and pieces that then faded away.

I removed my hands from my cheeks. Sigyn stirred, but didn't wake.

"And the amulet?" I said. "Did the gold hold?"

He nodded.

"The gold held," he said. "Ratatoskr buried the amulet within Yggdrasil's roots in the Below. We won't have any more trouble from Surtr now, because of what you did...what...what you gave."

What I gave?

I gave my chaos.

Cold snapped down my spine as the rest rushed back. I had hoped that splintered memory had been a hallucination. A nightmare.

I rubbed my chest over stickers and cords and wires. I felt so empty without my element, as if I were a hollowed out oak.

"What's wrong?" he asked.

"I didn't expect to feel this...this emptiness inside of me," I said. "It's like a part of me is missing, like if I'd lost my right leg."

He frowned and pain stitched his brow.

"A part of you *is* missing," he said. "It will take time getting used to not—"

"To not being a god anymore?"

His frown deepened.

"To not having your element," he said. "It was always there within you, even before you were a god. You ripped out a piece of yourself that has always been. It won't...it won't be easy to recover from this."

My breaths tightened, and a sadness took root in me from the finality of what I'd done. But it saved Sigyn, it saved everyone, and with that in mind, I think I could manage the rest of it.

I pulled in a breath, wanting to chase away the bites of sadness trying to take hold of me.

"I suppose I'm just a sack of meat and bones now," I said.

He shook his head and chuckled.

"You always are melodramatic," he said. "How about a thank you? I had to carry your 'sack of meat and bones' ass all the way here. For a moment we thought...we thought you were gone for good."

"You know I have a talent for surviving."

He smiled softly.

"I don't doubt that," he said. "But the fact is, you are mortal again. You will have to be more cautious. You can die now simply swallowing a piece of broccoli the wrong way."

I perked.

"You're right," I said. "I am mortal and exceedingly fragile."

He put his hand out to me.

"Wait, I know that look," he said. "That's not what I meant."

I smiled wider.

"Actually, I find this most thrilling," I said. "I have a new world awaiting me filled with fresh risks." I stretched my legs and flinched accidentally tugging on the tube running between my thighs. "Maybe the thrilling part will come later, but think of it! The perils of simply chopping a carrot. That, and cocaine will hit me much harder now, so I do have that to look forward to."

"Loki," he said. "Please contain yourself at least until the apple harvest and I can bring you a golden apple. It won't make you a god, but it will keep you from aging."

Aging. I forgot about that catch.

My exuberance plummeted into my stomach...but, wait...

"Apple?" I said. "What are you saying? That I won't have to endure growing old while watching Sigyn remain young?"

"What I'm saying." His breath caught. "What I'm saying is that I just want you to be happy. Because I figure one of us should be. For once."

I tilted my head.

"You're giving me my future with her?"

I glanced at Sigyn sleeping, her face calm and peaceful. Breaths deep.

"I just want you to be happy," he said, his voice husky.

I understood how much this hurt him. How much he wanted it to have been any other way.

I grasped his hand and surprise chased away a little of the sadness infecting him.

"I want you to be happy, too," I said. "And I want us to be free of this pain between us. I want us to move forward. The problem is, to do that, I think...I think we have to forgive each other."

He compressed his lips.

"I don't know if I'm ready," he said.

"That's alright, because I don't know if I'm ready, either," I said. "But maybe one day, we both will be."

He smiled softly.

"Maybe."

He squeezed my fingers and slid his hand out of mine.

Odin walked across the room towards the door. And I knew into what dragon's mouth he now walked because of me. Because of what he did *for* me and Sigyn.

"Odin," I said.

He sighed and stopped.

"What now?"

How to tell him...

"There's something you should be aware of," I said. "Something Bly told me before we left the Ironwood for Yggdrasil."

He turned.

"And what was that?"

"Frigg is the one who told everyone about my involvement in Ragnarok," I said. "Apparently, she is very much against the idea of me having any kind of life beyond cave walls."

He nodded stiffly and his fingers curled into fists at his sides. The fluorescent lights flickered and buzzed and a cold chill iced the room.

"I should have known it was her," he said. "She's always stirring the pot. She's not made life easy on me ever since...It doesn't matter anymore. I'm returning to Asgard now and finishing this. I'm going to make things right."

He always was so sure of himself.

But I knew better.

"Don't keep underestimating her," I said. "This time is different. She's out for blood, Odin. Your blood."

And Frigg would soon be out for mine as well. I was vulnerable now, and if she ever learned I was mortal—she could actually kill me this time.

37

THUNDER

I nestled deeper into the buttery leather of our sofa and enjoyed a riot of a film. I cackled—and regretted it immediately as my stitches pulled and stung my chest, forcing me to take shallow breaths.

This was getting boring.

I had already endured weeks of this nonsense. How much longer before I was finally mended? Who knew a measly stab wound from a twelve inch blade would be such a bitch to heal?

And then there was my shoulder that would spasm anytime I dared move the wrong way. Of course, *that* couldn't have healed completely before I lost my godhood. Just my luck.

Screams blared from the television and blood splattered over the white-tiled room. Seriously, if they just put a little effort into the sawing...

Sigyn walked into the living room furnished with teak furniture, books, and plants.

"What are you watching?" she said, holding a bowl and wearing her hair in a braid that I wanted nothing more than to untangle and run my fingers through.

"Some comedy about a serial killer who places people in games to test their will to live. It's the best thing I've ever seen—Oh, just break it off already!—Ow."

I clutched where my stitches tugged beneath my t-shirt that said *World's Best Dog Dad*.

Fenrir had gotten it for me as a gift months back. He laughed, and I laughed, and then I immediately stuffed the shirt in the back of my closet to forget about. Now, I had worn it every day for a week, along with Sigyn's pink striped pajama pants and fuzzy socks.

I don't know why I turned my nose up at Midgardian loungewear. The soft cotton was absolutely lovely against my skin. Gods. Who was I becoming?

Sigyn picked up the remote and switched the television off and tossed the controller aside. The room filled with the thunder of the Pacific Ocean crashing against the rocky shoreline outside.

"Perhaps some quiet time would be better for you."

I pouted.

"I've had enough quiet time, thank-you-very-much," I said. "And let me tell you why—"

"What about eating this instead?" Sigyn said, cutting me off. "It's double fudge. Your favorite."

She smiled and handed me the bowl piled with scoops of ice cream and topped with extra whipped cream and a mountain of sprinkles.

My mouth watered, but my stomach already heaved at the memory of last night's dairy experiment. I had felt parts of my insides I never wanted to feel again as everything twisted into cramps and prayers to the god of porcelain.

Not that it stopped me from experimenting again, and that's why I was still recovering from the glass of milk I'd drank earlier today.

"Thank you, but..."

I put the bowl on the smoked glass coffee table and laid my hand on my churning stomach.

She frowned.

"That too?" she said.

I shrugged, staring at the ice cream and wishing to taste one bite of the chocolate ribbons.

"Ever since I lost my element, my stomach only tolerates rice crackers and applesauce," I said. "I don't understand. I never experienced such issues before I was a god and lived in Jotunheim. I thought my mouth would never stop itching after I ate that pistachio last week."

Sigyn laid her hand on my good shoulder and squeezed in that reassuring way of hers that made me believe everything would be fine.

"Your body has undergone an immense amount of stress. Maybe it needs time to settle and adjust as you recover from the loss of your chaos?"

Maybe.

She sat next to me on the couch and looked so effortless and comfortable in her oversized navy sweatshirt and cuffed straight jeans. I couldn't help smiling as she nestled against me and wrapped her right arm around my torso and squeezed. I lowered my face to her hair and kissed the top of her head. I hadn't even realized I'd closed my eyes.

"I have an idea," I said, brushing her ear with my lips. "How about I take you to the bedroom and we can try the *Lioness and the Cheese Grater*? That should be an activity that won't make me break out into hives."

She pulled back and gave me a look as if I were mad, although the flush in her cheeks told me she considered the proposition. Perhaps there was hope after all...

"You remember what the doctor said." She stopped my hand trailing up her thigh. "Not until your stitches are removed."

"What if I just did the tongue thing?"

"No."

I slouched back into the sofa and groaned.

The novelty of mortality was wearing exceedingly thin.

"Can't do this, can't do that, can't eat onions after seven o'clock in the evening," I said. "Suffer, yes, that seems to be the only thing I'm allowed to do. How generous of the worlds."

She frowned.

"I know this is difficult for you," she said. "It's difficult for me to see you struggle so greatly with this new life you've been given. I wish I could take it all away, but...but at least Odin will bring you an apple. We can still have a life together, even if you aren't a god anymore."

My heart quickened at that one thread of silver lining, but that thread depended on an awful lot. I saw nothing but a maze of brambles ahead of Odin in retrieving an apple for me at all, and that was only if I survived until the Autumn harvest. I had already underestimated the slickness of wet tile when I tried to step out of the shower.

She kept staring at me, and her gaze deepened. She reached out and combed her fingers through my hair, and warmth flooded my body. I didn't want to be anywhere else than here. Now.

"Do you..." Her words melted into silence.

"Do I what?"

She exhaled sharply.

"Do you regret giving your chaos all away for me?" she said.

Bitterness wrenched harder at that gaping hole in my core. If there was one thing I wished to heal from, it was the unceasing sensation of emptiness inside of my body I couldn't quite shake—the sensation of being half of me. But it was what it was. My immortality and my chaos were gone, and I had to accept it. Because it had been my choice to give.

I took her hands and stared into her eyes, wanting her to understand.

"Everything I do for you, I never regret," I said. "Never."

I brushed my thumb over the tops of her hands and she smiled, the dimples I yearned to kiss tugging at her lips.

A warmth and sublime adoration bled from her eyes I couldn't stop searching. How was this woman mine?

"I don't understand," I said. "No matter how much I hurt you, you still love me."

Her adoration only grew.

"Is this so impossible to you?" she said. "You have cracks Loki, there's no denying that, but the cracks are where your light shines through."

Emotion built in my chest from all the love I had for her, and all the love I wanted to give her.

"It's just..." I said. "It's been my experience that every love has a condition."

She cradled my jaw in her hands and rested her fingertips on the sides of my face.

"We aren't just any love," she said. "And I'm not just any woman. I won't give up on you. I've made my choice, and I've chosen to love you. All of you. Unconditionally."

I smiled through my tears at the beautiful impossibility that we two beings, two opposites, should find each other. And in each other, find the purest of devotion. Strength. And I smiled at the amazement at how she still wanted me. After everything. After how many times I let her down.

Made her cry.

Made a mess.

I would strive every day to be worthy of her.

Because she was my light. My hope. Sigyn was fidelity, and loving fidelity meant loving something as steadfast and fixed as rock.

"Trust is something I've not done in a very long time, Sigyn," I said. "But I want to learn how to trust again. With you."

And I wouldn't wait a second more to...

To...

I patted my pockets.

Panic raced cold through my veins.

The ring was gone.

Sigyn tapped my arm and pulled out the gold ring from her own pocket. The thick band carved with knots and runes and Aesir symbols glinted in the warm lamp light.

"I found it in your things when you were in the hospital," she said. "I'm sorry if I ruined the surprise."

I smiled.

"This isn't how I imagined any of this taking place," I said. "I had wanted candles. Tablecloths..."

She chuckled.

"I think we have to accept nothing will ever go how we planned concerning us," she said. "And I think that makes everything more perfect, don't you?"

She slid the ring onto her finger and my mouth parted as if I'd wake from this dream any second.

"And you're sure?" I said.

"More than anything," she said. "I'm not saying we won't face storms together. They are guaranteed with us, but now, we will face them together."

She smiled and placed her palm over my heart. I dragged in a shivery breath.

"I am yours, until the end, Husband."

I laid my palm over her heart, loving every pulse beating through her chest.

"As I am yours, until the end, Wife."

I slid my hands behind her back, and she wound her fingers in my hair as we destroyed the space between us. She tilted her chin up to me as I moved my mouth to hers. Rosemary filled my breath.

Our lips met in a kiss. Our first bound together.

And I tasted the future.

I tasted happiness.

And it was ours.

We pulled apart and relaxed into each other's arms and looked out of the window at the night sky, the ocean reflecting the moon and a thousand constellations. Endless possibility.

"What now?" she said.

I smiled and held her tighter.

"We count the stars until they fall."

Our mouths met again and our kiss deepened until I thought I'd lose myself in her love forever. A rush of heat swept through my body like a wave of pins, but one pin nicked that empty space in my core sharper than all the others, like a single prick of a hot needle, almost as if...

No. That pinprick was just a memory, a phantom sensation, of what was.

But none of that mattered when I had Sigyn, and we finally had all our tomorrows.

Thunder quaked the house. The books and trinkets rattled on the shelves and fell to the floor.

Our kiss broke.

"What's that?" Sigyn said, her brow furrowing.

I drew in a bracing breath and slowly stood, grimacing at the sting of pain searing the length of my stitches.

A split of lightning shredded the sky that was clear with stars and filled our living room in flickering whites. A dark rumble shook the ground again, vibrating into the soles of my feet.

"That doesn't sound like normal thunder," she said.

"That's because it isn't."

I slowly walked to the window and looked out at veins and sheets of lightning.

And I knew what this meant.

Gods. No.

"Loki, what's happening?"

"It's Thor," I said. "Asgard is in trouble."

THE FIRE IN THE FROST

THE NINE WORLDS RISING BOOK 4

Loki will return in *The Fire in the Frost*, book 4 in *The Nine Worlds Rising* series.

THANK YOU!

I sincerely hope you enjoyed reading this book as much as I enjoyed writing it. If you did, I would greatly appreciate a short review on Amazon or your favorite book website, such as Goodreads or Bookbub! Reviews are crucial for any author, and even just a line or two (or only stars!) can make a huge difference.

ALSO BY LYRA WOLF

The Nine Worlds Rising

Novellas

Thunder, Blood, and Goats

Novels

Truth and Other Lies (Book 1)

The Order of Chaos (Book 2)

That Good Mischief (Book 3)

The Fire in the Frost (Book 4)

Untitled (Book 5)

Untitled (Book 6)

ACKNOWLEDGMENTS

I believe the first thank you needs to go to all of my family and friends who helped support me as I struggled to work through this book. Revision and editing usually takes me 3-6 months to complete. This book took me a year, which is shocking even to me. And I don't know how I would have gotten through without them.

I went into this book thinking I knew exactly what it would be about, and instead, I had every character throw the biggest tantrum because I was wrong. Originally, this was a book about acceptance, but what it became was a story about trust–how it can both tear you down and build you up. To throw more wrenches into the mix, it also became a story about what loving someone means. Very easy topics to stuff into 95k words.

But, it is because of the love and patience of my family and friends that this book finally came together.

Hannah, you have seen me through every book since the beginning and helped me weather so many storms (99.9% being ones Loki causes). I never can repay all the long discussions you have with me concerning different plot points, quizzing me on why a character is doing something this way instead of that way, and most importantly, how naked I should make certain scenes that take place beneath waterfalls. Thank you for always being there, and for reading a thousand terrible drafts. How you aren't tired of me yet is a miracle.

Rafi, thank you for letting me walk you through the various scenarios I was stuck between, and helping me find the right path every time. You kept my spirits up through all of my doubts, and never once stopped encouraging me to keep trying until I found the right notes. Not only that, you read three separate versions of this book without one sigh, and if that's not true love, I do not know what is.

Mom (and Dad!), who I informed to enjoy these next words because they shall never be repeated: you were right about that one chapter. I owe you so much for all those phone calls discussing angsty breakups, forgiveness, and love. You helped me finally find the tone I was searching for, and that one chapter is only what it is now because of your advice. Sorry I was stubborn about it at first, but you know me–I pour stubbornness into my coffee every morning.

Jenn, thank you for treading the dark waters of being the first reader of this book. The spit and polish and last minute tweaks you helped me make allowed me to finally say those blessed words "Hallelujah, this book is finished! Now, where's the Jack Daniels?" Yes, I know I said the book was finished a million times before, but because of you, it finally truly was. Your enthusiasm and excitement (and surprise!) about what I put Loki through gave me so much confidence for a book that gave me so much doubt. I can never thank you enough for that. The journey of this book may be at a close, but at least we will always have #Surtrgate. And, obviously, #TeamFenrir forever! Fenrir is waiting for you with the biggest strawberry smoothie in Colorado. ;) (Is this a hint for book 4? Hmmm...possibly.)

Cait, thank you for discussing with me probably the muddiest part of the whole book. There were so many fine lines, and you helped make sure I didn't cross any, except for the right ones. Because, you always gotta go for the pain, right? You are the one who started me on this journey of writing and becoming an author. I owe you every sleepless night I've had since, agonizing over the important things like "what ringtone would Loki have for his cellphone?" or "what car would he drive–correction–what car would Sigyn *allow* him to drive?"

Cat, thank you for reading the final version and proofing this book about our favorite chaos boy, even though you were going through a chaos storm of your own. Your catches helped ensure that this book was the best it could be, and that Loki's suffering was not dampened by those vile typos and awkward phrases. Not only this, but your commentary throughout the draft gave me life. I am so grateful to have your friendship in this very specific little niche of Norse fantasy.

To Kim, the God King of em dashes. Thank you for putting up with me that one day I threw you every em dash question I had, which were many. I told you I'd put you in the acknowledgements because of it, even though you didn't believe me. Jokes on you now.

And finally to you, the reader...it is to you I owe the biggest of thanks and gratitude. It is because of you I can keep writing Loki's journey at all. Every message you send me brings me so much joy. I am beyond happy knowing how much you love this world, and how much you love Loki. I wouldn't be where I am now if it wasn't for your support, and continued love for these books. To have readers like you is honestly an author's dream, and I count myself as extremely lucky to have found a home with you all.

.

ABOUT THE AUTHOR

Lyra Wolf is a Swiss-American author of fantasy and mythic fiction.

Raised in Indiana, home to a billion corn mazes, she now lives in Central Florida, home to a billion mosquitoes. She enjoys drinking espresso, wandering through old city streets, and being tragically drawn to 18th century rogues.

When Lyra isn't fulfilling the wishes of her overly demanding Chihuahua, you can find her writing about other worlds and the complicated people who live there.

Lyra has earned a B.A. in History and M.A. in English.

* * *

Sign up for the **Lyra Wolf Newsletter** for exclusive content, updates, and other delicious goodies.
Sign up Here

You can connect with Lyra on her website, or by following her on social media!

lyrawolf.com

Milton Keynes UK
Ingram Content Group UK Ltd.
UKHW011945240823
427459UK00012B/173/J

9 781944 912437